MW01705005

LAST OUT FROM ROARING BAY

by

Joe Lane

Grosvenor House
Publishing Limited

This book is published by
Grosvenor House Publishing Ltd
28-30 High Street, Guildford, Surrey, GU1 3EL.
www.grosvenorhousepublishing.co.uk

A CIP record for this book
is available from the British Library

ISBN 978-1-78148-619-1

Author's Note

In the context of this story I specified that a Japanese type C-3 cargo submarine, the I-52, was sunk by the Allies in the Atlantic in 1944 while rendezvousing with a German U-boat in the Bay of Biscay. The sinking of the submarine is a true wartime incident that occurred during the Second World War and therefore I cannot claim it as a piece of my creative imagination. As to the events surrounding the fate of I-52, and the role that Allied intelligence played, the Allies believed that the Japanese submarine carried amongst its cargo a quantity of gold bullion destined for the Third Reich to assist Adolf Hitler with the war. It was imperative that the Allies stopped the submarine before the transfer of cargo could be concluded. Whether there was any truth of gold aboard the I-52, all the evidence went down when the submarine was sunk.

In recent times, the I-52 was the subject of a television documentary featuring a team of American treasure hunters who had pinpointed the wreck site. Where the I-52 lay on the seabed, the submarine could only be reached with the use of submersibles and robotic cameras. The operation ended in disappointment, the team salvaging only tin ingots from the wreck and a few artefacts. There was no sign of the gold. The American salvage team presumed that the gold might never have existed in the first place, and if it had, then the mystery only deepened, probably never to be solved and the gold myth lost forever.

The incident concerning the I-52 came to my attention much earlier, before the documentary was made. I read of its fate in an English newspaper article. The thought of gold excites people. It makes good reading. It excited me too. The newspaper story had my imagination running wild: *what if* and *decoy* occupying my thoughts. Both sent my imagination dizzy. What the wartime incident did provide was the inspiration for me to develop and fantasize an intriguing deceptive plot and the chance to introduce my modern day metal detectorist* and renowned treasure hunter, Shackleton (Shacks) Speed, into the affray. More appealingly, to drench the readers thirst for adventure and my theory of what could have happened to the gold in that eventful year of 1944, so long ago. I often wonder if I am close to the truth of where the gold went during the war and, inadvertently, my story does mirror something that had actually occurred; uncovered a long lost secret perhaps. After all fiction is a dream and sometimes dreams come true. Perhaps my story holds hidden truths too, and out there, waiting to be exposed, there is a hoard of gold to be discovered. Who knows maybe 'Last out from Roaring Water Bay' points in that direction?

**Metal detectorist* is not a phrase printed in the English dictionary that I used. I refer to a *metal detectorist* as a person who skilfully locates buried treasure solely by the means of a hand held metal detecting device.

Acknowledgements:

Snake Jacobs in the USA, for his guidance and unselfish editing on my behalf.

JOE LANE

Chapter One

Fate powers life. It determines timing, the place, the day and the moment of action. It has its advantages. It has its disadvantages. It can be lucky. It can be cruel. Mixed with a pile of trouble it can be frigging dangerous and life threatening and I was somewhere in the middle.

I've never set out to find trouble; it usually finds me instead. I deal with trouble remarkably well, and eventually, I escape smelling of roses instead of human excrement. Certain antagonists had me down as an arrogant, lucky bastard who should be locked up and the key thrown away. Fortunately, I ride my luck well and I wasn't going to change the way I operated because of a few scares. I always thought I could handle awkward troubles. It seems I was wrong. The trouble hurtling towards me on my blind side, as I shuffled around in the hollow of a shallow gully nestling in the middle of a windswept Berkshire field using my metal detector, was trouble that bordered on destroying my confidence on how life in the fast lane had been good to me.

It all began inconspicuously enough when the metal detector sent a signal into my headphones indicating a buried object. The erratic bleeping more or less informed me that I'd located something big. What the bleeps didn't reveal, and something I would never have envisaged, is my next action would ultimately veer me along a road to unforeseen bedlam and the possibility that I would have to kill someone along the way.

I was too preoccupied listening to the strength of the bleeps to be thinking of such drastic circumstances. I was scanning the ground in front of me, ascertaining the true point of contact as to where I should dig first. Satisfied, I pushed the spade into the soil to mark the spot, put the detector down to one side, slipped the headphones down around my neck and turned over the grassy clump of dirt with high expectancy, only to be disappointed with what I'd unearthed.

Instead of the anticipated antiquity, I was staring at a length of rotting, dark brown braided electrical flex which wasn't even worth scrap value. False alarms are common amongst detectorists, but I don't usually fall into that category. I'm usually a lucky bastard through and through when it comes to finding something worthwhile. Not this time. In sheer frustration that I'd been conned, I pulled hard on the flex to dislodge it from the ground, probably too hard because it gave suddenly and I startled when a fist of skeletal knuckles flew out from the soil and tried to grab me by the throat.

I was probably overreacting on the 'grab my throat' theory but my gut reaction had me rearing away expecting the putrid smell of decaying flesh when in reality there was nothing but the smell of freshly dug peaty soil. I stood there wondering what I should do next, as this was my first grave find. A sensible person would have walked away immediately and contacted the police. Sensible people, on the other hand, make little headway in the pursuit of discovery. I'm different. I like a challenge, and I have an insatiable curiosity to meddle and learn, especially with things buried.

I didn't need much encouragement to coax me to continue digging. Ever so carefully I began to clear away the soil from around the hand bones, burrowing deeper into the grassy slope with my short handled miniature spade and ideally suited for delicate work. Within minutes I'd unearthed the skeleton's skull and left shoulder. I assessed what I'd found, and judging by the deterioration of the leather skullcap, flying jacket and tunic, glare goggles, the oxygen equipment and mouth inflatable life jacket, it was obvious that I'd found the remains of a wartime fighter pilot. Further digging showed the pilot was still harnessed inside the crumbling cockpit, which clearly suggested he never got the chance to escape before the plane crashed.

I gave a customary military style salute. My, "welcome home, Mister," was greeted by the unnerving movement of the skeleton's skull rolling slowly sideways as the supporting soil fell way. Something fell from behind the glare goggles and dangled there. It was the pilot's identity tags, or at least what was left of them. I leaned over and handled the tags with care while I cleaned the dirt from the metal with a little spit and finger rubbing, eventually revealing the faint indentations that were still visible. Corrosion had set in but one word showed through faintly, 'Craven'. I let the tags fall back and stepped away from the remains.

I didn't spend too much time pondering on whether Craven was the first or surname name of the pilot because I'd no intention to make this my problem. I wiped my soiled hands across my trousers, took the mobile phone from my jacket pocket and called the owner of the land.

"Tommy...Yes it's me, Shacks. Come down to the far field as quickly as you can...Don't ask questions, mobiles cost money. I'm down in a gully...Where? Look for the cows congregating...No I'm not in any trouble, but hurry anyway because I've something to show you."

While I was tucking my phone back into my pocket I noticed the flex I'd unearthed was attached to something still gripped in the skeleton's hand. Now I was well aware of the implications for desecrating a war grave but I've little patience of listening to what I can do and what I can't do, and bearing in mind that nobody was watching, I prised the finger bones apart to recover the device.

It was a push button mechanism made of Bakelite, its inners seized as I discovered when I tried to press the trigger. It had to have operated something of importance for the pilot to have kept hold of the device and I wanted to know what. I began tracing where the flex went, easing the cable gently from the crumbling soil so as not to snap and lose it, eager to find its origin before Tommy arrived.

The flex finally disappeared into what I assumed to be a corroding camera casing which dropped away from its attachment when I had moved the soil. In that instance I knew I'd found a WWII photographic reconnaissance plane. I wondered how much money old wartime footage would bring on the open market? With no hesitation I ripped the flex from the camera, crouched down onto one knee, slipped the large rucksack from my shoulder, wrapped the camera in a sheet of polythene and stuffed the camera inside the rucksack quicker than a Harrods shoplifter committing their crime behind a store detective's back.

I rose to my feet when I heard the clanging of Tommy's ancient tractor as it approached the top of the gully.

He was on foot when I caught sight of him peering down. He had his dog beside him, Winston, a strange looking beast, a cross between a Labrador and a Staffordshire bull terrier and despite the reputation of a half fighting dog, Tommy insisted Winston was a loveable character and he wouldn't hurt a fly. I'd no reason to disbelieve him. Nonetheless, this was a situation when no dog could be trusted.

I gestured for Tommy to join me in the gully. I said, "Leave Winston up there. I don't want the mutt running around the countryside with a bone clamped in his mouth."

Tommy was puzzled by what I said. His nose crinkled when he said, "Winston hasn't got a bone."

"He will have if he comes down *here*."

Still puzzled, Tommy finger signalled and told Winston to sit and stay. The dog obeyed. Tommy made his slow descent, his arms spread out for balance, not wanting the indignity of a clumsy slip onto his arse. I was amazed how agile he was for his age.

Tommy Bickermass had told me he was seventy two years old and the deep facial lines criss-crossing his leathery face verified his age. His day attending the farm began so early that it was rumoured he was solely responsible for waking up the crack of dawn before the cockerel even thought about it. He was dressed in his usual flashy woman pulling attire, a grubby flat cap, green checked tweed jacket covering a black satin waistcoat and a stained shirt. His brown cord trousers he had tucked into a pair of knee cap length Wellington boots that flopped when he walked. The thick curls of hair showing from beneath his hat was a mixture of yellow streaks mingling with grey and white, the yellow strands caused by the application of Grecian 2000, so he assured me.

When he saw the grisly remains his grey eyes popped out and most noticeably a peculiar shade of white varnished his red mottled complexion. Composing himself with a puff of his cheeks, he said, "Blimey!" then added something really stupid. "Is the bugger dead?"

I sighed, shook my head in dismay, and informed him sarcastically, "I suspect he's been buried here for years on the strength of being dead, Tommy."

He tilted back his flat cap to scratch an imaginary itch on his forehead. He shook his head in disbelief and said solemnly, "I wonder who the bugger is?"

"I'd say he was an R.A.F pilot shot down during the war, judging by the flying wings insignia badge on his tunic."

I thought it wise not to mention the camera or that it was a reconnaissance plane. I had my reasons, and the less others knew, the less chance of yours truly getting into serious trouble with the authorities. And then I noticed a strange trance like look in Tommy's eyes. He gave me the impression he was at the first stages of having a heart attack. He worried me. I asked him if he was alright. He didn't answer.

His silence annoyed me as he stood there in deep thought.

"Are you alright?" I snapped.

Finally, in a slow drawl he said, "I can't believe it."

"Believe what exactly?"

Tommy got a little excited. "That Billy Banter was right after all!"

"Who's Billy Banter if you don't mind me asking?"

"Billy! He's a bit of a strange fellow, a bit slow in the brain. You know backward. I've known him since we were kids. Aye, I remember it all now. It was a late summer evening, the sun dropping over the horizon; year of forty three or forty four; during the war. You'd find Billy running through the long grass pretending to be a fighter plane. He spent hours doing it; bags of energy he had. You were knackered just watching him play. Then one day he came up with this incredible tale that he had shot down a plane from the sky and he was sorry for what he'd done. I mean, it wasn't surprising that nobody took any notice of a nit-wit who hadn't all the cogs in his brain working correctly. And now...this turns up. It means Billy wasn't the crackpot we all thought he was, and ...well this wreck proves he was right after all. Billy still lives around here. I suppose I should tell him about this but I doubt he'd remember me or the war."

"It wouldn't have come to this if someone had believed him at the time. Quicker action could have saved the pilot's life," I added accusingly. "Instead the poor bastard perished, trapped in his cockpit. No doubt he suffocated to death buried in soil."

Tommy hit back. "Bugger off, Shacks! You make it sound so gruesome. We weren't to know. We were just kids. And there was nothing mentioned that a plane was missing."

"At least now you can rectify your mistake by calling the local constabulary to get this mess sorted."

Tommy arched a solitary eyebrow. "What about you? Are you not stopping?"

I was amazed he asked me that considering he knew my reputation first hand. "Frigging hell, I'm out of here! I may have found the wreck but I can't take any credit. The authorities and I don't exactly complement each other when it concerns digging up the countryside whether it's for a dead body or the crown jewels."

Tommy winked at me. "So you were never here then?"

"That's right. Besides, why share the honour? Think of the coverage you'll get. You'll be hailed a national hero in the papers."

Tommy's face gleamed at the thought of fame. "My name will be in the papers?" His smile widened when I nodded it would, and then his smile disappeared and he said with sadness in his voice, "Don't suppose the bracelet turned up?"

The excitement of my wreck find made me forget about the bracelet, the purpose of my trek to Berkshire in the first place. The bracelet was an inexpensive trinket that belonged to Tommy's deceased wife, a cherished memento he kept in his jacket pocket even while working in the fields; the silly sod had lost it two weeks previous. I quickly put him out of his misery and produced a clear polythene bag from my jacket pocket and handed it to him.

Tommy's eyes brightened as he examined the soiled contents inside the bag and realized what the bag held. "You found it!"

"Two hours ago, middle field. I thought I'd continue scanning the rest of the fields while I was in the vicinity so I can eliminate it from my map references. Good job too. Or else this poor saviour of our wretched country would have rotted into total oblivion, never to receive an honourable burial."

Tommy gripped the bracelet tightly. "Well, the pilot will have his military funeral and I've got this back. It means a lot to me, you know. You're a good un' Shacks."

"I know, Tommy, but don't forget; don't tell anyone I was here," I reminded him smartly.

I collected my equipment, hitched a ride on the tractor back to the farm, threw the gear into the boot of my Mercedes Benz 500K Roadster and headed back to London. My first stop was at a photography shop situated on the corner of Lambeth Road and Kennington Road. Larry 'the lens' Lazerow was the proprietor, a good friend of mine. I plonked the camera I'd got from the crash site on the counter with the instruction, "develop that if you can Lens!", and watched the astonishment creep across his Barbadian face as he studied the mess in front of him.

"But it's a bundle of rusting crap, Shacks."

"No, Lens, there's a roll of film inside that I'm interested in."

"You expect me to extract it from this lump?"

"I thought you said there's nothing you couldn't develop?"

He jabbed his finger at the mess. "This doesn't count."

"Don't give me limp excuses, Lens. Make it quick will you."

Before he could continue his protest I'd dashed from his shop leaving a trail of words in my wake, "Sorry, Lens. In a rush, important engagement," and went home expecting the good things to happen in my life.

Chapter Two

Since the discovery of the Spitfire wreck I decided to lay low for a while at home. I'm fortunate to have a sizable red bricked detached house, built in the fifties that nestled nicely in the grounds of a large plot. I like to think I live in the posh side of Hammersmith but it's nowhere near to the standards of *millionaires row* half a mile down the road.

The problem with inflicting self imprisonment is I've the tendency to think too much. Events at the farm were beginning to bother me. The reason: I hadn't heard a frigging thing from the farm concerning the Spitfire wreck since the day I'd left Tommy Bickermass to bask in all the glory. In all honesty I was a little perturbed as to why Tommy hadn't kept in touch. It wasn't like him to be so inconsiderate by keeping me in the dark. I could only assume he was being cautious because the investigation team was obviously still busy there at the farm, as they are a very meticulous lot when excavating WWII remains. I was thinking of giving him a call but decided it would be wise to refrain from doing so until I was absolutely sure the investigating team had finished their processing. Not that it mattered because I eventually located Tommy while shuffling through the morning newspaper while having a light breakfast.

Tommy had made it to page four, a quarter sized spread under the heading:

Lost in Action
WWII Hero's Body Unearthed in Farmer's Field

Tommy's short account of how he had found the plane wreck in the first place was brilliant. He'd been clever too, stating that his dog had actually made the initial discovery, which had accounted for the severe disturbance around the wreck. I had to congratulate Tommy on his improvisation and his passing the blame on a creature that couldn't defend himself. In fact his entire description was a masterful piece of fictitious nonsense, so realistic and believable, that I would have been proud to call it my own.

What surprised me about Tommy was the old sod never gave me the impression that he could be such a lying bastard. Though I shouldn't judge him too harshly because he had stuck to his word and never once mentioned my presence at the crash site. At least he'd done something in my favour.

I read on because something had caught my attention further down in another paragraph. It had me scratching the invisible itch on the end of my nose. The name of the exhumed pilot nowhere near matched the name I saw on the identity tags that hung around the skeletons neck. The Ministry of Defence had released the name Flying Officer Derek Rowland which was a ridiculously long way from the name *Craven* which I'd seen clearly hanging from the human remains. I knew I hadn't been mistaken and I certainly didn't need glasses. It was obvious somebody in the MoD, for whatever reason, had made an outstanding gaff along the process of identification. In simple terms, they're going to bury the wrong man in the wrong grave and if someone was to highlight their mistake then a lot of people were going to be really pissed off!

I should have got straight on the phone to complain about their incompetence. I would have too, only it would have been pretty stupid of me to arouse suspicion that I'd been present at the crash site. I shrugged. British history was full of mistakes so one more wouldn't make a frigging difference.

I cleared away the breakfast crockery, which was just as well because the rap on my front door thundered through the hallway like an echo through the dingy vaults of a medieval castle. I wasn't expecting anyone in particular, as most people I know call me first because they know I'm not readily available. And since I detest cold calling door hopping merchants, I ignored the intrusion rather hoping that whoever it was would go away in defeat.

The ploy never worked. The knocker was determined to grab my attention and a piece of my mind. At least I could disregard it was the police hammering on my door because they would have broken in forcibly; it wouldn't be the first time. I ran my fingers through my hair like a comb in a touch of vanity, and then marched down the hallway in a huff. I dragged open the door to remonstrate against the intrusion and was immediately struck dumb by the almost indescribable appearance of the two callers. They were ugly beyond ugly is the only way I could describe them: tall, slim men, dressed in smart dark silk suits who gave me the impression that they liked to scare people for a living. From their slicked back black hair, down to their highly polished shoes, both men had strikingly similar features. They could have easily been mistaken for brothers but they weren't. The slightly taller of the two, I noticed, had a jagged scar running up each side of his nose, as if some cannibalistic madman had tried to permanently detach it from his face with a blunt knife. The same man had also received an injury to his left hand, quite recently too, judging by the cleanliness of the bandage hiding the problem.

At a guess, I'd have put their ages in their early forties. Both remarkably had a similar shoulder deformity, a severe stoop developed by poor posture, probably while sitting hunched at a desk in a cold office with no central heating. Both had beady, dark eyes that stared unblinkingly. Their aquiline noses angled down above funny shaped mouths and their protruding thyroid cartilages gave the illusion of them having bent necks. If they were perched on the branch of a leafless tree on the African plains, they would quite easily pass as a pair of black African vultures waiting patiently for their next meal to die.

I wasn't about to die of fright and since I lack respect for people who supposedly represent authority, which I suspected they were in some category, I said snappily. "Whatever you're selling I don't want it. So fuck off!"

They'd obviously experienced obstinate shits like me before because they never flinched with my abrupt attitude. The scar-less one, stood to the left side of me, flipped open a warrant card and shoved it in front of my face and said just as quickly, "Inspector Filbert, Ministry of Defence Police."

I was a little worried but I wasn't impressed.

"You're Mister Shackleton Speed?" He wasn't politely asking, he was telling me in anticipation of my instant denial.

I never got chance to examine his credentials properly because he whipped the card back into his pocket. I didn't protest. I was too busy thinking aloud. And there could have been a number of reasons why the MDP should be stood on my doorstep. I could only think of one; a particular field in Berkshire and a certain farmer with bragging rights.

I didn't panic. I could have been wrong in my assumption. Mainly to distract them from their intended purpose, I said, "I'm a little too old to join the Forces. If it's recruitments you're after why don't you try further down the road, plenty of rich younger fodder there? Number seventy three, but don't bother knocking on the door, they'll be pie-eyed with expensive recreational drugs."

Two frighteningly aggressive expressions shot back at me. They shuffled forward in a way I considered a threat to my safety. I stood my ground as any true gladiator would.

Filbert's left eyeball seemed to wobble slightly when he spoke. "We're not recruiting, Mister Speed. We're here on a more serious matter."

I deliberately arched my eyebrows in surprise. "Has something happened?"

"It's a criminal matter; the desecration of a war grave."

Here we go! I thought and stabbed myself in the chest with my forefinger and pretended to be shocked. "You're accusing me of playing with the dead?"

Filbert smiled thinly. "You're very humorous, Mister Speed. Perhaps we should go inside to discuss things or would you prefer if we took a trip down to the local police station where you'll be questioned under caution?"

And a camera observing, no doubt, I thought tirelessly.

I didn't fancy the police station for a number of reasons, but I needed to know what they had on me before I decided on my next plan of action. I needed to know if Tommy Bickermass had accidentally dropped me deep in the shit; a slip of his tongue perhaps. It's easily done without thinking and when you're excited.

I let them in, closed the front door and ushered them into my study. I didn't offer them either a seat or refreshments; the quicker we got this over with, the better.

I remained standing too and looked Filbert straight in the eye. I said, "As I told you, I'm not ghoulish enough to visit graveyards."

I had a funny feeling the crafty bastards were recording the conversation, as I noted a slight bulge in Scar-face's breast pocket, where I presumed the voice recorder was hidden to catch my confession.

I went on with my defence and said, "Have you considered vandalism by juveniles? You can always find them hanging around graveyards, smoking, drinking and acting tough."

Filbert seethed. "I'm not referring to just any graveyard, Mister Speed. It concerns the recently discovered Spitfire in the Berkshire countryside."

I frowned first and then pretended to understand his meaning. "Is that the plane splashed across the morning papers? I've just finished reading the story when you decided to disturb my peace. I can't see how I can help you with that."

"It's surprising how you can help us, Mister Speed."

My mind was ticking over fast. *Frigging hell, Tommy, just how deep have you got me in?* "In what way can I help?"

Filbert struck for my jugular. "The ministry don't appreciate the interference of non-commissioned aviation archaeologists vandalizing war crash sites and stealing war memorabilia."

I pretended to be surprised. "No I don't think they would."

"Then you'd better return the piece of wreck you've taken from the crash site."

It was difficult to keep a straight face with such directness.

"Hold on there! Try impressing me with a better accusation."

Filbert's eyeball wobbled again, as it seemed to do when he was agitated. "What you removed from the crash site contravenes the War Graves Act. It's a crime which will send you to prison, if you don't cooperate."

My brow furrowed. "How about clarifying what I supposed to have moved?"

Filbert smirked. "Butter wouldn't melt in your mouth, Mister Speed. Perhaps I should highlight the situation more clearly. Then there'll be no misunderstanding."

"Feel free to proceed," I added.

You've *stolen* a vital piece of equipment from the crash site. We want it back!"

I had to accept that he wasn't in anyway going to be dissuaded by my plea of innocence. But in such tight situations it's always important to remain calm and to use the well rehearsed ploy to always act thick in circumstances where accusations can get you into a lot of trouble. I'm rather proud of my thespian aptitude. "What stolen equipment is that, considering I wasn't even there?"

"You're a fluent liar, Mister Speed!"

"It happens to be the truth."

Filbert sneered. "Don't insult our intelligence, Mister Speed. It didn't take much probing to understand that we're dealing with unscrupulous scum whose intention is to scavenge off the dead. Locating petty grave robbers like you hardly tests the versatility of our department."

"Steady on!" I snapped. "I invited you into my home in good faith. Not to be accused of something that doesn't concern me in the slightest. I was going to offer you refreshments but you can forget it!"

Filbert bared his teeth. "We're not here to socialize, Speed-," he'd soon dropped the niceties of Mister- "we're here to get our property back. Cooperate and we'll drop any impending charges of theft."

"There's nothing to drop. I've taken nothing. Who told you I was there?"

"Your name was mentioned."

"Who's my accuser?"

"That's strictly confidential."

"Then I'm afraid you're pestering the wrong Shackleton Speed."

Filbert smiled sinisterly. "I don't think so. The Shackleton Speed we require is a metallurgist."

I wondered how the hell he knew that. I shrugged. "So I've a qualification. Been checking on me?"

Filbert had more. "Renowned for plundering the land for lost treasure with a metal detector."

"It's a hobby enjoyed by thousands of others."

"Who happens to own a Mercedes Benz 500K Roadster?"

"So I have one in the garage."

"It was seen in Berkshire," he snapped.

"There's more than one on the road," I countered.

I couldn't help but shrivel inside knowing Tommy's narration had been far more detailed than I'd anticipated. He could have warned me. Yet it changed nothing. It was pointless for me to admit my guilt now as it would only get me in deeper bother, so I decided to allow them to do the speculating and I'd continue the denials. It wouldn't be the first time that I'd have to dig my way out of shit to save myself.

Much to my annoyance, Scar-face began mooching around the study desk and shelves. He probably felt he had to do something constructive instead of standing there with his finger up his arse. He further angered me when he began touching the items on the study desk, his greasy hands picking up a picture frame of my late parents for closer inspection and the unceremonious way he roughly replaced it. With the tip of his forefinger he flicked loose papers and envelopes giving me the impression he was memorizing all that caught his eye.

I said meaningfully. "Break anything and I'll frigging sue your department!"

Scar-face directed a searing glare at me. In a deep drawl he said, "I suggest you start giving the right answers or else you might not be around to enjoy your luxuries."

I took his remark as being physically threatening and I suppose it could have been quite frightening to a weaker minded person. But I don't scare easily whether the threats are violent or verbal. I snubbed my nose up at him in defiance and said, "If you want to carry on wiping your grubby hands on my belongings I suggest you show me a search warrant!?" Which I knew never existed in a month of Sundays. So I added cockily, "*You* don't have one?"

Scar-face's complexion turned purple with rage. Within a few minutes of our paths crossing I'd managed to make his guts ache. I thrived on those sorts of annoyances. Yet as I observed his transition from a mild mannered official to a snarling beast, I began to have my doubts about his authenticity as a ministry official. I'd never seen a person of authority deliver the face of a deranged madman as he did. I kept my eyes firmly on him or at least I thought I had until I realized much later what the crafty bastard had done.

As for the present situation, it was plainly obvious that they lied better than I did because there was one outstanding flaw in their story. Tommy never saw me take anything from the wreck and neither did I tell him I had. I believed they were guessing that anything was taken at all. Now was probably the right time to find out before I decided to eject them out of my home.

I said, "Even though I wasn't where you say I was, what is it that I've allegedly stolen?"

Filbert sneered. "You've a bad memory. Try the reconnaissance camera."

"Oh I see...Now let me get this straight. A plane crashes from a great height and probably disintegrated on impact, and after all these years you still expect to pick up all the pieces?" I shook my head. "I don't think that's possible. Do you?"

I still couldn't sway Filbert. "You must think we're gullible, Speed. You dug it from the wreck. You stole it!"

I'd no intention of falling into any verbal trap. "Look! I suggest you go and ask the dog involved because the papers said the dog found the wreck. You can't go around blaming innocent people because you're incapable of finding whatever you've lost. Now if you're absolutely convinced there is something out there to be found, then I'll lend you my metal detector if you can't afford one. For the right price you could even hire me to find it for you. But I don't come cheap!"

"Cut the crap, Speed, and hand over the camera," Filbert seethed.

"I seem to be having trouble convincing you of my innocence."

"It's your last chance!"

I knew at that precise moment that they'd nothing to connect me directly to Berkshire. I decided to call their bluff. Stone faced, I said, "If I'm under suspicion then arrest me now because I'm beginning to get bored with your wild accusations." I paused for an answer. "So what is it to be, handcuffs or are you two going to hold hands and skip off back to Whitehall?"

I expected a backlash and Scar face didn't disappoint. He snarled, baring a dentist's paradise of profitable work to be done, chipped and horribly stained teeth. "Your arrogance can get you seriously hurt, Speed."

I was ready to grapple with him if necessary.

Filbert stepped between us, a thin smile on his face. I suppose I should be thankful for his intervention as it certainly prevented a lot of damage to my furniture. He said, "Fortunately for you, Speed, we have far more important matters that require our immediate attention. Don't assume this is the end. Next time the search warrant will be intact and pinned to your forehead for closer inspection."

I'd no need to direct them out of my home with the assistance of my faithful defensive baton that I keep in a handy position just behind the study door. They left hurriedly, without even a glance over their shoulders. Their rushed exit had me puzzled. I watched their retreat and final departure with added interest. They climbed into a black saloon, which was parked half on the pavement in front of my driveway to prevent any escape by a vehicle, and then accelerated away like boy-racers.

I'd no doubts that I would see them again. Not that I wanted to, but it seemed inevitable. I closed the door and secured the bolt in place just in case they returned unannounced and tried to force their way inside. I went and made a pot of tea, thoughtful of my initial experience with the men from the MDP. There were a number of questions bouncing inside my head.

I sipped my tea at the kitchen table thinking of what excuse I could concoct if the MDP returned with reinforcements and with a warrant for my arrest. There weren't many excuses I could think of at that moment other than a straightforward denial. And then again what proof had they? Nothing substantial I was guessing. I'd no need to worry and, strangely, I didn't think there would be any problems now they had gone. And if they did persist on pestering me over the subject, then I'd have them on a charge of harassment. I should have felt a little better knowing the law would be on my side for a change but I'd a funny feeling that I wasn't the only person they'd been harassing.

Late in the afternoon the telephone rang. Before I'd the chance to lift the receiver it had stopped ringing and within seconds my mobile phone rang. My cheery, "hello", was engulfed by a hype of hysteria that savaged my eardrum.

"He's dead, Shacks! He's dead!"

At first I struggled to distinguish the owner of the emotional voice before I clicked. "Tim! Is that you?"

"Who the fuck do you think it is, Shacks?" There was a stifled sob mixed with his anger.

"Tim, calm down. Take a deep breath and tell me again."

His intake of breath sounded as if he was sucking in air between his teeth. "It's Uncle Tommy!"

He was referring to Tommy Bickermass, the farmer where the Spitfire was found.

"What about him?" I asked, feeling a sudden cold shiver bumping down my spine.

"He-he's dead."

Frigging hell! I thought. I felt my blood drain from me. My legs weakened as I stood there gripping the phone in shock. And then the invisible hand grabbed hold of my heart and ripped it clean from my chest. My voice stiffened. "Tommy...he's dead? When was this?"

I heard Tim suck in more breath. "He was found yesterday."

"What happened?"

"His body was pulled from the slurry tank at the farm."

I had to think hard about what he had just said, trying to establish a mental picture of the farm. I said, "Let me get this right. Do you mean the large steel tank they fill with cow shit?"

I assumed it was because Tim rambled on, not confirming my curiosity. "The police think it was a terrible accident. Reckoned he must have been stood on the gantry at the top of the tank; probably lost his footing and fell in. Reckoned for an old man it would have been like trying to swim through porridge; the quicksand effect; the more he struggled the more he sank. Christ Shacks! It's too awful to think about."

"Tommy drowned in cow shit, is that what you're saying?" I didn't mean it to sound corny or in anyway disrespectful of the dead.

"That's what I'm saying, Shacks."

"Who found him?"

The farm hand, poor sod."

"Benny, you mean?"

"Yes Benny. Said he found Tommy's cap at the foot of the tank ladder when he arrived early at the farm. He checked the top of the tank but there was no sign of Tommy. But he noticed the usually crusted topped slurry had been broken, like cracked ice, as he described it. Said he saw something half submerged and when he hooked it with a pole to find out what it was,"-I heard a faint sniffle-"well he pulled Uncle Tommy out as quick as he could, but...it was all too late."

"Frigging hell, Benny must have been heartbroken."

Another sniffle, "He had to be sedated when the paramedics arrived."

"I'm not surprised. Tommy was like a father to him."

"Benny had told the police that he was baffled as to how Tommy had climbed onto the tank gantry in the first place."

"Tommy was scared of heights?"

"No. He suffered from a frozen knee. He couldn't have climbed the vertical ladder even if he wanted to...well not without a struggle or help."

"Tommy could have climbed regardless...if he had to?"

"I suppose so. But why should he want to? Benny said he never climbed the ladder at all. That was Benny's job; always."

There was obviously a good reason why Tommy had decided to make the effort up onto the gantry, but I'd be guessing wildly for the answer. I said, "What's happening at the farm now?"

"The police are still investigating."

"So they're not certain what happened to Tommy?"

"I'm not sure what they think, Shacks..." I heard Tim sniffle. "It's wrong...it's wrong that a good man has to die horribly, alone; no one there to help him."

I couldn't have agreed with him more. I could think of a number of people I'd rather see dead than poor Tommy Bickermass. How ironic I thought. The hero splashed across the news one minute, dead the next. There's no justice in life and fate has such a pathetic way of running its business. As for the appropriate condolences I have to admit I'm useless in such delicate situations.

"Is there anything you want me to do, Tim?"

"No, nothing Shacks. Everything is being done and his immediate family are there now. I rang you because I knew you'd want to know about the tragedy before you heard it elsewhere."

"I appreciate that, Tim. I'd gotten quite attached to the old fellow recently."

"I'm going over later today. I'll ring you when I know more."

"Okay, Tim. Take care."

"You'll be at his funeral, won't you Shacks? He'd want you there."

I hate funerals; they're morbid, depressing and give a false image that there's something to look forward to on the other side. "I'll be there, Tim."

The call ended.

I pressed the off button on my mobile. I realized I was still trembling slightly. I cured the hypertension with swift straight dark rum, gulped down in one, poured another and wandered aimlessly to the sofa where I slumped down and slouched back dejectedly. I stared blankly up at the ceiling, trawling the term tragic accident back and forth through my mind. My eyelids went heavy and weary. I closed them. I tried to blank Tommy's death from my thoughts but I couldn't. By the time I'd finished churning everything inside my head I was as far away from Tommy's death being an accident as I could ever be. Tommy didn't strike me as being that stupid to have fallen in a tank of shit. He always had a careful aptitude when running his farm; a stickler towards safe farming; everything fenced off properly; things in their rightful places. I saw all that for myself firsthand. And Benny, well he'd confirmed that Tommy never scaled the slurry tank because of his bad knee. That knowledge in itself made the theory of an accident vulnerably weak.

I sighed. Tommy would be sadly missed. I finished the second rum and found myself twirling the glass through my fingers, thinking how Tommy could have climbed onto the gantry in the first place? What had attracted him to make the mammoth effort? Those were the questions the police should be asking, not skulking around with their heads stuck up their arses taking the easy option of an accident. The police should be listening to the people who knew Tommy instead of relying totally on their professional opinions which most of the time is guesswork and probably nowhere near the truth.

The insides of my stomach knotted the more I delved into his death. I'm not psychic, nor do I ever pretend to be, but I had this awful feeling that somewhere, other developments were mounting. There's a saying: things happen in three's. That worried me immensely. I was suddenly connecting the events at the farm with other imaginable contenders.

The two men from the MDP, who had pestered me earlier making idle threats, were back in contention. Perhaps I'd misjudged their seriousness. I wondered how much they knew about Tommy's death because I'd gotten the impression they'd been at the farm to question Tommy about the plane wreck. And what an idiot I'd been. I had failed to double check or verify their credentials before allowing them access. Come to think of it, Scar-face didn't even show any credentials and neither did he reveal his name. Perhaps they had contributed to Tommy's fall into the slurry tank? There was only Tommy who knew I'd been at the farm. Perhaps they threatened him into revealing the location of the reconnaissance camera after dragging him up onto the gantry to scare him? Perhaps a titanic struggle had occurred and Tommy had struggled too much and had fallen in. Or maybe the MDP officers had pushed him? Or was I perhaps searching for truths that weren't there to be found. It wasn't exactly difficult to concoct a number of storylines to fit my inquisitive questions. I was desperate for any excuse.

What I could confidently conclude was the two ministry policemen knew the reconnaissance camera had gone from the wreck. So what importance did the camera have that it was the sole subject of conversation with me? Historic military archives came to mind, exactly what I thought when I pinched the frigging thing. Yet if they were genuine MDP eager to retrieve government property, and they were confident that I had it, then why did they leave me alone so easily without making more of a fuss? They could have called the local constabulary and had me arrested on suspicion of theft, but they didn't.

I was just getting more and more confused and giving myself an almighty headache. And then to my horror it clicked. Why indeed did they leave so easily? Because...?

I sat upright and opened my eyes in sheer terror. My eyes flicked in the direction of the study. I remembered Scar-face was messing around with my belongings, being too nosey. It was shortly after that when they left in a hurry and without a threatening word from either.

I jumped up from the sofa, put the glass down on the coffee table and dashed to the study where I ran a careful eye over everything that Scar-face had mooched through or displaced. I checked the moveable items and various papers that he had disturbed. I checked the bureau and scanned the book shelves. I did notice he had shifted the telephone to a different angle.

The telephone!

I realized there was something missing that I'd left next to the telephone.

The sad bastard had stolen my pad of telephone numbers and addresses.

Why bother?

To check names and addresses obviously...names and addresses? I suddenly had visions of the photography shop where I'd left the camera. My heart raced as

I thought of the dreadful possibility that I may have put Lens's life in jeopardy. I snatched the phone from its cradle and pressed in a set of numbers; waited impatiently as the ringing tone searched for a connection. I suddenly became clammy. I'd palpitations.

My anxiety eased when Lens finally raised the receiver and went through the motions of announcing the name of his business in his laid back Barbadian voice.

"Larry's photographic agency-"

I burst into his rehearsed announcement before he had time to finish and asked him if he was alright. My enquiry must have confused him because it's not something I would normally ask him. For an eerie few seconds he didn't answer. I could hear him breathing down the line. My anxiety was back again.

His reluctance to speak angered me. Lens was about to witness a different side of me. "Frigging hell, speak to me you dumb bastard!"

"Hey Shacks, man!" his voice finally drifted through. "Stay cool. Hard to take in, man, cos I didn't realize you'd a heart."

I pushed on. "Listen to me! Has anyone come asking about the camera I gave you?"

Another pause didn't help matters though I imagined his wide eyes rolling in their sockets in sheer panic. He didn't care for dishonest activities, especially mine.

"Shacks, is the damn thing hot?"

"No! If you remember I told you I dug it from the ground."

"Yeah, man, but whose ground? No, don't say, man, I'd only have bad illusions of being thrown in piss smelling prison, served sloppy dinners and have nasty shit stabbers molesting my cute arse."

"Lens, you're avoiding my question! Has anybody asked about the camera? Think Lens. It's important!"

"Nobody asked. Why?"

"You're sure? No phone calls or anything out of the ordinary?"

"Yeah, I'm sure, man; you're the only one asking."

I puffed out my cheeks, the weight of anxiety lifting from my shoulders knowing Lens was safe.

Lens said, "By the way, Shacks. This lump of rust you brought in is a complete bag of mutilated crap."

"I wasn't considering displaying the thing, Lens. Did you manage to retrieve anything worthwhile from it or not?"

"Scrap, that's what I got. In a thousand twisted pieces now. I had to go in with the surgical expertise of a brain surgeon to remove the film. Rubber gloves, dissecting tool, pliers, the works, man!"

"Stop pissing around, Lens!"

"Okay man!" he finally conceded and raced through his findings. "Found four pictures which I masterly extracted. Damned lucky I got that many. The rest of the film roll, I'm afraid, is a complete waste of my effort; the film's watermarked beyond recognition."

"Lens, I'm amazed you found any at all."

"Shacks, you know me and the miracles I can do. I've put the pictures and negatives in the post this morning. What do you want me to do with the scrap pieces and watermarked negatives that are left?"

"Dump them, Lens." It was pointless keeping hold of the evidence."

"Consider it done, Shacks."

"What do I owe you?"

"The usual fee, Shacks: a Chinese meal and plenty of beer to swill down the food. Throw in a few loose woman and we'll call it straight."

"Don't want much then," I quipped.

"I'm a healthy guy, Shacks. Oh! Did I mention a night in the West End too; with spending money?" he added cheekily. "There's a new nightclub I'd like to boogie on down to and strut my stuff."

He always reminded me of a jelly man when he danced, he was that flexible.

I'd began to open my mouth and ready to give him a slice of verbal abuse concerning his exuberant fee when I heard something else echo in the receiver that took me a moment to register what it was. What I'd clearly heard was the chink of the photography shop doorbell interfering with Len's voice. Then Lens hurriedly said, "Got to go, Shacks, paying customers," and after a low whistle, he added, "Hell man, what a couple of weirdoes. Last time I saw a pair like these I was watching wild life in Africa and they were devouring the carcass of some half eaten Lion spoils."

I then heard him speak to whoever had entered the shop before his voice faded away from the receiver.

At first I wondered what the frigging hell Lens meant when he mentioned *Africa* and *Lion spoils,* until my brain registered. By then Lens had already replaced his receiver and I was shouting into a tunnel of emptiness. "Lens, Lens! Get out of there!"

I pressed the shop's telephone numbers into the handset frantically. It rang a few times and then I was cut off. My heart rate accelerated. I pressed the same numbers again, whispering the words, "pick up the phone, Lens, pick up the phone!", as I waited. All I received was the tinny echo of a discontinued line.

I threw the receiver down and sprinted for my car keys and was out of the house. I roared the Roadster into life and began driving hard and furious, breaking every road rule in the book. I didn't frigging care how dangerous I drove. I just hoped no police car would try to halt my progress because I was in no mood to stop.

I slammed down the accelerator pedal to the floor, the engine growling as I crashed through the gears. I tore down street after street, road after road, dangerously overtaking, tyres screeching as I negotiated tight bends, ignoring blaring car-horns and the probable and deserved fingered gestures. But I wasn't looking who I passed on the road. I was too focused driving like a man possessed to save a friends life.

On reaching Lambeth Road I maddened because the traffic was at a standstill. I could see a police roadblock ahead. In the distance I saw the large plume of black smoke rising above the buildings. Fire engines had just arrived at the scene and were in immediate action; more fire engines were on the way with a police escort to get the engines through the traffic. I pulled the Roadster into the side of the road, got out and began running between vehicles in the direction of the fire. My frantic running had me gasping for breath. My lungs hurt and the taste of acrid smoke tainted my mouth. When I neared the row of shops and my final destination my stride stiffened and I grinded to a halt, in disbelief. It was Lens's photography shop that was on fire.

The initial shock had me gob smacked. I could only stare at the spectacle I was witnessing and my mouth was dry as if it had been swabbed with blotting paper.

I mustered enough spit and shouted out, “Lens!”, and then I continued running towards the building and slap bang into a policeman’s huge hand in my chest that brought my progress to an abrupt halt.

“Sorry sir! He advised me assertively. “You must step back. There’s danger of an explosion ahead.”

His prediction came true and a muffled bang blew out one of the photography shop windows. Shattered glass forced the fire-fighters to cower as they aimed their hoses into the flames and the mushroom of orange and black smoke whooshing into the air. The policeman and I ducked instinctively, even though the debris never reached us. The flames were horrendously hot even at the proposed safe distance. And I noticed that the westerly breeze was spreading the flames to other premises along the road.

The explosion only served to make me fearless and more determined to push on towards the building. I had to find Lens. I made another attempt to pass my holder and get closer to the burning premises. The policeman held me back, almost wrestling me to the ground. I was shouting out Lens’s name. Two, three times I called, still grappling with the policeman. I never went to ground. Some inner strength kept me on my feet as I pushed hard, struggling for freedom from the policeman’s powerful grip.

The policeman suddenly had his face in front of mine. “Is there someone still inside the building?” he quickly asked, shaking me to get me focused on what he was asking, staring into my eyes for a definite answer. “Listen to me, please sir! Is there still someone inside?”

“Larry Lazerow, the proprietor. It’s his shop on fire! He got out, didn’t he? He’s a coloured guy, medium height. Tell me he’s okay?”

My heart sank somewhere inside my bowel as I watched the policeman's expression of uncertainty before he confirmed the inevitable. "We-I-er-thought everybody was accounted for, sir. Are you sure he was still inside the shop?"

"I spoke to him not twenty minutes ago on the telephone," I said frantically. "The line went dead. I thought something was wrong, so I came straight here. You must have seen him?"

I didn't think it was due to the heat of the fire when I noticed the beads of sweat leak from beneath the policeman's helmet and trickle down the sides of his face. It was the defining moment when I knew Lens was still trapped inside his photography shop, trapped in the inferno. Lens was probably dead, engulfed by the flames. I always thought I was a strong person in such tragic circumstances and that I could handle terrible moments. I was wrong. Inside I fell to pieces. Uncontrollably my legs quivered and buckled. I found myself sitting on the kerbside with my head in my hands listening to the policeman shouting across to the chief fire officer that there might be a casualty inside the building. I knew then it was too late. The damage was done. Not even the Devil himself could have survived the ferocious flames that lit-up the smoke filled street.

I hung around more in hope than anticipation. And just maybe Lens had escaped and was lying injured somewhere. That hope turned to despair when there was still no news of him after the hour it had taken the fire brigade to bring the blaze under reasonable control. My insides churned and ached in frustration. I'd failed Lens twice. I'd put him in danger and I was too late to save him. After a further thirty minutes the fire team entered the building, damping down the burning embers. Another thirty minutes later the fire investigators went inside the burnt shell followed by the forensic team. The news leaked out. They had found a charred body but they couldn't make a positive identification. I stayed long enough to watch the fire team return with a bulging and strangely deformed body bag. What contents from breakfast I still had left in my stomach ended on the ground between my legs.

"Excuse me, sir," the same policeman addressed me, his tone neutral.

I looked up hopefully. Expressions tell a great deal and the policeman's hadn't changed for the better.

"I suppose it was Larry they've dragged out of there?" I asked, a large lump swelling in my throat and choking me.

"It's impossible to confirm anything at the moment, sir. They've retrieved a body and it's being taken away for examination; that's all I can tell you; sorry."

My head dropped back into my hands and I exhaled long and heavy.

"I'll need to take your name and address, sir, as a statement will be required for the investigation team later."

I nodded and squeaked out my relevant details which he noted in his black notebook. I couldn't recall exactly where I went afterwards, when I'd finally found the strength in my legs to get to my feet and walk away from the carnage. It was some pub close by, its name by-passing my memory. I can only remember the pub was quiet and I had somewhere to think. I drank until the dark rum numbed my brain and the barman finally refused to serve me any more. I can't remember how I got home but my Roadster was at an angle in my driveway the following afternoon.

I was informed three days later that the charred body of Larry Lazerow was identified not by any physical part of his anatomy but by the gold ring he had pieced through the end of his foreskin. I remembered Larry telling me that the girls adored it. Not anymore they won't.

Chapter Three

Nobody should have to endure a double tragedy. The police in Berkshire were satisfied that Tommy Bickermass had been the unfortunate victim of circumstances. That he had slipped and had fallen into the slurry tank; a forgone conclusion, signed, sealed and delivered. I wasn't convinced-well not after the death of Lens, which at least was still under investigation although not in the direction it should have taken.

I had all the time in the world to blame myself for Lens. I'd dragged him into the frame. Quicker thinking on my part and I could have warned Lens much earlier, probably got him away from the photography shop with some lame excuse without scaring him. But how the frigging hell was I to know he'd been added to some death list. I say death list because two accidents relating to something that connects me just doesn't happen. My troubles are usually my own; they don't involve others, well not serious enough to be killed for.

Lens had been got at alright, that I was sure. But the most frightening part of the whole situation is no police fingers were pointing to any particular suspects other than Lens was a victim of his own making and therefore Lens would become another unfortunate accident report.

Lens had died by sinister means; I'd no doubt about that. I had an inclination of who was to blame for his death and the two sad bastards from the MDP were clearly embedded in mind. They'd been in contact with Tommy. They'd turned up on my doorstep swinging threats at me and had most definitely stolen my telephone pad, which I now recall I'd left opened on the page with Lens's photographic shop telephone number and address clearly visible. I'm positive it was the same two that had arrived at the photography shop on that fatal day. It made sense it was them.

Lens wasn't renowned for his toughness and he would have succumbed to anything when threatened with violence. Lens was too much of a nice guy. He wasn't particularly a strong man either and he would have undoubtedly struggled to fight them off. The fact was Lens couldn't even fight his way out of a wet paper bag even when he got angry enough. I imagined his resistance to an assault would have been nonexistent because he probably never thought he was going to die in his own shop.

What really nailed my brain to the floor was why should anyone want to commit murder over a battered WWII camera, which was unquestionably the link, and then create the impression they were accidents. I mean killing someone to make it look like an accident had been practiced since the first lawman arrived. The problem I had now would be trying to persuade the police that they had a murder enquiry on their doorstep.

I soon got my chance.

I was summoned to Kennington Road Police station on a wet and miserable morning: 10 AM on the dot. I was early for a change but that was more to me not sleeping properly since the tragedies. On principle I'm not normally cooperative with the police, but on this occasion I had to reassure myself that the police fully understood the seriousness of what was going on right under their noses. And if they had already done their job thoroughly I'm sure the evidence accumulated would be sufficient to arrest the culprits and for me to identify the bastards from the MDP.

I approached the desk sergeant apprehensively and told him who I was and why I was here. He made an internal phone call. While I waited for a response, I glanced around. Police stations, wherever situated in the world, always gave me the feeling of uneasiness, mainly because I had frequented too many in the past in order to defend myself against false accusations, but that's another dozen or so stories.

I was shown into an interview room and told to take a seat. Within minutes the interviewer arrived, carrying a green paper folder and pen. He closed the door behind him and introduced himself as Detective Constable Stevens. He was a tall, young fresh looking chap with well groomed dark hair and had a lean build. He had a determined look and one that gave me the distinct impression that he could go a long way through the police ranks. The more I studied him, the more I concluded he was just another ambitious copper who would ignore common sense to get a prosecution in order to build up an impressive CV to show his bosses for when the promotions were up for grabs.

Stevens smoothed his trousers down with his hands before he sat, opened the folder and looked briefly at the contents, which I assumed was my statement I had made the day after the fire which had killed Lens. He flicked his eyes in my direction and said, "You are Mister Shackleton Speed?" His tone resembled more of a prosecuting Barrister.

I nodded. "Yes, that's right."

"I'm sorry to drag you down to the station on such a horrible rainy day," he sounded sincere but his lying eyes betrayed him, "and I hope not to detain you any longer than necessary." He coughed lightly to clear his throat. "Now I'm led to believe you actually spoke to Mister Lazerow shortly before his unfortunate death. Is this correct?"

"Yes, by telephone."

He ticked the document in front of him, looked at me with a powerful stare, which made me shift uncomfortably in my chair. "You seem agitated, Mister Speed?"

"I'm tired. I haven't been sleeping well. It's hard to accept the death of a friend."

Stevens nodded in agreement. "I quite understand. This-ah," he glanced at his notes, "telephone conversation with Mister Lazerow, anything special you discussed?"

"Just to ask if he'd completed some work for me."

"Work of any importance?"

"No!" I was getting a bit peeved already.

"How did he sound to you over the phone?"

"How did he sound? I'm not following."

"Did he sound distressed or was there anything he said that was out character?"

I should have realized sooner than I did what Stevens was getting at, and that his thoughts, I feared, nowhere near matched mine. "No." I said assured. "He sounded like he always sounded, happy and content."

His eyes flicked up. "So what induced you to dash over to the photography shop?"

"The call was cut off without warning."

The eyes still probed. "You redialled?"

"Yes."

"What occurred?"

"The line was dead. I guess I panicked."

"You panicked?"

"Yes. It happens sometimes when I'm under stress. Has this anything to do with his murder?"

I hit a nerve in the Detective's back teeth as he sat up straight, slightly shocked by what I had just said. But he recovered quickly and said, "I'm sorry, but I think there's been a misunderstanding. This is not a murder inquiry I'm conducting."

"Then why-"

"To iron out a few points," he jumped in.

I hate to be interrupted and have my sentence anticipated. "What sort of points?"

He smiled weakly. "We need to establish the last known movements of the deceased and his state of his mind at the time. You were the last person to talk to him."

"That maybe so but what's the purpose of all this?"

"We have to prepare a report for the Coroner's office. Every minute detail has to be established for a correct verdict in court."

"And what is the verdict likely to be, out of curiosity?"

"I'm not at liberty to say."

"There's nothing suspicious about the way he died?"

"There's nothing that we are aware of. Fire investigators pinpointed the probable cause of the fire was by a small explosion of chemicals relating to the processing of photographs. They concluded that the owner of the photography shop, Mister Lazerow, probably mixed the wrong chemicals which then created an explosive reaction that ignited flammable material. Or he may have been smoking at the time."

I jumped straight down his throat in protest. "That can't be right! For starters Larry never smoked and he never made mistakes. His expertise in photography was legendary."

The Detective wasn't for listening. "It's what the fire investigators confirmed, taking in consideration of where the body was positioned and the intensity of the blaze. They're extremely professional in their field, I can assure you, Mister Speed."

"They've got it wrong this time."

"Is that so, sir?"

"Larry could do his job with his eyes closed and three parts pissed."

"So he drank a lot too?"

Typical police twister, I wanted to tell him and simultaneously expressed my disgust with his feeble accusation. I held back my anger when I said, "He never drank during the working week and that's a fact. What I said was a figure of speech. I was trying to emphasize that Larry was careful beyond being careful. Mistakes by him would be unthinkable. Someone else started that fire."

"I know you're upset."

"I'm not upset!"

"I hope you don't mind me asking, Mister Speed. But has a doctor prescribed any medication for your trauma?"

"I don't need medication."

"Maybe it would be best if you booked an appointment to see a doctor."

"I don't need to see a doctor."

He tried to allay me. "You've lost a good friend and it's understandable that his death is distorting the way you're thinking, Mister Speed."

"Look! I've got over his death. It's what you're trying to tell me that upsets me. It just doesn't add up. I knew Larry inside out and he wouldn't be that clumsy."

"It's evident how you feel, but I can categorically state that the fire investigators are extremely confident with their findings. They're a pretty accurate bunch and I can vouch for their competence."

"I'm not disputing their skills. I'm saying Larry Lazerow didn't make those kind of mistakes. He was too damn *good* at his job. The fire, I believe, was started by someone else and made to appear as an incompetent accident."

The policeman's eyebrows lifted. "Then perhaps you can throw some light over the proceedings, Mister Speed? You seem to have very strong opinions on the matter. Do you have any notions to support your theory? Perhaps some suspects?"

"I know two men entered the shop while he was in conversation with me on the telephone. That's when the line went dead. The fire started not long after that."

"There's nothing in your statement referring to the two men."

"It had slipped my mind. It was hard to think clearly at the time."

"These two men you refer to; they were customers?"

"More than customers, they were from the Ministry of Defence Police."

"How could you have possibly known that considering it was a phone call?"

"I heard it mentioned in the background before the line went dead." I had to lie in order to get him thinking my way.

"Why should the MDP want to call upon, Mister Lazerow?"

My brain went into constructive overdrive as I concocted what I considered to be a decent enough story. "It concerned the recent discovery of a war plane in Berkshire?"

He nodded. "I've read something about it in the papers."

I thought I'd better explain the situation, eradicating myself from the scene, of course. "Well the owner the land, where the plane was unearthed, asked Larry to take some photographs of him standing near the wreck. Tommy, that's Tommy Bickermass the farmer, wanted the pictures for his scrapbook."

"Put pictures into a scrap book." He sounded incredibly bored.

"Yes. To capture the memories so he could show his grand-children." Sarcastically, I added, "It's what normal families usually do!"

"To show grand-children plane wrecks?"

I wondered if he ridiculed everyone he interviewed. As big as he was he needed a good smack across the chin and I was certainly strong and fit enough and certainly in the mood to do just that. But somehow I didn't rate my chances of exiting the building without the assistance of a stretcher if I did. Instead I gave him something else to mix into his thin dossier for the Coroner.

I said, "What about Tommy Bickermass? He also died recently in mysterious circumstances shortly after the discovery of the plane."

He looked disappointed with me. "Mister Speed, please. Surely you're not implying the MDP had something to do with both deaths?"

"That's precisely what I'm saying."

"Good heavens, Mister Speed! Why should that be?" The slight conviction in his tone suggested he could be taking me seriously, but I was only kidding myself.

"How the frigging hell should I know why!" I barked. "That's what I believe."

Steven smirked. "It's hardly in the best interest of the MDP to exterminate people because of an old fighter plane being exhumed. This country wants to recover all its dead heroes not get rid of new ones. Being paranoid isn't going to solve very much. Life is full of unlucky people making fatal mistakes which end in tragedy."

"I'm not being paranoid." I protested. "I suppose the two MDP officers that came pestering me at my home was a figment of my imagination, especially when they accused me of vandalizing the wreck." I could have shrivelled up like a prune at that moment knowing what I said. I quickly added, "Even though I wasn't even at the crash site."

He was onto my gaff in an instance. "You *weren't*?"

"No I wasn't. And I've no idea why they thought that I was there."

Stevens scratched the end of his nose with the pen. "Do you have any names for these MDP officers?"

"I caught only the one name; an Inspector Filbert."

I assumed I'd triggered something important because the Detective suddenly rose from his chair and said, "Excuse me for a moment." And he promptly left the room as if he was in a hurry.

Twenty minutes the slimy Peeler kept me waiting. Being isolated in a police station within four tight walls, no windows, and a whining wall-fan that irritated me to the point of insanity, can be tediously daunting at the best of times. The wait certainly tested my patience because I found myself drumming my fingertips hard upon the table with no true rhythmical beat but I did manage a brief shufti at his notes he'd left on the table. There was nothing in the notes that I didn't know already.

When he finally returned he was carrying a thick brown, A4 cardboard folder which he slapped onto the table with the deliberate intention of sending a gust of wind flying into my face to wake me from my boredom. He also had an accusing stare when he sat down.

I leaned forward and said, enthusiastically, "Got something already?"

The detective's slow and deliberate action had me retracting in my chair. He said, "I've been in contact with the MDP. They state, categorically, that there are no impending investigations regarding the crash site in question. They assure me all normal procedures have been carried out and completed. The pilot's body was exhumed in readiness for a military funeral. The crash site has been logged and is now a protected area. As for a Inspector Filbert, you might be interested to know, he retired from the ministry ten years ago and would have gladly made the journey to see you if he'd been able to get out of his wheelchair. So I'm afraid whoever came knocking on your door, Mister Speed, it certainly had nothing to do with the MDP. Perhaps you've been infuriating someone else?"

I had no reason to doubt the information Steven's had received from the MDP concerning Filbert. And it was plainly obvious that cold callers such as those two creeps who had come thumping on my front door were hardly going to leave behind their true calling cards. I decided in my best interest not to press on about them. Instead

I watched with intrigue as Stevens opened the folder he had brought into the room and began to flick through individual pages with eye-popping reactions of what appeared to be photo-copied script. I could tell by the sudden gleam in his eye that he had found something incriminating against me.

Finally, he said, "I've acquired this special piece of information from the police computer that should interest you, Mister Speed."

More like he's been checking up on me, I thought. "Have you really!" I said.

"My-my-you have been extremely busy over the past few years. Eleven court appearances in front of the judge concerning non-declaration of treasure trove."

I struck back sharply. "It should also mention that I was acquitted eleven times?" I said, defensively.

His brow scrunched with my untimely interruption. "*And,* neither has your exploits escaped the attention of Interpol. It seems that you have been plying your infamous trade among the scallywags in the black market labyrinths of Amsterdam, Brussels, Hamburg, and other various seedy parts of Europe as far as Turkey. Yes, Mister Speed, this suggests to me you've been a very *busy* man on the wrong side of the law."

The smarmy bastard, I thought. So I dug a few English antiquities from the ground and sold them on in Europe. What's the big fuss? It's not my fault the highest bidder happens to be in Amsterdam or Brussels or Hamburg. It was time to defend myself before he got too carried away.

I said, "You'll find all the allegations are untrue. Is there a point to all this? Only I thought the reason for coming here today was to discuss Larry Lazerow's demise. Not if I've been a naughty boy in the past!"

"Most definitely there's a point, Mister Speed," his tone was sharper now, "It's a warning really, to stay away from the crash site."

"There's no law against looking," I said stubbornly.

"I was referring to the use of a metal detector. Because if I get word from the Berkshire constabulary that anything has gone missing, I'll make sure the next conviction against you will stick forever. Is that clear?"

I stood up and looked him straight in the eye with the strong urge to tell the sad bastard he was a week too late, but I resisted the temptation. "I guess you've finished with me over the photography shop?"

"I don't think I'll be bothering you again on the matter."

I headed for the door hastily only for the Detective to stop me in my tracks.

"There is another issue that you should be aware of, Mister Speed."

I didn't bother to turn and face him; I already knew what was coming. Over my shoulder I said, "Yes!"

"It's advisable that you refrain from spreading rumours concerning your inappropriate theories, especially to the newspapers, until after the Coroners verdict has been announced. Remember, Mister Lazerow died as a consequence of his own misfortune and nothing else. We've concluded a thorough investigation and we're confident of our findings. Is that understood?"

I said nothing in return and was halfway through the door when he added: "Please convey my condolences to Mister Lazerow's family. Good day, Mister Speed."

I left sharply before I said something I would never regret and probably end up in gaol for the night.

I left the police station in a state of frustration. It was maddening to think that I'd gone there with the good intentions of persuading the investigation team that they had a murder enquiry on their hands and instead they turned the whole episode into an inquisition against me. Back in the Roadster my anger blurred my concentration. In a better frame of mind I might have noticed the black saloon slipping in behind the Roadster sooner than I did.

When I finally noticed I was being tailed, it wasn't difficult to guess the occupants of the vehicle behind me and I wouldn't be far wrong in assuming that the two vultures I'd previously encountered were circling their intended prey. I prepared myself mentally, my sweaty palm hovering over the gear lever for a racing gear change in case of a sudden attack. They weren't going to catch me out as easily as they caught Larry or Tommy. With every manoeuvre I made, I double-checked the rear view mirror, mainly to confirm by sight if it was the two bogus MDP officials. But in a blink of the eye I'd lost them. I'd turned around a corner and the car didn't follow. I was alone again and my panic subsided.

I detest being labelled 'paranoid', as detective Stevens had suggested. Paranoid people require treatment for their mental state and I wasn't ready for the asylum just yet. There were questions buzzing around inside my head that required an answer and I was determined to get them regardless of whose nose I got up. For me now, I would have to rethink my strategy because I suddenly realized that I wasn't going to get any help from anybody who represented the badge of a Peeler.

Chapter Four

I declined the opportunity to attend the inquest on Lens's death and have my say. There was no point? My presence at the official hearing would have had no bearing whatsoever on the eventual outcome, well not without the hard evidence that a murder had been committed. Accidental death was firmly planted in the minds of everyone concerned and any interference from me would change nothing other than to infuriate those officials in attendance at the Coroner's court.

I had to start thinking about myself and my own safety. Naturally I was pensive as to why I walked this crazy wretched earth still in one piece and why they hadn't made a positive attempt to silence me for good. Surely I was on their list for extermination just as Tommy and Lens were. I could only assume that they hadn't finished with me. Knowing that, the sensible solution would have been for me to go into hiding. Loose myself amid other tourists in some over-crowded resort far away. Frigging hell I was fooling myself! That was the easy way out. I wanted to kick arse. I wanted to avenge Lens's death. But my most disturbing thoughts centred on how far I would be willing to go to achieve my revenge.

I began to devise a plan of where I should start. Since I'm no super sleuth I considered hiring a private detective but I didn't want the responsibility of another death on my hands regardless of how professional the person was at their job. Besides, when it came to chasing answers, I'd spent a good part of my life in the pursuit of lost treasure and I'd gained considerable notoriety when outwitting the Treasure Valuation Committee, all of which puts me in a position of not being a complete novice after all. I could be tough and vicious if I needed to be and with no remorse whatsoever.

I knew my situation wasn't favourable. I would be a one man army with no fire-arms experience and up against...what was I up against? Two vicious, nameless men insisting I hand over a battered camera, for starters. That frigging camera! I cursed.

Something pinged in my brain. I suddenly remembered what Lens had told me over the phone. Without even doing anything outrageous I already had my start; the camera! I went to retrieve the mail I'd thrown unceremoniously into the waste-bin by the study door and sifted through the pile. I could tell Lens's handwriting straight away when I selected the A5 size brown envelope, ripped open the seal and studied the contents. I was looking at four black and white photographs of poor quality and water-marked badly around the edges. Each photograph showed the same surfaced submarine, but at slightly different angles, with what appeared to be a plume of smoke coming from its stern. I got the impression the craft was sinking by the angle of the submarine riding in the water.

I went down into the privacy of my cellar studio, the place where I clean all the artefacts I've unearthed in the past. I put each photograph in turn onto the enlargement projector and examined them in more detail. The submarine was positioned approximately half a mile off a rocky shoreline but I'd no idea where other than it being a European shoreline. On the submarine's conning tower

I could barely make out the symbol of the Rising Sun and the faint lettering I-52. I was looking at a Japanese submarine which was clearly in dire trouble. But I was thinking deeper. Wondering why a Japanese submarine should have attracted the attention of a British reconnaissance craft instead of a battle cruiser. It all seemed a bit strange especially when the Japanese did their fighting in and around Asia. And then I remembered there were liaisons between the German U-boats and Japanese submarines in order to transfer vital supplies. But those transfers were usually conducted out in the Atlantic or in or around the security of German held territories.

I could have continued searching forever for the right answers. Whatever the photographs were trying to tell me I couldn't make head or tail of it, yet these photos were redeemed to be worth the lives of two men. I placed the pictures in the wall safe where nothing less than a nuclear bomb would extract them.

*

The following day I was back in Berkshire for Tommy Bickermass's funeral. There's a saying: *you suddenly realize you're getting old by the number of funerals you attend*, and I suppose my sudden increase of two dead friends rather made my thirty-five years feel more like seventy-five. I'm not a religious man by any means nor do I disrespect another person's faith. I believe in fate and luck and it's served me well so far in life.

I stayed away from the church service only attending the burial itself. The whole occasion was a quiet funeral for a nice quiet man who lived for nothing more than the chance to make an honest crumb. I felt as if I had let him down in a lot of departments.

I never mentioned to any of the congregation about my suspicions of how Tommy died. Perhaps I should have but I didn't, mainly because they were upset enough. If I'd begun spreading dodgy presumptions amongst family and friends, and they turned out to be untrue, I could imagine my arrival in these parts again would be repelled by the barrel of a twelve bore shotgun or a pitchfork shoved up my backside.

It was at the defining moment when the priest mentioned *dust to dust* that I heard Tommy's dog, Winston, pining for his master. I glanced down at the poor beast noticing that Winston had received a nasty looking wound above his left eye. I waited until after the service before I asked Tommy's daughter, Debbie, how Winston had acquired his wound.

"Nobody seems to know," she said sombrely, her eyes red, still the odd floating tear ready to seep and trickle down her cheek. "The poor dog was cowering in the barn covered in dried blood the day after my...father was found..." She wiped away a tear. "The vet had to put six stitches in a deep cut."

I gave the dog a sympathetic pat. "Look, I know this isn't the right time to be asking but have you ever heard of a chap named Billy Banter? It's a name I recall Tommy-sorry-your father-mentioning after the discovery of the plane wreck."

Debbie looked at me strangely. "Yes I know of him. But that isn't his real name; it's Billy Slade. Why do you want know, if you don't mind me asking?"

"Your father said that when he and Billy were kids, during the war, Billy had been ranting on about a plane crashing in the fields at the time."

Her lips pursed in surprise. "My father never told me that story."

"Well actually there was no story to tell because no one believed Billy at the time. Now, after the discovery of the wreck, your father felt a bit guilty for not believing Billy and I think he wanted to make amends, but he never got the chance with...well...the accident intervened. I thought it would be a good gesture to have a word with Billy myself and finish what your father intended. Do you know where I can find him?"

"He's still in the area. He's in a nursing home at the far side of the village. It's an old converted mansion called 'Three Trees'. You do know he has learning difficulties?"

"Your father did tell me about his condition."

"Well I don't think it'll do any harm you visiting him, Mister Speed."

"Please, call me Shacks."

"Well, Shacks, I just can't imagine Billy actually remembering anything that far back in time."

"I know it's a long shot but think I should still try. It's what your father would have wanted."

I felt Winston nudged past our legs. I glanced at him concerned. His ears were pricked and he begun to growl, pulling on his restraint, his eyes seemed to be focused on the stone wall at the far side of the church. She had to drag him back forcibly.

"Something's seemed to have spooked the dog," I said, forgetting where I was; not that I believe in ghosts.

"He's not usually this agitated. He's quite placid normally."

It got me thinking that perhaps there was something more logical concerning the dog's behaviour. That maybe Winston was on the same wavelength that I was on and he was sensing that we were being watched from unknowns. Winston's antics gave me a fantastic idea.

"What's going to happen to Winston now?" I asked seriously.

Obviously Debbie hadn't given the matter much consideration. "I don't really know. I guess he'll have to stay with us for a while."

"What if I look after him? It's the least I can do until you sort things out here at the farm."

She was delighted with my proposal. "Are you sure, Shacks? It'll be a great help. I must confess I'm a little reluctant to keep him at my house. I'm actually allergic to animal hairs."

"That's settled then."

"You *will* you take care of him properly?"

I assured her I would and I would keep in constant touch.

She was alarmed. "You're not coming back to the farm? There's food and drink laid on for everybody. Oh please do, Shacks."

It had been my intention to return immediately to London to formulate my plan of action. One look at her desperate expression changed my mind. I smiled, "I wouldn't dream of missing the occasion."

"Good. While you're there at the farm you can collect Winston's dog bowls, his tins of meat and biscuits; he needs regular feeding and watering. And you'll need his doggie-do bags for when he does a number two on the pavements or grass verges."

"Doggie-do bags," I said unappealingly.

"Yes, to pick up his smelly bits."

"Can't I just leave it for the flies to disperse?"

"Not a pleasant experience I grant you, but it has to be done. The local council are very strict on people who inconsiderately leave dog poo on the public walkways."

"He should have gotten a cat instead. There are no laws to govern where they leave their crap, and it's usually in some unsuspecting corner in my garden."

She smiled at my dig at the feline world and handed me the dog lead. "Here, you might as well get used to handling him."

I flicked my head into the air wondering if I made the right choice and headed back to the Roadster with a new recruit to my regular army obediently by my heels. Yet there was still something bothering Winston as we walked back to the car park. There was nothing or nobody I could see but Winston still had issues with the stone wall at the far side of the church. In Winston I now had an ally. I would use him as my early warning system to sniff out the enemy before I did, or at least I hoped he'd respond quicker than I would.

Back at the farmhouse, eating a freshly cut sandwich, I happened to gaze out of the kitchen window and saw young Benny going about his daily business of taking the herd in for milking; somebody had to keep the farm running. I felt aggrieved for young Benny, as the farmhand he must find it eerily strange to be without the old man about the place. I only wished the whole frigging drama had been a bad dream and I would see Tommy come wandering out of the cow shed wearing the same clothes as when I last saw him...

Debbie disrupted my thoughts when she entered the kitchen and offered me another sandwich. I politely declined. I wasn't really hungry but I did accept the offer of a sweet sherry though I could have done with something stronger. When the chance came I slipped away from the depressing atmosphere, left the farmhouse and went to see for myself where everything had happened to cause this unhappy occasion.

I located the slurry tank where Tommy had died and decided to climb to the top. I was about to mount the first rung of the vertical steel ladder that was attached to the side of the galvanized tank when I hesitated. Something on the ground had caught my eye. I reached down and picked up a large, rusty adjustable spanner which had been concealed by overgrown grass at the base of the tank. On examining the tool I noticed the tip of the adjustable jaws had a small piece, of what I assumed it to be, dried skin with a few strands of short black hair. I didn't need any forensic freak to confirm to me that the piece of tissue was the missing piece from Winston's skull. It wasn't surprising they found Winston concussed having received a crack across the head with such a heavy tool as he probably tried to protect Tommy.

I cursed suddenly when I realized what I had just done and how naive I'd been as I held the spanner tight in my hand. My fingerprints were all over the handle. Worse, and without thinking about my actions, I'd just contaminated the possible finger-prints of the previous holder, because I was sure that Winston would have gone berserk if I had shown him the weapon that had clobbered him. What a shame the police had missed what would be vital evidence, but then again, they were investigating the death of Tommy and not his dog.

I threw the spanner to the ground in the almost identical spot from where I'd retrieved it and climbed to the top of the tank. I stood on the inspection platform spanning across the edge of the tank and ran a few things through my mind. The platform was long and wide enough to hold at least three men. I say three men because I could well imagine Tommy being forcibly dragged up here and threatened by the bogus MDP men that had come calling at my home. And after they had gotten the information they wanted from him, they threw Tommy into the tank of cow shit and probably held his head under until he drowned. It was a horrible thought but it all sounded too feasible to be ignored.

Apart from my imagination working overtime, there wasn't much else to see. The tank had now been emptied yet the smell of cow shit still lingered. I suddenly felt sick. It was time for me to leave. I made my way back to the farmhouse and found Debbie to tell her I was leaving. I collected Winston and his doggie belonging, and went to see Billy Slade. On the way I called into a toy shop.

*

I found Three Trees nursing home and drove the obligatory ten miles an hour along the driveway and parked near the main entrance of a 1920 red brick building. I took a carry bag from the rear seat and told Winston to guard the car, which he seemed to understand. I got out and approached the large oak door and rang the doorbell. A nubile girl with her hair in plaits, dressed in a white tunic, answered the door. I asked to see the matron of the establishment. She smiled pleasantly and ushered me inside, through another set of coloured glass doors and told me to wait at reception. I immediately smelled hospital bleach. It reminded me of my childhood memories and my first encounter with a syringe the size of a javelin.

"Can I help you?" A woman's stern voice came from behind me.

I turned and was greeted by a woman with peroxide blond hair, wearing a dark blue uniform and with a face like thunder.

I smiled politely. “Is it possible I could talk to Billy Slade?”

She looked at me quizzically. “Are you a relative of Billy’s?”

“No, Matron. I won’t keep him long.”

“What is it you wish to speak to Billy about, Mister Ah?”

“Shackleton Speed, Matron. I’m here on behalf of an old friend of Billy’s; the friend I refer to has died recently and I have something to pass on to Billy from him.”

At first she didn’t appear to take kindly to my intrusion into her highly efficiently run nursing home and greeted my request to spend some time with Billy Slade with open hostility. “The normal procedure is to arrange an appointment, Mister Speed; not just turn up when it’s convenient for you.”

“I know I’ve been a little rash not arranging a proper time, and I can only apologize for the inconvenience. I only arrived from London this morning and unfortunately, I have to return to London tonight.”

“It’s not just your timing, Mister Speed; more that it’s very unusual for Billy to receive visitors. In fact, it’s never.”

I was determined that she let me see him. “I’ve just come from the funeral.”

“Oh I see.”

“The deceased had left me instructions that I was to pass on this gift to Billy-,” I showed her what I had in the carry bag, "-and to convey a message to him, an important and confidential message."

Talk of death softened her up. "Very well Mister Speed. I will allow it to pass on this occasion, but for future reference, you must make an appointment in advance."

I assured her I would; well I grovelled really.

"Now I feel I must warn you that it's important you're patient with Billy, as he sometimes struggles to understand what's going on around him." She pointed the way. "Go through the lounge and out of the French windows. You'll find Billy at the bottom of the garden on his favourite bench; it overlooks the wheat fields. Please avoid walking on the grass; keep to the gravel pathways at all times."

I sensed Matron watching me closely as I exited through the French doors and set off down the pathway searching for somebody I'd never seen before. Eventually I came across an old chap, sitting alone on a wooden bench donated by some benefactor. The chap was gazing skyward in a world of his own, oblivious to my presence as I approached. I wondered if he even heard me and he was perhaps deaf. I presumed I was looking down at Billy Slade.

Billy Slade had tight cropped white hair and a sunken mouth where his teeth should have been. He was dressed in a thick, blue woolly jumper that was tucked into the waist of a pair of grey baggy trousers which were secured by a leather belt and a pair of red braces. This I could see was a man who lacked confidence and I wondered if I was doing the right thing being here.

"Hello, Billy!" I said pleasantly, trying not to scare him with my sudden introduction.

His head turned to face me. He obviously wasn't deaf after all.

"My name is Shacks," I told him, a slight smile to assure that I was no threat to him.

He smiled back, displaying a set of gums. His, "hello", came out slow and in an instance he was up onto his feet wobbling slowly up and down the pathway with his arms outstretched and between rasping the sound of engine noises, shouting out at the top of his voice, "I...like...planes."

Embarrassed by his strange antics and the attention he might attract, I said. "Why don't you come in to land, Billy, I want to talk to you."

I did feel a bit of an idiot saying that and hoped no one heard my off-the-cuff remark to him.

He sat down eventually, exhausted after completing ten paces out and ten paces back. In between catching his breath he spoke wearily. "I was a pilot...you know... during the war...against the Germans."

I played along. "Yes I know you were, Billy. That's what I want to talk to you about; during the war. You remember the war?"

"Oh...heard then...I was a pilot?"

"Yes, Billy, I heard you were a good pilot."

"I...like...planes!"

"Yes, Billy, I know you do."

I reached into the plastic bag I'd brought with me and retrieved a metal replica of a Spitfire plane I'd purchased at the toy shop on the way over and showed it to him. Billy was delighted. He made a grab for the plane but I selfishly drew it away from his grasp. I said, "It's yours,

Billy, only if you listen and concentrate on what I'm going to ask you. Okay?"

By his enthusiastic nod I assumed he understood. I talked slowly and clearly so he could fully absorb exactly what I was saying. "Think back, Billy, when you were a young boy during the war. Remember the war Billy? A plane, just like this one in my hand, crashed in the local fields. Remember that, when you were a little boy?"

The vacant stare he portrayed didn't quite instil the confidence from him that I was hoping for. To be honest I was probably wasting my time on him. Debbie did give me ample warning that I would fail on all accounts. But prevail I must because illiterate Billy was all I had to go on. I pressed him again. "Remember telling people that you saw the crash. No one believed you, did they, Billy?"

"I was...a pilot! No one believed...I was...a pilot."

I was losing patience quicker than I could think and the frustration was clear in my voice. I said sharply, "I believe you, Billy. You were an excellent pilot, but do you remember the frigging plane?"

He stared at me like a frightened child. I'd lost before I'd even started. I sighed heavily, disappointed by my failure to communicate with Billy. I suppose my tactical approach was doomed because I'd no experience in dealing with people like Billy. It had been a long shot anyway and though I hate the word defeat, it was pointless pursuing something that was going to lead nowhere.

I shoved the replica plane in Billy's hands and his eyes suddenly brightened. At least I would leave him happy but it left me at a dead end. Where I went from here I'd no idea other than I'd be dragging my feet for the rest of the day wondering what I could have achieved. I was about to rise from the bench when Billy, twisting the plane through the air playing, said something quite unbelievable.

"It's like the one...that got shot down," he said, and without any prompting.

I tried not to show too much excitement but inside I was bursting at the seams.

"What do you mean, Billy?"

Billy tapped his new toy with his finger. "There... there were...two of these planes. Have you...got another one for me?"

"No Billy, I'm sorry, but I promise I'll bring you another one the next time I come to see you. Would you like that?"

Billy's head was nodding so hard that I thought it was attached to a piece of thick rubber.

"You saw two planes in the sky?" I prompted him before he forgot.

"Two planes...yes two planes-two planes and they all fell down!"

"In what way did they fall down?"

Billy stopped playing with the replica. His face went blank. I assumed it must be his usual expression when thinking hard. Finally he said, "One was...chasing...the other one."

Billy's account of events was really beginning to interest me.

He put his hand to his mouth sniggering. "I play...chasing. I chase...all the girls, kissed them...when I catch them."

"Yes, Billy I bet that's good fun. Now forget about girls. We can talk about them later. Remember the planes. What did you mean by the planes *chasing each other*, were they playing chasing games? Perhaps they were having fun too? Maybe they were fooling about, to show their flying skills." I demonstrated with my hands.

"Oh no...I saw it...I was in my...plane, flying... through the field. I was only...a small plane. I was hiding. No one saw me. I was...scared...I hid...in the long grass."

"What did you see, Billy?"

The plane...behind the other one...its guns... shooting...rat-tat-tat-tat-tat. The plane...it made the other one...crash. I watched it...it came down from the sky...smoke coming...from here." He demonstrated the entire scene with the replica Spitfire very convincingly.

"You're sure of what you saw, Billy? It was a long time ago."

"It was...on fire...it crashed in the field. I never...saw it again." He smiled impishly, "I set fire...to my paper airplanes. Matron doesn't like me doing that." His face saddened. "She shouts at me...for being a bad boy...send me to bed early...with no supper. I've stopped doing it...now. I like my supper!"

I looked at him incredulously and wondered if this nursing home was the right place for him. I guess it was ideal.

Billy glanced at me with speculative eyes. "You believe me...don't you?"

"You must understand, Billy. What you've told me would sound ludicrous to someone who never saw those two planes. Two friendly Spitfires battling against each other over the skies of England when effectively, they should be fighting Germans? It doesn't make any sense."

Poor Billy, he never understood a word I'd said. He was happy twisting the replica plane through the air in his imaginary battle, rasping the sound of an attacking Spitfire.

As for Billy's account of that day it was so far fetched it wasn't surprising no one believed an illiterate boy during the war. If just one person had taken the time to verify his story, well, I wouldn't have found the wreck when I did, nor find myself in the precarious position of looking over my shoulder every five minutes waiting for the inevitable hit-man. I left Billy in peace flying his new toy and headed back to the Mansion.

Before leaving Three Trees I had a quiet word with Matron about the possibility that Billy might have other visitors, nasty reporters trying to make a fast pound or two. I told her of the plane that had been recently discovered, and how Billy and the deceased had seen it crash during the war. I suggested that if uninvited callers insisted on speaking to Billy she should have them removed from the premises immediately. Her waspish glare convinced me she would oblige.

"Don't you worry, Mister Speed, Billy won't be pestered by anyone. Will you be coming again to visit him?"

In all honesty, I'd no reason to ever see Billy again. "Yes, of course I will." I'd never found lying a hard task ever since childhood. I wasn't about to change my ways.

On the return journey back to London I found a nice eating place with a quiet corner where I could unravel the complexity of the entire situation so far and chew over a piece of skulduggery. Why would a R.A.F. Spitfire shoot another Spitfire from the sky? It didn't make any sense. Perhaps what Billy saw was an incident of friendly fire, a regular occurrence during wartime night-fights, but not during daylight? Unless the pilot needed spectacles, it's a mistake that couldn't be made. Perhaps Billy had got the identification wrong and it had been a German plane that shot down the Spitfire. Overall it meant nothing conclusive to me. Then in reality, could I trust the mind of Billy Slade?

Chapter Five

The following morning I went to the London Imperial War Museum on Lambeth Road determined to find out all I could about Craven, the pilot that had flown the crashed Spitfire I'd unearthed in Berkshire. One of the curators, a grey haired, grey winged moustached chap, who introduced himself by the title of Flying officer Captain Wright, retired, was keen to help me with my hesitant approach to where I could find the correct information.

"Can I be of assistance, sir?"

"Yes. Pilots missing in action during the second world," I asked. "Is it possible to view records?"

"Yes, of course, sir. Are you perhaps a journalist, Mister-ah?"

I steered him away from wanting to know my name.

"What makes you think I'm a journalist?"

He tapped the side of his pock marked nose. "This tells me a lot, sir."

I gestured with my finger how right he was.

"Follow me, sir."

The curator walked along the corridor in military fashion and funny as it might sound I found myself walking in the same manner. He ushered me to a table, pottered around the reference bookshelves and moments later plonked a thick hardback book in front of me. "If he's missing in action,"-he tapped the book cover-"his name will be listed in here, sir."

I thanked him and he left me to dwindle through the pages at my leisure.

There were two Cravens unaccounted for during the war. I could forget about the rear gunner on a Lancaster Bomber and concentrate on Wing Commander Ralph Craven, and the impressive number of honours that followed his name. I took out a pad and pen and began to make notes of importance. After gaining enough material to write a short story I went back to have a chat with the same curator.

"Is there any relevant information on the particular missions the pilots were involved in at the time they went missing?'

He expressed his surprise. "Now there's a first. Not a usual request at this museum." He shook his head unfavourably. "I'm afraid such information falls within the classified format and can only be obtained directly from the Ministry of Defence. For that you'll require an appointment, and more appropriately, security clearance to view the sensitive material I should imagine. It'll be the usual red tape affair, I'm afraid, sir."

There ended my day at the museum because it was one appointment with the MoD that I wouldn't be making, and with my reputation, I'd be lucky to even stand outside the main entrance without getting clobbered by a police truncheon.

Back outside I checked the notes I'd jotted down. During the war Craven had been stationed at R.A.F. Duxford. It seemed a favourable place to visit and it was open to the public as a war museum too. I drove straight over to Cambridgeshire with Winston by my side. And just in case I was being tailed I took a route around London that even a professionally organized surveillance team from MI5 couldn't follow, never mind the intelligible mind of a London cabbie. I also thought I was in for a relaxing day. I was wrong.

*

My arrival at the Imperial War Museum R.A.F. Duxford placed me in the middle of a spectacular air show buzzing over the airfield. I parked the Roadster, leaving Winston inside the car with the window slightly open for fresh air, as I didn't want to be accused of animal cruelty.

Once inside the grounds I made my way along the pathways towards the exhibition buildings while an old Bi-plane groaned across the skies above the airfield. Wandering through the different building I concentrated on only what the war museum had to offer in respect of various mementos of the war; reading inscriptions and accounts of air battles. Basically I didn't have a clue as to what I was looking for and was rather hoping that if there was anything significant it would immediately jump out and catch my attention.

I concentrated heavily on glass framed photographs scattered around the walls and came across a collection that showed the resident pilots stationed at Duxford in the autumn of 1943. There was one particular photograph that attracted me; a large group photograph listing all the pilot's names and ranks which I studied carefully. Finally, figuratively speaking, I came face to face with Wing Commander Ralph Craven standing proudly in the centre of a group photograph of all pilots ready for action in their fatigues and customary flying jackets. I would never have thought that such a handsome face had once lined the skeleton I found.

From the way he portrayed himself Craven appeared to be a very confident person, which you would expect from a leader of men. He was noticeably young. In fact they were all noticeably young. No one, I guessed, above the age of twenty-one. I wrote down every name listed on the photograph. I wondered how many were still alive with whom I could talk with, and then it struck me, a sudden chill gliding down the curve of my spine as I contemplated that just maybe one of the men in the photograph with Craven might be his murderer and if I was to confront the alleged killer straight to his face he might decide to kill me on the spot.

I was overreacting. What possible harm could a man do to me when he was probably in his eighties or nineties, also taking into consideration he might be dead, wheel chair bound, or simply lapsed into dementia that he couldn't recall the last time he had a shit, never mind shoot someone in the frigging back?

With the names of the pilots noted, I went back outside to speculate everything I'd collected on the matter while I watched the air-show with little enthusiasm until I caught sight of an elderly chap who marvelled and applauded every manoeuvre the planes made. He obviously knew a great deal about the relics flying in the sky so I decided I'd pinch some of his knowledge. I moved through the crowd and stood beside him.

"Wonderful old rust buckets," I said, as any true admirer would.

"Old rust buckets!" he countered, his throat hoarse and dry.

I pointed skywards as a Spitfire roared overhead followed by a second plane which I had no chance of identifying in a month of Sundays.

He scowled at me and replied acidly, "They're more than rust buckets, lad." His voice warbled as he talked. "Those magnificent 1030 horse-power machines helped save England from certain destruction during war, lad, and don't you forget it!"

"Oh don't get me wrong. I'm not ridiculing the crafts," I said reassuringly. "But for comfort, compared to modern planes, they must have felt like carpet handbags."

I touched a nerve with that one too.

"They weren't built for comfort, lad," he scowled fiercely. "Fighting machines, that's what they were. The finest in their time and as fast as they come; swift, so manoeuvrable it could turn on a sixpence."

"You obviously know a lot about them?"

"Know lad! During the war I happened to be part of the ground crew that kept those beauties air worthy when they were needed. 'Erks', we were nicknamed but we were a skilled bunch with it. When those battle battered Spits returned we would work through the night to patch them back up again in readiness for the next flight."

"So you were actually stationed here during the war?"

"Aye lad, I was."

"The war certainly kept you busy."

"Aye, it did that, lad, and more. In a short space of time, when the V12 Rolls Royce Merlin engines became the power of the Spitfire, we had to become experts. We didn't have time to be taught the intricate workings of those engines. 'Erks had to quickly require the skills to repair stressed skin, split flaps, hydraulics, pneumatics, and the electrics; some wage packet if you could do all that nowadays! Aye lad, needless to say those wonderful crafts didn't require much love and care to fight. They were awesome fighters."

This chap was beginning to interest me. "What about the pilots based here during the war, did you get know any of them?"

"Vaguely; they came and went for various reasons. The war took a lot of good young men. I didn't exactly socialize with them personally; you didn't have the time for niceties; too busy."

"Do you know if any of the pilots are still alive today?"

"Hard to say, lad, but I wouldn't count on any of them holding a pilots licence anymore." His chuckle of laughter was drowned by the sound of an ancient plane rattling overhead.

"I wasn't looking for flying lessons."

"Aye, I know, lad, just having a bit of fun."

I pushed ahead. "Do you remember a pilot stationed here who went by the name of Wing Commander Ralph Craven?"

His saggy eyes lit up. "Now that chap I'll never forget. Such a considerate man too. He always had a kind word to say and he made sure we had piping hot mugs of tea and lashings of toast when we grafted during the cold nights. Sometimes he would stay with us in the hangars while we worked, reminiscing on the good days before the outbreak of war. Aye, he was a grand chap alright. Went out on a mission one day and never came back, missing in action. That was the problem with the damn war, a pilots life seemed more expendable than most."

"Yes, I'm already aware of Ralph Craven's fate. I'm more interested in talking to any surviving war veterans who served with him here at Duxford. Someone he may have been chummy with."

"Are you related to Craven? If you don't mind me asking?"

"He was my Grandfather."

His jawbone drooped, as if he'd said something dreadfully wrong. "How tactless of me, I never stopped to think."

"There's no problem; honestly! It was all a long time ago." Frigging hell, I was beginning to sound so sincere I began to believe every bit of bullshit I spoke. I now knew how a thespian feels when he plays a character so believable he has problems distinguishing what was fictional and what was reality. It was a strange feeling to have. I prompted him to continue. "I was asking about any of his flying chums?"

I waited impatiently for the rusty cogs of his brain to clanged into action, the skies exploding above our heads when two modern fighter planes zoomed across, the sound of the jet engines blasting my eardrums to the point of insanity that I wanted to scream. As for the old man remembering ex-patriots it was probably a long shot but then I was desperate for any scrap of information.

I could have sworn I heard a metallic ping echo from between his ears just a second before he got all excited and raised a finger of remembrance. "Group Captain Bane!" he suddenly bellowed above the racket. "He's still alive. Or at least he was."

Stooping to hear him because of a noisy jet overhead, I said, "Who did you say?"

"Group Captain Bane. I spoke to him here two years ago. Never saw him last year though. He told me he always made the annual pilgrim to Duxford to honour the fallen."

I actually felt deflated. "Two years is a long time. He must be getting on a bit with his age; he could have passed away by now?"

"Aye, lad, he may well have. But I doubt it."

"How can you be sure?"

"Bane gave me the impression that he looked after himself physically; he didn't half look youthful for his age, made me feel like his father. We were gossiping about the war like two old women. He knew his planes alright. He said he made the trip every year from Yorkshire, though I only ever saw him that one time, two years ago."

"Yorkshire's a big place. Did the chap mention whereabouts in Yorkshire he lived?"

He nodded. "He did as a matter of fact."

I hurried him along. "Can you remember where exactly?"

"It was a village with a funny name."

"Can you remember the name of the village? It's important that I meet and talk to him."

He suddenly snapped his fingers. "It's Gaggle or something that sounds just like that." He frowned. "Gagglestone I think. No not Gagglestone." His face creased in deep thought.

I couldn't help him in any way as I'd no idea where he was trying pinpoint. Seconds seem like minutes before he sprung back to life.

"It's Giggle-something. Yes, that sounds more like the place he lived." I could feel the heat of his brain going into uncontrollable overdrive and then he was talking excitedly as he remembered. "I've got it! Giggleswick! That's where he said he lived."

"It was definitely Giggleswick?"

"Yes I'm sure that was the place he mentioned."

"Would that be Giggleswick near, Settle?" I prompted.

He looked at me vacantly. "I wouldn't know that. To be truthful, I've never been further north than Birmingham."

"Did he happen to mention if he'd retired there? What I mean: do you think he still lives in Giggleswick?"

"I wouldn't know that either, lad. I'd be guessing."

I didn't prompt him for any further details. I would have to hunt down Bane myself and hoped he still resided there. I mean: how big is the village of Giggleswick? At least I'd a trail to follow which was a lot more than I had yesterday.

I made my excuses for not stopping any longer, thanked him for the information and left the commotion and fuss of the air show with more enthusiasm in my step than I had an hour ago. Strangely, I was beginning to enjoy my days as a detective and I was seriously considering it as a secondary occupation for when the treasure trails slackened during the winter when the ground was frozen hard. I smiled. Me! A private dick! Shackleton Speed P.I. It sounded great, adventurous.

Yes I was seriously thinking along those lines as I trundled along. But isn't it funny how ideas can change so dramatically? And suddenly the thought of being a competent detective didn't seem logical anymore, as I was about to discover as I approached the Roadster.

I was focusing too much on Winston at the time, wondering why he was bouncing insanely around the car's interior. I should have anticipated something was wrong only I'd relaxed on my security, and inadvertently, I never noticed nor heard anything untoward other than the roar of aircraft engines hurtling across the skies. Some detective I'd make because there was good reason for the dog's madness only I didn't see the problem until it was almost too late.

By sheer luck, out of the corner of my eye, I caught a glimpse of the rampaging steel bull hurtling straight at me. Somehow I jumped and twisted in one movement and scaled the bonnet of a blue car a tenth of a second before the large van smashed into the side frame of the vehicle precisely where my legs and midriff would have been. So violent the crash, the van shunted the car clear of its path. The impact sent me sprawling from the bonnet and as I crunched to the ground I managed to roll onto my knees, picking up the sound of the van accelerating away as erratically as it had approached.

I'd had a lucky escape, and a few inches either way I'd have been telling a different tale, if any at all. Okay, I'd have a few bumps and the inevitable bruises would show later, but I was still in one piece and I was quickly up on my feet watching the back end of a battered white van leaving the scene. I attempted to make a mental note of the registration but I was wasting my time because the van didn't have one. The only visible identification I saw was on the right hand rear door and highlighted in the dirt in big letters was the impoverish scrawl of 'wash me'.

By the time I'd considered giving chase the frigging van had disappeared from the car-park and could have taken a number of routes to escape. I cursed my incompetence for not being more alert and cursed even more knowing that my flash with death was no accident. Therefore, even though I'd taken a great deal of effort to prevent such a thing occurring, it was obvious someone had tagged me. I'd been followed. And not only had my body been bruised but also my ego.

I hand brushed the dust from my clothing, glancing around for any witnesses to the serious attempt on my life and found precisely none. I approached the Roadster with extreme caution this time. I suppose after what had just happened it would be my moral and lawful duty to alert someone to the mess of smashed vehicles. I did consider it, but that was as far as it went. It was important that I got out of there fast. Some idiot had tried to run me over. They might return for a second attempt and I didn't wish to be around if they did. I climbed into the Roadster and patted Winston.

"Good boy! You certainly scared them off good and proper."

I drove away from the car park and half a mile down the road, slowed and pulled in at the side of the road. Something bothered me. I couldn't help wondering how they had found me so easily. I had this ridiculous, unimaginable thought. I got out and began a search of the exterior of the Roadster for some sort of tracking device. Checked under the bonnet, probed under the wheel hubs, finger searched along the underside of the body, bobbed my head underneath and found nothing but grime. I checked if the boot had been forced, it hadn't. I checked inside anyway to be certain. There was nothing untoward.

I stood back away from the car scratching the back of head and totally confused. It hadn't been sheer luck that they had found me. I was too far from London to be that unfortunate. I gave the Roadster another scan in case I'd missed anything, circling the vehicle one way then the other. At the rear of the car I felt my bootlace had loosened and bobbed down to tighten the lace. That's when I saw the interesting piece of hardware that I'm sure wasn't in the price when I bought the Roadster. There inside the mouth of the exhaust tail-pipe was a small device, black in colour and no bigger than my thumbnail. It was attached magnetically as I found out when I forcibly pulled it free. It gave no indication of being a tracking device, no blips, no sign of an L.E.D., no audible sounds of operation, but I had to assume it was some sort of tracker because I didn't put it there and it made sense on how they found me so easily.

I thought about throwing the device into the hedgerow but I assumed they'd realized I found the frigging thing because the tracker wouldn't show any movement. I was considering my options as what to do with the device when a passing motorist slowed down to admire the Roadster. The driver nodded his approval. I smiled and discreetly attached the device to the side of the passing car. I got back into the Roadster and drove on. The car, I'd attached the tracking device to, turned south. I turned north and accelerated as far away from Duxford as quickly as possible and joined the M1.

Chapter Six

Yorkshire in early summer in the afternoon is without contradiction a splendid piece of green and fresh English countryside. In comparison to the appalling air pollution across London, here I could fill my lungs and not have to cough or collapse into an asthmatic heap. Not that I suffered such ailments, but I might do in later years.

Finding Group Captain Josh Bane in the village of Giggleswick had all the adventurous excitement of scouring a tatty directory inside a piss smelling telephone kiosk I located in the vicinity. I rang him first to explain my predicament and the urgency to discuss the recent discovery of the crashed Spitfire. Thankfully he was at home and willingly invited me for a chat. I suspected he was probably lonely and needed the company and would have probably agreed to anything, even a bogus salesman with the intention of depriving him of his hard earned money.

Sweet-pea cottage, where Josh Bane lived, was awash with an abundance of flowering colour and fragrance. I followed the narrow brick pathway and rapped my knuckles on the solid oak wood door. It took him a while to answer. When he finally did the door creaked opened and I saw a frail bent man clutching a Zimmer frame for support. If he had appeared youthful to others two years ago then something had savaged his complexion to a gauntly sick grey, and without being too distasteful or unkind, I found him just before the grim reaper did.

It was hard to imagine this white haired bony old man capable of commanding the skies of Britain during the war. His suspicious watery, grey eyes scanned me with inescapable apprehension.

I smiled to reassure him I wasn't the enemy. "Hello, Mister Bane. Shackleton Speed. I rang a little while ago. I'm here to talk about the Spitfire discovered in Berkshire."

A slight glow of life brightened his eyes. "Ah, yes, yes, young man! Come in," he beckoned, his voice slow and slightly hoarse, yet within that mixture of an aged larynx there was the educated posh tone of an ex-Cambridgeshire man.

I said, "It's good of you to see me at such short notice."

"I'm always one for a good chat, young man. If you can just squeeze past the old Zimmer chariot and head straight on to the sun lounge, I've got a pot of tea and some digestive biscuits ready on the table."

I slipped past him. I heard him close the door. I walked slowly through, trying to avoid being nosey, an almost impossible thing to do in a strangers home. I heard Josh Bane scraping along after me, his bout of genuine asthmatic breathing sounding as if a stalking dragon followed my every footstep.

On reaching the sun lounge a faint flow of fresh air brushed my face and rustled the leaves of various potted plants that filled the window sills, some plants like towers and filtering the sun-light entering the room. I was impressed with the spectacular rear view of the rolling hillside.

As he shuffled into the room, I said, "Very pleasant in these parts."

"Yes, we've been lucky these past years with Yorkshire summers."

Josh Bane puffed out his cheeks as he eased himself into one of the cushioned basket chairs placed around the pine coffee table. "Sit yourself down, young man, can't have guests standing about. If you would be so kind as to pour the tea, my shaky hands never seem to fill a cup properly anymore."

The chair creaked as I made myself comfortable. I talked while I poured. "When I phoned, you confirmed that you were stationed at Duxford air field during the war?"

I noticed colour returning to his cheeks as he reminisced. "Indeed I was, young man. 66 Squadron based at Duxford fighter command." His tired eyes widened. Those were exciting times, dangerous, but exciting nevertheless. I flew a Spitfire."

He was obviously proud of his past and he would have surely brought out his ribbon of war medals to prove it, if his legs had been more stable. I handed him a cup and took a taste of mine while observing the old boy, noticing his hands did shake slightly as he slurped his drink.

Josh Bane nodded towards the table. "Help yourself to biscuits. They're very nice dipped in tea."

I politely declined as I wasn't particularly peckish, though if I'd allowed Winston inside the cottage I knew he'd have scoffed the lot without introduction.

"Do you recall a pilot by the name of Ralph Craven?"

"Wing Commander Ralph Craven! Indeed I do. Never forgot the chap. Ralph Craven was an outstanding

Officer. The type of comrade you wanted beside you in those bitter times of conflict. A strong willed chap, as I remember, admirably respected amongst the men. In comparison to the other pilots under my command, I could trust him totally with anything." His eyes dropped from mine. "Alas...one day he went out on a mission and never returned. He was listed as 'lost in action'."

"You obviously knew him better than most?"

"He's the kind of chap you can never forget. But he had no connection to the fighter plane found recently?"

"You mustn't believe everything you read in the papers. It was Craven, or what was left of him, strapped in the cockpit."

He nearly choked on the mouthful of tea he had just sipped into his mouth. He swallowed hard, coughed and said, "Absolutely impossible young man! I might be old and withered but my eyes are still pretty damn good. The newspapers categorically stated the pilots name as being Flying Officer Derek Rowland, missing in action in 1943."

"The information was wrong. Or the wrong information was given to the media deliberately."

"I very much doubt that the military would make such a massive mistake when it comes to missing personal, young man." And then he added, "Don't let your tea get cold."

I took another sip. "That's what I found strange. The name given in the papers didn't correspond with the identification tag still attached around the neck of the pilot's remains. To be blunt, they buried the wrong man in the wrong military grave. I should know I found the wreck with my metal detector. I clearly saw the name Craven."

Josh Bane raised an eyebrow inquisitively. "A farmer and his dog discovered the wreck."

"Ah-yes-well, that's not strictly true. At the time I thought it would be best that I should let someone else take the credit."

Josh Bane tapped the side of his wrinkled nose. "This tells me you're missing some important narration, young man?"

I didn't want to alarm him in anyway, so I tried to play it down. I said, "There isn't much to say really."

He just screwed up his eyes at me. "There's enough for you to come seeking me out. I'm listening, young man."

I shrugged. "It's a little awkward to explain. What I mean is I couldn't afford to take any credit for the find. To certain authorities I'm a bit of a renegade, a rogue really. I sell on the artefacts I dig from the ground. I won't bore you with the details of what I've found over the years, but put it this way, if the Tower of London still housed hardened criminals then Customs & Excise and the Treasure Valuation Committee would have jointly locked me up forever. I preferred to be invisible on such delicate issues and unearthing the Spitfire was one of them."

"I see," Josh Bane said probingly. "Let me get this clear. You discovered the plane with a metal detector and you were afraid of being arrested?"

I nodded. "That's sounds about it."

"That's poppy-cock! Finding a wreck doesn't warrant an arrest. How about stretching the truth a little wider? That you actually feared being arrested because of another reason?"

There was no fooling Josh Bane despite his frailty.

"Well I did find one of the reconnaissance cameras amongst the wreck."

"You stole the camera?"

I shrugged, expressing my guilt.

"That's damned despicable! Robbing war graves is against the Law!"

"I know," I said humbly.

"You're going to get into a lot of trouble."

"I'm already in a lot of trouble. And before you ask, I didn't take anything that belonged to the pilot. All I took was a rusty old camera that would have probably been scraped for what it was worth. Or so I thought. Somebody had other ideas and decided that the camera was worth killing for."

His cup and saucer rattled violently. "What do you mean by *killing for*?"

"I mean exactly that. The only other two people who knew of the camera's existence were the victims of nasty but questionable accidents. I'm sure they were silenced on purpose. I'm a little concerned that I might be next"

"Good gracious young man! You must inform the police at once."

I shook my head. "I've already been down that avenue."

"What did they say?"

"They practicably laughed in my face and instead accused me of inciting trouble."

"Well I'm sure the police would have done their investigation thoroughly on the two people you knew."

"They've been hoodwinked. The killings were made to look like accidents, that I'm certain, only I can't prove a thing. The only way I can shove it back up police noses, is to venture out there in the wilderness of uncertainty and prove they weren't accidents but murders."

Josh Bane flustered. "I can't see how I can possibly help you?"

I finished the drops of my tea and placed the cup and saucer onto the table. I said, "There's a tremendous amount you can help me with. Like beginning with the day Wing Commander Craven went missing. I need to know everything that happened; any minor detail you can remember. It's important so I can piece together a few facts that are disturbing me."

Josh Bane puffed out his cheeks to prepare himself. "To be perfectly honest I remember the day as if it was happening right now. It was the day of my birthday; not that there was much time for a celebration. Though some of the events of the day are a little hazy...a lot of years have past under the bridge since then."

"My integrity depends on what you can tell me."

"I'll try, young man, but my accuracy may stray a little."

"Anything you remember will be worthwhile, even minimal scraps of information will be appreciated," I said encouragingly.

He was on the verge of beginning his narration but stopped. He leaned forward, placed his cup and saucer shakily down on the table, leaned back into his chair, and all completed in one continual movement of incredible slow motion, as if he was preparing for a nap. The wait narked me.

"Now then," he finally began, "The mission-ah-yes the impossible mission, as us pilots called it that day." He paused and his lips twisted as he thought of something he wasn't sure about.

"Is there a problem?" I asked.

"I'm not quite sure, young man. I'm a little bothered that I could be contravening the Official Secrets Act by relaying military information to a civilian."

I was about to casually mention 'that went out with the Ark' when he beat me to the mark.

Josh Bane slapped his hand down on his thigh. "No. How damned silly of me! How can I be accused of such damnability when the TV nowadays is splattered with war documentaries? Now let us get on with the mission in question. Duxford fighter command received orders from the War Office that was of vital importance. At our pre-flight briefing we were told that an operation, involving British Intelligence and the American Atlantic fleet, was in motion at that very moment while we were sat on our arses listening to a piece of summarizing. The Allies were tracking a Japanese submarine attempting to rendezvous with a German U-boat out in the Atlantic to transfer essential cargo. We weren't told what the cargo was but rumours had it that the Jap submarine was carrying gold bullion, allegedly, to assist the Germans financially in continuing the war in Europe.

"I did learn later the full details of that Atlantic operation. The Allies had cracked a number of German codes. This enabled the Allies to track a Japanese submarine from its base in the Southern hemisphere all the way to the Atlantic for a rendezvous with the German U-boat. Using ships modified into small aircraft carriers, the Americans launched their attack and caught the Japanese submarine far out in the Bay of Biscay and sank her to the bottom of the sea. That is historical fact.

"I recollect there was a documentary on the television concerning the discovery of that very same submarine; the I-52, a transport class submarine capable of staying beneath the waves for long distances. The documentary involved a team of American treasure hunters. They were convinced that the sunken sub still had gold aboard. The same old riff-raff excuses; treasure seekers pretending that the historical intrigue of the lost submarine held precedence over the importance of finding gold bullion; cods-wobble! But as it was, to add insult to injury, the greedy sods never found any gold and probably never will. Serves them right too!"

"Do I hear a little animosity in your voice, Mister Bane?" I asked cheekily.

"You must understand, young man, disturbing the dead serves no purpose at all. Bloody treasure seekers are a pain in the arse."

I wondered if that included me.

"The Japanese may have been the enemy," he went on. "But, by god, they were still true warriors and were willing to give their lives for what they believed; a lot of brave men died that day when the Allies hit the submarine with all they had."

I hurried him along. "What was your squadron's mission?"

"Give me time, young man! I'm coming round to that." He coughed to clear his throat. "While the Americans were playing war games in mid-Atlantic and chasing submarines for real, R.A.F. Duxford command had been given a pointless exercise of trying to locate an apparent renegade Japanese submarine. The Allies were reacting to an independent intelligence source that came from deep within Japan, so we were told. The information received indicated the departure of a second submarine apparently displaying the same prefix I-52, which set sail at precisely the same time as the first I-52 but from a different port and its destination, supposedly, was German held territory. Because there was no codename from the mysterious informant, the Allies, understandably, suspected that the information regarding the second submarine was a diversion to throw them off the scent of the initial target they were tracking. But in war those vital scraps of intelligence can prove to be priceless, so the search for the second submarine went ahead.

"Duxford was chosen mainly because our squadron had Super-marine Spitfires that had been previously redesigned for the purpose of long flights to protect Bomber Command on their raids over Germany. It meant our Spits could cover a large area in quick time." He drifted into a tediously boring explanation of the intricate modifications done to the crafts. I tried to look interested, "The mission was given the code-name 'Huggermugger'. It involved reconnaissance flights as far wide as the Spitfires fuel tanks would take them; the North Atlantic; the North Sea. It was hit and miss really; like searching for a ghost submarine. In all truth we'd have probably found a needle down a dark passageway at the height of the blackout period far quicker. There were no reports of any sighting whatsoever."

"Not quite that difficult to find needles if you look in the right places," I said and slipped the photographs from my inside jacket pocket and gave them to him for inspection.

He looked long and hard at the photographs. Finally, he said, "The qualities bad. How did you come by these?"

"The camera I took from Ralph Cravens wrecked plane."

His eyes illuminated. "Good grief! That means Ralph must have taken these photographs on the same day he went missing. They always put fresh film into the cameras for every mission so there's no confusion."

"I thought they'd be of interest to you."

"Quickly now," he pointed to a small writing desk sat in a corner, "there's a magnifying glass in the top drawer. Can you get it for me, please?" There was excitement in his voice, a new lease of life.

I did as he asked, sat down again, observing his reactions as he meticulously scanned every millimetre of each photograph. Finally, with a slight shake of his head in disbelief, he said, "This submarine carries the identification I-52. The shape alone tells me it's the design of a Japanese cargo submarine, and one that's in some considerable trouble."

"Could that be the mysterious submarine that set sail the same time as the Atlantic bound submarine?"

He looked up. "You're certain that these photographs came from the crash site?"

"I should know."

"Well there can be no doubt then." He handed the photographs to me and I slipped them back inside my jacket pocket. He went on thoughtfully. "You're positive you saw the identity tags with Ralph Craven's name on?"

"I could only make out Craven, but I did check war records which confirmed that Ralph Craven was listed as still missing in action."

"Then we can disregard that these photographs are connected to the recorded Atlantic sinking of the I-52.

Craven's Spitfire never went anywhere near there. So there had to have been two submarines carrying the same prefix I-52. Blimey! Craven found the elusive sub after all. It's incredible! Ralph found the needle in a haystack and died for his troubles. What a shame 'Sniffer' Deveron never got a glimpse of the submarine too. He could have taken the glory in finding the submarine."

"Who's Sniffer?" I asked curiously.

"It was just a nickname we'd given to another pilot based at Duxford. Squadron Leader Dillon 'Sniffer' Deveron, as I knew him at the time. He was Ralph's wing protector on that fatal day."

My eyes illuminated. "This wing protector, does that means he flew with Craven?"

"That's what a wing protector does, young man. Anyway, when Deveron landed back at Duxford he reported his Spitfire had developed engine trouble and he had lost sight of Ralph's Spitfire somewhere over the Welsh mountains. After twenty-four hours Craven was finally reported missing."

"Was anything done to find Craven at the time?"

"There was plenty done, young man. The moment he was reported missing, naturally; a sea and air search was implemented; normal procedure when one of our Boy's fails to come home. No wreckage was ever found along his predicted flight path, so the next procedure was to inform the local police in all counties and the Home Guard. All we could do was to continue our attempt to win the war. I'm afraid the dead soon became a distance memory especially when the war in Europe intensified."

"What happened to Deveron afterwards?"

"Within three months he'd jumped up a rank, which wasn't surprising."

"He was a popular fellow then?"

"Popular in the right places more like. Better known for his brown-nosing when in the company of senior officers; hence the nickname 'Sniffer'. He was a damn good pilot, admittedly, but boy, could he shift up to the higher command's backsides when he got the chance. By the end of the war he'd raised a few more ranks so there was no great surprise when he continued his service in the Air Force after the war finished."

"Trustworthy type of chap, was he?"

"That would depend on how you definc trustworthy?" The look in his eyes told me he was suspicious with my line of questioning. "I certainly wouldn't have verbally insulted a higher ranking officer in his presence for the fear of him splitting on me and I'd have been hauled before a military court. But other than that, we got along without any major disagreements."

"Would you trust him with your life?" I tried not to sound dramatic.

"In war time you had no choice but to trust your comrades."

"How well did you know him?"

"Personally, you mean?"

I nodded.

"There was very little time to get to know anyone personally at Duxford. The war took its toil on a regular basis; eat, sleep and fly and that was about your lot. After Ralph went missing, a few months on I was deployed to a European airbase helping the Allies drive the Germans back to Berlin. Deveron remained at Duxford."

"How did Craven get on with Deveron?"

"They got on together, if that's what you mean."

"They never fell out at anytime?"

"I wasn't aware of any disturbance between them."

"What about the flight path Ralph Craven flew that day?"

"Ah-well, that's difficult to remember. But I think his flight path would have taken him around the coast of Ireland, probably twenty or thirty miles out into the Atlantic before heading north, circling the Scottish Isles and then back down the West of England. It's hard to be precise. And Ralph was a bit of a Tally Ho man; he loved the thrill of fast flying."

"And this Squadron Leader Deveron, he also took the same route?"

"As I told you, young man, Deveron was Ralph's escort. His job was to protect Ralph's plane if he came under hostile fire, say from the submarines gun cannons or even a marauding German fighter. It was virtually impossible for a pilot to defend his craft and snap pictures at the same time. And even if the task of doing both was mastered, it didn't make any difference to a converted reconnaissance plane because the craft didn't carry any weapons."

"So Craven wouldn't have been able to defend himself if he came under attack?"

"That's correct, young man; totally vulnerable. It took a brave man to fly photographic reconnaissance, especially on those lonely flights across Europe and into enemy territory. The Spitfire MK X1 had a Merlin 60 series engine. It was incredibly fast and powerful and speed was the essential defence for reconnaissance flights; speed and larger fuel tanks. Even then the power of the Merlin engine wasn't fast enough with the excess weight the Spitfire carried. A directive came from the high command to strip the craft of every conceivable item the Spitfire didn't need in order to achieve that excessive speed. All weapons, radio equipment, everything that wasn't welded or bolted down was dismantled and disregarded. The Spitfire became a shell but a hell of a lot lighter and faster."

"Would there be any reason for a third Spitfire to fly alongside Craven and Deveron?"

Josh bane frowned with my question. "I shouldn't think so, young man. Not unless they'd defied orders. And may I add proudly, insubordination was rare to nonexistent in the RAF."

I thought of what Billy Slade had told me. "Would this Deveron fellow be crazy enough to shoot down another Spitfire?"

"That's a strange question. I suppose friendly fire has been known to occur on occasions. A plane gets caught in the crossfire. It can happen in an aerial fire-fight. But there was nothing in Deveron's report suggesting that they'd experienced an enemy attack."

He hadn't clicked to what I was getting at. I took a deep breath, hoping that what I was about to reveal to him didn't cause his heart to seize into a solid lump.

"No. I meant deliberately shoot another Spitfire from the sky."

Josh Bane stared at me in astonishment, his mouth half open, his lips trembling as he tried to speak. He swallowed hard and said, "Are you implying that Deveron downed Ralph's Spitfire on purpose?"

"It's what I think happened out there on that fateful day."

"Deveron left Ralph to die?"

"Crude I know."

Josh Bane waved a hand in disgust. "Perish the thought!" He spat out angrily, glaring at me with the intention of throwing me out of his home, if he could have found the strength to do so. I wouldn't have blamed him. He immediately appeared to me as being the British stiff upper lip type of guy. He never let the subject drop either and was straight back on the defence of his fellow airman.

"It's a ludicrous assumption for a start. A man doesn't become Chief Air Marshall Sir Dillon Deveron on the grounds of being a traitor and a murderer. He would never have got away with such cowardice."

"What if he had got away with it, until now?"

"That's preposterous and unthinkable."

"What if it was proven?"

"I'd shoot the bugger myself. But things like that just didn't happen during the war. Craven was the victim of circumstances beyond control."

"Frigging right he was! Deveron shot him from the sky."

"You have a vivid imagination, Mister Speed."

"I have a reliable living witness who watched the entire sequence on that fateful day in 1944. The witness saw a Spitfire open its guns on another Spitfire. When the witness reported the incident it was dismissed as fantasy. Nobody followed up to check the story." I considered it inadvisable to mention the mental state of my star attendee at the scene of the crime.

Josh Bane was in a state of shock. "No, no, it's too incredible to comprehend. There has to be a mistake? Where was this person watching at the time?"

"Close enough to see the incident, but probably too far away to pinpoint exactly where the Spitfire crashed."

"Then it's possible the witness was mistaken."

"The witness didn't hesitate when describing the attack to me."

"Why didn't this person come forward at the time?"

"He was a kid and probably scared in case he received a clip around the ear for his troubles. Or he never really understood the consequences of what had happened at the time."

"Deveron…shoots down Craven's Spitfire?"

"Admittedly I'm not a hundred percent if this Deveron was the pilot responsible."

Josh Bane shook his head at me in disgust. "I shouldn't even be discussing the matter with you. Do you realize the consequences of such a treacherous act if it had been known at the time?"

"I think he would have been hanged for the crime," I said, casually.

"Try hung, drawn and quartered, more like, and that would be from his fellow warriors at Duxford even before Deveron had got the chance to plead his innocence in a military court." He calmed and sank in his chair, shaking his head in retrospect of what I'd told him. "It's unthinkable. Why should Deveron want to commit such an awful act on a fellow brother in arms? It beggars belief."

"The rumour of gold bullion sounds a feasible reason."

"I can't believe he would do such a despicable act on a myth?"

"Stranger things have happened."

"Deveron fought hard for his country, not for self glory."

"I don't doubt that," I said. "But even a myth can change the way a person thinks and acts."

"Nobody could be sure if the gold even existed never mind if any was aboard the second I-52."

"Deveron gambled with Craven's life on the assumption there was gold. He shot Craven from the sky and concocted the story of losing sight of him."

"He did loose sight of Craven. He reported having engine trouble and that Craven had continued on alone. And then there was confirmation that a lone Spitfire was spotted by a Home Guard observer between the Welsh and Scottish borders on the time and day stated."

I paused for a few seconds to think it over. "So Craven obviously located the sub somewhere during his lone flight, snapped the photographs and on his return back to base, rendezvoused with Deveron. Somehow I think he told Deveron what he'd found and the rest is elusive history which only Deveron himself would have known."

"Who's to say that the submarine didn't scarper to another destination after being spotted by Craven? That would be the logical thoughts of the submarine captain. It would make the death of Craven seem pointless."

"Not really, the evidence was on film. The photographs I've shown you prove the submarine itself was in dire trouble; listing and on the verge of sinking. That submarine was going nowhere. Deveron must have known this too."

"It doesn't make sense, Mister Speed. Why would Deveron continue serving in the RAF after the war had finished if there was gold to be found?"

"That's because the location of where the submarine was anchored was stored on Craven's reconnaissance camera. Only Deveron couldn't find Craven's crashed Spitfire. The plane had buried itself two feet under the earth inside a gully. The summer grasses were high and easily camouflaged the craft. After the war in Europe it became a matter of time. Summers came and went, the plane lost forever. But that didn't deter Deveron. Riches beyond belief drove him on in his pursuit. The search for the plane became his career. With every discovered crash site around the United Kingdom he could have monitored the situation; checked every missing craft as they were unearthed. His only problem was time itself. The search became years, a lifetime, in fact. Now that's changed; the plane has been found, and let me tell you there are a lot of undesirables in hot pursuit to discover if the submarine really existed and are willing to kill for that information."

Josh Bane absorbed what I'd said thoughtfully. "It's a very scary situation you have fallen into, young man. It would be better to let the police handle the problem and safer for you. Perhaps you should report it to the Ministry of Defence?"

"I've already had a run in with some dodgy officials from the Ministry of Defence Police."

"You can't possibly manage the situation on your own."

"I've no other choice."

Josh Bane nodded but seemed genuinely concerned with my plight. Then we were back on the subject of Deveron. "Still," he said, "I do find it rather difficult to imagine a man, Dillon Deveron's age, would be running amok, killing innocent people for what I still believe to be nonexistent gold. Yes, the pictures you have do prove the existence of another submarine. It doesn't prove there was gold bullion on board in 1944. Would you go on a killing spree on those pretences? Would you risk the probable wrath of British justice if you were wrong? Have the dishonour of such a cowardly act splattered over every newspaper in the country, your life in complete ruins. Would Deveron have risked all that? I certainly wouldn't have."

There seemed no point in me pressing on about whether Deveron was guilty or not. I felt as if I was heading in the right direction and I wasn't going to be distracted by Josh Bane's defence of the 'stiff-upper-lip brigade'. Josh Bane had no chance of changing my mind. Yes, Deveron could be in the same position as Josh Bane and is probably scuttling around with the aid of a Zimmer frame. Hardly killer potential if that's the case. But anyone can give orders or hire the right kind of villains. It would only take a phone call. No, I couldn't excuse Deveron from guilt, at least not until I'd confirmed his innocence and that was very unlikely because Deveron was the last man to see Craven alive.

"Have you seen or heard of Deveron recently?" I asked.

Josh Bane was flabbergasted. "Surely you're not thinking of asking him to his face if he's a murderer?"

"The thought had crossed my mind."

"Well I'm sorry but I can't help you."

"You won't reveal where he might be just in case I upset his feelings?"

"Oh-no-no, I don't even know where he is and neither do I know if he's still alive. Yes, I've seen him on occasions many years ago attending the odd reunion and at Remembrance Day. As for his present whereabouts, I haven't the foggiest."

And that more or less ended my conversation with Josh Bane. I eased from the chair and stood, apologising for leaving. "I have to get back to London. You've been a tremendous help, Mister Bane and I appreciate the time you've given me. There's no need for you to get up. I'll see myself out."

Josh Bane's gaunt sunken face had me worried. I'd seen that type of expression before. That traumatized look of a man about to witness the imminent death of a condemned man. It sent a shiver down my spine.

"Take care, young man," he said kindly. "Intuition tells me you're turning over a barrowful of rotting maggots. Finding that submarine might favour your quest for the truth but it might also be your death warrant."

"I'll be fine," I assured him.

"That might be so, young man. I only hope that when I pick up a morning newspaper in the future I'll be reading about the greatest gold find ever, though I pray I don't read your name in the obituaries column instead."

I rather hoped he was joking, but I sensed he wasn't. In the meantime what he had given me was a lead to the whereabouts of one elusive submarine, which without doubt, would stir interest among the natives, especially those I was after. What a perfect excuse to flush those cockroaches from their hiding hole with the faint whiff of gold in the air.

*

I headed back to London nursing an overactive mind, a bad headache and the bruises from my earlier clash at Duxford aerodrome, now beginning to remind me exactly where they were. And I was badly in need of sleep. Winston was already snoozing. Nothing seemed to stop the wretched hound from sleeping. He'd flaked out on the passenger seat the moment I turned the engine. I also made an astonishing discovery. I never realized dogs snored and farted when they slept and with such an annoying effect, which at least prompted me not to drop asleep while driving back down the motorway.

When I'd finally reached the dark street where I lived I came back alive and alert. I say *Dark Street* because none of the street lights were illuminated; the odd one extinguished sometimes but not usually all of them. The road was darker than the deepest depths of an abandoned coal mine. Not just that. None of my security lights came on as I swung the Roadster into my extensive driveway; they were definitely working yesterday. I immediately thought of a power-cut in the area but I'd noticed other houses in the vicinity still had electricity on. My suspicions of something more sinister were confirmed in the blink of an eye. And considering there was no breeze that evening, I could have sworn the shrubbery to my right began to move as I drove up to my garage door.

Chapter Seven

The bushes had stopped moving by the time I switched off the engine and stepped from the Roadster. I didn't require psychic powers to know that I had hostile company. Winston had already indicated trouble when he shot out from the car to be by my side. The dog was agitated but controlled and neither did he bark or growl. He waited patiently. I think his intention was to allow the danger to come out into the open. The dog obviously knew more than I did because the ploy worked and out from the shadows of the shrubbery stepped two beady-eyed vultures. I knew them as Filbert and his bogyman minder, alias the two fraud ministry policemen.

The pair approached me with a quick pace. They failed to notice Winston tucked in behind my left leg. Any anxiety I had when I got out of the Roadster had dispersed the moment I prepared myself for the inevitable attack.

"You're frigging trespassing!" I said, assertively. "So you'd better get your skinny arses off my property before the police arrive."

They were impervious to my threats; cold blooded killers usually are when they know differently. I heard the double click a second after I felt Winston's body tense against my leg. Although no switchblades were shown or swished in a frantic arc of rage as they neared, the distinct positioning of their hands hanging limply by their sides told me all I needed to know.

Winston reacted far quicker than I did. The moment the bogyman's hand twitched, Winston had latched onto the striking wrist and I had parried Filbert's upward strike and caught hold of his blade hand, twisting the weapon away from my stomach. The threat on my life turned me into a raving lunatic. I hit the bogus Filbert with every thing I had: head, hands, knees and feet, and not necessarily in that order. It was ten years since I'd thrown a decent punch in anger and I hadn't lost my touch. My attack on him was vicious and frantic but I didn't cease the bombardment until I heard the sound of the blade crashing to the ground.

I didn't stop there. I hit him again with a flurry of body punches before finishing off with a terrific uppercut that dropped him to the floor with a crunching thud. He lay there, groaning and then silenced. I'd knocked the bastard out.

With the feeling of invincibility I quickly switched my attention to the fracas behind me. Winston had his fangs buried in the side of his victims face with the expected savagery of a pit bull dogfight. I thought of intervening but changed my mind when human screams of agony ghoulishly crept through the night air and I decided that my hand wasn't going anywhere in between the action.

I turned back to Filbert when I heard him moan, knelt down beside him, grabbed him by the hair and yanked his head up. He might have been groggy but I didn't care. I wanted answers.

"Right you piece of shit! Start by telling me your proper employer? And don't give me verbal diarrhoea that *the Ministry* are because I know differently." I shook his head hard to grab his attention. I got carried away and slapped his face a few times. "You'd better start talking shit breath!"

I was distracted by noise behind me.

My head spun round to see Winston's piece of meat had broken free and the bogeyman was off and running down the driveway with the dog snapping at he heels with every stride. I let Filbert's head hit the ground and rose to my feet to watch the pursuit, making my way to the roadside. I made the wrong move. Stupidly I'd given Filbert the chance to scarper, which he did, straight through the shrubbery and scaled the high garden wall that surrounded my home. I heard him drop to the pavement and then the sound of running feet. I reached the end of the driveway in time to see Filbert scampering away in the same direction as his companion.

I cursed loudly and gave chase. I would have caught him if a dark coloured car hadn't raced past me and screeched to a crawl. This allowed Filbert and his bogeyman to scramble into the rear of the vehicle before the car accelerated away with Winston in gamely pursuit of the tailpipe.

I whistled the dog back from his pointless pursuit and gave him a pat for his gallant effort. "Good boy, Winston. Sure showed those sad bastards who's the boss." And the dog promptly spat out half an ear. I winced. "Didn't like the taste, hey boy! I don't blame you. Never mind, I've a juicy piece of proper meat in the fridge that's far more appetising than bits of scum."

I watched until the red tail-lights of the car had disappeared in case they decided to double back for another attempt on my person. I didn't think they'd take the chance of a return. They didn't. I turned round and headed for my driveway only to be startled by a man's voice beckoning me from the shadows across the road. I'd missed his presence because of all the commotion.

"Mister Speed, I presume?"

I glanced across, vaguely making out the lurking figure standing there with his hands down by his side. He didn't appear to be a threat and I think Winston agreed with me, as the dog made no move.

"Depends who wants me?"

The stranger approached warily, a bulky man of medium height, which was about as much as I could make out in the dark. I was ready to repel another attack and so was Winston until we noticed he had raised the palms of his hands to show he carried nothing to endanger us.

"You're certainly a hard man to track down," the stranger said, slightly out of breath. "I've been waiting your return for hours. I'd actually dropped to sleep in my car," he threw a thumb over his right shoulder to indicate where he had parked down the road. "The fracas woke me up."

"Well-I'm really sorry about *that*," I said sarcastically. "But I shouldn't be disturbing you again tonight"

"We need to talk, Mister Speed."

His timing was wrong for starters. I wasn't in the mood to talk or listen and my answer was obnoxious and quick. "It's late. I'm knackered. I'm damned well agitated. So fuck off!"

The stranger took a cautious step back and said, "I fully intend to leave after watching your heroics. Yet if you can spare the time, I must speak with you on urgent matters. I appreciate the situation is momentarily inconvenient, so I posted my credentials through your letterbox. You can give them back to me later, if you're interested."

He was certainly a calm character and a person not used to taking no for an answer.

"Why should I want to talk to you?"

"If I'm right, I can probably put a name to your attackers for starters."

He had my attention.

"But since you're in a foul mood, and obviously in need of sleep, perhaps we can meet later today. Breakfast perhaps? I'll be at the establishment called, 'The Greaseless Grill'. Do you know it?"

"King's Road," I said. "And you're paying?"

"Indeed, Mister Speed. Shall we say ten AM?" He gave a flick type wave and toddled off down the road. I heard the click and slam of a car door, the engine starting up and he drove away.

I looked down at Winston and he returned the look. "What a frigging day it's been."

Winston responded with a whine.

Before going inside I inspected the security lights around the front of my home. I wasn't surprised to discover that the light fittings had been vandalized beyond repair and I guessed the street lamps had suffered the same treatment.

I picked up the stranger's credentials as I entered, closed the door and studied the details. They were impressive so I had no excuse not to accept that Inspector Dan Hamer of the Ministry of Defence Police was the genuine article. There was a telephone number and extension number for me to check if the details matched the visitor, which, after some sleep,

I rang. Everything about him was confirmed. Why he had turned up on my doorstep was a mystery, and I detest not knowing what the frigging hell was going on. I left Winston behind to watch the house and went to meet Hamer.

*

'The Greaseless Grill', serves a gourmet breakfast equal to any of the top restaurants in and around London, everything cooked to absolute perfection. Fresh crisp bacon, perfect yellow eggs, large flat mushrooms in a delicious sauce, cooked tomatoes, and toast that melts in the mouth. All swilled down the gullet with a pot of proper brewed tea, none of that dry tasting paper tea bags, just pure leaves soaked in boiling water for a minute before adding a splash of silver top milk. It's an expensive place to eat but understandably busy and I was going to enjoy breakfast immensely because I wasn't dipping my hand into the money pocket.

I found Inspector Dan Hamer seated at a window table drinking what appeared to be coffee. The daylight did him no favours. By the deep age lines around his eyes, I guessed he was touching the age of fifty. His physique bordered a person whose love affair with the gymnasium had all but gone and if he had made the effort to improve his level of fitness, it'd have probably killed him. He wasn't grossly fat by any means, but the loss of a few pounds of flesh would have improved his health tremendously.

Hamer half rose from the comfort of his chair for the courtesy shake of hands, his grip strong and commanding. I estimated his height to be around five feet ten inches which carried his plump figure adequately.

There were streaks of grey running through his neatly trimmed brown hair. He had deep set hazel coloured eyes, a slightly bent nose, and a strong square chin that I reckon could take a decent punch.

"Glad you accepted the offer, Mister Speed. Please, sit down."

As he re-seated I gave him back his credentials. "I did check them."

He smiled thinly and slipped the documents inside his jacket pocket. "I'd have been disappointed if you hadn't."

I sat down and pulled the chair in. I said, "I don't usually accept offers from strangers but I'm notoriously weak minded with the offer of free food and hopefully some answers."

"I won't have all the answers, Mister Speed, but I'll try my best."

My first impressions of Hamer had me thinking that I was dealing with a polite chap, but first impressions mean nothing. Anyone can be polite when they want something and Hamer wanted something.

"I gather those two Neanderthals didn't return last night?" he sounded genuinely concerned.

"Nothing disturbed me, and Winston slept like a log."

Hamer smiled at my quip and nodded his approval. "Good. I must say you certainly look in better shape after a few hours sleep. And how's your dog?"

"Winston's fine. He's still chewing a piece of his victim."

"It must be a tough piece of meat to last so long."

"Not really. It's just that he likes to savour his meal slowly."

"And where's the dog now?"

"I left him at home, on guard. Besides, I thought the other diners wouldn't appreciate his slobbering jowls when he's after food from their plates."

"He's an incredible animal and a cleverly vicious one too! That was some display last night. I'm glad I stayed on the opposite side of the road."

"He's not usually that vicious."

"Isn't that something all dog owners plead after their dog's bitten somebody."

"I wouldn't know. He's not actually mine. His owner died recently. I'm just looking after him for a while until things have been sorted."

"I'd say that he was looking after you, Mister Speed. And such a strange looking beast too! I'm not familiar with the breed?"

"He's cross bred between a Labrador and a Staffordshire-Bull Terrier."

"Ah! Now I understand his ferociousness in battle."

"Winston's a softy at heart. He just detests anyone attacking his friends, as you duly witnessed."

Breakfast arrived. The aroma drifting from the plate making me swallow saliva quickly before it excreted down the sides of my chin. I was famished and tucked in heartily asking the appropriate questions in-between mouthfuls.

"How come your card landed through my letterbox, I've already had a bad experience with the ministry police."

Hamer swallowed the mouthful of food he was chewing. "You mean the two thugs from last night? They certainly don't work for the MDP."

"I thought as much at the time. Their approach to their work didn't have the same panache that I would have expected from government officials."

"What did they want with you?"

"I got the impression they were trying to kill me."

"Well you're still alive. They were obviously after something from you?"

"They accused me of having something that belonged to them."

"Have you?"

"Never found out. So who are they?"

"If I'm right, you've got a major problem on your hands, Mister Speed. They're dangerous people."

"How dangerous should I be worried about?"

Hamer lowered his voice as he spoke, "Professional killers from the Eastern European regions. They go by the names of Damian Love and Theodore Hate. Nobody knows their real nationality. For recognition purposes you tackled Love and the dog had hold of Hate. Love is the mouthpiece of the two. Not to be underestimated, as his brutality is on equal terms with Hate. They have no preference of victim as long as there's a paymaster. They butcher people mercilessly, quietly and without fuss. They're well known throughout the European police forces, yet no force has managed to make anything stick against them; never any witnesses to their crimes. They are usually highly efficient bastards, and if they mark their target for death then it's usually funeral arranging time. You've had a lucky escape, Mister Speed."

"You seem to know a lot about them?"

"They're on our wanted list too; a little incident in Cyprus five years ago when a British army sergeant was murdered on the orders of a Turkish Mafia boss. We knew the slimy toad sergeant was up to no good, and we were on to him. Love and Hate got to him before we did; knifed him to death. On whose orders we've no idea. End of our investigation."

"Well they're at it again." I thought I'd mention the fact to him.

Hamer jabbed his fork towards me. "It doesn't surprise me. They've obviously been brought into the country to cause havoc in London by someone."

"Have you any idea who would want to hire that calibre of men?"

"The only suspect we have is a chap named McClusky. He runs an Irish-American import and export and storage business at the docklands. Does that name sound familiar to you?"

I shook my head. "I can't say it does."

"We've never heard of him either."

"You've proof that they work for this McClusky character?"

"The car used by your attackers last night is registered to McClusky; I traced the registration through the DVLA at Swansea this morning. But let's not get carried away. I wouldn't be at all surprised if the vehicle hasn't already been crushed into a cube at a local scrap-yard. Or they'll probably say it's been stolen."

"Obviously you checked to find out if it had been reported stolen?"

"There's been nothing yet reported concerning the vehicle."

"What about McClusky himself?"

"He's clean; a bona-fide business man who deals in raw materials for the animal feed industry."

"Then how come I'm at the top of everybody's forthcoming Christmas card list?"

"That's clearly obvious. You piss people off, Mister Speed. Somebody wants their retribution."

"I only piss off authoritarians."

"That's exactly what a certain Detective Constable Stevens told me after he rang the MDP to enquire if we were conducting an investigation concerning you."

"Were you investigating me?"

"Not then, but we're interested now."

"So where do I fit into your investigation?"

"I'm not sure of that either."

"What are you sure of then?"

"I know that two enforcers from the dregs of Europe are connected to a stolen identity in regards to an ex officer of the MDP. I know that you've a passing interest in a recently exhumed world war two Spitfire fighter plane. What I don't know is what connects the two. Maybe you can throw some light on the matter."

I sighed. "I knew the farmer who owned the land, but that's as far as it goes."

"Yes, I did speak to Mister Bickermass when I was overseeing the salvage operation at his farm; such a nice, pleasant chap. Strange that he never mentioned your presence at the crash site."

"It's hardly surprising since I wasn't *there,* as I explained to DC Stevens, when he interviewed me over another matter. Did you know that the farmer died in mysterious circumstances shortly after the recovery of the plane?"

"I'd heard that he had been killed in an unfortunate accident. Fell into a slurry tank, I was led to believe."

"Rather strange don't you think considering there are two known killers floating around unchallenged and posing as MDP?"

I could have easily taken up some serious issues with Hamer on how I thought Lens had died, but I suspected it would only fall on another pair of deaf ears. I drank some tea and stuffed a piece of bacon into my mouth.

"Please understand, Mister Speed, I'm not here to take over official constabulary business. And neither am I here to persecute you over a plane wreck. It's your help on a different matter that I really sought."

He wants my help? I almost choked on my food with the request. I said, "I'm listening."

Hamer wiped the corners of his mouth with a napkin.

"I'm not one bit interested in any active part you had in the discovery of the Spitfire, Mister Speed." I was about to protest my innocence when his hand rose. "Please hear me out."

I shrugged and carried on eating before the food went cold.

He jerked an appreciative smile. "I believe, Mister Speed, that it was you who first discovered the wreck with your metal detector. I believe you allowed Mister Bickermass to take the credit; a nice gesture Mister Speed. I assume the number of arrest warrants you've accumulated over the years for non-remittance of treasure trove obviously accounted for your silence. How am I doing so far?"

"You should take up writing fiction. And you've obviously had an extensive chat with that Peeler DC Stevens."

He ignored my remarks and pushed on. "Look at it from my point of view. The plane is found, exhumed, and the pilot, a chap by the name of Rowlands, is given a military funeral. After cross-referencing, everything is logged and stored in the archives for eternity. Another chapter in history concluded. Sounds so simple don't you think? But out of nowhere questions are asked by a local police station enquiring about you and a retired MDP official who has had his name used by criminals, all because of a piece of wreckage and a military uniform full of bones."

I was thinking about something else. What had happened to the identity tags around the skeletons neck bone which would have identified the body correctly? I hadn't removed the tags, so where did they get the name Rowland from?

Hamer went on. "There has to be a connection surrounding the wreck of a Spitfire with a renowned treasure hunter and two killers from Europe."

"It does seem a strange concoction, doesn't it, Inspector?" I said, and promptly wiped my plate clean with a slice of cold toast.

He frowned at my indifferent response. I suppose I should have eased his mind and told him the name I saw on the tags, but why should I stupidly strangle myself by admitting I was there at the scene. I was deep in it enough to want more additions.

"I feel that you're not taking me seriously, Mister Speed?"

"I'm not clear as to what you're getting at?"

"I think there was something else at the wreck site which isn't there now."

"What might that be?"

"I'm not sure."

"You could have asked Tommy Bickermass what he saw, if he hadn't been killed *accidentally*."

"You sound as if you don't think it was an accident?"

"At last I've got someone following in my direction. I believe Winston has met those two thugs before at the farm. He proved that by his reaction. He was old Tom's dog, and as I said before, he reacts against anybody who harms his friends, especially his master."

"Have you any proof?"

"That Love and Hate killed Tommy? Yes if I can get the dog to talk."

"Being facetious won't help, Mister Speed."

"What difference would I make? I couldn't even convince the local police to investigate the suspicious death of a good friend of mine; another statistic of the Love and Hate crime consortium. Why don't you try and persuade the police otherwise, since you're on friendly terms with that Peeler Stevens."

"I'm hardly on friendly terms, Mister Speed. But you could still prove to the police that they were wrong if you move without delay."

"I'm hardly in a position to take the law into my own hands without having them slapped for unnecessary intimidation. DC Stevens did warn me to watch where I stepped."

"But if you could, would you like to bring those responsible to justice?" His expression was serious.

"Damn right, if I knew where to begin."

"Begin by telling me everything you haven't told me? Like what you saw or found at the wreck site that has got people spooked enough to bring killers into the affray."

Hamer was pushing his luck. He'd chosen the wrong line of approach to ask for my help. My reaction towards his clever ploy to get me to reveal information for his benefit and a possible prosecution against me probably sounded a little hostile. I didn't care a toss!

"I've already told you I wasn't there at the farm. So why push it? Inside the ministry you probably carry a lot of whack. Outside in the real world you're way out of your jurisdiction. If you really want to be a good policeman, why don't you work alongside our wonderful police force scattered around good old London and between you, hopefully you can find the two unscrupulous characters roaming the streets bothering people with the intention of wanting to murder them." I stood to leave. "Thanks for the wonderful breakfast. I only hope I don't vomit on the way home when I think of what you tried to pull."

Hamer was certainly persistent and being the typical policeman, he attempted to put the frighteners on me.

"Be warned, Mister Speed. This is far from over. I implore you to reconsider working alongside me. Those two brutish fiends are still a threat to you. It isn't going to go away. All you've achieved is to stand on the tails of a couple of rattlesnakes without getting bit. You're treading a dangerous path. I know them; how their devious minds work. They'll want retribution. They'll strike back and they might be successful next time. I can't protect you unless you help me. Hand your problems over to the professionals who get paid for dealing with dangerous villains."

I smiled confidently. "Don't fret. I'm a big boy. Must get back or Winston will start tearing my place apart in search of food."

I turned to leave but checked my stride. I thought he deserved something for buying me breakfast. I asked him, "Ever heard of a wartime operation 'Huggermugger'?" His expression said he hadn't. "Look it up in the military archives," I told him. "It's very interesting. World War Two, I'm informed. R.A.F. Duxford carried out the operation."

I probably should have kept my mouth shut because when he finds out what I know, he'll no doubt be even more suspicious of how I know so much. By giving him that information I was thinking more on the lines that the military might rectify their mistake and bury Craven under his own name with full military honours; then again, the inevitable embarrassment of owning up to their gaff would have them sweeping the mess under the carpet as usual. As for my own enquiries, the right direction had me heading towards McClusky's which I located at Greenland dock in Greenwich.

I parked the Roadster and went on foot to the dock gate. It was busy when I got there; bustling with traffic passing through security. I used the confusion and sneaked past the security hut alongside a long wheeled-based lorry trundling through the gate. When I'd reached the warehouse where McClusky's resided, a large red brick and concrete structured building with an array of warning signs indicating a fragile roof, I peeped through the large opened steel doors.

There wasn't much happening inside; just the horrible scraping noise of a solitary bucket loader shovelling piles of grain into sectioned bays. I noticed to the left a steel stairway leading to what appeared to be raised offices which would be worth a look inside. I decided I would return later. In the middle of the night when it was nice and dark, perhaps bring along a selection of tools to break-in and have a look inside when nobody was around. What I would be searching for I've no idea.

*

I was back at McClusky's just after midnight. I was prepared this time, dressed in black combat type clothing, a zipped and buttoned bomber jacket, trousers and black soft soled boots. I considered a balaclava with slits for eyes as a little excessive in case I got caught and it would be hard to explain away. I parked the car down the road, collected a leather bag, something similar to a doctor's bag, from the boot and walked fast-paced to the main gate and past the security gatehouse with unimaginable ease. I suspected that the lapse of disciplined security was duly down to the attitude of the two guards within the gatehouse, who probably decided that first class security requires first class pay and the pittance that they were probably paid didn't warrant the effort to get off their backsides in too much of a hurry; such consideration only served to make my task simple.

I didn't want to use my flashlight with the fear of the beam being seen. Luckily the moonlight flickering through the night clouds lit my way sufficiently to scamper across the compound, having to clutch the leather bag tightly to stop the tools from playing a metallic jingle as I bounced along. I checked that everywhere was clear at the front of the warehouse before making my way to the rear. It was there where I saw a light emitting from a lower window underneath a steel stairway that led to a first floor doorway which I assumed was a fire exit.

I angled across, away from the building and pushed my back tight against a large steel container and waited there for a few minutes thinking there might be lookouts wandering around the perimeter. Satisfied I was alone I circled the container to check what was on the other side. There I found a lorry tarpaulin covering what I thought was a medium sized vehicle. I peeled back the corner of the sheet and the momentary flash of moonlight lit up, 'wash me', finger written in the dirt on the right rear door of a white van. Things were looking promising, and if I was to examine the vehicle closely, I'd have probably discovered a large dent on the front offside with car paint matching the blue colour of the vehicle that the van had hit while attempting to dissect me at Duxford.

I let the sheet fall and tip-toed across to the window under the stairway and crouched, carefully placing the tool bag down on the ground. I peered through the grain dusted glass. I could see men using hand pulled hydraulic stack lifts, in the motion of shifting large wooden crates in readiness to load onto a flat-backed truck parked inside the building. I counted a total of five men altogether, though there could easily have been more that I couldn't see. It would be five men too many for me to handle in one go; one or two men, yes, three at a push if I was desperate. In reality I'd chosen the wrong night to risk an attempted break-in. It was time to get out of there before I was seen.

I eased away from the window, grabbed my tool bag, straightened my posture and back tracked my steps. I was on the verge of turning when something struck the back of my head with such force that I'd thought my skull had been cracked open. I almost blacked out but realized I was falling to the ground. In my semi-conscious state something or somebody had caught my fall. For a moment or two my head throbbed, the feeling of a lump swelling at the base of my skull, stretching my skin. I felt my heels dragging along the ground before I was dropped onto something cold, as if I was a large fish being slapped down on the fishmongers dissecting table. I think I died at that moment because everything went black and quiet.

Chapter Eight

I knew I wasn't dead when I came round from my induced sleep. God only knows where I was. My eyes were glued shut. At least I thought they were. I raised my head and my neck cracked. The pain pumping at the back of my skull reminded me of the wise meaning: *watch your back at all times in enemy territory.* Something I'd neglected to do. At least my sense of smell hadn't deserted me because I could smell the badness of congealed blood that had soaked into the neck of my black polo-necked sweater.

I quickly abandoned my first attempt to open my eyes when the incoming light tired to split my eyeballs in two. What fraction of feeling I still had in my body made me realize that I was still upright but slouched in some sort of harness. I had numbness around my crutch region and all my limbs and joints were a mixture of aches and pins and needles. I forced open my eyelids to a slit and stood the few inches required to support my own weight. I tried to move about to get the blood circulation going through my veins but all I could do was squirm as the harness seem to hold all my limbs tight.

My eyes flickered open fully and I became aware of what held me. The harness wasn't a harness as such. Some inconsiderate bastard had nailed every conceivable part of my clothing to a wooden stanchion and I was pinned there in the form of a crucifix and no matter how hard I twisted, turned, or pulled, I wasn't going anywhere, indefinitely.

I got a sudden strong whiff of damp walls. I looked around at what appeared to be the attic room of an old house. A single light pendant hung from the rafters dingily illuminating the room, its clear glass lamp diffused by its coating of fly excrement. In the corner of the room, abandoned on a small stool, I saw the culprit for my imprisonment; the nail gun that had attacked my clothing. Apart from the stool, there was no other furniture I could see. The attic room had no skylight so I couldn't tell if it was day or night. The only entrance into the room was by a narrow, wood panelled door directly in front of me. In all honesty, I couldn't visualize much hope of escape until I heard a bout of laughter and voices drifting from the other side the door.

I made an attempt to make myself heard but it came out as a disappointing squeak because my throat was dry. Gathering what saliva I had left in the crevices of my mouth, I swallowed painfully and tried again.

"Is there anyone listening?" I bellowed the best I could.

The response was quick, direct and threatening. Straight away I knew I was dealing with a non-negotiator.

"Shut your fucking mouth!" The voice belonged to an arrogant piece of shit with a strong Irish accent.

"I need a piss!" I shouted back angrily. I wasn't lying neither.

"Piss down your leg," a different Irish voice bellowed back.

"You might enjoy standing in a pool of stinking fluid but I happen to have more class and dignity. I need a piss, like right now!"

Ten seconds later I heard the clatter of hard soled boots scaling a creaky stairway. I watched in anticipation as the latch lifted with a metallic clap and the door squeaked open. A tall, young man in army fatigues, reluctantly shuffled through the door. He had a spotty complexion and scraggy medium length hair tied back in a short ponytail. As he approached I noticed he had a mouthful of disorientated teeth that a dentist would have ripped out and started again.

More appropriately, he had brought the bathroom to me in the form of a dented metal bucket that he must have pinched from a local scrap yard.

I smiled, amused with the feeble effort. "How nice, personal service, I see."

He scowled at me; the looks could kill type of expression.

"What's going on?" I asked sharply. "Why am I being held prisoner? Who the frigging hell are you lot?"

He seemed surprised that I didn't know the answer to my own question, but he refrained from saying anything. I wondered if he was under strict orders not to speak to me. In that case I would be right to assume he was the youngest of the bunch to earn the right to be handed the task of errand boy and his sour faced expression hardly disguised that he detested the responsibility. He placed the bucket down on the floor in front of me and was about to leave.

I stopped him with an almighty 'Whoa!', and superimposed a stare of astonishment, I glanced down at the bucket, then to him, then the bucket, then to him again. I said mildly, "What am I suppose to do with that?"

Again he expressed surprise at my inability to understand the procedure to use the bucket. "You some sort of idiot?" His Irish accent differed from the others I'd already heard; therefore I was dealing with at least three warders "You piss in it!"

"From here?"

The lines on his forehead furrowed deeper

I said, "You're not too bright, are you?"

His teeth gritted. "You're asking for a smack in the mouth, Mister!"

"I'm more likely to get wet pants because I'm not renowned for any magical attributes, so I'm going to find it rather difficult to unzip my flies and direct my dick towards the centre of the bucket. Catch on?"

His dormant brain suddenly clicked. He blushed. "If you think I'm holding your prick, you can get fucked, you gay bastard!" With that outburst he left in an almighty hurry.

"Touchy!" I said, and watched him disappear down the stairway.

I could overhear Spotty-face moaning to his comrades about the audacity of my request and the roars of laughter that followed. Served the frigging bastard right, I thought. I would have laughed along with them only I was still desperate to avoid wet pants. I shouted through again. "I still need a piss you selfish bastards!"

The response was swifter than I anticipated. A pair of boots thundered up the stairway and to my surprise they'd sent a woman instead to attend to my needs. I'd no complaints about the choice. She was pretty for starters, slim and quite tall. She had short boyish styled brown hair swept back. Her attire consisted of tight dark military pants, a black round-necked T-shirt that stretched enticingly over the smoothness of her cone shaped breasts and she had taut muscles in her arms and shoulders. She was my type of woman; an Amazon warrior.

She frowned as she approached me. She did look more capable of smacking me in the mouth for misbehaving than Spotty-face's feeble threat. She picked up the metal bucket. Her sparkling green eyes burned into mine and without taking her eyes from mine, she'd unzipped my flies, rustled around inside my pants and flopped out my dick with staggering speed and tucked the cold steel rim under my scrotum. Now this was a woman with talent and dominance I just had to have forever.

"Piss, Buster! I haven't got all day!" she was bossy too, I'll give her that much. And neither was she Irish. Her accent had me estimating North American.

While I pissed, I said, "What's the idea of holding me against my will?"

She eyeballed me but said nothing.

"I don't know what I've done to offend you, but surely we can work something out together?"

Her silence annoyed me and interrupted my flow.

"Kidnapping is against the law," I snapped.

"Just concentrate on your bodily function, Buster."

"I've a right to know why I'm being held!"

"Know this, Buster! Wet me and you'll be wearing this bucket on your head."

I didn't miss and when I had finished she put the bucket unceremoniously down, tucked my dick back inside my pants and re-zipped my flies which caused me to cringe with the thought of my scrotum being caught in the zipper; it's something you always remembered happening during your childhood.

The bitch playfully tapped the front of my pants, sort of grinned, and said, "Happy now, Buster?"

"No I'm not happy; not one bit. I'll be happy when you tell me what the frigging hell's going on?"

She slid the bucket across the floor with her foot. "Save your pleas for when your interrogation begins. We have a lot to discuss."

My eyes popped out of their sockets. "What interrogation?"

She'd no intention of telling me anything further and turned to leave.

"What interrogation?" I repeated.

She closed the door behind her leaving me to swirl in my own fear.

I didn't like the sound of this *interrogation* lark. It can make a person think too deeply about torture. I wondered if she'd said it on purpose in an attempt to weaken my resistance to questioning. Frigging hell, what could they inflict on the human body to make a person talk? A damned lot came to mind in a flash. Realistically, all they had to do with me was to tickle the bottom of my feet with a feather and I'd have told them anything they wanted to know. If she'd planned to worry me, it was working.

I could be certain of one thing. Wherever this place was that held me prisoner; it was nowhere near McClusky's warehouse or any other frequented place. Inflicting severe pain on a person and the impending screams of agony from the unfortunate victim would be clearly heard for miles and I suspected we were miles from anywhere.

It suddenly occurred to me as to why there was a delay to interrogate me. What were they waiting for? I was awake. In prime condition to crack under extreme pressure, but they weren't pushing ahead with their questioning. Why? Were they actually expecting me to worry myself to death instead? No. There was a more obvious reason. They were waiting for the arrival of some other mean bastard. They were waiting for the interrogator.

My body tensed. I swallowed hard with a feeling of dread. Where they waiting for Damian Love and Theodore Hate to show? Was that the reason? I'd this mental picture forming inside my head; a clear indication of them eagerly climbing the stairs in anticipation of slicing lumps out of my flesh. Frigging hell! I had to get out of here. I couldn't hang about waiting for the worst to happen. I jerked my body forward in a frantic attempt to free my clothing from the nails. I twisted and pulled and jerked forward again. I didn't want those bastards enjoying their revenge. I don't mind being hit providing I'm in a position to defend myself and give back as good as I got. Yet I don't think such callous killers would give me the chance.

Again I was jolting about like a madman in a straight-jacket, but all my efforts for freedom were useless. The clothing was too tightly nailed to get a good pull and all I achieved was to exhaust myself into submission. All I could do now was to wait for the expected consequences for prying into something I was too badly equipped to handle.

I didn't have to wait too long before I heard the clattering of heavy boots storming up the stairs. The door flew open and bodies piled in. Stood in front of me were the woman, Spotty-face, and two bulldogs in the form of brutish looking Irishman in fatigues who moved towards me menacingly. Both men were tall and powerful looking with short cropped dark hair, and round deep-set brown eyes. They were obviously brothers, almost twin-like but separated by one of them having the mangled and battered face of a pugilist. There was no immediate sign of Love or Hate and I wondered if I'd been reprieved or even mistaken that they would be involved in this farce.

I said defiantly. "Have I done something to offend you chaps? Only I'm not usually so bad that it warrants being trussed up like this. It's ruined my clothes I'll have you know!"

"That's exactly what we're going to soon find out!"

The deep toned Irish voice echoed from behind the group and when they fanned out, a grey haired, bulbous nosed middle-aged man of medium height and supremely smart in army fatigues was standing there rigid, chest pouted, both his hands behind his back holding a short cane. He had all the hallmarks of a proud man who'd taken considerable care over his appearance and everything that should have shined did indeed shine: combat boots and the buckle on his belt.

Big-nose, (since he didn't introduce himself, I'll refer to him by that name) walked slowly towards me, purposely clumping down his boots on the wooden floor boards with every step, his hands still clasped behind his back.

As he neared, I said, "Great! Now perhaps you can tell me why I'm here playing frigging Jesus when it isn't even Christmas?"

Big-nose quickened his final steps towards me and lashed me across the face with his cane. My teeth gritted both in anger and to absorb the stinging pain. His grey eyes bore into mine. "Don't take the Lord's name in vain you imbecile."

"It's just a name to me. I'm an atheist."

Big-nose suddenly rammed the tip of his cane into my throat, which left me gargling for breath. "You'll be a dead atheist if you speak out of turn again." He removed the cane and repositioned himself to one side of me. I wondered why and instinctively my eyes strained to follow his every movement in anticipation of another assault with his cane. He went on. "Now shall we begin by establishing that you are one of McClusky's men?"

"I knew it!" I spurted out with relief. "You've abducted the wrong man."

Big-nose arched an enquiring eyebrow. "You were guarding the rear of the warehouse."

"The hell I was! I was spying through the window."

"Lies won't save your hide."

"I intended to rob the place."

"Hence the bag of tools found in your possession?"

"A burglar needs his tools," I said.

"It's a grain warehouse, not a rich man's house."

"There's a safe." I was guessing there was.

Big-nose still wasn't convinced because his temper was something to witness as he laid into me. "Don't lie to me! You're one of McClusky's men?"

"No. I'm a burglar," I said with a touch of cockiness and almost paid the price for my insolence.

The object thrown at me from an unknown source whizzed past my face and embedded into the wooden stanchion just inches from my left ear. My head shot round. I saw Spotty face standing there with a twisted smile, displaying his horrendous bulk of teeth while holding two pub darts in his hand. I realized now that he was responsible for the embedded dart that had threatened to pin my face to the stanchion.

I eyeballed Spotty-face. "That wasn't necessary, you creep!"

Big-nose pointed his cane at me. "Admit it. You're one of McClusky's men?"

I kept one eye on Spotty face's raised hand, a dart rolling between finger and thumb. "No, I'm actually an innocent bystander."

Big-nose tapped my shoulder with his cane. "A moment ago you were a burglar."

"A moment ago you didn't believe me," I retorted.

No sooner had I finished my denial, Spotty-face threw the dart into the fleshy part of my right hand. I grimaced with the stinging sensation and quickly examined the damage. There was no blood oozing from where the dart was embedded, just a blob of pulled white skin where the dart dangled from my hand.

I threw Spotty-face a revengeful glare because given the chance I was going to ram those darts down his throat and pull them out of his arse.

Within seconds something horrible happened to me which I couldn't control. The pain increased in my injured hand, a feeling of burning as if the dart was attempting to bury deeper into my flesh all by itself.

Big-nose smiled and thoroughly enjoyed explaining the situation to me. "You're no doubt feeling the intensified pain-yes? Each dart tip is coated with a solution of muscle distorting serum ZX 34, originally created in Russian laboratories by bored chemists. It's used extensively now in the Middle Eastern countries, heavily administered to prisoners inside illegal prison camps. It's a civilised form of torture; it leaves no physical marks like a severe beating would. The serum gradually found its way to the shores of Ireland for use in nail bombs during the campaign for freedom. For the purpose of interrogation, the serum is usually injected into a chosen muscle with a syringe," he snorted a smirk. "But our way is far more exciting."

The pain I was experiencing made me feel sick.

Big-nose went on. "Now for the intriguing part of this exercise, when the muscle goes into spasm and you feel a tight, twisting pain, which I believe, although I have never experience the devilish stuff, is equivalent to having your muscle squashed in a mechanical vice. The suffering probably lasts approximately one minute, but whose counting. Exciting isn't it! There is, of course, an antidote. Correct answers to simple questions."

I just hate that moment when the tormenter proves to be right. I did feel precisely what he told me I'd feel and it hurt badly. I couldn't even move my fingers. The pain intensified to excruciating. That invisible vice wouldn't stop turning and there was nothing I could do until the pain finally subsided and I was left gasping for breath.

Big-nose was relentless and began tearing into my mind again. "What's McClusky planning?" he bellowed in my ear.

"How the frigging hell should I know! I don't even know him."

"Talk, now!"

"I don't know."

Big-nose gave a hand signal and out of the corner of my eye I saw Spotty-face unleashing another dart. My body tensed as the dart smashed into my left thigh with a sickening thud. I arched and squirmed, clenching my teeth in readiness for the oncoming blast of pain. I soon realized that the bigger the muscle, the more intensified the agony and I was hurting inside. When the pain eased

I was dripping with sweat and I couldn't stop my body from shaking.

Big-nose was at me again. "What's McClusky planning?"

"I've no frigging idea!"

Another dart penetrated my right thigh.

Big-nose pushed his face into mine. "Is it wise to suffer for a mere piece of information?" He said and moved away.

I had no time to plead. The pain had already kicked in and began to rip through my thigh. I thought I was screaming but I couldn't be sure. I wanted the pain to stop, but I had to show these bastards that I'm not easily intimidated despite what they inflicted on me. *Mind over matter! Mind over matter!* I kept telling myself. And the more I held on, the more Big-nose got agitated and frustrated because his ingenious plan was failing right in front of his eyes.

Spotty-face still had that horrible grin when he approached me to retrieve the darts dangling from my body. The bastard deliberately retracted each dart slowly as he watched me wince with each pull. He took particular delight when removing the dart from my hand, observing the spectacle with vampirism asperity, fascinatingly amused as the blood oozed from the wound. He then returned to his starting position, dipped the tips of the darts into a liquid solution, and waited eagerly for the signal for him to unleash his darts into my body.

Big-nose went on, "Be the hero. We've all the time in the world to break your resistance. Now tell me what McClusky is planning to do with our merchandise and I assure you the pain will stop?"

"You're going beyond the extremes of stupidity, Mister! I don't kn..."

I never got the chance to finish as two darts, one after the other, rammed into my left and right breast muscles, penetrating the thickness of my Bomber jacket with ease. Within seconds the pain was unbearable. My chest was on fire and caving in. I struggled to catch my breath and in between my agonies Big-nose was shouting quick-fire questions in my face.

"Tell me what McClusky has planned?

"Where are my weapons?

"Why suffer for scum like McClusky; he'd sell you out with a click of his fingers."

Through the hurt and gritted teeth I fought back. "I don't...know," I said weakly.

"How many men does he have at the warehouse?"

I shook my head.

"Tell me the strength of their armaments?"

"How many...times...do I have...to say, I...don't know," I gasped.

"You will tell me now!" he ravaged in my eardrum.

I found some inner strength from somewhere and flew into a short rage. "Frigging ask him yourself!"

The dart that penetrated my left shoulder muscle put me in deep trouble. I was so disorientated that for a moment I couldn't even scream anymore. I screwed my eyes so tight to fight the onslaught of pain that I never even felt the stinging force of Big-nose's cane as he slashed it against the side of my face in a burst of uncontrollable rage.

"Talk you scraping of excrement!" he ranted "What deviousness is McClusky contemplating in his sick mind?"

As my suffering eased, I said, "Aren't you the one that's sick, using me as a pincushion. Asking me questions I can't possibly answer. How many times do I have to say, I don't work for McClusky."

In a remarkable turn-around, Big-nose was calm again. "Either you've an incredible resistance to pain and have such loyalty to a traitor like McClusky or you obviously don't know anything worth pursuing. If you did, you'd be squealing like a pig to tell me what I want to know. So big hero, who are you, besides an incompetent burglar?"

"Does it matter who I am?"

Big-nose quickly raised his hand to stop Spotty-face from throwing another dart. "Your name or the pain continues."

For awkwardness, I said, "Noddy!"

Big-nose slashed his cane across my mouth. I howled a mixture of obscenities, feeling the instant trickle of warm blood leaking from my throbbing split lips.

He pulled a quick smile, and said, "Strange how the details we found inside your wallet spell Shackleton Speed. Or just maybe you are a thief or a damned good liar."

"I still don't work for McClusky!"

"I'll be the judge of *that*."

"Why don't you ask him? He might even tell you how he tried to kill me; twice."

"Kill you!" Big-nose scoffed. "Why should he want to do that?"

"How should I know? I might have found out but someone decided to smash the back of my skull and drag me away."

"What were you hoping to achieve at his warehouse all alone?"

There seemed no point holding back any longer. "Blow it to smithereens if I had to. I intended to break-in hoping to find some evidence against him. He's responsible for murdering friends of mine. I needed to know what I was up against. I didn't think it was wise to introduce myself at his front door, mainly as a precaution to prevent him shooting my frigging head off."

"And what were your intentions afterwards?"

"Pass what information I can find onto the police and let them deal with him."

"You should have mentioned all this earlier. It might have saved you a lot of anxiety and pain."

"You never gave me the frigging chance. I was battered unconscious, kidnapped and trussed up as if I was a trophy. And then you had one hundred and eighty over there displaying his future darting ambitions upon my body."

Big-nose showed no remorse. "It'll teach you to stick to whatever you do best. Now why should McClusky want to kill your friends?"

I shrugged. At least I think my shoulders twitched visibly considering my clothing was nailed tight to the stanchion. "I'm not sure," I said.

"Perhaps you were interfering with one of their operations?"

"I hardly think that's the problem. Until a few hours ago I'd never even heard the name McClusky. Not until two of his henchmen came harassing and threatening me."

"What did they want?"

"It's a long story.

"Going somewhere, Speed?"

As only a fool would take unnecessary punishment for the sake of a slice of truth, I told them everything that had happened, that was, everything they needed to know to convince them I would be no threat to Big-nose and his army. I went through the entire episode from the discovery of the plane, through to my untimely presence at the docks, though I did make a few alterations along the narrative route, a few white lies to protect the innocent and wisely forgot to mention the gold bullion. When I'd finished I waited for their reactions.

I sensed Big-nose wasn't convinced. "McClusky wouldn't make all that fuss over a piece of plane wreckage, a few war relics, a corpse and a ghost submarine locked in someone's imaginary head. There has to be more."

"There is no more."

"What did you intend to do if you found this submarine?"

"Claim the salvage rights and sell it of course! People are willing to pay for pieces of unseen war memorabilia, even a war museum."

"Good grief!" Big-nose exploded angrily. "This is what our planning has achieved, the capture of a grieving metal detector enthusiast out for revenge, who still has his wits about him to make a dishonest profit." He looked me sternly in the face. "Honour and greed don't mix, I can assure you. As for lurking around McClusky's I think you fell lucky to drop into our hands rather than his or you'd have been mixed up with animal feed and fed to the pigs by now."

Frigging hell I nearly burst out laughing. *Lucky,* after what they'd inflicted on my suffering body. Given the choice, I think I would have seriously taken my chances of being fed to the pigs.

The girl edged forward in military fashion, stood straight almost to attention, hands behind her back, eyes forward, not looking directly at her commander. "Have I permission to speak, sir?"

Now it could have been my imagination concerning the woman, but I had noticed on a couple of occasions, when I came under attack from spotty face, that beneath her hard exterior I thought I glimpsed a softer side, a slight squirm when the dart penetrated my flesh. I did, of course, change my opinion when she smirked afterwards.

Big-nose nodded his approval for her to speak.

"I've heard the name, Shackleton Speed mentioned before," she said. "This guy is headline news in Europe and America, regarded as renegade by treasure trove officialdom. Many historical artefacts that have illegally left British shores are down to him alone. There were two accusations I recall; both made the newspapers here and in America. One concerned a medallion reputedly lost by the Parliamentarian Oliver Cromwell while in battle. The medallion turned up in an American's private collection. It didn't please the English heritage who regarded this prisoner as nothing but a criminal."

This woman had some memory, I admired. I said in my defence, "Speculative nonsense. Nothing was proven so less of the criminal."

She ignored me and went on. "And only last year, a jewel encrusted broach belonging to Mary Queen of Scots, which she apparently lost on a coach journey to London, mysteriously turned up at New York jewellers. I've seen the jewel. A magnificent piece displayed in such grandeur. Again the name Shackleton Speed was linked." She looked me accusingly in the eyes. "Do you deny that also?"

"I do, categorically! I'm a man of honour. I would never sell a lady's jewels for money."

She didn't stop there. "Roman coins in abundance and Saxon gold bracelets. The list is endless. This guy is your modern day marauding archaeologist whose historical value on items he finds means nothing more than making the next dollar or two."

Big-nose wasn't amused by any of my antics and said, "So you're nothing but a fucking thief and a useless commodity to us."

"Thanks," I said under my breath.

"It's apparent you were in the wrong place at the wrong time. That is unfortunate. It's a pity you couldn't tell us anything about McClusky."

As Big-nose turned to leave the room, I said sharply, "Surely you're not intending to keep me here, only I'm in need of medical attention. And I'm frigging hungry!"

Without warning the girl struck me twice across the face and rammed her knee into my groin with such power and precision it sent my balls splaying at different angles inside my pants.

"Speak when you're told to, Buster," and she meant it.

I tried to say something else. "I'm only-."

But she cut me off by ramming her clenched fist into my solar plexus with some considerable power for a female, leaving me gasping for breath. "Keep your mouth closed tightly, if you know what's good for you!"

Big-nose smiled thinly. "That's my girl," he said with satisfaction.

I guess Big-nose was still agitated as he left, something I defined by his continual slashing of the cane against his thigh. The others followed silently. The door shut and I was left alone in a state of discomfort. I was also very concerned about what was going to happen to me next. That didn't mean I'd given up any hope of escaping as I had made some solid observations. I knew the door wasn't locked and I worked out that only the top two treads of the stairway squeaked. My only real problem was freeing my clothing.

At least I'd something to smile about when I heard Big-nose bawling at his troops, calling them incompetent imbeciles for capturing the wrong man. He finished by stating that their entire mission had been a diabolical shambles and that they were a disgrace to the regiment. I wondered what regiment he meant because I was unsure if terrorists did have regiments. I did suspect they were IRA but I quickly changed my mind because I was still alive.

It went quiet downstairs. Half an hour later I heard a vehicle door slam shut and an engine start up, and then the crunching of tyres on gravel as the vehicle drove away. I wondered how many of them had left the building. The moment worried me. Straining my ears listening, I finally heard light footsteps climbing the stairs and the woman entered carrying a tray of food and drink. I didn't dare ask if it was the last meal for the condemned man in case she threw the contents straight into my face and punched the hell out of me again.

"You're fortunate to be getting this meal," She said, noticing my untrustworthy look. "Don't worry it's not poisoned."

On a matter of principal I should have refused the offer, but the rumble of hunger had my stomach thinking my throat had been cut. To be truthful, I was that hungry I would have eaten a scabby donkey between two slices of mouldy bread, but I was quite content with the plate of cold greasy fried chicken.

I nodded my approval for nourishment, and said, "How about a little freedom while I eat, it's uncomfortable in this position."

"Not permitted, Buster."

"I promise I won't run off."

With gunslingers speed she had drawn a handgun from somewhere and bent my nose with the nozzle, all skilfully done without disturbing any of the contents on the tray, not even a spill of coffee. She said confidently, "How far do you think you would get?"

My Adam's apple rippled as I gulped and I was relieved when she replaced the gun into the holster strapped to the side of her leg and then she promptly rammed a chicken leg in my mouth. I took a bite and chewed. My jaw ached.

"I heard a vehicle drive away," I said, trying to avoid spitting food from my mouth as I talked. "Has the big boss gone?"

She tapped my nose with a chicken leg. "You ask too many questions, Buster."

"I enjoy conversation when I'm eating. Which terrorist group are you?"

She shook her head in disbelief. "Never give up, do you?"

I swallowed. "Are you a splinter group from the IRA?"

"Does it matter?"

"To me it does."

"Why?"

"I like to know which terror group intends to kill me so I can haunt them from hell."

She smiled. "Are you afraid of dying?'

I was thoughtful, but the answer came pretty quick. "I guess not."

"Extremely brave you are, Shackleton Speed."

"Not really. If you can't remember being born, then you're unlikely to remember dying."

"Then it matters very little you knowing anything."

I made no attempt to decipher what she meant. I said, "Do your kind of terrorists eventually release their prisoners?"

Her eyes narrowed. "I dislike the term *terrorist*. We are Urban Guerrillas fighting for freedom from tyrannical rule."

"Whose eyes are you covering up?"

"Obstinate cretins like you who don't understand what we are trying to achieve."

I pulled a disapproving expression. "I've heard all this frigging bullshit baloney before: fighting for a unified Ireland: throw out the repressors. All that and the frigging rest of the compulsive crap scraped together into a dirty pile."

"Spare me the boring lecture."

"I'm a shit lecturer. I'm more confused by the necessity for so much destruction. Ireland is a beautiful place, including Northern Ireland. People like you fuck it up with your trumpet for freedom. And you all miss one important fact."

"What's that?" She sounded bored.

"Have you or any other of those self appointed gladiators ever considered asking the people of Ireland if it was what they wanted? I doubt very much. Why, because you are all nothing but a bunch of Irish gangsters using the excuse of a campaign against tyranny to gain power and supremacy by intimidation and brutality. What you have running about is a regime of self proclaimed degenerates pretending to fight the good fight and hiding behind democracy to prolong their greed to accumulate wealth. You're on equal terms with the Mafia. No. I'm afraid terrorism doesn't come into the equation, just greedy gangsters accumulating a mass of money."

I think I twitched her conscience because she didn't strike me with anything. But she was still verbally aggressive.

"You sound just like a politician!"

Before I'd the chance to counteract, she shut me up promptly by ramming another chicken leg into my mouth forcing me to frantically chew or choke to death. I tried to eat quickly and half swallowed.

"We don't operate on that pretence," she said with pride in her tone.

I managed to gulp down what I was still chewing and carried on the debate. "You blow up innocent people."

"Casualties of war are inevitable."

"How frigging reassuring is *that* to the families of those victims."

"Listen, Buster! Instead of blaming us, try blaming the cowards who run the British government."

"By restructuring the blame it makes you sleep easy at night?"

"Like a log."

"Well how comforting for you," I said sarcastically. "But if it's attention you seek, why don't you try a different approach and chain yourselves to a steel gate. That way you might just convince the good people of Ireland that there is another alternative than murder."

Her mouth twisted with hate. "Meddlers like you know nothing."

"I know that true gladiators fight in the battlefield and not behind a remote controlled detonator far away from the destruction of a shopping mall full of women and children, without a soldier in sight."

"Then the quicker the politics are sorted within Ireland, the better!"

"I couldn't agree more. Yet there is one slight problem within a terrorist policy."

"Being?"

"The gangsters that run the organizations don't want an end to the proceedings. They don't want peace because their source of income would dramatically shrivel. Less income means their comfortable lifestyle of luxury would diminish and the unfortunate bastards would have to work for a living instead."

"We're not gangsters."

"That's your opinion."

"You're not exactly high on God's list of achievers."

"At the back of the queue, I should imagine. But at least I would be in the queue if I wanted to be; you wouldn't."

She stuffed another piece of chicken in my mouth. She sneered. "You talk too much for someone in the precarious position you happened to be."

I gave up at that point. I devoured the last piece of chicken and accepted a few mouthfuls of lukewarm coffee she offered me and without another word said she loaded the tray with the leftovers and left the room. She never even gave me the chance to thank her for the meagre offerings. I think she took offence to my insensitive attitude towards her. At least I could belch in peace without any complaint.

Half an hour later she was back carrying a bowl of steaming water and a towel over her arm. I had to look twice at her. She was different and no longer had the warrior queen appearance I'd associated her with earlier. She'd obviously showered. Her hair was damp and brushed back and she was wearing a black silk bathrobe that clung to her damp skin, but the combat boots she'd kept on hardly graced the occasion.

I noticed she wasn't as hostile as before, though I wondered if that was a bad thing or not. She was unpredictable as I'd already experienced, and there's nothing worst than an unpredictable woman who might be out for revenge.

She placed the bowl down on the floor.

Unsure of her intentions, I said, "Am I beginning to smell that bad?"

"Yeah, it might attract the rats."

"I thought it had already." I said sullenly. "Am I to be sold into slavery?"

"Don't be so ridiculous. Unless you think you're worth anything?"

"I like to think I am."

She squatted and squeezed the excess water from a flannel, rose and stepped closer to me. She had a sweet smell about her. Even without a lick of makeup on her face she was pretty. She began gently washing and drying my face. For a girl who displayed such a brutish attitude towards me earlier, she had a soft touch when it came to playing nursemaid. I'd no complaints. This was far more rewarding than having, Spotty-face, pin my skin to the stanchion.

She rinsed the flannel only this time I became a little worried when her hand dropped to my crutch and undid my trouser zipper.

"I don't need to piss."

"No, but you need to wash."

I don't use underwear, so it was easy for her hand to slip in between the slot of my pants zipper. At first I thought she might be making a fool of me, deliberately teasing, but there was something about the way the flannel worked over my flaccid penis that alerted me that this girl wasn't teasing. No. This was blatant foreplay and I wasn't in any position to do anything about it. She might be the sybaritic kind and usually I'm all for it, but uncertainty steered me away from temptation.

She came close to me and nibbled my ear lobe. She whispered. "Isn't this nicer?"

I almost agreed until I remembered that the bitch was part of a consortium hell bent on damaging my body. With that in mind I'd no intention of playing along.

I said, with a sudden hoarseness in my throat. "What's to become of me?"

"Wait and see," she said softly, the flannel sliding over my scrotum.

"I want to know now!"

"Be quiet! I hate these interruptions when I'm busy."

And before I knew what was happening she had flopped my penis out of my pants and was washing the length of shaft in a gentle pulling motion.

Well I wasn't having any of this bad captor-good captor shit! I said, "I think its clean enough now."

She kissed me on the lips.

I didn't respond. Kept my lips rigid to the movement of hers and stubborn as I was, in reality I wanted to kiss those pouting, luscious warm lips. I nearly did respond but my biggest problem was keeping my manhood limp.

I managed to get a word in when I turned my head sideways. I said, "Am I being cleaned up for my release?"

Her face pulled away from mine. "Hey, wake up dumb-ass! This is the captor's prerogative. To do what they want with their prisoner. There are no rules to abide. I want to fuck. It's as simple as that."

"Why don't you go and pick on one of your studs downstairs."

"I'm picking on you! I fuck who I want to fuck. Besides, they've have all gone and we're alone."

Stupidly, I said, "I might not want to participate."

"You're not exactly in a position to argue."

"It's sexual harassment."

"So fill in a report, Buster!"

"I'm going to play hard to get."

"Please do, I like a challenge."

The contest ended when she began caressing my dormant penis. Despite my resistance I wanted her but I wanted her on my own terms, not strapped to this stanchion like a side of beef. I had to defy her advances by thinking negatively. I thought of horrible things about her to distract from succumbing to her delicate advances. Clap, came to mind. She might have syphilis or large ulcerating scabs around her vagina? I sighed heavily. It was useless. She was too good for a feeble mind like mine. She knew how to handle a man and my resistance was dramatically failing.

She looked me in the eyes. "Fighting me are you?"

She went down on me and that first gentle flick of her tongue as she mouthed the tip of my penis all but sealed my fate. I'd lost the battle of wills because she discovered my ultimate weakness; let's be fair, it was probably every man's weakness and without doubt the oral sex finally mellowed my resistance. No man in this entire world could resist the warmth of a woman's mouth as she sucks and moves her warm lips up and down the shaft. My dick swelled hard in her mouth. She knew that the way to a man's heart isn't through his stomach like most women suggest. She knew differently. She knew it was how a woman performed and she was exceptionally good, as if she did it for a living. I was bursting at the seams with no way back.

She rose to her feet, and said, "Now that didn't take long."

She untied her robe and let it fall open. I was spellbound as I gawped at her muscular body and firm breasts. She reached for the stanchion over my shoulders and raised herself onto my erect manhood, slowly lowering, that wonderful feeling as my dick pierced the moist lips of her vagina. I listened to her soft groans as she clung on. By her arm strength alone she moved herself up and down rhythmically, squirming side to side, finding her love spots that threw her into spasms of ecstasy. Her groans became frantic jerky screams as she thrust her hips up and down, her rhythm increasing with ever flick of her hip movement until she suddenly squeezed tight into my body and bit my neck vampire style to stem her scream. I grimaced. I felt the hotness of her vaginal juices explode as her muscles squeezed against the girth of my erection. Harder and furious she bounced her hips to reach her ultimate orgasm. I was rather glad that her nails dug into the stanchion rather than my flesh as she held on, exhaling huge gasps of air with every spasmodic jerk of her body, before she gently slowed, panting, catching her breath and I think deeply satisfied. It hadn't taken her long.

I was horrified when she dismounted me.

Hell! What about me? I wanted to shout out.

I hadn't finished. She had frigging left me there, unfulfilled, on the verge of eruption and was calmly tying her robe together. I was frantic with the frustration of not being finished off. I couldn't even thrust myself off because I was pinned tight to the stanchion.

"Are you frigging kidding?" I yelled.

She pretended to be surprised. "What's wrong?"

"*What's wrong?* Are you blind woman? I've this huge hard on and with no end product. No satisfaction. That's the problem!"

"On the contrary, Buster, you've just been had. Used is a better term. It's called womanpower, full control of the situation. How does it feel to be used and left dissatisfied? Fucking awful, I hope?"

"What a bitch! I should have filled your mouth with semen when I had the chance." I retorted defiantly.

"Naughty. And if you had done, I'd have spat it back in your face and watched the fluid dribble down your chin."

By this time my erection had all but gone, hanging limply, defeated. She glanced down at my useless piece of dejection.

"Lost interest?" She said, as if it really mattered.

"Fuck off!" I snapped.

"Suppose I should put it back into your pants, wouldn't want it to get cold."

After zipping me back up, to add insult to injury, she patted my dejected lump and said, "Better luck next time, Buster."

"There's going to be a next time?" I said.

"Depends?"

"Oh!"

"Depends on whether or not we decide to kill you."

She picked up the towel and bowl and left the room with a swing in her step, leaving me in a state of shock. Frigging hell! I was furious with myself for being weak-minded. Now I've been raped by a girl whose name I don't even know and now she wants to kill me!

But how might they dispose of me? A firing squad came to mind, since I was already trussed up and ready. They could have at least untied me and allow me to die with honour, maybe allow me to fight and die like a Viking, with a sword in my hand, even if it was only a wooden one.

The crunching of tyres along the gravel driveway an hour later suggested the men had returned. I guessed I was about to discover my fate.

Chapter Nine

I wasn't exactly grovelling when the big terrorist with pugilist features came at me brandishing a claw hammer and a huge commando knife because my heart was somewhere in my mouth trying to escape. As the condemned man, I considered, I deserved at least a dignified death. A bullet through the head would end it quick. When he raised the hammer the natural progression was for me to shut my eyes and wait for the first fatal blow and the blade ripping into my stomach.

Of all my expectations none of those happened apart from a ripping sound. I dared to open one eye just in time to see the big guy pulling the nails from the stanchion and what nails he failed to pull he simply hacked at my clothing with the knife until my aching body drooped with every disconnection. My weakened legs failed to hold me. The big guy caught me easily, yanked me upright and literally carried me out of the room, manoeuvred me down three flights of stairs and out into the pitch dark of the night where he effortlessly threw me into the back of a large dark coloured van, climbed in after me and sat down on the side seating with his foot resting near my face. I caught a glimpse of the girl sitting there too looking rather subdued. She obviously felt she ought to have been sat in the front seats

Spotty-face climbed in last and made to slam the van doors shut. I managed to catch a fleeting glimpse of the moon lit country house that had held me prisoner; it was a rundown place. I heard the passenger door slam and then the engine was started. We set off at a roaring pace and wherever our mystery destination was, it seems it was important to get there in a frigging hurry.

Within the confines of the blacked-out van the American bitch and the two other idiots were sitting there in comfort while I rolled about the floor like a steel ball in a pinball machine. We were approximately ten minutes into the trip when an array of armoury came magically from nowhere and a sequence of metallic clicking began. The way they handled their weapons in the dark strongly suggested that this wasn't their first venture. Military precision requires time and a meticulous training schedule. This sudden response of loaded weaponry clearly indicated they weren't intended for me, a simple silenced handgun would have concluded that matter. We were heading for a battle.

I guessed we had been travelling for about thirty minutes before we came to a stop. The driver opened his door and got out. I heard the rattle of chain against steel followed by the clunk of something heavy hitting the ground. The sound I heard next indicated that a huge hinged gate was opening. The driver, who I presumed was the second big guy, got back into the van and the vehicle moved slowly along an uneven trail. Within three minutes we had stopped again and the engine was switched off.

The American bitch (yes I was still angry with her) got out of the van pointing her large automatic hand gun at an imaginary figure in front of her; a little over cautious

I thought. The big guy dragged me out with him, the cold steel of his machine-pistol rubbing against my face. If I wanted to make a run for it I didn't stand a chance. He'd have cut me to ribbons. Besides, my legs were still weak. I could hardly stand up straight let alone scarper. I was in lousy shape and did I know it. I ached from head to foot. The dart wounds were aggravatingly sore, and all I wanted to do was to stand there until the strength came back into my legs. No such luck; the sight of the handgun being waved in my face prompted me to ignore my hurt and I reluctantly headed towards a familiar building.

We were back at Mcklusky's warehouse, approaching the building from the rear. The big Irishman frogmarched me all the way, the coward using me as a shield from any surprise attacks. Neither did I appreciate him using my shoulder as a rest for his machine pistol. He pushed me up the same flight of steel stairs where I'd been clobbered earlier. At the top I was encouraged to move a little faster along a short gantry with a shove in the back until we had reached a closed door. There was no ceremonious knock on the door to let those inside know we'd arrived. Pugilist features lifted his size twelve boot and effortlessly kicked the door open, smashing the mortise lock in the process. Before I knew what was happening, our entourage had burst through the doorway and we took the group that was inside by surprise.

We were all standing in a large office threatening three startled men sitting round a large oak desk smoking cigars and drinking Irish whiskey. Or at least the others were doing the threatening because I was then pushed to one side leaving Spotty-face to dig his machine pistol into my ribs.

The man sitting behind the desk, with thick, bushy grey hair and a fat beer gut rose sharply to his feet, knocking his chair back with the momentum. I considered him to be an extremely brave idiot to attempt such dramatic movements with three sets of guns cocked and ready to fire at him. He obviously knew them because they didn't riddle him with bullets.

"Damn fools! Put those guns away!" Beer gut ranted.

"Sit down, you fat fuck," Big nose ordered, raising his machine pistol to Beer gut's head.

Beer gut picked up his chair and sat down, but he was still defiant when he continued his protest. "Are you all mad?" he said, searching the faces of each gunman.

We can't be seen here together. It's too dangerous. You'll get us all killed."

Big-nose extended his gun arm. "You'll be dead in two seconds if you don't shut your fat mouth, McClusky. Where's my merchandise?"

"It's-it's- in a safe place." McClusky murmured his assurance.

I assumed this unscheduled get together had a lot to do with gunrunning.

Big-nose was at him again. "You were paid in advance. You failed to complete the transaction. You fucked us!"

McClusky had the shamed look of a guilty man. He was sweating under the pressure, and he was a practiced pleader. "Listen! I had to change plans at the last minute."

"You didn't tell me, you fat fuck!"

"Listen-I tried. Honestly I tried."

"It made my men vulnerable to capture. My men were sitting ducks; two hours they spent waiting for the delivery at the arranged rendezvous; two fucking hours,

McClusky. And in all that time you couldn't be bothered to even inform us of a change of plan. You put my men in peril. Your inconsiderate actions could have got my men killed! It's almost as if you were trying to set us up, you fat fuck!"

"No, no! It was nothing like that. I was ready to make the delivery. But all my plans went wrong. Something of more importance was sprung on me at the last minute."

"So you don't consider your customers important?"

"No-I mean yes, of course you're important, but the timing was wrong."

"You're damn fucking right the timing was wrong. You didn't deliver!"

"You'll have your merchandise. I promise."

"When will I have my merchandise?"

It was a simple enough question and one McClusky struggled to answer. "When-ah-well-"

"I want the stuff, now!" Big nose interrupted.

It wasn't difficult to see that McClusky didn't have Big nose's merchandise. The look on his face said it all. "What, right now?"

"Is there a problem?"

"Listen," McClusky was playing the sniffling weasel again. "It would be awkward moving the merchandise at the present time."

Big nose hated negativity. I should know. He was maddening every time McClusky concocted an excuse. "It'll be fucking more awkward for you if I stick a bomb up you fat arse. Where's my equipment?"

McClusky lowered his stare as if he were embarrassed with the entire situation. "It's not here. But it's in a secured place."

"Well it should be fucking here! Not unless, you conniving sewer rat, you've spent the money on personal preferences."

"I have all your requirements that you highlighted on your list, but not here at the warehouse. I'm scared of moving it at the moment. There's been a major disruption in outside operations that I have no control over and that has forced me to cancel my personal business transactions."

"You're full of shit, McClusky. I should never have trusted a greasy Irishman like you to do a deal."

"I'll honour our agreement, but I need more time to sort things out."

"Who scares you more than I, McClusky?"

"He's someone who can wipe me out in an instant with a click of his fingers."

"And I can't?" Who is this scaremonger you fear more than me?"

"He goes by the name of 'The Housekeeper'."

"Where do I find this *Housekeeper*?"

I was absorbing all this information for future reference. So McClusky has a boss. But who's to say this Housekeeper is only part of the chain and not the man at the top? Nevertheless, he interested me. It suggests a person who cleans up all the mess; disregards the rubbish; probably kills people in the process or hires villains such as Love and Hate to do the dirty work. Yes. I could probably learn a great deal from this 'Housekeeper', only McClusky wasn't for telling where to find him."

McClusky shrugged. "I don't know where. He contacts me."

"How does he make contact?"

"He sends his errand boys."

"How often do they show up?"

"It depends."

"Be more specific, McClusky?"

"He contacts me when he wants important material transporting to certain ports."

Big-nose was thoughtful. He lowered his gun from McClusky's head to McClusky's stomach, and said with satisfaction. "I want a meeting with this *Housekeeper*."

McClusky combined suspicion with a worried look. "What the hell for?"

Big nose smiled sinisterly. I'd seen the same smile twice before during my captivity and interrogation. "Perhaps he can give me my merchandise instead."

I quickly worked out that McClusky's worried look probably stemmed from the fact that he had been fiddling the inventory accounts and had also double-crossed this Housekeeper character by pilfering the Housekeepers armaments behind his back. I smiled inside. How naughty of you McClusky. I think Big nose also latched onto the way I was thinking.

"Make the arrangement for a meeting," Big nose insisted.

McClusky found a lame excuse to avoid any confrontation. "He'd kill me if I were to bring outsiders who hadn't been scrutinized or vetted."

"I'll fucking kill you if don't make the arrangement." Big nose threatened. "Then maybe you're just scared that he'll discover your secret arms dealing; the fact that you're selling the same equipment you stole from your employer behind his unsuspecting back."

McClusky clasped his hands together into a prose of pray. "There's no need to go to those extremes. I assure you that your merchandise is safe. We can still do the deal together. I just need more time."

"Your problems are not my problems. You had the money up front, as we agreed. Since you failed to deliver the weapons on time, I shall have to take my business elsewhere, either to the mystery 'Housekeeper' or whoever gives me a better deal than you have."

McClusky went white. His eyes widened and he clutched his chest where his heart was. "You...want the money back instead of the weapons?"

Big-nose arched his eyebrows. "There's a problem with my request?"

"I've invested the money in another project."

"That's tough, McClusky. I want my money now. And I don't take cheques."

"I-er-I don't keep that much cash here on the premises."

Big-nose yelled at McClusky. "That's fucking bullshit!"

"It's the truth!"

"You're a crook, McClusky, and crooks always have plenty of money stashed away for a rainy day. And it's pissing down outside."

Spotty face actually turned to look to see if it was raining outside. The fool! I should have taken the opportunity to clobber him and make a run for the exit door while his head was turned, but the intrigue of what I was hearing held me back.

McClusky was pleading once more. "I'll get it tomorrow."

I suspected Big-nose wasn't going to fall for anymore of McClusky's drivel.

"Tomorrow's too late."

"I'll get it as soon as the bank opens."

"You're a double crossing piece of Irish shit. Shall we try again? I want to see two hundred thousand Euros on the table, now!"

Big-nose levelled his machine pistol to McClusky's head.

McClusky put the palms of his hands up in front of him and gulp hard. "Okay! Okay! Calm down. The safe is downstairs, in the warehouse."

Big-nose waved his gun in the direction of the office door. "Get moving McClusky, along with your merry men. No tricks or I'll decorate the wall with different patterns of your brain."

Spotty face shoved me forward and I followed the troupe down a flight of stairs into the main warehouse. Nervous eyes watched each other. McClusky led the way, as he angled across the grain dusted warehouse floor. He stopped beside a broken fridge/freezer unit and from inside the freezer compartment he produced a bulk of money wrapped in a plastic bag. I noticed his hand was shaking as he gave the wad to Big-nose. I guessed by the size of the money package the amount was going to be considerably short.

Big-nose snatched the money from McClusky's grasp and then rammed his gun into McClusky's grovelling face. Spittle flew from Big-nose as he talked. "You don't value your fucking life do you? Where's the rest of the money?"

"I-I said I don't keep that kind of money on the premises. There's twenty grand, that's all. I'll get the rest tomorrow. I swear on my mother's grave."

Big-nose was ready to explode but somehow managed to keep control of his temper. He tossed the wad over to Spotty-face. It was then McClusky looked suspiciously at me, if only to use me as a distraction from his imminent death.

"Who's the rag merchant you've got there?" He asked carefully. "He isn't one of my men."

My minder shoved me to the front so McClusky could get a better view of me.

Big-nose said, "Ah-yes. He wants to rob your place; steal a bag of corn or two."

McClusky frowned with uncertainty, not sure if Big nose was taking the piss or not.

Big nose was quick to put things in their true perspective. "Actually, he's a vigilante. He wants to know why you had his friends killed."

McClusky looked hard at me. "I've never seen him before."

That was it! I'd had enough. I made an attempt to move towards McClusky but a huge arm from pugilist features blocked my path. I still had plenty to say despite not being able to land a punch on McClusky's chubby face.

"You're going to know me, McClusky! I have you down for ordering your murdering heavies to kill an old farmer and a photographer, you frigging bastard!"

I could see McClusky was confused. "What's this vagabond talking about?"

Big-nose laughed. "It seems everybody knows what you're like, hey McClusky?"

McClusky's face slowly turned to shock as he worked it out what I meant. His eyes widened. "You're the metal detector man?"

"Bravo, McClusky," Big-nose scoffed.

"How come you have him?"

Big-nose beamed with confidence. "He belongs to us, McClusky."

McClusky flustered. "I want him! He can get me out of a jam."

I was surprised to witness McCluskly's rediscovered courage despite the threat of his head being splattered with bullets.

"You're in no position to demand anything," Big-nose snarled. "What's so special about him?"

"'The Housekeeper' wants him."

Big nose was amused. "What for, McClusky?"

"He has something the 'Housekeeper' wants."

"Which is?"

"I don't rightly know what."

"Okay, McClusky. I'm going to give you the chance to sort out the mess you've created. The money or the merchandise by tomorrow night, and then I might forget you tried to double-cross me. And as a bonus, I'll hand over, Mister Special here afterwards."

"I've already explained, I can't move the merchandise; not without 'the Housekeeper' discovering my side line."

Veins popped from Big-nose's forehead. "You're not listening, McClusky."

McClusky pointed at me. "I can't do anything because of *him!*"

Big-nose gazed at me, a cunning smirk on his face. "What makes you so special?"

I shrugged. "I guess I'm just a popular guy with the criminal fraternity."

Big nose smiled. To McClusky, he said, "The money or the weapons you fucking imbecile or I'll be making arrangements to meet your boss. I can use our captive here as a bargaining chip, and just maybe your employer might satisfy my demands in a more professional manner rather than the amateurish spectacle of your feeble attempt."

"Give me a chance," McClusky was back to his pleading and self pity, which told me he was more scared of the Housekeeper than he was of Big-Nose.

"You had your chance, McClusky. You fucked it. You should have honoured the delivery date instead of forcing me to risk more exposure by coming to London. The blame is entirely with you, McClusky, no one else."

Whatever was going to happen next, it would have no bearing on whether Big nose or McClusky sorted out their differences. Something above us had caught my eye. There were a number of dark figures advancing from the office we'd vacated. Somehow I knew this get together wasn't going to be resolved in an orderly manner because two of the figures circling our position I recognized in an instance. Damien Love and Theodore Hate and three or four others were packing machine-pistols themselves. Some smart commander Big-nose proved to be. General bodge-up had failed to cover his arse. Made it easy for Love and Hate to sneak up on us by not securing the very fire escape we'd used.

I had perhaps only seconds to think of what I should do before all hell let loose because that was the inevitable outcome as the menacing assailants positioned themselves behind wooden crates in readiness to open fire. I should have made a dash for it and fucked the rest of them, but where would I have run to? I did the only sensible thing I could think of at the time. I yelled out a warning.

"Watch out!"

And all hell did break loose. Deafening gunfire exploded as bullets zinged in all direction as the automatic pistols kicked into action. I crouched so I wouldn't become an instant target, my hands protecting my face from splintered fragments flying through the air. I'd no idea where to run; I just ran. I couldn't fathom a safe enough passage. Bodies dived for cover including mine. I found temporary sanctuary behind a pile of dusty sacking before scrambling for the metallic security of a bag-stitching machine. I spat wheat dust from my mouth, deciding there and then that the first chance I got to save myself I wouldn't hesitate to take the opportunity: women and children first and me leading from the front. The only problem with my plan was finding the right moment to move and in what direction I should take.

I was getting worried at this stage. The bullets continued to zip past me forcing me to huddle tighter against my metallic protector. With the noise of gunfire increasing I put a finger in each ear. I tried to focus on the mayhem. See where everybody was. I witnessed a couple of bodies fall to the far side of me, riddled with red spots. Which group they belonged to I couldn't identify the victims. I shouldn't really have been bothered. I needed to concentrate on my own welfare. I searched for a safe way out, scanning the interior of the building before I became the victim of a stray bullet.

I sneaked a risky glance from around my protective shield to assess the situation; a stupid move. I'd been seen. The screaming attacker suddenly charging towards me shooting at everything that protected me indicated that. Splintered wood struck me in the face like pins, and I was shitting myself. Bullets ricocheted off the metal stitching machine and all I could do was cower behind the sacking pile in hope that someone would hit him before he reached me. Instead a handgun slithered across the floor hitting my legs and before I'd the chance to understand the consequences of what I was doing I had the gun in my hand and I was frantically shooting at the oncoming assailant with my eyes half shut and without knowing if I was shooting with accuracy. It became apparent I was a better shot than I thought.

I knew the bullets had hit my assailant directly in his chest because his upper body jerked back a couple of times and he dropped to his knees before keeling over, twisting into a slow spin and onto his back spread-eagled. I was in shock. The body just laid there in front of a sack bale, the eyes wide and motionless. I was certain he was dead because he looked dead. I'd killed him. All I could do was to stare at the body, my gun hand shaking uncontrollably. I sank back behind the sacking for protection and sucked in deep breaths to steady myself; to clear my mind of what had just happened. I was brought back to reality when a deafening explosion shook the building. I found myself covered in larger wood fragments and concrete dust floating down from the huge plume of thick smoke that had engulfed the building. I assumed that whatever was inside one of the wooden crates it must have exploded after being hit with a stray bullet? Through the cloud of dust and choking smoke I became aware of street lighting beaming into the building from where the explosion occurred. I saw the gaping hole in the wall where a door had once been. I didn't hesitate. I was up in a crouching position and scampering for my life. I'm not sure how fast I was travelling when the line of bullets peppered after me but I was moving faster than I thought as I made the mad dash for freedom. I'd survived with no apparent injuries. I was out in the night air and up and running even harder.

I kept on running, anticipating that gunmen would be in hot pursuit of me. The thought of the chase made me sprint. I soon became breathless and my mouth was dry from the wheat dust still in my lungs. I kept moving towards the main gate, stretching my stride. In the distance I could see the two security men from the gatehouse trotting hesitantly towards me in no particular rush. I'll always remember their shocked expressions as I shot pass them. I suppose I must have appeared to them as if I'd taken the brunt of the explosion judging by my tattered clothing flapping in the breeze. But I was desperate, in a hurry and with no time to explain the danger behind me. They would inevitably stumble across the problem themselves, and if they'd any sense they'd be running in the direction I was running, like a frightened rabbit. While I ran I thought of something accusingly against my name. It occurred to me the possibility that I could stand trial for murdering a man, even though he had tried to kill me. To make matters worse, I still had the gun gripped tight in the palm of my hand. I panicked. I wondered if the security guards had seen the gun I held. Point the accusing finger at me in a criminal court case. The thought only increased my anxiety and the palpitations. Whatever damage I was doing to myself, I didn't stop running until I'd reached the Roadster I'd parked down the road earlier that evening.

I considered what I should do with the gun. I had to dispose of the weapon quickly. But where would it be safe? I couldn't just throw it in a river or even bury it because it had my fingerprints all over the frigging thing, and in the all the right places for a successful prosecution. I'd no time to wipe the prints off so I slipped the weapon into the only pocket that hadn't been savagely ripped. I searched my rags frantically for the car keys before remembering the terrorists had pillaged all my possessions. I flexed my foot, felt the metallic movement of a spare key at the bottom of my sock. I removed my boot and sock and retrieved the key, not bothering to put the sock back on just the footwear. No one had tampered with the car and I was glad of the growling power of the Roadster as it pulled away from the kerb. By a miracle I'd escaped and I wasn't going to return to the warehouse in a hurry even if I had reinforcements.

Chapter Ten

The beginning of dawn crept over the roof tops as I approached home. I was tired beyond being tired and my bones ached in places I didn't think could ache. But I soon forgot my personal health problems and quickly switched off the car headlights as I entered my driveway. I'm usually very thorough when it comes to routine and I definitely recall switching off all my houselights before leaving that evening carrying my bag of burglar's tools with me. Two of my ground floor rooms were ablaze with illumination behind drawn curtains. I'd uninvited visitors who it seemed, weren't afraid to show their presence. Either that or they weren't expecting me to return at all.

I dug out a set of spare house keys I kept in the glove compartment, got out of the car and closed the car door gently. I cautiously scanned the driveway with extreme caution. I couldn't take the chance of being attacked again when I least expected it. Satisfied there was nothing that smelled of danger lurking, I moved quietly up to the house and listened at the door.

There was one valued bit of knowledge that I knew about my own front door; the hinges were well oiled and were very unlikely to squeak when opened. I eased the key into the Yale-lock, twisted, pushed the door ajar, just wide enough for me to creep inside, closed the door behind me and listened before I made my move. There was a strange noise coming from my lounge that I couldn't relate to.

I crept down the hallway on tip-toe, stopping at every doorway to check for any nasty surprises ready to strike out at me when I passed. There wasn't any. Four strides further on I stopped outside the lounge door and listened. I startled slightly. Someone was there. I definitely heard a noise; a distinctive noise which sounded like crispy paper being rustled. And then there was the sound of crunching biscuits that was familiar to me. I relaxed. Winston began to bark. The mutt had sussed me out. I palmed the lounge door open and went into the room headlong into unexpected company.

"Come and sit down, Speed and take the weight off your feet," my visitor beckoned with a cocky attitude.

I found myself gawping at my uninvited guest who I didn't appreciate in the slightest. And neither did I appreciate that he was sprawled majestically across my expensive leather sofa, drinking my beer and feeding Winston with crunchy dog biscuits straight from the cardboard box the biscuits were packaged in. My first inclination was to throw Hamer out on his arse and I probably should have; only I was too knackered to raise the effort of even bawling at him.

I threw my thumb over my shoulder, and added, "The front door's that way and be sharp about it."

His reaction was to burst out laughing.

I didn't think what I'd said was funny. I allowed him a moment to suppress his outburst, regain his composure, and then I told him straight. "If you've been evicted from your own home and you're expecting, out of the kindness of my heart, to doss here for the night, forget it!"

In between the odd splutter or two, he said, "Which hawthorn hedge was you dragged through? You've got to tell me what happened to you."

I'd almost forgotten how bad I looked, but I wasn't to be distracted.

"Never mind what happened to me," I said snappily. "I would have thought you being some sort of policeman, you should know better than to enter a suspects home unannounced and uninvited. It could construe as breaking and entering, which, in police legislation, is classed as a criminal offence. Not unless, naturally, you have in your possession a piece of legitimate court paper allowing you the privilege to break into my home and pinch my goodies?"

"Go and examine your doors and windows, you'll duly observe there's no sign of a forced entry."

"That's strange since I don't recall giving you a key. Maybe you've a sideline as a pickpocket and acquired one for yourself?" I should have searched the smug bastards clothing in which, no doubt, I'd have probably uncovered his special bunch of keys that would open any kind of lock, but I wasn't in the mood for a scuffle. I added, "I neither left the door unlocked and the dog certainly didn't let you in. Yet amazingly you managed to get in somehow. I find that rather baffling."

"Gaining access to properties is a speciality of mine."

I didn't like his conceited attitude either. I said, "They teach you that at the school of ministry misdemeanours?"

"Self taught I'll have you know. I'll wager that I could break into Buckingham Palace, sneak into the Queens bedroom and land a kiss on the cheeks of her arse, and get out of there unnoticed in ten minutes flat."

"I'm impressed Inspector. But don't get any ideas of wanting to kiss my arse cheeks because I've no homosexual tendencies. I'm a straight man myself; have been ever since I was squeezed out from a vagina, and I've been trying my hardest to get back into as many as I can since."

"That's it, Speed; misread what I'm trying to explain."

"Well then, stop practicing your breaking in skills on my home. Oh and I see you've got Winston eating out your hand too. Is that another specialist job of yours, stealing guard dogs?"

Hamer patted Winston on the head. "He remembered me from the other night and he certainly has a fondness of these doggie biscuits. They say that a dog won't bite the hand that feeds it?"

I glared at Winston. "Traitor," I said. Strangely the dog seemed to understand exactly what I meant. He whined and hung his head in shame.

"Look, Speed, the truth is I did knock on the door first. The dog started barking hysterically. You never answered. There are two killers still on the loose. Hell! I panicked thinking they'd returned. You may have even been hurt; lying on the floor terribly injured. Could I take the chance and just walk away? Hell, Speed! I was only doing my job. I swear."

"It's still trespassing regardless."

Hamer pulled a face. "You're such an ungrateful fucker, Speed!"

"It's something you shouldn't forget."

"What right have you to be angry just because you've got a bad tailor?"

I almost laughed myself with the thought of my excursions into madness. "Well let me see now; considering I've been shot at: physically abused: mentally tortured: been used as a pin cushion: shagged: ridiculed: kicked: thumped: dumped, and not necessarily in that order, to make matters worst, I come home to find you enjoying the comforts of my graft and drinking my cans of hard earned cold beer. Yes, you might say I'm in an angry mood. But please don't concern yourself on my behalf." I pointed to the pile of beer cans he had stacked on the coffee table, and said sarcastically, as I reached for one, "Do you mind?"

He shrugged. "Help yourself."

I pulled the ring pull, sucking the bubbled gases escaping from the hole. The beer was warm. It told me Hamer had been here for a while.

Hamer eased his legs from the sofa and sat upright. He'd thought of something unbelievable. "Hang on a minute! You went to McClusky's warehouse-didn't you?"

I wiped my wet lips on the back of my hand. "You're speculating, Hamer."

"There's been a report of a major explosion there, in fact not that long ago."

"Is that so? How would you know what happened at McClusky's if you've been here waiting for me?"

He tapped his jacket breast pocket. "My mobile has all the facilities for up-to-date news and police information direct to my screen; the cleverness of modern electronics."

"Then why are you still here pestering me? I thought you'd be over there reminding McClusky and his two goons, Love and Hate, of their constitutional rights that they're not entitled to in a month of Sundays."

Hamer expressed his shock. "Love and Hate! They were there?"

"Shooting the frigging place to pieces, no less."

"They did that to your clothes?"

"No. That's another disappointing story which I'm not prepared to discuss."

"How did you escape from the bastards this time?"

"I ran like the frigging clappers!"

"Then we've missed them."

"Not if you hurry. They were busy battling it out with a group of Irish terrorists."

Hamer expressed his concern. "The IRA? INLA? Who?"

I shrugged. "I've no frigging idea who they represented," and then I drank some more warm beer.

"This is going to be a job for Scotland Yard's Anti-Terrorist Squad."

"I might be wrong, but I got the impression this McClusky fellow had pissed them off and the terrorists were after an instant refund," I said, wiping a beer drip from my chin. "Why don't you go and find out and do us both a favour."

"It'll be too late now. I should think erratic gunfire would have already attracted the local blue-bodies; they'll be swarming all over the warehouse picking up what's left of the pieces. The MDP are not ready to get involved with the constabulary just yet or Scotland Yard. They'd ask too many awkward questions as to why we're investigating known and wanted criminals without informing them. No. We'll leave them to clean up the mess. They'll conclude that it's gang warfare among the Irish contingencies. So we'd better leave it at that for the time being; not unless you want to get involved in the proceedings?"

I'd no intentions of spitting into a hot frying pan and having it spit back. "No point. I'd just deny I was there."

"Did you see what happened to Love and Hate?"

The shake of my head disappointed Hamer. "You must be joking! I kept my frigging head down when the shooting began, and then I got out of there fast."

I decided against divulging bragging rights of my first kill.

Hamer was thoughtful. "That's not good," he said, dejectedly. "They've mastered the art of escapism down to a fine line. Hell! They could be anywhere now."

"I could have hung around and asked which hotel they were staying in?"

"You're not funny, Speed. Besides, you should be taking this with a bit more seriousness. You're part of the set up whether you like it or not."

I drank what was left of my beer, crushed the can and tossed it into a waste bin sited near the stone fireplace.

"Well, Speed. How about giving me an accurate rundown of tonight's events?"

"What so you can gloat on my misfortune?"

"It might help me on my assignment."

"Well it won't."

"I need to know so I can establish where we go from here."

"Your next move is going home."

"You have an uncanny knack of upsetting guests, Speed."

"What is it you want at this ungodly hour, anyway?"

"I have two issues I want to take up with you."

"You only have two, and so early in the morning. This is definitely a police tactic; catch the unsuspecting recipient when he's half asleep."

Hamer ignored my moaning. "First of all, I couldn't find any encouraging documentation relating to an 'Operation Huggermugger'. It better not be something you made up?"

I wondered if Josh Bane had perhaps made a mistake with his recollection of events on the day Craven's Spitfire went missing. "You did check that the mission was conducted from Duxford airfield?"

"I'm not a fool, Speed. Damn fucking right I checked. I double-checked and nothing even remotely relates to 'Huggermugger'."

"There's the possibility the mission went under a different name, maybe in order to fool German spy rings. You did check all the war archives thoroughly?"

Hamer smiled thinly, "Those under the letter H I did."

"You need to check deeper. Maybe expand your search."

"Do you realize the archives down at Whitehall have tons of documentation hiding away in deep vaults? I could spend my life searching and Morgan might not appreciate me wasting my time."

"Your approach to work is a little disappointing."

"Then why don't you tell me what you know about "Operation Huggermugger'?"

"I don't know anything worthwhile."

"Where did you get the information from in the first place?"

"I read about it somewhere."

Hamer frowned. "Where exactly did you read it?"

"I've forgotten where."

"Don't you be holding back on me, Speed?"

I smiled impishly. "And the other issue?"

"Ah-well now this is the real laughable bit. My superior wants to meet the indelible, super sleuth, Shackleton Speed, with the assumption he can personally convince you to work alongside us. Really pathetic, don't you agree? I can't convince you so why does a professional pen-pusher think he can do better than me in trying to turn a stray boy into a useful commodity."

I stopped him right there. "I've no intention of entering any government building to be interrogated, whether it is done over a cup of tea, or by cruelty."

"Scared we'll never let you out?"

"It's a phobia I have. I prefer open spaces with plenty of witnesses."

"Well don't fret, Speed. We'll find a suitable place so the hairs on the back of your neck don't stand up."

"Who's this superior of yours anyway?"

"Commander Harris Morgan. He's okay; a little bit of a pompous git but he knows the right people and has a certain whack if we require the assistance of the Metropolitan Police or any other force we need to call upon. He knows enough high ranking principles to pull the right strings."

"He sounds like a dependable chap."

"He wants to meet you."

"What can I possibly offer him?"

Hamer shook his head. I think he was disappointed with me. "Stop the innocent act for fucks sake. This is me you're talking to, not some idiot. It concerns the plane. It concerns Love and Hate. It concerns you! We need you on our side if we're to go after Love and Hate and whoever controls them."

"There's nothing I can tell you that you don't know already."

By Hamer's expression I knew he wasn't going to leave me alone. "Come off it! Are you not a little intrigued to hear what he has to say? Just meet the fellow. What harm can it do?"

I thought it through. Hamer was right. I'd nothing to lose by meeting this Morgan fellow. Who knows, he might relay some information that would be useful to me. It would mean defying my strict rules of non-engagement with authoritarians, not unless I'd been arrested and then I wouldn't have had any choice. I had to think positively about my present situation. The dangers were still out there. And Love and Hate were still a threat. If I'm to stay in one piece then the more back-up force behind me the longer I'd stay alive. And it has always been my intention to live to a ripe old age.

Meeting Morgan made sense.

"It might be interesting," I said finally.

Hamer jerked back in pretence shock. "Fucking hell, are you feeling alright? You're actually considering accepting something constructive from me?"

"I accepted breakfast."

"That was different. I was paying for the damn meal."

"No, the taxpayer was paying for the meal... expenses, remember Hamer? Tell Commander Morgan I'll listen but that's all I'm prepared to do for the moment. Now I need a shower and sleep."

I turned to leave the lounge and over my shoulder, I said, "Finish your beer, Hamer. And on your way out shut the door properly. I don't want another burglar or vagabond thinking my home is an open invitation to the unworthy."

I climb the stairs wearily and thoughtfully, wondering if I'd done the right thing in accepting the meeting with

Morgan. I considered it was and if I wanted to change my mind I was probably a little too late, as I imagine, even at this early hour, Hamer would be on his mobile sending a message.

I heard the front door slam. Hamer had gone. And then I heard the patter of Winston's feet climbing the stairway. Alone again I eased my battered body under the shower spray, shut my eyes, and let the water power against my face. I thought about the man I'd killed, as spontaneous as it was. I couldn't picture his face just a set of opened eyes staring into space. I realized how easy it is to squeeze the trigger when your own life is threatened; too frigging easy for my liking. My actions were self defence so what had I to worry about. Frigging hell! I'd a lot to be worried about. I was a murderer! I was no better than Love or Hate.

My head dropped dejectedly. I stared at the water swirling down the shower drain hole, wondering if a warrant for my arrest was being drawn up at this very moment. Would the witnesses to my actions at McClusky's warehouse, being criminals themselves, dare to step forward and point the accusing finger of guilt directly at my face? I brightened. Would they frigging hell as like! They'd have dispersed just as fast as I did. End of story. End of worry.

Thinking of criminals, the girl terrorist came to mind. I could picture her face quite clearly. I didn't recall seeing her again once the battle started. I did wonder, briefly, if she'd got out of the warehouse alive. Strangely, I rather hoped the bitch had escaped the pitched battle.

Chapter Eleven

The explosive shootout at McClusky's dominated the news headlines both on the TV and the radio broadcasts on every station. I listened to the dramatic events on the car radio; a battle between two Irish gangs at London Docks, the eventual outcome given by Scotland Yard. There'd been no names released of the casualties. Blah-blah-blah, it went on. The problem was none of the story resembled anything I was involved in. The truth had been so far stretched that it was ready to split wide open. The blame for the misinterpretation of events lay with the conflicting statements given by the two dock security guards who had ran past me that evening while I was escaping, who funnily enough, had seen a hell of a lot considering their sleepy confinement inside the security hut. There was one part of their story that was coherent with the truth. They'd witnessed an armed scarecrow running away from the premises. That joint statement alone should have convinced the investigating police team that the two guards had been drinking and taking drugs while on the job.

I'd received a phone call from Hamer later that morning to confirm the arranged appointment with his superior, Harris Morgan for the following afternoon, at one O clock. I agreed. Best to get this over with quickly so I could press on with other lines of investigation; yes

I was back to the detective role. I'd no other avenue to follow but my own.

I stopped off on the way to meet Harris Morgan. I called in at the Imperial College in South Kensington. I'd no appointment just a purpose. I left a large brown envelope at the reception for the immediate attention of a Professor Cyril Squires. I collected a can of Coke from the reception drinks machine and drank it on my journey to Hyde Park and the Italian Gardens, the prearranged place for our meeting. At least the sun was shining if nothing else.

I spotted Hamer before he spotted me. He was in deep discussion with a tall, lean chap with flaming red hair who was chomping on a fat cigar while he listened to whatever Hamer was telling him. They ceased talking when they caught sight of me in the distance. I must admit I was a little tense as I approached them. There was no friendly wave from either man, just two stern expressions watching my every movement. By the time I'd reached their position, the tension inside me had gone. I was rock solid and ready for anything they threw at me.

The stranger's hand reached out to shake mine and with his cigar still clamped between his teeth, he said: "Commander Harris Morgan," he said sharp and precise. "I appreciate your attendance at short notice, Mister Speed."

"Hello Commander," I said with a slight smile to make it look as if I was happy to be shaking his hand. While doing so, I made a quick assessment of Harris Morgan as a person. He had enough wrinkles about his face to suggest he was in his middle or late fifties and he either suffered heavily from stress or was a heavy drinker. He had a vice like grip, deliberately imposed,

I thought, to show me I wasn't dealing with a powder puff desk clerk but a man whose career strengths had powered him to the position he now held. I could only admire him for that. He was clean shaven with a strong smell of an aftershave which I couldn't put a name to, but I thought it smelled cheap.

I broke off the hand shake, noticing that what he lacked in lavishing expense on aftershave, he more than made up for it with expensive clothes. He was wearing a light-weight, dark suit, immaculately tailored no doubt by one of the best makers in London. His white shirt was silk and his tie matched perfectly. I'd noticed his shiny black leather shoes when I'd first approached them, deciding that if the opportunity arose, it was possible to see up a woman's skirt if the shoe were to be positioned in the right place. Not that I thought he was that type of person.

Morgan pulled the cigar from his mouth and twirled it through his fingers. "I believe you have an extraordinary occupation involving metal detecting?"

"Hardly extraordinary," I said.

"Boring I'd say."

"You've obviously never tried the excursions into the wild side of Blighty."

"I can't say I know anyone that does, apart from you, that is."

"You'd be surprised by the amount of detectorist's out there who have fun scouring the lands for buried trinkets."

"You don't scour the land for fun, Mister Speed."

"I thought I did."

"No, Mister Speed. I've heard that you're quite an exceptional finder of things that nobody else could possibly find."

"I guess I've had my fair share of luck in the past."

"You're too modest Mister Speed." He smiled and waved his hand over the landscape. "These surroundings meet your approval, Mister Speed?"

I nodded. "It's relaxing providing you don't suffer from hay fever or agoraphobia."

"Good gracious! It's a good thing you don't suffer from either of those, Mister Speed. It would certainly prove a stumbling block on your outdoor pursuits."

Morgan then changed his approach and his eyes probed deeply into mine. He gave me the impression that he could make a person feel uncomfortable while in his presence. He said, "No disrespect, Mister Speed, but Inspector Hamer thinks we shouldn't be dealing with crooks who despise paying their taxes, amongst other eventful cases of improbity. Are you a crook, Mister Speed?"

I flashed Hamer a searing glare that made the two-faced coward redden. I calmly said, "We are all entitled to express our opinions of a person we meet for the first time."

Morgan clamped his cigar in the corner of his mouth. It distorted his speech. "Quite right too, Mister Speed. Well, in my opinion, I don't think you're a crook. As a matter of fact we all despise paying our taxes. I admire your stand against fattening the coffers of the Treasury. I too despise the governments continued misuse of the public funds wrenched from our diminishing pay packets. Instead of financing the influx of asylum seekers, and other non-productive morons, they should spend the money on a more proficient professional police force. The Treasury are worst than any crooks, I'd say."

I stopped him right there. I felt as if he was still accusing me of a financial swindle. "Let's get one thing straight. I'm not a crook and I have never seen the inside of a prison where crooks are supposedly confined."

"What about police cells, Mister Speed?"

"They don't count. You can be in a drunken mess and still end up in a cell for the night."

Morgan snatched his cigar from his mouth and blew out a cloud of cigar smoke and said, "As I correctly assessed, Mister Speed, you're nothing of the kind. Crooks usually do end up in prison."

I didn't care for the way he said that, either, but I kept quiet.

Morgan pressed on. "Regardless of your alleged reputation, Mister Speed, I feel confident that you'll not divulge to anyone that this meeting took place." He paused. I think he was waiting for my reassurance to keep a secret, but I didn't give it. He pressed on. "Between you and me and the big blue sky, within the walls and corridors of Whitehall there has been some devilish activity going on."

"There's nothing new there then?" I said.

"I'm not referring to the politicians and their unreserved attitude to things, Mister Speed. I'm talking about simple military records kept in the vaults of Whitehall. Military records kept since records began on all fronts of battle through the ages. If a historian wanted certain information in regards to certain military events, then the historian would expect to locate those records within the vaults. I would expect to locate records too. Not so, it seems. What I found was a gaping hole where there should have been an abundance of information. I'm talking about Duxford airfield and the fact that the airfield played an important and active part in World War Two. I therefore would have expected to browse through records filled with literature regarding the events and incidents at Duxford between 1942 and 1944. Only there isn't any-well-not anymore. How do I know this, you may wonder? I went looking for certain information in relation to the remains of the exhumed pilot we recovered from the Berkshire wreck. The files I was after just weren't there. We could assume the files were the consequences of bad management. Perhaps misplaced or they've even been misfiled; it happens; no one is perfect. Whatever the verdict those files have disappeared. Gone from the vaults I'm sure. Now you might be wondering what the hell does it matter after all these years and who really cares? The past is the past and gone forever.

"I care, Mister Speed. In my position I have a moral duty to fill in certain gaps relating to the war, as and when I find them. In the depths of Whitehall I could produce a mountain of documentation that has those huge gaps; that lack the necessary information to know the truth. On this occasion I'm referring to pilots lost in action. What happened to those pilots and was it accidental or an act of war. We can only determine that when the good Lord decides to give up the dead and we're fortunate to locate them and assess the true situation of how they met their fate. I'm talking about the recovered Spitfire in Berkshire. I'm talking about the pilot whose name was assigned to that Berkshire Spitfire. The pilot's name was Rowland."

"The Berkshire wreck has drawn a lot of attention just lately," I said casually.

"It has indeed, Mister Speed. And the startling events that have arisen in relation to the wreck at Berkshire have forced the MDP to reopen the file on Rowland. We decided to rebuild our intricate jigsaw all over again because some of the pieces don't fit in the right slots. Add all this with two known assassins from Europe, and the alarm bells began clanging away in my head. I began reinvestigating this war hero, Flying Officer Derek Rowland, whose remains were apparently recovered from the crash site. Digging deep into the archives, interestingly I found that his last recorded flight was in the cockpit of a Spitfire mark one; a wonderful machine so I'm informed. I had the wreckage from Berkshire carefully re-examined and discovered that the similarities ended there. What we had was the wreckage of the Super Marine Spitfire class. The problem with that is Rowland had no recorded flying time in a Super Marine.

"Official military records show that Derek Rowland was stationed along with the Americans at Burtonwood airbase in Warrington, Lancashire. Now according to those military records, no Super-marine Spitfires were ever stationed there. So the intriguing question is how did Rowland get into our wreck in the first place?"

"Perhaps someone made a huge gaff when identifying the pilot," I said conceitedly.

"A huge clanger it seems, Mister Speed. Along with another problem; the files relating to the crash site may have been fiddled with deliberately with the intention of deflecting the interests of a nosey parker from obtaining the true name of the pilot. I asked myself the question: why should someone want to go to all that trouble to hide the true identity of the body found in the wreck of a World War Two plane?"

"If you've dragged me all the way out here to ask if I had anything to do with them, then you've wasted both our time," I said.

"You'd never have passed the threshold of Whitehall to obtain them, Mister Speed. Your recent revival of popularity would ensure automatic expulsion. We have you down on record as a threat to security since you've come to our attention."

"I've never regarded myself as a threat to the nation."

"Well you are, and you wouldn't get past the boundary line without being shot."

"Not even if I said please?"

"Not even if you were invisible."

"You're quite a callous bunch you Whitehall fellows."

"No, I'm talking about internal sabotage here. Someone already established inside Whitehall; someone so deep inside Whitehall that they would never be suspected. It happens on occasions; a world wide epidemic, in fact. And that very same person causing us problems, I've decided, is also responsible for the recruiting the likes of Love and Hate to do the conspirators revolting deeds. This brings me to the reason for this meeting, Mister Speed."

"Don't look at me! I've no idea who's behind it all."

"Let's talk about another immediate problem that concerns us both; the sightings of Damien Love and Theodore Hate, the two murderous cretins who have mysteriously surfaced in London and are posing as MDP. And even more baffling, their interest in a plane wreck and their connection with an entrepreneur by the name of McClusky, who, unfortunately, has been killed after a bloody shootout at his warehouse. So we're not going to get any explanations from him."

"You're going to be busy for a while," I said.

Hamer chirped in. "Evasive as ever, Speed."

I stared hard at Hamer and then back at Morgan. "I've already explained to Inspector Hamer that I'm the wrong person to be asking for help. Why don't you liaise with the police involved in the McClusky affair, they might offer some answers."

"I'm afraid it doesn't work that way, Mister Speed."

"I can't see a problem conversing with them."

"There's always a problem, Mister Speed. Our first duty is ministry investigations are conducted privately before even thinking of liaising with other forces. We simply cannot have outside interference on our internal affairs no matter how difficult the task ahead. Yet that doesn't mean we can't involve a neutral, an outsider working for us."

"Meaning yours truly, me?"

"That's precisely what I mean, Mister Speed. Now, with regards to your present situation, there has to be a good reason why Love and Hate have paid particular attention to *you!*"

"I was under the impression they wanted to kill me!"

"Yes, yes! I'm well aware of what they intended, but why?" Morgan was getting agitated. He threw his cigar butt into the Serpentine. It hissed loudly as it hit the water. "They're cold-blooded assassins who follow orders. And if McClusky had hired them, then for what purpose did McClusky want with you?"

I shrugged. "I never got the chance to ask him. His death has complicated matters"

"There's more disappointing news. I made a few discreet enquires regarding the incident at McClusky's warehouse. It's apparent that Love and Hate weren't among the dead or injured. They're still out there somewhere."

"They're probably running back to that shit hole from whence they came from, now their boss has perished," I said, confidently.

"I disagree, Mister Speed. I've concluded that McClusky didn't hire their services at all. It's more the reverse. They were controlling him. If McClusky wanted to be Mister Nasty, I'm sure he would have hired any number of Irish thugs to do his dirty work for him. No, I'm can categorically state that Love and Hate are in the gainful employment from another paymaster; a more sinister and deadly adversary."

"There's no point in asking me." I said.

"It's you they're after for whatever reasons, Mister Speed."

"They've made a mistake chasing after me. They've got me mixed up with somebody else."

"Love and Hate don't make mistakes."

"How would you know?"

"We have a wanted file two inches thick on them. We've been searching for their whereabouts for years. They murdered a British army officer a few years back. The problem is they're not as well known here in our country and were more difficult to apprehend. But they're known by other European police forces. Yes, all those forces have constructive files on Love and Hate but nothing that's steel-tight for a conviction; they can't even get them for spitting on the pavement. Now they're in London, probably sneaked in on false documents. They'll be very difficult to pinpoint."

"You should complain to border control for their slackness."

"We did, Mister Speed. And border control's incompetence is being dealt with. In the meantime, for what reasons they're here, it's essential we find the two scoundrels before they can cause anymore damage, and then we can at least hold them on illegal entry if nothing else. Regrettably, our actions have come a little too late to prevent the tragedies that have occurred so far. And I believe, as you do, Mister Speed, that they *were* responsible for the deaths of a Thomas Bickermass and Larry Lazerow,"

I said, "I only wished others saw it that way."

"You can't blame the police for ignoring suspicious circumstances as both incidents. Nothing pointed to anything other than what the Coroners verdict clearly stated: death was caused by misadventure."

"The police have their heads up their arses," I said. "They write with blunt pencils because they can't be bothered to sharpen them. They didn't want the excessive paperwork involved in a murder enquiry."

"You sound bitter towards the constabulary, Mister Speed?"

"They failed me."

"So you're adamant that the deaths are connected to the Berkshire wreck site?"

"I've no idea what they're connected to. But two people I knew are dead and it stinks of Love and Hate."

"Then changing the minds of the police will be difficult, Mister Speed."

I shrugged. "I'd say virtually impossible unless the killers confess their guilt."

"What did Love and Hate want when they came knocking on your door?"

I wondered when he'd get around to that. I calmly said, "Did Inspector Hamer not fill you in with the dull details? For some reason they thought I'd tampered with the wreck site in Berkshire. The whole world knows that the owner's dog disturbed the site."

Morgan gave me a disapproving look. "Be honest, Mister Speed. You're amongst friends and allies here."

I tossed my head in the air in disbelief. "Give me a break! I've just told you they made a mistake because I wasn't anywhere near the wreck."

"Love and Hate obviously made a connection somehow?"

"They probably didn't understand English. Besides, I hardly think a pile of junk and the bones of a British pilot are worth murdering somebody for."

"There has to be more to it than rusting junk and dried bones?"

"As I said before, you're going to be busy finding the right answers, Commander Morgan. And good luck in trying to convince the Peelers there's a lot they're missing."

"We'll do our utmost best, Mister Speed. That's after we have finished our internal investigation to find the insider who's deviously removed incriminating material concerning the recently exhumed Spitfire. We have to find this insider before we lose control of the situation, and it has to be done in complete secrecy. Any other way just won't work. And it has to be done without treading on too many toes"

"Can you do all that without attracting attention to yourselves?"

"We damn well have to, Mister Speed! Our careers will be at risk. We balls this up and it'll be more than our pensions at stake. There'll be ridicule and humiliation and we'll be the fall guys; probably get the sack to add to our woes and be disgraced through the media."

"I'm sure you'll make the right decisions."

"That's where you can help us, Mister Speed. If we can locate Love and Hate first, not only will we prevent further tragedy, but we might get them to direct a true course to their employer and the possible mole inside Whitehall."

"When you eventually find Love and Hate, you have my permission to throw them in the Tower of London and squeeze the truth out of them in any way you redeem to be acceptable."

"Something I would enjoy immensely, Mister Speed; only we British have morals to maintain. We're not a third rate country so we can't simply snatch them from the street and throw them in prison before a question is asked. We have to stick to European guidelines. Hard proof is required for the D.P.P. to even sniff at the case. An incident that happened three years ago in Cyprus doesn't warrant an instant arrest on two men who have no positive criminal convictions. Yes they're on a long list of police files as suspects but there are no outstanding warrants for their arrest. No jack-shit! We need something stronger to use other than immigration defaults."

"They attacked me. Hamer witnessed everything. Get them arrested on those grounds."

"That would be an acceptable solution but for one stumbling block. I see little evidence on your person of any kind of assault, and from what Inspector Hamer reported, I digested that it was the viciousness of yourself and dog that were the aggressors and victors. A top barrister would have a field day with us and have you arrested for assault instead."

"That's British Law for you!" I said, condemningly. "And you've got your work cut out."

"Not if you are willing to work alongside us. Mister Speed."

"You want to use me as bait to attract a pair of rats?"

"It's an interesting thought. But that'll only draw out Love and Hate. I want the top dog behind this outrage. You can help us penetrate the solid mass that blocks our way to the truth. What you decide to divulge to us will be treated with the strictest of confidentiality, naturally. The discovery of the Spitfire hides a story, Mister Speed. It has resulted in some very serious incidents which require explaining and I feel you can help us uncover the truth."

I was finding it more and more difficult to control my feeling of persecution. "I seem to be having a lot of trouble convincing people I know nothing of the crashed plane, which is obviously what you're referring to, other than what I've read in the papers and have been told."

"You will be well rewarded, Mister Speed."

"Whoopee!" I said sarcastically.

"Further more, any involvement you had concerning the matter, I'll guarantee you'll be free from any form of prosecution; in writing of course, in return for adequate information. We can't have ruthless villains posing as MDP officials and causing havoc. We need to apprehend the villains quickly, Mister Speed; time is of the essence."

"Then there's not much hope, since I've nothing else to add to your dilemma."

"There is always hope, Mister Speed. I suspect you know a lot more than you're willing to tell. Work with us, not against us. We get the right convictions and you'll be adequately paid for your efforts. That means easy money in your bank account and no questions asked. Does that sound tempting?"

I smiled. "Sounds more like a frigging bribe."

Morgan's forehead deeply lined. "It's not a bribe, more like what the constabulary describe as informers payments. It's all quite legit. Now do we have a deal?"

"I'm not certain I can give you anything of value, Commander."

"It all began somewhere, Mister Speed. Start by explaining the reason why so many infuriating criminals showed interest in a metal detector enthusiast who, I might add, has gained a renowned notoriety for selling antiquities on the black markets of Europe."

I shrugged. "Beats me"

"You have something in your possession, possibly passed on to you by your friends, that maybe is destined for the black market?"

"I don't sell on the black market!" I said decisively.

I noticed that Morgan was beginning to get extremely frustrated. "Come now, Mister Speed. You're known in the European black markets as the Norseman-a highly respected trader of illegal antiquities. I suspect years of elusiveness from the law has somewhat dampened your enthusiasm to cooperate. Nevertheless, we still require your help to round up these monsters and I'm not really concerned about what you do for a living."

"I don't want to get involved."

Morgan's face muscles tightened. "Whichever way you look at it, Mister Speed, you are involved, whether you want to be or not."

"And if I choose not to help, what then?" I thought I'd better ask the question.

Morgan smiled. "I'm sure you'll want to cooperate voluntarily."

"You sound confident?" I asked warily.

"We have our methods of persuasion."

"Torture chamber, you mean? I better warn you that I'm used to that method of persuasion."

"That's the primitive alternative, Mister Speed. What I was actually getting at borders more on the victimization side of life. To put it bluntly, help us and we won't consider putting you on trial for vandalizing a war grave and stealing the pilot's personal equipment."

"You'll never make it stick, Commander," I said calmly.

Morgan attempted to brush-off his bullying tactics. "It's pitiful, I know. But we are desperate, Mister Speed, and desperate people revert to desperate measures. Additions can be arranged to strengthen our bargaining powers."

"In other words, Commander, you telling me you can falsify evidence against me to ensure a conviction of grave robbing."

Morgan smiled. "Not that we would wish to."

"And you're supposed to be the good guys," I scoffed.

"I'd think things through very carefully what is on offer. We can make your life very difficult, Mister Speed."

I'd no doubts that Morgan wasn't bluffing either, and normally I don't surrender to threats. Yet, if I'm honest, and I thoroughly understand my predicament on both fronts, to progress further along my lines of enquiry, I was certainly going to require help and who better than the government themselves.

So I told him straight. "If you want to use me as bait, I want written immunity from prosecution first, information of what I know you get after."

"That can be promptly arranged," Morgan announced, and he reached into his pocket for a pen.

I stopped him there.

"It has to be presented on official government paper, signed, stamped, and sealed, so I can arrange for my solicitor to hold it in storage; just in case, or there's no deal."

Morgan's face tightened, as if he was to explode with anger. "That's damned impertinent of you to mistrust my promise."

"No, Commander. That's damned sensible on my part."

"This is preposterous! I offer you immunity from spending time in prison, and you fail to take me on my word. Good gracious, you philistine! What do you take me for? Do you realize it entails a trip back to my office? Time is against us, man! We need to press on. We can't allow two murderous villains to abscond a second time. The longer we take the further they stretch from our reach."

I stood my ground. "Your office isn't far, Commander. Without the official documentation there is nothing. If I'm to get involved in something dubious I want to be in a position where I come out unscathed." I shuffled my feet in readiness to leave. "It's up to you."

I could tell by the frowns on their face's they detested my stubbornness. I rather enjoyed watching Morgan bite his bottom lip as he relented.

"Very well Mister Speed. I shall deal with the matter the moment I return to my office. Where can we contact you?"

"Inspector Hamer knows the exact location," I said. "He thinks he's my lodger."

Morgan turned and walked away in a huff. I caught Hamer by the arm and asked him if he could locate the whereabouts of Sir Dillon Deveron for me. I did rather expect a volley of abusive language from him in retaliation, especially as I hadn't exactly been cooperative myself, only he took me completely by surprise and nodded agreeably. Perhaps he was in a state of shock. And then again, I could only assume that they'd already anticipated my agreed involvement and that Hamer was under strict orders to fulfil any reasonable demands I made. I actually found that amusing. Yet I'd no doubt that the questions of my interest would come later. In my opinion Hamer was too much of a nosey bastard not to ask them.

Chapter Twelve

I returned to the Imperial College and went in search of a Professor Cyril Squires. I found him where I expected to find him at three o'clock in the afternoon, sitting in his office, eating his lunch after he'd finished his tutorial sessions. I knocked courteously on his door and waited for him to answer. His slow, articulated voice said, "Enter."

I went in and closed the door behind me. Professor Cyril Squires was behind his desk comfortably embedded in his favourite well-worn green leather executive type chair and with a napkin on his lap catching the minute crumbs falling from his triangular cut wholemeal sandwich with no crusts. *Posh sod,* I thought with a smile. His bulging round eyes caught my approach to him.

He had grey, wiry hair, kept in place with the application of a wet comb, and his high forehead gave his face the appearance of being long and stretched. He was sixty three years old but to his credit his clean and healthy complexion made him appear younger. His long, thin forefinger wiggled to direct me to the chair opposite him. I made myself comfortable.

He quickly swallowed what he was chewing and said, "Nice to see you again, Shacks. Been keeping away from trouble?"

"I've built a steel wall around myself," I reassured him.

"That's not what I've been hearing lately. And those photographs you left at reception; old aerial footage from the war. Not something I would have associated with you. Now whatever you're presently into, keep the details well away from me unless you're willing to tell me the whole truth and nothing but the truth, to help me fend off the police when they come knocking on my door."

I ignored his lecture and pressed on. "Did you get a chance to look at the photographs?"

"A fleetingly observation since I do have lectures to conduct."

"Did you deduce anything from them worthwhile?"

Professor Squires expressed alarm. "Slow down. Why are you always in a hurry, Shacks?"

"I don't want to be caught in the rush-hour traffic." I lied. Being stuck in traffic had never bothered me. My excuse was more in line that I didn't really want to hang around for a chit-chat over a cup of tea in the canteen afterwards, where he would undoubtedly start asking me awkward questions and force me to lie through my teeth. I'd always had an open and an almost honest relationship with him, but the way the present situation was panning out, I didn't want him deeply involved in my present caper.

He laid his napkin on the desk, rose and drifted over to the filing cabinet that sat in the corner. There was one thing that struck me about old Squires. I can't recall ever having seen the professor dressed in any other clothing other than what he wore for the office: brown tweed jacket with leather patches sewn on the elbow regions, a green shirt and dark brown cord trousers held in place with red elastic braces. I guessed he'd a full wardrobe of familiar attire.

On his way back to his desk with the envelope I'd left him earlier, I noticed how the hems of his trousers lifted above his ankles due to the tight pull of the braces he wore, his every step revealing an awful looking pair of grey patterned socks beneath. He re-seated, pulled his chair closer to the desk and spread the contents of the envelope onto the desk.

"Hmm," he muttered, and then put on a pair of reading spectacles and selected one of the reconnaissance photographs.

Besides being an excellent, if not boring, tutor on the subject of metallurgy, he knew a great deal about rock formations around the world that no serious person could possibly know, and despite it being the most menial of subjects that a person could ever sit and read about, it was the rock formations in the photographs that I required his knowledge.

He sipped in a mouthful of water, flushing the fluid around his mouth, this he does regularly to dislodge food particles in his mouth, and swallowed. He cleared his throat with a slight cough. "These are terribly old photographs and badly water marked too. My initial findings earlier have somewhat changed since I've had more time to reflect on the images."

He was beginning to sound negative but he soon rebuilt my confidence in him.

"It's a good job old Squires isn't a quitter, and it'll take a lot more than crap photography to dampen my enthusiasm. Can I assume that these are something you found or stole? Or should I not be asking?"

"Both and don't ask," I said.

He didn't flinch at my reluctance to divulge details because he knew me too well.

With a sharp suck of breath, he went on: "These are interesting rock formations, but as I stated the quality of the pictures does rather hinder the process of their true locations. Yet challenges I thrive on, and I detest defeatism."

I interrupted him and told him what I knew, "It's somewhere along the West side of the British Isles, if that helps any."

The Professor's eyes lit-up. "Ah! So you have learned something worthwhile from me in the past?"

"Not really, professor. Information received pointed me in that general direction, I just took the persons word for granted."

Professor Squires wasn't amused. He said solemnly, "Shackleton Speed, (he always called me by my full name when he was annoyed), you greatly disappoint. If you had taken the time to attend my lectures with a bit more regularity and the commitment to learn, you might have achieved the ability to be in the same position as I am instead of messing around in muddy fields. It pays handsomely well, and you don't have to get your hands dirty."

"I like to get my hands dirty," I said seriously.

"And that's your choice. Now pay attention to someone who knows what he's talking about. Oh! Before I forget, you still owe me a liquid lunch for verifying to the police that you attended one of my lectures when I know damn well you were in Berlin attending-what was the excuse you gave me-ah yes-a seminar in structural engineering. Utter bollocks! More like a slice of your black market involvement. You're damned lucky I'm on your side or else you'd have had a lot of explaining to do."

"I did thank you for it," I corrected him.

"Verbally is insufficient! You can thank me by taking some weight off your illegal gains and buy me a ticket to the opera of my choice instead."

I agreed hastily; wanting to move things along.

"Good. Now let's return to the necessities."

Professor Squires meticulously packed away the remnants of his lunch into a briefcase and resumed his study of the photographs. When he began speaking it was if he was lecturing a class.

"The sweeping angle of the waves hitting the coastline is most definitely a western coast, as you rightly suggested," he said, looking at me to see if I was paying attention, which I was for a change.

He picked up a magnifying glass and repetitively re-scanned the four pictures with equal amounts of time. His studious silence had me drumming my fingers on my thigh with no rhythmical pattern as I grew impatient.

Finally he said, "These rocks don't relate to any United Kingdom shorelines, that I'm certain. No. I'd be more prone to suggest that the distinct contours of the rocky shorelines actually point me more in the direction of the South coast of Ireland."

I was actually disappointed with his findings; expecting an exact location.

"It's still a fair amount of coastline," I moaned.

The Professor raised his head alarmingly and told me off. "You have the patience of a Wildebeest spooked by a stalking Lion, Shackleton Speed!"

I shrugged apologetically and he resumed his study of the photographs.

Without looking away from the photographs he reached for the folded paper map on the corner of his desk. It was an enlarged map of the Republic of Ireland. He began flitting from the photographs to the map as if he was participating in a game of bobbing for apples and continued the motions for approximately two minutes before I saw the smile of satisfaction across his face. Then he infuriated me by flitting through for a second opinion, map-picture-map before he lay back in his chair and clasped his hands behind his head in a gentle stretch.

"Well?" I probed anxiously.

"I've no doubt whatsoever it's the coastline of South or South-west of Ireland. I'd say roughly coastline between Skibbereen and Bantry. I'd like to speculate further, but without actually attending the area, and taking in consideration the water damage on the photographs, it's the best I can do at the moment, Shacks."

"You can tell all that from those photographs?"

"The way the waves hit the coastline concedes the information. I've studied enough coastlines around the world in the past to know the differences, believe me, Shacks"

I thought initially what a boring life he must lead to take up such a subject and spend endless hours studying, but I'm glad he did. His knowledge would guide me along a different road; to where exactly only my own intuition would take me.

I smiled. "You've done more than enough, Professor. I can't thank you enough."

"My pleasure, Shacks, though I don't issue freebies. I'll add the consultancy fee to the drinks bill when you decide to honour your previous debt. Now be off with you!"

I placed the photographs back into the envelope and went home. I poured myself a cold beer, dug out a road atlas and began scrutinizing the southernmost point of Ireland. The professor's estimation of the possible coastline was filled with bays, crevices, inlets, and rivers, which I estimated would take me a multitude of time to explore. I'd no complaints because it was a starting place regardless, and one I wasn't about to ignore.

I threw some belongings into a small travel suitcase, shaved, showered and dressed into suitable driving clothes. I fed Winston with a hearty meal of diced best steak mixed with biscuit cereal, and while I watched in amazement as his slobbering jaws devoured the contents, the telephone rang. It was Professor Squires.

"Glad I caught you before you left."

"Who said I was going anywhere?"

"Just say, I'm a good guesser and I know you too well. Now, pay attention! Forget my previous prediction on the location of the rock formations and concentrate on the surrounding coastlines in and around Baltimore and Roaring Water Bay. Don't forget to send me a postcard," he added just before he broke off his call.

Reluctantly I decided to leave Winston at the home of an acquaintance of mine, a nice girl called Judy; she does my daily housekeeping. Okay the mutt had been a marvellous ally up to now, but I hardly think rock climbing or snorkelling would be suitable for a dog. Besides I couldn't possibly concentrate on his welfare and mine too especially now the minefield had widened considerably. And if my pursuers were willing to kill me they wouldn't think twice about shooting a dog whose acquired reputation of taking no prisoners in battle had probably now become legendary.

Incredibly I'd suddenly lost all interest in Hamer and Morgan. They would have to wait for my help. I packed everything into the Roadster, drove down the M4 to Swansea where I caught the next available night car ferry to the Republic of Ireland. I was too late to book a cabin so I found a comfortable chair and slept a few hours. There was one important thing I promised myself as I began to snooze. Whatever happens to me in the following days it was important that I was back for Len's funeral, even if it meant I would have to share his coffin too.

Chapter Thirteen

It was raining hard when the ferry sailed into Cork harbour. From Cork I eased the Roadster along the N71 coastal route to Skibbereen. Even though Professor Squires had pinpointed the area of Baltimore, I thought I would check out his first prediction anyway and then make my way back. On my arrival I wasted no time in touring the roads close to the coastline that I'd marked on my road map. Mile after mile, I travelled, stopping at various points that looked something similar to those on the photographs I had spread across the passenger seat. It soon became apparent I was getting nowhere fast, other than sending myself daft. There was nothing on the photographs that I could relate to the landscapes or coastlines I came across. Then I shouldn't really be surprised since structural changes to the landscapes had obviously occurred over the passing years.

Overall I found little of significance. It had been a long day. I was tired and hungry and I was developing the first signs of a crunching headache. I decided to give up for the day. There was no point in pushing myself beyond exhaustion. Dejectedly, I drove back to Baltimore to locate the hotel where I'd booked a reservation over the telephone before I'd left London.

The Baltimore Harbour Hotel was busy and perfect to blend in without attracting too much attention to myself. After dinner in the hotel I went out to familiarize myself with the area. If this was going to be my base camp for the duration then I would need to know every nook and cranny of the area. It would also give me the opportunity to double check if I had been followed across to Ireland. I didn't expect to be followed, and I soon discovered I hadn't. Though to be absolutely sure I ventured into a pub called Bushe's Bar. I ordered a cold Guinness and sat at a suitable table with my back against a wall and to keep watch on the entrance while I listened to the lively tunes and Irish songs from a local folk band.

During a short intermission from the music I took the opportunity to pester Inspector Hamer. I needed to ask him something. I rang the mobile number he'd given me and kept it blunt. "Got anything on Deveron?"

Naturally, Hamer was pleased to hear from me. "Oh it's you Speed! So nice of you to surface from your hiding place! I've been searching London for you."

"Why?"

"I have your required document stating immunity from prosecution over the matter of Ministry property at Berkshire, signed, sealed, as you asked for. Remember?"

"So?"

"So how the fuck do you expect me to deliver it when you elect to disappear?"

"Well don't bother breaking into my home. Post it!"

I sensed I'd rattled him.

"You have the gratitude of a male spider being killed after mating! Where exactly are you?"

"I'm in a safe place. Did you locate Deveron?"

"Not exactly, he retired from the Ministry years ago."

"I already know *that!* Where did he go?"

"He never left a forwarding address, so I guess he didn't want to be traced."

"I thought you chaps were good?"

"Shut it you facetious swine. Anyway, the old bastard is probably dead. What's so special about Deveron?"

"He's a war hero. I want his autograph."

"Well I hope you have better luck than I did trying to find him. Now are you going to tell me where you are, Speed?"

"I'm on holiday."

"Oh! A pleasant place is it?"

"Are you asking or probing?"

"I haven't decided."

"Well then, when you've decided I'll ring you back."

Hamer began to mutter some obscenities but I cut him off and switched my mobile to silence and straight to the answer phone.

While I was replacing the mobile back into my pocket I became aware of a rugged looking fellow of medium height standing at the bar, probably in his middle fifties, wearing a flat cap and knee length coat opened to reveal a checked shirt. I'd no doubt whatsoever that he was staring directly at me. He actually made me nervous. I sipped some Guinness to steady myself, watching his distorted shape through the rim of the glass. If it was me that the fellow was interested in then I was about to find out what he wanted because he moved away from the bar and headed in my direction.

I continued my observation of him through the beer glass while I pretended to take a long drink. When he got within spitting distance I placed the glass down onto the table in anticipation of trouble. He had a determined look in his eyes but I soon realized he presented no danger to me. Anyone preparing for a fight wouldn't have had a clay pipe clamped between their front teeth and carrying a glass of beer ever so careful so as not to spill a drop. I continued to be minding my own business but remained wary of him.

On closer observation the man had red veined cheeks associated with someone who had spent a good deal of life in the open air. I could tell even before he spoke he was touting for some relevant business and as he hovered over me I got a distinct smell of fish which narrowed down the options of what he did for a living quite conclusively.

He removed the pipe from between his teeth and smiled at me. I could clearly see the arch shape chipped away in his tobacco stained upper two front teeth where the pipe stem had fitted perfectly, the indentation probably achieved after a lifetime of clamping the pipe stem.

"Hullo there, sir!" He said with a cheerful southern Irish voice.

I acknowledged half heartedly with a false smile, nodded and looked away to discourage his approach. In truth, I wasn't in the best of moods for small talk, as my mind had yet to clear from the disappointments of the day. But the Irish fellow was persistent.

"Would it be work or pleasure that brings yer to these shores, sir?"

"A bit of both," I said, dryly.

"Yer're wouldn't be one of those poets looking for a bit of inspiration, would yer be, sir?"

"Not really-Mister-ah?" I thought I might as well know who I'm talking to.

"It is I, sir, Shamus O'Malley, at yer service, and owner of a pleasure fishing boat. Do yer perhaps want to fish these waters?"

"I detest sea fishing." And I did.

He expressed his disappointment. "O that's a shame yer don't like fishing, sir."

But he had me contemplating an idea. "How big is this boat of yours?" I asked, thoughtfully.

"It's very big, sir. And the finest in Baltimore harbour. She's in readiness for a fine customer as yerself. Yer be thinking of a cruise then, sir?"

"Yes, cruising, Shamus; amongst other things."

I could sense his suspicion creeping into the conversation. "And what would this other thing be, sir? I'm not a smuggler or anything of that nature. My hearts as pure as the water I drink."

"You're drinking Guinness," I reminded him.

"That I am, sir."

I smiled. "Relax, Shamus. I'm actually a journalist researching for material on the possibility of an attempted Japanese invasion on these very shores in 1944."

"You'd be kidding me, sir? A Japanese invasion indeed! Here in Ireland?"

"It's perfectly true. I thought an excursion around the bay might reveal some relevant details."

I was half expecting him to assume I was crackers. That I'd maybe lost a few screws that held my brain in place. I was wrong. He didn't rate me as an escapee from a mental institution because he began to rub the grey bristles on his chin while delving into the depths of his mind in search for a speck of information to extend our conversation. He raised a forefinger. I assumed he'd suddenly remembered some important detail he needed to tell me.

"An invasion you say, sir? I might just be able to help yer on that one," he said, proudly.

For a moment I found myself staring at him vacantly before my mouth clicked into gear. "You've knowledge of such an incident?"

"It's more second-hand knowledge, sir."

He put his glass down on the table, removed his hat, revealing short cropped dark ginger hair, pulled in a chair and sat down opposite me. I didn't protest that he'd invited himself, but I did notice his clay pipe wasn't even lit. I suppose listening to a rambling old Irishman wouldn't do me any harm, though I was perhaps being a little harsh on calling him old. He looked older than he probably was due to his weathered face and stubbly chin; neither did him any favours in the beauty department. He had deep set, grey blue eyes and bushy eyebrows. By the time he'd told me everything about his tale, we had drank a few beers.

"It's an incredible story, Shamus. Can you verify any of this?"

The Irishman's eyes narrowed. "Yer wouldn't be thinking, Shamus O'Malley was to be telling yer lies, would yer, sir?"

"I'm sure you're not, Shamus, because nobody could create a story quite like yours. And I'm sure you can prove it?"

"Indeed, sir," he announced solidly. "Take yer to the graveyard where the body's buried."

"It's a start. Now tell me the story again but leave out the intricate details."

Shamus slurped down a mouthful of beer. Ran the back of his hand over his mouth and began, "As I said, sir. Me uncle told me that during the war this wee lad was strolling along the beach at Gollen, a place where I've lived all me life; a beautiful place, sir. So this wee lad had been collecting drift wood from the beach when he stumbled on the ghoulish thing washed up on the rocks. A real mess it was, sir; a badly sea battered body with squinty eyes, smashing against the rocks. That I'm as sure as being sat here holding me empty glass."

I got the hint and reordered. I was going to suffer with a frigging bad head the following morning there was no doubt about that, but I thought this conversation was worth the pain. Go on!" I pushed. "You can clearly remember all what you were told?"

"Clear as a twinkle in me Mother's glass eye. Isn't the sort of memory yer can forget, sir, as a lad. I were scared stiff for weeks just thinking about it."

"Did anyone know how the body became washed up on the rocks?"

"I'd heard a rumour much later that the body may have had something to do with the Americans sinking some Japanese submarine out in the Atlantic at the time, and the body had probably drifted towards Ireland on the currents."

"I suppose the body could have carried that far. What happened to the body after it was retrieved from the water?"

"It was buried, sir."

"What, straight away? No autopsy, no coroner's inquest?"

"I wouldn't know about the medical details, sir. But as the tale goes the body was buried within days, sir. It was beginning to rot a bit. There was no such thing as fridges around here at the time to be storing bodies."

"Buried here in Ireland?"

"So my uncle assured me, sir."

"Can you remember where the burial took place?"

Shamus raised his finger in the air. "Indeed I do, sir."

"Will you take me there tomorrow?"

"Ah-well, sir..." He began slowly. "...I'm a very busy man, indeed."

"I would be paying for your time handsomely, naturally."

I had read him well because there was an immediate sparkle in the Irishman's eyes, and he said, "Now the mere mention of those immortal words is enough to send a leprechaun running for his golden pot to be filled. Is there any particular time in the morning, sir?"

"Don't make it too early, I've a feeling I'll need some aspirins."

"Yer disappoint me, sir. A few pots of the black magic and yer've a hangover before getting one. What yer need, sir, is to drink a glass of Irish water before yer go to bed, and yer'll be as fresh as dew on the morning meadow."

I rose and told him where I was staying, and to be early: eight AM, no later.

I left the bar and staggered back to my hotel. I ordered a pot of tea to be brought to my room on the way through reception. When I eventually turned off the light and lay down on the bed, the room began to spin and so did the thoughts in my head. I nodded off, sinking into a quagmire of nightmares from which I thought I would never return.

Chapter Fourteen

The spear of sunlight pieced the crack in the curtain and hit me directly between the eyes. I climbed out of bed laboriously, drowned my body under a cool shower to wake me up and went down to breakfast. I ate a full traditional Irish breakfast consisting of rashers, grilled tomatoes, sausage, black and white pudding slices and potato cake, all washed down with a refreshing pot of tea. I had just finished when Shamus O'Malley arrived.

"Top of the morning, sir!" he said cheerily. "It's a fine day to wander the beautiful lands of Ireland, it is."

"I hardly regard stomping about in a graveyard as a charming excursion." I reminded him.

"O' no, sir, I meant the views on the way. Yer did mention sightseeing to me last night. That I remember, sir?"

"I'm sure I did, Shamus. Shall we get going?"

Outside Shamus proudly showed me the battered remnants of his Land-Rover, that and the need for a trip through the car wash.

I said casually, "Is it roadworthy?"

Shamus was astonished with my mistrust of his vehicle. "O don't be fooled by the looks, sir. She's a fine, fine runner, indeed."

"I'll have to take your word for it. What about insurance?"

"She's very safe, sir."

"No-not assurance...a driver's insurance?"

"What might that be, sir?"

I looked at him vacantly. I'd two options: go or stay. I said, "I've a little complaint before we set off."

His eyes bulged in anticipation. "Yer've a complaint already, sir? And what might that be?"

"For goodness sake, please stop calling me 'sir' every five minutes. You can call me, Shacks, okay?"

"It's a fine name, Shacks sir, a fine name indeed."

This was one Irishman whose vocabulary I'd struggle to change in a million years.

Shamus O'Malley drove with the same perception as a learner driver with pace, as he took full advantage of the entire road width available when he decided to take his eyes off the road to point out relevant landmarks of interest. I shouldn't moan, as it's not often I have the privilege of being chauffeur driven even if it made me feel uncomfortable. But I overcame my fears the longer the journey went.

We made decent progress along the country roads and despite the country air flowing through the open window I still couldn't relax because of two annoying factors: Shamus's constant crunching of the gears combined equally with his crunching on pieces of dried pork morsels he rustled up from a bag beside him. I've seen a pregnant sow scoffing slops from a bucket eat more quietly.

From Baltimore we took the same scenic route I'd taken the day before until we reach Ballydehob, then onto to the R592, passing a mushroomed topped mountain as we headed for the village of Schull. Keeping right, as we went through Schull, Shamus veered the vehicle off the road and we headed down a narrow country lane until we approached a derelict church minus its roof. At first I thought Shamus was taking me on a sight-seeing trip after all to liven the day, but he hadn't. This was the place.

"We're here, Shacks sir." He announced as if introducing me to something fantastically special.

I stepped from the vehicle unimpressed and stretched my legs. I followed Shamus through a broken oak gate hanging by one rusty hinge and along an overgrown grassy stone pathway to the rear of the ruins.

"So what's the story of this sorrowful place?" I asked as we went along.

"O it is a shame, Shacks sir," he said over his shoulder. "A violent storm in the twenties ripped the roof clean off, so I was told."

Shamus stopped and swept his hand in an arc to show the area where I assumed the body was buried, but he refused to go any closer. I saw nothing but overgrown vegetation and total neglect. It was obvious nobody had been here for years.

Bewilderment on my face, I said: "This is the graveyard?"

Shamus nodded.

"Where are all the headstones?"

"O well, Shacks sir, this church was never actually used for Irish burials."

"Then what are we doing here?"

"The authorities at the time, Shacks sir, made an exception and had the body from the shore buried here. It's over there, Shacks sir, under the overgrown hedgerow."

I followed his outstretched arm to the spot he was pointing to and said, disappointedly, "Hardly distinctive as a grave."

"O believes me it is, Shacks sir. I swear on me Mother's grave it is. If you flatten the long grass down you'll find it. I'd do it meself, only I'm a rather superstitious kind of man, and the thought of leaning over another mans grave only heightens me fear of being taken before me time."

"You're scared, Shamus?"

Shamus blushed because it certainly wasn't exertion. "Scared? Me?"

"You're afraid of a ghoulish hand suddenly shooting from the ground to drag you down into Hell?"

Shamus owned up to his phobia. "That's precisely what I'd be thinking, Shacks sir." And he immediately made the sign of the cross over his chest.

Even I hesitated before crouching down in front of the supposed grave. I parted the grass and found the evidence that proved Shamus was right.

"There's no headstone of any type," I bellowed over my shoulder. "But there's a wooden plaque. It's a bit twisted and faded, but I can still read part of the inscription."

"What does it say, Shacks sir?"

"Let your God-something-something-soul: rest-something-something; probably rest in peace."

It was hardly an impressive piece of writing and proved nothing to confirm this was the last resting place of a Japanese sailor. I rose to my feet, contemplating the possibility of hiring a couple of gravediggers to exhume the body for verification, but there's a law against doing that without the proper authorization and paperwork and to be accused of grave-robbing didn't really appeal to me.

"Are you sure this is the grave?"

"As sure as me name is Shamus O'Malley," he said seriously.

"Why did they decide to bury the body here at the ruins, some Irish custom?"

"O well, yer see, Shacks sir, the priest at the time, Father Brady, O he was a fine man indeed and a devout Roman Catholic, well he wouldn't allow a non Catholic to be buried on sacred ground. I'm afraid Father Brady wasn't quite prepared for the religions associated with the Far East, so it was decided that this forgotten church would be sufficient until the body was claimed."

"Very thoughtful, only it seems nobody bothered to pass the information on."

"O it's an awful thing, Shacks sir," again his fingers shifted across his chest as he made the sign of the cross, "time simply passed by. No one came looking. No one remembered, until now. Is it helping at all?"

"Not directly, but I should think the Japanese government will want to know the body exists."

"Does that mean the forgotten soul will be going home?"

"No doubt the Japanese government will reclaim the body and would want its return immediately. They're an honourable bunch when it comes to their hero's. Send them a shoe and that's sufficient for a full military honour."

"It's a fine, fine thing, Shacks sir, a fine thing indeed."

"Yes, but we'll not mention anything about it just yet, Shamus. Shall we move on to the part of the coast where the body was discovered? You do remember?"

"Indeed I do, Shacks sir."

Back onto the main road, Shamus eased the Land-Rover through a sweeping bend that took us into Toormore Bay. We had small talk as we drove along, Shamus did all the talking and I just pretended to listen. My head was too full of *'ifs, buts and why's.*

We left the vehicle in the car park, made our way down to the beach and walked along the waters edge until we came to a piece of rocky beach. Shamus stopped and looked about as if he was lost, moved perhaps two steps back, muttered something, turned, took another two steps and stopped. He didn't exactly fill me with confidence when he began scratching the back of his head and looking rather perturbed.

"Is there a problem?" I asked.

"Indeed there is, Shacks sir, I'm having a little trouble remembering on which side of the large rock the body was washed up."

"I hardly think it matters, Shamus." I assured him. "Can you recall being told the state of the body when it was found?"

Shamus gave me a strange look. "O dead, Shacks sir, very dead indeed."

"No! I meant the condition of the body. How did it look?"

"I was told it was battered to a pulp as I said last night, Shacks sir."

At that moment a huge wave smashed into a number of large rocks a few metres out and sprayed me with saltwater. It didn't distract me. "No I meant was the body bloated, swelled like a balloon?"

"O no, I distinctly recall my uncle referring to a skinny little runt with squinty eyes and his skin white and wrinkly."

Skinny little runt told me a great deal. It meant the body could never have travelled from mid-Atlantic without suffering such deformities as severe bloating and rotting flesh. It meant the body could have come from a closer source. The thought gave me a nip of inspiration.

Excitedly I said, "How deep is the water around Roaring Water Bay?"

"That would depend on your intentions, Shacks sir."

"I've suddenly acquired the urge to go fishing, Shamus."

Shamus broke into a short Irish jig. "I knew yer were a fisherman the minute I first cast eyes on yer. Is it the big fish that appeals, Shacks sir?"

"Sort of, Shamus. How big did you say your boat was?"

"The biggest in the harbour she is, Shacks sir, and ready at a special price to you."

"Good because I hope you don't mind fishing for submarines."

Shamus ceased his jiggery dance gave me a long hard look. "Submarines yer say, Shacks, sir?"

"Yes Shamus. We are going hunting for a great big metallic Japanese submarine which I'm absolutely positive went missing while on a secret mission, here in Roaring Water bay. But keep it to yourself, if you don't mind."

Shamus grinned. "O yer be pulling me leg, Shacks sir? The devil yer are."

"I'm too serious to be pulling your leg, Shamus. My sanity is riding on the hunch."

"O yer're insane and working on a hunch, is it, Shacks sir?"

"A bit more towards probability actually."

"O well, yer see, Shacks sir, I don't want to disappoint yer, but I've been sailing and fishing these waters for a long time now. I'm rather proud to say me expertise on these waters is as equal to any seafaring mariner. And apart from the odd rumour of old sunken galleons, I'm afraid that a Japanese submarine never quite reached me imagination. If you know what I'm saying?"

"My hunches have in the past have been noted as being rather spectacular."

"I think you're a crazy Englishman!"

"Yes, Shamus, but this crazy Englishman is paying frigging good money for the privilege of being crazy."

"That's very true, Shacks sir. A crazy mans money is as good as any other crazy mans money. Hunting submarines it is!"

"It's settled then, Shamus. Now let me explain something about the body washed up on the beach. You described the condition of the Oriental after being dragged from the sea as skinny. There was no sign of bloating so it hadn't been in the water long. Does that not arouse some suspicion that maybe the body came from a closer source?"

"As a young boy, Shacks sir, the talk of the dead had me hiding under me blankets and suffering from terrible nightmares. That I did, sir." He half smiled, "Have yer never thought it rather strange how bad things tend to stick in the mind longer than good things."

He had a point there.

I showed him the photographs I had safely tucked away in the inside of my new zipped bomber jacket. I said, "That, Shamus is a Japanese submarine in a lot of trouble somewhere off the coastline in this area. Do any of these rocks or shorelines look familiar?"

He studied them and then with a negative shake of his head, he said, "Nothing I can put me finger, Shacks sir."

"I've had an authority on the subject of rock formations pinpointing these parts as the area on the photographs," I assured him. "He's pretty damn good at his job."

"O I don't doubt the integrity of the person Shacks sir. But the pictures are more angled towards the coastline. We'd see things more clearly out there on the open water."

"Frigging hell, Shamus, I can't venture out there on the open seas in my condition."

Shamus appeared concerned. "Why? Does the rough sea bother you some, Shacks sir?"

"No. But going without lunch does. This sea air is playing havoc with my stomach. I noticed a seafood restaurant at the quayside; my treat."

I didn't expect Shamus to disagree with the offer, and he didn't disappoint me.

We left the beach and made our way back to the Land-Rover. While doing so I felt that we weren't alone and that we were being watched from a distance. I stopped for a moment and looked around. There was nobody I could see in the vicinity but I still sensed a presence and close enough to be nosey of our actions. I think the observer had us in a pair of binoculars.

*

Shamus dropped me back at my hotel so I could change into the appropriate clothing to combat the inevitable cold expected across the Bay. What hadn't changed by the time I slid the electronic key into the door entry and entered my room was the same paranoia I'd experienced at Toormore Bay earlier which had now reached the interior of my room. I looked around. Immediately I realized my room had been searched. There was definitely something amiss. Certain items had been moved minimally. Some of my clothing had been disturbed, obviously not conducted by an inconsiderate searcher intent on throwing my belongings all over the room in frustration of not finding whatever they were looking for. No this searcher was a calculated, neat person, whose expertise in such matters meant only the minor interruption, but there was enough detail to make me suspicious.

I stepped inside the room and closed the door quietly behind me.

I was alert to what I thought was a faint scraping noise coming from the bathroom. I quickly picked up the nearest weapon I could locate in a flash, which happened to be a statuette from the coffee table, only noticing afterwards that I had manhandled a statue of the Virgin Mary by her breasts. But it hardly concerned me at the time. What I had in my hand was heavy and dangerous. I raised the statue aloft, club-like and advanced towards the bathroom door ready to strike the first lethal blow. I definitely knew I'd a heart inside my chest because it bounced against my ribs with the sound of a bass drum. I sucked in a deep breath and rushed through the door, wailing like a banshee, hoping to frighten the lurking assailant into surrendering.

What a fool I would have appeared if I was being watched. The lone fly buzzing around my head with extreme confidence was hardly a threat. I shattered the annoying insect with a flick of a hand towel and retreated to the bedroom. I replaced the statue on the table and instantly became aware of a distinct smell of perfume, not too strong, just enough to have me thinking of where I'd smelled it before. I noticed the bed had been made and accepted my intruder was probably no other than the chambermaid attending the room.

With the panic over I changed my clothes for a cream coloured thick roll-neck jumper, jeans, suitable boots and a decent jacket and went back down to the harbour which was clogged with people busily attending their various array of expensive yachts and cruisers.

I located Shamus on the deck of his boat going about his business, whistling a lively tune, while he prepared for the sea journey ahead. I was disappointed with the way he looked. I'd visions of him wearing a pirate's hat and a black patch over his right eye. Not that I thought he was the type to rip me off, but I was a little deflated with the elegance of his boat compared to rest of the fine boats scattered around the harbour.

The name *Muff* highlighted on the bow of Shamus's fishing boat had me wondering how the vessel's name had originated in the first place. I was tempted to ask him but finally decided against it. As long as the frigging boat didn't sink then that's all that mattered. Underneath its lick of blue and white winter maintenance paint, the exterior of the *Muff* showed all the signs of taking a battering by the Atlantic swells. Still, it appeared seaworthy and I doubt Shamus would risk his reputation of providing an un-seaworthy vessel because I assumed he valued his own life far too much to take unnecessary risks.

As I came alongside I shouted down to him "Ahoy there shipmate, have I permission to come aboard?"

Shamus looked up at me far from impressed with my maritime quip which he obviously considered was originality long past its sell by date. He gestured me aboard, and when I had scrambled on deck, he said, "Changeable weather approaches the Bay, Shacks sir. Possible rain, heavy too, But don't worry yerself, I've a

Sou'wester or two aboard ship. If yer're thirsty there's cold Guinness in the fridge down in the Galley, or yer might want a Paddy's Irish whiskey that'll warm the toggles of yer heart. We set sail in ten minutes."

I nodded and glanced around the harbour. "Lot's of activity, Shamus. What's with all the fancy yachts?"

"The regatta starts next week, Shacks sir. The amateurish sailors are a pain in the backside but Baltimore prospers with the extra revenue it brings."

I de-capped two bottles of beer and put one into Shamus's large leathery hand. He promptly gulped down half of the contents, placed the bottle down on the chart table and resumed his radio check, informing the harbour master of our intended journey around the shorelines of Roaring Water Bay and our return expectancy before dusk. With final checks completed I assisted Shamus with uncoupling the mooring ropes before climbing back on board. I had a strange feeling come over me as the *Muff* chugged over the water; a strange surge of anxious excitement, mixed with apprehension and delight, as I thought of what was out there waiting for me.

I was soon distracted from what lay ahead when the roughness of the sea hit us. I was thrown to one side, not fully prepared when the first heavy wave smashed into the bow of the boat with the effect of driving the vessel backwards rather than making headway. I'd sailed rough seas before but I had to confess that the conditions now had me gripping every conceivable piece of apparatus on the bridge to prevent falling flat on my face.

I tapped Shamus on the arm. "Whoever named this bay wasn't kidding."

"O yes Shacks sir, a rough Bay she is, just like the Irish, tough and beautiful. If yer're thinking the boat can't handle the conditions, don't concern yerself, she's sailed these waters endlessly for thirty five years."

"I'm sure with a Captain like you behind the helm, Shamus, I've no worries."

"O yer a very kind man, Shacks sir."

"So where are we heading?"

"I think it best if we start where the body washed ashore and follow the shoreline back to Baltimore. If we come up empty and there's still time, we'll circumnavigate the Islands."

"You're the Captain, Shamus."

I placed the four photographs in a position where it was beneficial for the two of us to check them against the shoreline and hopefully we would find a match. In all honesty I would be depending on Shamus's knowledge of the shoreline because everywhere looked the same to me.

Shamus was right about the changeable weather. What began as a reasonably bright day, the weather suddenly turned and smacked the *Muff* with a bout of heavy rain, which, inevitably, was always accompanied with a gusty wind that howled and whistled through every nook and cranny of the boat. Add the creaking sound of twisting wood with the added edition of the window wipers flicking side to side, and with careful listening, the entire accompaniment had the makings of an orchestral beginning on its way to Davy's Locker.

I soon discovered there was one disadvantage to the pounding rain lashing against the window pane. It made viewing of the shoreline a lot harder to see, so I was forced, or for a more correct application, encouraged by Shamus to venture from the wheelhouse whenever we spotted a place of resemblance. On my first venture out into the elements I stupidly ignored Shamus's advisory words and didn't bother with waterproof protection. A good drenching remedied my ignorance so that the next time I ventured outside I was better equipped to resist the weather, and more importantly, I could wipe that cheeky grin from the Irishman's face.

Apart from the cheap entertainment I provided for Shamus, and some hairy moments close to the shoreline when I thought the boat would be dragged against the rocks and smashed to pieces, overall, it turned out to be another long frustrating day.

"As I said, Shacks sir, the photographs don't give a clear picture. The landscape has changed dramatically through the years. I think we're wasting our time. I think we should get the photographs enlarged? See things a little more clearly."

"That sounds like a sensible idea." It had never occurred to me to think of such an easy solution. Then Lens Lazerow drifted into my thoughts. If he had still been alive he would have certainly made the suggestion.

"Have you somewhere to take them, Shamus?"

"Indeed I do Shacks sir."

"Okay, let's get back to Baltimore harbour and call it a day."

*

With the *Muff* securely moored, I went ashore. I said to Shamus before leaving, "Don't lose the photographs. They're the only ones I have."

Shamus tapped the side of his nose; it flexed like rubber. "You can trust old Shamus, Shacks sir."

"How long do you think it'll take?"

"It'll not be today, Shacks sir. Will tomorrow morning do?"

"Fine, and If there's any problems call me at my hotel. I should be there for the rest of the day as I need to rid the taste of sea salt from the back of my throat."

On my arrival back at my hotel reception informed me that a new guest had arrived at the hotel and had requested to see me and that the enquirer was presently having a drink in the lounge. I was, understandably, stunned by the announcement because I'd told nobody my true destination to Baltimore. I approached the lounge with great caution and nearly dropped through the floor when I caught sight of the man sitting there at a table looking directly at me with smugness written all over his fat face. I quickly ordered a straight dark rum from the bar, swallowed the lot, and with great reluctance I crossed over and sat down opposite the man from the MDP. I think my expression of displeasure for Inspector Hamer was justifiable once again.

I said sharply, "You've a nasty habit of following me?"

"I missed your presence in London."

"I'm sure you did."

"Morgan's not happy with you absconding after he went to all that trouble to compile your immunity from prosecution."

"So he sent you to drag me back?"

"I follow orders. Why the sudden disappearing act?"

"What business is it of yours?"

"I'm your protector."

"Am I supposed to be impressed?"

"You might be if you didn't keep on running away all the time"

"I don't need protecting. I need to be left alone."

"I'll leave you alone when you agree to cooperate with the Ministry police."

"How long have you been in Ireland?"

"Why?"

"Is the question too difficult for you?"

"I flew in on a morning flight."

"How did you know where to find me?"

"You're not a hard man to find when you use a credit card and ring me from your mobile phone. GPS is a fantastic piece of equipment."

"I wasn't thinking straight. Thanks for the tip."

"It's a little too late, Speed. We're not a bunch of amateurs. We use the same sophisticated equipment equal to any major police force or security agency to acquire intelligence."

"That's how you found my hotel room then?"

Hamer frowned. "Which one's your room?"

"The one you searched while I was preoccupied elsewhere?"

That question threw him off balance.

"What are you drivelling on about?"

"Don't give me that verbal claptrap! You're supposed to be clever and you never even asked reception for my room number? Maybe you're not Raffles, the gentleman thief, but you've already proved your skills of passing a security lock whether it's mechanical or electronic. What were you expecting to find in my room?"

"Your mind's deranged, Speed. I've been down here since I arrived. Ask reception. Ask the barman if you don't believe me; go on!"

I silenced with uncertainty and instead tried to read his facial expressions to ascertain if he was telling me anywhere near the truth. I suspected Hamer could tell bare faced lies far better than I could. It wouldn't have taken much for him to have slipped away when the barman was busy. Though Hamer had one saving grace; the perfume I smelled in my room didn't match the cologne he'd splashed on his face that morning.

"Which fat bee flew up your arse, Speed?"

"I think that's an inappropriate question since you're sitting there. Where's Commander Morgan now?"

"He's at his London office, fretting. The paranoid sod thinks his office has been bugged because of the stink he's caused over the missing documentation concerning flight operations during the final years of WW2. He suspects the perpetrators are watching his every movement. You really got him hooked with this Huggermugger operation, and he's chasing answers and hitting a brick wall."

"Is his office bugged?"

Hamer shrugged. "I wouldn't be at all surprised. The rumours are rife that the corridors of Whitehall hide a mass of electronic listening devices and surveillance cameras. Why do you think ministers arrange secret meetings away from Whitehall? Open spaces are much harder to monitor, especially the golf courses. Morgan does the same thing. But at the moment it isn't just missing documentation that's worrying him. There are still the two killers on the loose: Love and Hate."

"You haven't located them yet?"

"We're working on it. And when we finally nail the bastards, Morgan will no doubt take all the credit as per usual."

"You sound as if you're pissed off with him?"

"Doesn't everybody with their respective employer? Unlike a freelancer such as you, Speed, I'm suppressed. Morgan, he likes to do things his way and is deaf to other people's suggestions. He thinks I'm his lap dog; throw a stick and I'll go and fetch it back."

"I'll agree with you on that," I said.

Hamer frowned, trying to work out if I was ridiculing him. I kept a straight face and said, "So he insisted you come here then to pester me?"

"Your fault entirely, Speed. Remember what was discussed in London about solidarity? Together we battle against the enemy? If we can connect Love and Hate to the killing of your friends we'll be half way to solving the mystery of the Spitfire wreck."

"Where do you think Love and Hate have gone?"

"They could be anywhere. And since I can't force you back to London, I'm here to watch your back."

"That's very heroic of you, Inspector, but who's watching your back?"

"It's not me they want"

"You've had a wasted journey. If I'd have needed a minder, I'd have hired one."

"I come free of charge, Speed. And I'm here to stay. Commander Morgan insists I remain here. Who am I to argue? My insubordination would only lead to him slapping a P45 in my hand; we're all vulnerable to the sack."

"This is harassment and an infringement of my privacy."

Hamer tossed his head in the air. "Then complain to Morgan, not me. Now apart from practicing being a moaning bastard, what are you doing hiding in these parts?"

"I'm hardly hiding. I'm on holiday, convalescing from the rigours of being abused by thugs and picked on by authoritarians."

"You're talking bollocks!"

"No, it does include the thugs?"

"It's still bollocks!"

"You're getting tiresome, Hamer."

"You still won't accept you need our help, will you Speed?"

"Is it that noticeable?"

Hamer fumed. "You're an ungrateful sod!"

I shrugged.

Hamer insisted on scolding me more than I was willing to take. "Get yourself killed. See if I care a toss! I'd be happy to slap your dead carcass on Morgan's office desk and tell him the case is closed."

"You're staying then?"

"Damn right I am."

"Not too close I hope?"

"Close enough, Speed." This is a splendid hotel."

"I was under the impression this hotel was fully booked with summer sailors?"

"There's been a cancellation on the Bridal suite."

"How appropriate-eh- the last room at the inn."

"I've no complaints."

"It's a big room that's made for sharing," I said smartly. "I don't want you knocking on my door when you get scared in the middle of the night."

"How would you feel if I camped right outside your door instead?"

"It would be like a cold draft up the crack of my arse," I said, and rose to my feet. "No doubt you'll be dining here this evening?"

"You'll not get a free meal out of me twice."

I smiled and walked off. Over my shoulder, I said, "You want to bet, Hamer!"

Through a reflection of glass I caught Hamer flashing me a two fingered gesture behind my back. I thought about returning to shove his two offensive digits up his fat nose. Instead I focused on Love and Hate, as I made my way to my room. Their disappearance rather put a different complexion on proceedings. I wondered where and what the two vultures were doing right now. I imagined them staking out my home. Even worse I imagined my place burnt to the ground with them thinking I might be hiding inside.

If Hamer was right about the two goons and their determination to hunt me down relentlessly, then I guessed they still wanted the reel of film I'd taken from the wreck. I stopped off and used the hotel payphone, a security precaution against an illegal line tap on my mobile. Hamer had certainly managed to make me feel uneasy with his brag about of being able to track people down by their personal equipment. I rang Judy, my daily housekeeper, to check if everything was all right back in London and how Winston was treating her. She told me everything was fine and Winston was such an adorable dog that she wanted to keep him forever. I said we'd talk about that when I got back.

I left the phone booth and enquired at reception if Hamer had asked for my room number at any time. He had, but as far as they were aware, after Hamer had been shown to his room by the bellboy, he'd returned immediately down to the lounge to wait for me.

I checked my room again when I got back. It hadn't been breached a second time because the small piece of paper I'd wedged between the lower door hinge and door jamb was still in place and immediately fell to the floor when I went inside; pathetically simple but effective. I locked the door behind me, something I don't usually have concerns over when occupying the room at the time, but I thought it was a wise decision considering. Without thinking about it I'd become jittery and I'm usually never that.

I had a shower, shaved, put on a bathrobe and crashed out onto the bed, closing my aching eyes. Eventually I expelled the thoughts that were criss-crossing through my mind and I drifted into a world of ambivalence and absolution. I slept for twenty minutes and when I awakened I was refreshed and I dressed for dinner.

*

Hamer was already sat at a table in the hotel restaurant. He was staring thoughtfully through the window and seemed absorbed with the view across the bay. I startled him as I approached. I rather enjoyed his reaction considering he was supposed to be a tough guy.

He looked up at me in disbelief, his eyes glued to the tuxedo I was wearing. I didn't think I was overdressed for the occasion. The hotel management most definitely didn't think I was overdressed, appreciating my effort to impress, as it would enhance the reputation of the hotel. The ladies were impressed too because I was getting the right stares of approval. Hamer wasn't impressed. He didn't appreciate my effort at all and he didn't mix his words either.

"You overgrown snob!" he commented rudely.

"You don't appreciate quality," I told him.

"This isn't the Caribbean, Speed."

"It's closer to the Caribbean than London will ever be," I pointed out.

"Sit down Speed, before your swelled ego knocks you down."

I sat down opposite him.

He gave me a low whistle. "I guess grave robbing is a profitable business."

I attracted the attention of a waitress to take our orders. I chose a meal of seafood, washed down with a splendid bottle of Muscatel, followed by coffee and Cognac. Hamer selected a more hearty meat dinner and had the appetite to match, as he scoffed his food down in a mannerism that had all the grace of a divulging barbarian.

We spoke very little while we ate, Hamer the instigator of the main conversation, in between stuffing his face. I wasn't even listening to him gabbing on, not that he noticed. I was thinking deeply. Trying to piece together what information I had gathered so far. When in deep thought my eyes have a habit of wandering and I found myself staring across the room at a table occupied by three couples. I could overhear the men at that table bragging over the size of their yachts while two of the women sat with them pretended to be interested. I caught the third woman at the table eyeing me up before she shyly turned away disinterestedly.

Hamer belched loudly followed by his out of date comment 'compliments to the chef'.

"Enjoyable was it, Inspector?"

Hamer raised a hand as if he was stopping the local traffic. "Let's cut the formalities crap. While I'm here, (he belched again loudly much to the annoyance of other diners), call me Dan; much more friendly. Do you prefer me to call you Shackleton?"

"You can call me anything you want Dan, apart from Shackleton or Shacks. Those names I reserve for my friends."

Hamer could tell by my expression that I wasn't joking. He burst into a tantrum which attracted more attention than he would have probably wanted.

"You're such an awkward bastard, Speed!"

"We understand each other then?" I said placidly, which angered him even more.

"That you're a slapped arse because I'm babysitting you? Yes I fully understand."

"How close do you intend to stick to me, Danny boy?"

He groaned disapprovingly at being called *Danny*. "As close as I fucking can."

"I'm that important?"

"You're the only target that's ever survived Love and Hate. You've seriously dented their reputations as professional killers. They'll want to make amends for the mess they left behind. A witness is too dangerous to them; witnesses can testify. They'll want to rectify the problem fairly quickly I should imagine. They'll want to slash your throat, Speed!"

"Is that all? I'm really disappointed with their style."

"Listen for once. Why don't you return to London? We can set you up in a safe house; provide you with around the clock protection."

"I'm not playing the bait. Beside they won't know I'm here in Ireland."

"I found you easy enough."

"Frigging hell, you want them to find me anyway so what's the difference if I'm here or in London?"

"Here's more difficult to protect you; too many open spaces to cover; a sniper could take you out at two hundred yards."

"A sniper could take me out anywhere; not unless you have me enclosed in an armoured vehicle, preferably with a large calibre machine gun mounted on the front, and then there shouldn't be any frigging problem at all."

"There's no need for such waggishness, Speed."

"I take it you're armed?" I assumed he was. A small calibre weapon could easily be concealed on a person quite comfortably.

He disappointed me with a shake of his head.

"You've no armoury at all?"

"Sorry, Speed. I'm just your bodyguard. You'll have to trust my abilities in unarmed combat."

"Oh I see, you're going to deflect the bullets with your hands?"

"No. I'll use you as a shield. Does that scare you?"

"I'm shaking in my boots. Yet there's one problem you need to consider before you get too over confident in your assumption that I'm controllable and safe in your competent hands."

"What's that, Speed?"

"I've no intentions of going under a protection scheme until I've completed my business here in Ireland. So I suggest you don't fall under my feet. By all means, hover like a fly looking for a bad smell, but don't keep pushing me into complying with pitiful requests. I'm not pliable and I can't be moved in different directions."

I expected another backlash from Hamer, but to my surprise he shrugged in defeat. I think he was feeling tired and probably three parts pissed too.

"Have it your own way. Your arrogance blinds common sense. Why should I care? You're just an arrogant meddler, with an attitude problem, and layered with dishonesty."

"Dishonesty," I said in disbelief. "Show me an establishment of authority that doesn't deal in dishonesty and I'll show my arse in Burton's shop window all day with my cheeks squashed against the glass plate for all the pedestrians to see."

"There you are, exactly what I'm getting at, attitude problem."

"No, Hamer. It's the attitude of a person who's had enough of snub-nosed pin-striped bureaucrats throwing their weight around in my affairs."

It was the frown Hamer expressed that made me realize that together we'd no chance of creating a workable team. There can't be two team leaders within one group. Yet despite my reluctance to have him under my feet and his blatant openness that he was playing with my life, I still thought he could be useful to me.

"Look! I'm here to offer my protection. I intend to carry out my duty."

"That's very chivalrous of you, Hamer. Since you're going to be attached to me, you'll no doubt enjoy the pleasure of a cruise around the bay on my expense account?"

"You're going to waste a day cruising?"

"There'll be deep sea fishing, sight-seeing and scuba diving. Do you scuba-dive?"

"You're damned serious about this being a holiday?"

"What else? If I'm going to die I might as well enjoy myself in the meantime"

"Well you won't find me sticking my head beneath the sea. I prefer my head above the waterline breathing natural air and my feet on terra firma. I'm very experienced in paddling. When is this great event to watch you drown?"

"Tomorrow morning. I'd advise you wear some warm clothing; the chill factor out in the bay is appalling. And if swimming isn't a strong point I suggest you check on whether life-jackets are readily available."

Hamer's eyebrows lifted in terror. "Is it going to be that bad?"

"Have you seen the weather forecast predicted for tomorrow?"

Chapter Fifteen

I was drinking tea in the hotel lounge when Shamus arrived and presented me with the enlarged photographs he had rolled together carefully. "Did you get my diving gear from the boot of my car?"

"Indeed I did Shacks sir, safely transferred to the boat in readiness."

"Excellent."

I unravelled and studied each enlargement in turn. On one of the photographs, what I'd first thought were just black dots on the hazy originals, now clearly showed three small rubber crafts with at least two men aboard each craft seemingly in the process of attaching implements to the stern of the submarine.

I pointed to the spot I was looking at on the photograph. "What do you make of this, Shamus?"

Shamus leaned over. "Straight forward, I'd say. The submarine's under attack, Shacks sir. I examined the photos with a magnifying glass. The people in the dinghies are attaching black discs. I'd be guessing explosives."

I agreed with him. "Limpet mines, Shamus. It would seriously explain the smoke bellowing from the rear of the submarine in the other photographs. I think their intention was to immobilize the steering controls to stop the sub sailing away."

"The attackers were trying to capture the sub, Shacks sir?"

"I think the intention was to sink the sub."

"Why would they want to sink it, Shacks, sir?"

For the gold bullion I was tempted to tell him. Instead I said, "I'm not sure, Shamus. Ireland declared neutrality during the war. Perhaps the Japanese thought it was a safe haven. There's no records of the Allies attacking a submarine in these waters because they were too busy battering a similar sub in the Atlantic. So why indeed should anyone attack a submarine in Irish waters? I wouldn't mind betting there's nothing written in any of the history books concerning this slice of wartime activity."

"History or not, Shacks sir. Old Shamus now knows which shoreline the sub lies off. Look carefully at the second photo, just to the top, right side, there's a faint image showing through the watermark. It's a landmark, a piece of rock rising from the water. I've seen it before! If I'm not mistaken, that splinter of rock holds the ruins of O'Driscoll's fort. Dun an Oir, 'the golden fort'. The historic fortress is on the West side of Clear Island."

"Good man, Shamus! You've just earned yourself a double bonus."

My jubilation lasted all of three seconds when a shadow loomed over our shoulders. Hamer leaned over to view the photographs.

"What have we here, Speed?"

"My holiday snaps in three D, Inspector."

He looked hard at Shamus. "Who's this chap then? Is he trying to sell you some postcards, Speed?"

"Shamus, meet Inspector Hamer, Ministry of Defence police investigator who's volunteered to assist us in our quest for fishing for the big one. Inspector Hamer, meet Shamus our tour operator and guide."

Shamus appeared concerned. "He's a policeman, yer mean, Shacks, sir?"

"No Shamus. He's a Ministry of Defence policeman. Don't worry, he's not after you. His jurisdiction ended the moment he touched Irish soil. But be warned. You touch even a flake of paint that resembles military hardware and he'll have you strung up by your balls and carted off to the nearest gaol without your feet touching the ground. Isn't that right Inspector?"

Hamer curled his top lip and resumed his interest in the enlargements. "That's a Japanese cargo submarine used during WWII?"

"You're very observant, Sherlock."

"Cut the crap, Speed! Is that why you're here in Ireland, to find a submarine?"

"I happen to have a passion for wreck diving."

"You're wasting your time even looking, Speed."

Shamus jumped in. "Exactly what I told him, sir."

Hamer scowled at the interruption. "There aren't any such wrecks in these parts."

"You're just as bad as Shamus; spoiling my dreams."

"I'd say we're doing you a favour."

"I take it that you're an expert on the subject of wrecks, Hamer?"

"I know enough to tell you there are no sunken submarines in these waters. There was only ever one Japanese submarine sunk in this part of the world during the war." He flicked his head sideways. "And that was out there in the deep blue ocean of the Atlantic in 1944. That's historical fact. And that particular submarine has already been located by the yanks in recent times, pinpointed and recorded. Besides, Speed, if you're thinking of an Atlantic rendezvous, I'd give up now. It's far too deep for you and your flippers."

"Have you any idea how long I can hold my breath?"

"Not long enough, Speed. Save your air tanks. Let's instead have a nice cruise around the harbour, collect our things and get ourselves back to London to sort out our problems. Then we can think about a holiday to somewhere warm and pleasant and away from the smell of fish. I'll even get Morgan to finance the arrangement."

I gave him a stern look and said, "You're trying to be bossy again."

"I want to go home."

"Nobody's stopping you."

"You're forgetting Morgan."

"You just decide whether you want to come along and play pirates or not?"

*

Hamer made the trip with us to Clear Island after all. His presence suited me. At least I could keep an eye on him. It turned out that Hamer made a lousy sailor. He suffered miserably with seasickness throughout the rough voyage. He grasped whatever he could in the wheelhouse providing it didn't move and he wouldn't let go. Not even for a beer. I left him to suffer alone in the corner of the wheelhouse.

Me! I was excited with the prospect of solving the mystery of the elusive I-52 when we arrived at the proposed diving site; the position Shamus and I had calculated where the submarine would have been at the time when the photograph was taken by Craven's Spitfire. Shamus dropped the *Muff's* anchor.

I changed into my diving gear. While doing so I explained to Shamus the importance of conducting a rigorous training session for a surface coordinator on line duty and the various pulling signs he must know to communicate and understand the diver below. I also stressed the fact that this practice was what a diver's life depended on. Twice I went through the procedure with him. Twice I didn't get the responsive confidence I'd hoped for. Just his expression alone told me he didn't fancy taking on the responsibility alone. When Hamer made an appearance on deck I asked him if he understood the procedure, but he shrugged, made a mad dash for the starboard side and promptly threw up his half digested morning meal.

Again I went through the communication rope pulling signals with him while I slipped into the neoprene dry suit, attached the aqualung (double tri-mix air tanks-air regulator-buoyancy compensator), put on an adjustable buoyancy life jacket, weight-belt, fins and silicon facemask resting on my forehead. I illuminated the rubber torch to check it was working; checked the knives were in position, one on my arm and one attached to the side of my leg; checked the wrist attached dive computer (calculated depth, temperature and compass bearings). I attached the safety line and I was ready to dive.

"Right, Shamus! Listen again! You are the shore and I'm the diver. Okay?"

"I've got that, Shacks sir."

"One pull on the rope by shore indicates, 'are you okay' to the diver. If the diver pulls the rope once, it indicates, 'I'm okay'. Understand?"

"Indeed I do, Shacks, sir. It's one pull and you're okay."

"Two pulls by shore, indicates, 'stay still'. Two pulls by diver, indicates, 'I'm still'. Three pulls by shore, indicates, 'go down'. Three pulls by diver, indicates, 'going down'. Four pulls by shore, indicates, 'come up'. Four pulls by diver, indicates, 'coming up'. Continuous pulls by shore, indicates, 'emergency bring you up'. Continuous pulls by diver, indicates, 'bring me up'. Have you got all that?"

"Indeed, I do, Shacks, sir." He prodded the side of his head. "All here, within the confines of me head."

"It better had be there, Shamus because I'm depending on you," I warned him. "Now is the blue flag flying to show other crafts a diver is down in the water?"

"It is, Shacks, sir, flapping in the wind, it is."

I pulled the goggles down over my eyes, put the aqualung mouthpiece in and sucked in some air to test it was working correctly. And then I made a walk-in dive and dropped beneath the water line, brought my knees up to my midriff and threw my head down, kicked the fins and made my descent into the depths of Roaring Water Bay.

I descended at an energy saving pace. The water darkened the deeper I dived and the water temperature dropped rapidly; not exactly a diver's paradise. Further down I had to revert to switching on the powerful rubber torch I'd brought with me.

I made routine checks of my depth on the wrist computer until I'd reached the bottom vegetation. If a large vessel of any description was down on the seabed, especially a submarine of such a massive length, I was confident I would find the frigging thing, that's if it hadn't sailed away in 1944, as Shamus had already suggested plus making the annoying point that *if it was here why hadn't it been discovered before now?* But I wasn't to have my confidence dampened by wasteful thoughts so I pressed on regardless; there was a lot of seabed to search and breathing time under water is limited.

In a short time I'd covered a fair section of seabed, establishing a grid reference search which took me in towards the rocky shores and back out again. I marked the areas I'd covered on my submersible chart. It was tiring work which wasn't surprising considering the strong currents I had to swim against. I decided to take a break and warm my bones with a hot cup of tea mixed with a tot of paddy's whiskey. I pulled the rope four times to indicate to Shamus that I was coming to the surface. I began the surfacing procedure with the utmost of care and if I were to apply the wrong application on my return to the surface, I would have ended up inside a decompression chamber with the bends, and that's not regarded as having a thumping headache but more in line as a close to death experience. I should know because I've been there before.

It was ten years ago now and it hadn't been through stupidity that I'd surfaced too quickly and found myself abandoned inside the scary atmosphere of a decompression chamber. But it wasn't as scary as having a great white shark bearing in on me, forcing me to swim for my life. The choice I made was simple. I'd rather experience the agonizing bends than have half my limbs shredded with a set of razor sharp teeth. Apart from that one unfortunate incident of the bends, my competence in scuba-diving was down to being taught under the guidance and supervision of the great Jacque-Yves Cousteau and his simple application: never allow yourself to ascend faster than your last air bubble. *Watch the bubbles or you will suffer*, he used to harp on...

When I broke the surface, Shamus's large hand was there to haul me aboard. I removed my facemask. Shamus stood there with a cocky grin on his red veined face.

"Now didn't Shamus O'Malley say there wasn't anything of interest down there, Shacks, sir?"

I removed my aqualung. "Take that smug look off your face, Shamus. I haven't finished the search yet."

"O' well, I be thinking how boring it must be looking for the mysterious one. If yer fancy a change, I'd noticed a shoal of fish off the portside. We'll catch a pan-full that I promise."

"Sod off, Shamus! I'll take a two hour rest, change of tanks and I'll make a second dive. Where's Hamer gone?"

"He's down below, Shacks sir; from under my feet."

"Better join him while you make a mug of tea. And don't be selfish with the added whiskey or else I'll dock your wages."

*

In less than two hours I was back down beneath the murkiness of the bay scavenging the seabed once more, swimming in a cross-directional search pattern, interweaving through the vegetation, with small playful fish darting across the torch beam in a game of dare. I checked meticulously every conceivable object large or small that was encrusted with sea-life in-case the submarine had exploded and fragmented over the seabed. Up-turned everything and frustratingly I found nothing remotely resembling even a scrap of submarine.

I stretched my search area further left, approximately the size of half a football field. Frustrating as it was turning out to be, it's moments like this when some searchers would be ready for chucking in the towel; that self doubt tapping the back of their skull that they were wasting time and effort. I'd never reached that stage yet but I was getting rather close to quitting myself.

My overall assessments had me thinking I was looking in the wrong place. Not my fault entirely. It stands to reason that a submarine the size of the I-52 just doesn't evaporate to metal filings unless it had been lost for a thousand years. There would be pieces scattered along the seabed; big pieces that wouldn't need even an underwater metal detector to locate. Maybe Shamus was right after all and there would be nothing to find. Perhaps he knew more than he was telling me and was quite happy to leave me to my own devices. It stands to reason that the longer I'm unsuccessful the more he's paid. I wondered if Shamus was playing the artful dodger underneath his jovial expression. Or perhaps I was just deflecting my own failures on Shamus which was unfair to him.

I snapped out of my negative thoughts quickly. I was no quitter and I wasn't about to begin now. My success in finding objects was down purely to perseverance; that and the thrill of the challenge. And if I were to falter in the belief of my abilities I now had the back-up to drive me on: Tommy and Lens, and the horrific way they died.

I was back into my swimming, concentrating and focusing on the seabed. I'd covered a fair section when I felt the first signs of fatigue beginning to slow me down. I checked my air gauge, my aqualung was showing low. I twisted to make one last run and was about to kick out the fins when something caught my eye.

I floated over a section of seabed vegetation which I'd noticed was behaving in an abnormal pattern; swaying differently to the rest of the surrounding vegetation

So minute the deviation, that at first I thought it was an optical illusion, that was, until I viewed it from three different angles to confirm the phenomenon. The clumps of long sea grasses definitely swayed in the opposite direction than the surrounding forms of mixed vegetation. In theory, the sea grass was being pulled towards the shore, as if in some sort of slipstream. I swam down amongst the swaying grasses. The current was stronger in this area; a sort of vortex. I could physically feel an ebbing flow, to and fro, like the waves crashing against the shoreline of a rocky beach. Using the palm of my hand I traced the flow towards the rock face and came across a large split in the rocks which, strangely, reminded me of a giant woman's vagina on the verge of penetration. The split rock was approximately two feet wide at its centre point before narrowing at the top and bottom of its approximate four feet in length. It was nowhere near wide enough for me to squeeze through to investigate there and then. I shone the torch beam through the gap and into a fissure, the light losing its way the deeper it penetrated, and I did get the impression that the fissure widened the further it went.

I dwindled over a few possibilities: the time scale and strenuous effort it would take to widen the split in the rock to fit my frame through? And what would I find on the other side if there was another side to discover?

I'd plenty to think about as I swam away from the rock face a short distance and surveyed it at another angle. I floated there, seeing an alternative picture. I got the impression that at sometime in the past that particular part of the rock face had been the opening to an underwater cave and an eruption of great magnitude had caused a rock fall which eventually covered the entrance. Right or wrong, whichever outcome, it needed checking. I'd strong urges now, the same urges and tingles I get when I'm close to finding lost treasure in the vastness of an open field, and that in built directional finder I had was at it again.

I considered what options I had for enlarging the gap. Other than a mechanical digger or a few sticks of underwater explosives, I guessed I'd be limited to a long, strong steel engineers lever, and even then there could be repercussions, as I had no way of knowing if my actions would cause a subsidence that could endanger my life. To understand the principals of what I intended to do, it would require a second opinion from an expert, but that would take time, involve more people, and attract too much attention to myself and it was the attention I was trying to avoid.

I studied the terrain intensely, shining the torch beam up and down, following the cracks and crevices of the rock-face. I finally came to the conclusion that the formation of the rocks around that particular area was the result of a severe disturbance sometime in the past. When in the past I wasn't sure about. I marked the area on my chart and kicked for the surface because at that precise moment my safety line was pulled four times: come up!

Back on board, Shamus shouted in my ear as if he assumed that being below water made you deaf for a while. "Weather's changing for worse, Shacks sir."

I flicked my head towards Hamer who was now sitting in the wheelhouse. "It's not the only thing that's changing," I grinned.

"He's in a bad state, Shacks, sir. I don't think the idea of him coming along was a good choice."

"O yes it was," I winked.

I glanced up at the darkening skies and felt the sudden rush of a strengthening wind. The crack of lightening far to the West encouraged me to shape myself and quickly squeezed out of my diving gear while I talked to Shamus. "Do you know if there are any charted underwater caves around Clear Island?"

Shamus rubbed the bristles on his chin in thought. "I wouldn't be sure of that. I've never been one for diving meself, Shacks, sir."

"So the possibility's there then?"

"We could take a peek into maritime records, Shacks, sir. Maybe ask the locals around the harbour. And there's a diving school a couple of miles out of Baltimore. We could ask them."

"I'd rather not involve anybody else at this time."

"Yer found something, haven't yer?"

"I'm not sure what I've found, Shamus. But I'll know better on the next dive."

Hamer disturbed us when he poked his head out of the wheelhouse; death had almost caught up with him He didn't look at all well, but he still had a sense of humour when he said, "You still with us, Speed? I came to see you drown and you're disappointing me."

"Why don't you accompany me on my next dive? There's nothing like a close encounter to witness a drowning man. You could ensure I'd drowned if you held me under water until I ran out of air."

"I'd savour the moment, Speed! Only how the fuck am I expected to get back to shore; you know I'm a lousy swimmer?"

"Yes, there is that scenario. You might also want to consider this: what if the boat sinks before we get back to Baltimore?"

Hamer did consider the possibility and took it badly. He dashed to the portside and promptly vomited into the sea. I pulled a squeamish expression, and who could blame me after I saw what Hamer had just ejected over the side.

The return journey to Baltimore harbour turned out to be an absolute nightmare with the heavy swell challenging the *Muff's* durability. None of the conditions bothered Shamus in the slightest; in fact he looked like he was enjoying the occasion immensely. I soldiered on with the pretence that nothing bothered me. Hamer, as it was, disappointed me considering how he'd bragged about his toughness. The sea definitely wasn't for him.

I looked away and beyond where Hamer stood spewing. I'd caught site of what appeared to be a large fishing trawler about a half mile off our position. There's nothing sinister about a fishing vessel operating in these waters and in fairness I shouldn't have had any concerns, but I had. The trawler gave me the distinct impression that it was shadowing us. I couldn't be rightly sure and there was nothing to suggest that the trawler showed interest in the *Muff*. If anything the trawler was probably and wisely heading for the safety of Baltimore to shelter from the storm, as we were.

Still, there was something pecking away at my skull trying to get to my brain. The more I observed the trawler, the more I found the whole set-up strange, though I couldn't quite work out what was missing from the scene. And I would have expected a ship of that size to have the horsepower to stretch its distance between itself and the *Muff* instead of maintaining equal knots.

I grabbed a pair of binoculars and went out on deck to check the trawler over. I remembered I'd seen the trawler before, anchored just outside Baltimore harbour that morning. When the binoculars fell on the bridge of the trawler my suspicions were proven right. I was literally staring into another set of binoculars. We were under observation. The problem was, the distance between the two vessels made identification of the watcher difficult for me. The situation reminded me of the cold war days when Russian trawlers use to stalk Navy ships. I say Russian because the trawler was flying a Russian flag.

I went back inside the wheelhouse and gave Shamus a nudge to distract him from his concentration, shoving the binoculars in hand. "What do you make of that trawler off the starboard bow?"

Shamus rammed the glasses hard into his deeply wrinkled eye-sockets. "She's not a regular at Baltimore, Shacks sir. And she isn't there for the fishing."

"How can you tell that?"

"She carries no nets, Shacks sir."

I snatched the binoculars back and looked for myself. He was right. "She's been with us all day, I'm sure.

"That she has, Shacks sir."

"Then I'm not imagining the trawlers tagging us?"

"That she is, Shacks sir."

"You noticed too?"

"Wouldn't be much of a seaman if I didn't, now would I, Shacks sir. Should I change course? Give her a once over."

"Shamus, you're on my wavelength."

Shamus spun the wheel and angled the *Muff* towards the ship, as if on a collision course.

In between swallowing bile, Hamer chirped up. "What's going on?"

"We're sightseeing," I told him.

"Fuck the sightseeing! Get me back to shore! I need to lie down for a while."

"The cabin bunk is for the mentally sick."

"Ha-fucking-ha, Speed," Hamer said dully. "I want to lie down on something that doesn't move."

Hamer twisted his head and wretched, unleashing a torrent of indescribable fluid into a plastic bucket Shamus had found for him, all of which even made my stomach tighten.

"I did warn you it would be rough out in the bay," I told Hamer harshly.

"I've…" He gagged. "I've never suffered like this before. I've got food poisoning."

"More like you were too greedy at breakfast."

I left Hamer alone to battle with his stomach problems and continued my observation of the Russian trawler. On approaching the trawler I noticed Shamus had a sudden cob-on, but to be perfectly honest I suspected something had been bothering him for a while.

"What's wrong, Shamus, you've gone quiet?" I asked him.

He flicked his head towards Hamer and then whispered to me. "What's *gut churner* hanging around fer? You shouldn't have brought him along. He makes me nervous. There's something about him I don't trust. He should *beggar off* back to whence he came."

I kept my voice low too. "Don't concern yourself with him. He thinks I need protecting from a couple of villains."

"In his state, Shacks sir, I'd be a little concerned if he were watching my rear."

"You steer the boat, Shamus and forget about Hamer."

Shamus brought the *Muff* round in an arc and straightened the bow until we were parallel with the trawler, keeping a reasonably safe distance as we chugged along in an attempt to catch her. I managed to glimpse the Trawler's name on its bow; *Flying Fish*.

What I found strange was the lack of attention from the rest of the ships crew. Apart from the watcher, who had now disappeared, not one other face peered over the side for a curious look. I would have thought we were worth at least one interested glance. Not wanting to give the impression that we'd sussed the trawler, if a crewman had decided to make an effort, I signalled to Shamus to steer the *Muff* away.

I went astern, mainly to get away from Hamer and his horrible gagging sounds he continued to make when he thought he was about to vomit. I found a space to sit and to reflect on the entire episode so far; to assess the information I'd gathered which wasn't very much, but it certainly amounted to a lot more than I had yesterday. I thought again on what method I should use to excavate the split I'd discovered in the rock face beneath Roaring Water Bay. I wondered how thick the rock would be and the length of time it would take me to create an opening. I decided against the use of air powered tools as that would take time to set up for action. Another alternative would be explosives but that would require the expertise of an underwater rock blaster, which was never going to happen. It left me the only possible answer: physical force and the use of an engineers levering bar. Not that there would be any guarantee of success, more of an increase of danger to myself if I'm honest. And if I was to accidentally cause an underwater rock fall then I could be trapped or even worse crushed to death. It would mean I would have to depend entirely on Hamer to raise the alarm. I would have preferred to be more dependent on Shamus but I think he'd have panicked beyond sensibility if he knew I was in trouble. Hamer would be better equipped to arrange a rescue. Used a calmer approach because he'd have been in no rush to save me straightaway. He'd have probably wanted me to suffer first before he started swinging his badge of authority. Yes, he could certainly help me tremendously in that department. That's providing I haven't sent Hamer insane before the jobs finished.

*

Back at the harbour we secured the *Muff*. Hamer seemed to make a remarkable recovery the minute his feet touched solid ground. Without a word he toddled off in the direction of our hotel and I wasn't far behind him.

I collected my room key from reception and was also given an envelope with my name neatly hand written on the front. And even though I hadn't advertised my whereabouts, I'd suddenly become very popular in these parts of Ireland. Hamer had warned me that if he could find me easily then others could follow; he wasn't fibbing. And then again, what had I to fear? I doubt very much if anyone, who had hostile intentions against me, would want to leave me a warning of their presence. That didn't mean I should drop my guard. I had to be positive I was safe from harm, regardless.

I studied the exterior of the envelope with interest. My name was spelled correctly, so the writer knew me. No address, no stamp or any other mark, which suggested the letter, had been delivered personally. I attracted the spectacled fellow on reception who had given me the envelope and called him over. I asked, quietly, "Did you see who delivered this letter?"

"O yes sir, a very fine looking Lady." He winked at me as if he understood that I'd some sort of sexual rendezvous unfolding.

I said snappily, "What did this woman look like; was she young, old?"

His eyes lifted in a gazed look. "Do you know, sir, I'm not quite sure."

"Would this *you're not too sure* have anything to do with you were too busy looking at her tits and arse?"

His cheeks reddened, his eyes flicking in all directions searching for listening ears. "Now you've put it that way, sir, I must admit both parts were a most appreciable sight. And she was wearing sunglasses."

"Dark glasses no doubt?" I humoured without smiling.

"Designer too," he added.

"How observant you were. What about the colour of her hair?"

"Blonde! No-let me think- more a reddish blonde, if such a colour exists. Short cropped too, boyish style."

"Anything distinctive she was wearing?"

"A pair of tight jeans comes to mind."

"How long ago was the letter delivered?"

"Quite recently, maybe fifteen not twenty minutes ago."

"Is she still on the premises?"

"No, Mister Speed. I watched her leave."

"Was that every step of the way?"

He frowned with uncertainty. "I'm sorry?"

"You followed her arse as she left," I said casually.

"Guilty as charged, Mister Speed. It was just a discreet, gentlemanly glance, to watch poetry in motion."

His eyes lifted again. "Then spell bound, you ask yourself, how can-"

"Something so full of shit can look so beautiful!" I intervened.

Dream boy expressed his disgust in me for such a tasteless remark. "Not quite what I had in mind, Mister Speed."

"Did you notice what direction she took when she left the hotel; right or left?" I was thinking of going after her.

"I was interrupted by a guest attending the counter at the time."

I nodded my thanks and moved away from the reception desk, revolving the letter full circle, and thinking about its credibility. I wondered if I'd an admirer in the hotel. The woman the other night staring across at me while I was having dinner with Hamer came to mind. Perhaps the letter was an invitation for a rendezvous? But that was wishful thinking because I hadn't seen the woman since.

I examined the envelope thoroughly because my instincts told me it might be a letter bomb. I stopped twirling the envelope around and held it more delicately and contemplated whether to throw it down to the floor and run like hell. I held my nerve, mainly because I remembered that letter bombs only explode when opened. The envelope was of quality paper, not the thin cheap brand that comes wrapped, twenty for a pound. The envelope had class, bought from an expensive store. I fingered the contents inside the envelope, feeling for any unusual lumps of putty like material, wires, bi-metal strips, things I would have expected if it were a bomb. But there was nothing lumpy or squashy and satisfied my fingers wouldn't be blown off, I opened the envelope and removed the folded piece of paper I found inside. Again the quality of the paper signified upper class connections. I unfolded the paper. Nothing exploded but the words in the letter had the same effect as if a bomb had just exploded in my face.

Dear, Mister Shackleton Speed.

I write this letter of introduction in anticipation that you will do me the honour of accepting an invitation to grace my humble home with your presence. I would have dearly enjoyed the journey to the South of Ireland to meet you personally, but unfortunately due to illness I'm unable to travel. We have a lot to discuss about the past, about the crashed plane in Berkshire, which I should imagine will fascinate your appetite for the truth, because it is indeed the truth you seek. If you are wondering how I know so much about you and where you are staying it is because of the information I received alerting me to your presence in the Republic of Ireland. I will understand if you totally ignore this letter and do not make the journey. If you do decide to accept the invitation then you will not be disappointed. If it is the unknown you fear then let me stress that your safety will be guaranteed at all times. If I have calculated the kind of man you are, Mister Speed, I think the inquisitive side of you will not resist the challenge.

I do hope you will join me. Overleaf you will find a return ticket to Dublin and the time and place where my representative will meet you.

This is no hoax, I assure you, Mister Speed. Nor will there be any sort of entrapment if you do accept my offer. My intentions are honourable and sincere.

Yours sincerely
Chief Air Marshall Sir Dillon Deveron. (Retired)

My eyes lifted from the letter in sheer disbelief, staring ahead into nothingness, blanking everything that passed before me. The first thing that struck me was how the hell did Deveron know I was here in Baltimore? How would he have known I was looking for him? Hamer came to mind. That the crafty bastard had indeed located Deveron and had warned him I was looking for him; military men sticking together syndrome. Frigging hell! You can't trust anybody to keep quiet. And Deveron mentioned Berkshire in his letter. I wondered if he knew that I was aware of his deadly past. How though? Only I and Billy Slade knew that deadly sin. Did he also think that I suspected him of being involved with the deaths of Tommy and Lens? If so, then the situation had reversed. Now the hunted had turned into the hunter and I didn't know if that was a good omen or a bad omen and where it exactly left me now that my cover was blown sky-high.

I'd now become the prime target from all sides. I quickly weighed up the risks if I were to accept his invitation. I'd be heading into the unknown with the disadvantage of a blind person walking along a pitch black alleyway with cotton wool stuffed inside their ears, for starters.

Could I trust Deveron to keep his word and guarantee me the safe passage that he'd promised? I wasn't sure. Was Deveron involved with McClusky's operation? It pointed that way. And then there was Love and Hate and their connection with Deveron. And to really mix Deveron in the affray, didn't Commander Harris Morgan suspect someone in Whitehall was stealing the files regarding the Berkshire wreck? Deveron was connected to Whitehall during his career and he probably still has a strong influence within the military.

Deveron could have had an abundance of information placed in front of him with the click of his fingers.

Now Deveron openly wants to meet me.

The plot thickens.

It left me pondering on one serious question: could I really trust Deveron?

The answer was simple and clear: could I frigging hell as like!

If I'd any sense of self preservation I should have hotfooted out of Baltimore and proceeded to relocate my base camp elsewhere, and done in the next five minutes. But Deveron had been right about my curiosity never fails to get the better of me, and that carrot he'd dangled in front of my nose was a tempting offer. Then I'd to consider why I was here in the first place. It wasn't just about finding Japanese gold. Deveron had to be dealt with firsthand. I couldn't let Deveron weasel his way out from his evil past. He was a murderer on all accounts. He'd murdered Craven in 1944 and somehow he was connected to the deaths of Tommy and Lens. No. Deveron had questions to answer; incriminating, awkward questions that should make him squirm with guilt. Frigging hell, he owed me a huge explanation. He had the answers to the demons that were running havoc inside my head, and I didn't care how old he was or what army he would have standing in front of him for protection, I'd still throttle the frigging bastard till he squealed the truth.

I rang mobile to mobile and contacted Shamus to explain that I wouldn't need him tomorrow. By the sounds he was making when he mumbled down the line, 'hullo', he was obviously munching on a bag of his favourite dried pork pieces.

"Is there any particular reason, Shacks sir?"

I sensed he thought he might be losing a client, but I didn't want to relay too much information to him for a number of reasons. I told him as much as he needed to know. "I'm going to see someone."

He didn't pressurize me for a name. "Will it be for long, Shacks sir?"

"I'm not sure. Don't worry the payment meter is still running. If for some unforeseen circumstances that I don't return, feel free to sell my diving gear."

"O no, Shacks, sir, I couldn't do that. What about the Hamer fella?"

"Sell him too!"

"No, Shacks sir, I meant what if he comes pestering me?"

"Why should he?"

"He's a nosey bastard, isn't he?"

"That's true, Shamus."

"Do you want me to tell him your business?"

"No. Let him sweat. Tell him I've disappeared from the face of the earth."

"Won't that make him angry, Shacks sir?"

"Naturally, but he operates better when he worries over me."

"Yer can be a bit of a bastard when you want to, if you don't mind me saying, Shacks sir."

"Yes Shamus, I can be a real bastard when I want. And while you're doing nothing and idling about on my time, you can find out information on the *Flying Fish*. I want to know what it's doing in Baltimore."

Chapter Sixteen

I dressed casual, nothing too impressive: driving jacket, round necked sweater, and a pair of slacks and comfortable shoes. I left a message at reception to say that if anybody came looking for me, I'd be away for the day and possibly the evening too, thinking I might stop at a hotel if I'm too tired to travel back.

I drove to the railway station at Cork and parked the Roadster on the long stay car park, used the ticket Deveron sent me and boarded the train for Dublin. There was plenty to think about during the journey. Hard thinking that produces the inevitable headache. Here I was hurtling towards Dublin not knowing what to expect and my only source for protection was a letter assuring my safety from a man who I had never seen before; a man I secretly despised for a number of reasons; a man who had escaped the gallows in 1944.

There was also the strong probability I was walking into a trap and the killers searching for me may even be waiting for me at the end of the line. Yes, it was hard to relax when knowingly going to a place with the same intention of raiding honey from a bee-hive and expecting not to get stung because you're not wearing the appropriate protective clothing; mine should have been a military tank.

*

Somehow I slept for the latter half of the journey only stirring when the train approached Dublin. I sat up straight and rubbed the sleep from my eyes. Within seconds I was focused again on the reasons for the train journey. And then I experienced my first concern of the day which actually frightened me.

I was calm. Some super cool character when I should have been twitching with nervousness. Not even a tingle in the stomach region. No apprehension whatsoever. I'd arrived at my destination with the accolade of a fearless warrior ready to take on whatever they threw at me. I'd no idea how I'd adopted such nerves of steel, though I probably had always possessed that toughness but had never really noticed before.

I stayed in my seat as the train pulled in at Tara Street Station. I didn't rush to disembark. I carefully observed anyone who remotely appeared to be observing my presence. No one did. When I was the last person on the train I left the carriage, vacated the station and walked down towards the River Liffey, glancing back a few times to see if I had picked up a follower from the station. I turned left into Burgh Quay. I followed the river upstream. With another quick glance over my shoulder, I walked with pace onto Aston Quay until I had reached the painted steel construction of the Ha'penny Bridge arching over to the north side of the River.

I could see why Deveron had chosen this particular iron bridge construction as a meeting point, as it wasn't the ideal place for me to spring a trap, if I had wanted to. They could watch me from a comfortable distance; the first sign of trouble and they could walk away unchallenged. I moved onto the bridge, made my way to the middle where I stopped, as instructed in the letter from Deveron, and waited for my contact.

I soon grew impatient after ten minutes had lapsed. I've never been a good waiter of time. I wasn't clock watching intentionally, just sending myself daft as I glanced at every person that passed me by, half expecting one of them to approach me. I turned round and placed my arms through the gaps in the bridge railings and leaned lazily on them, staring down into the flowing river, focusing on the reflection of the bridge but still observing from the corners of my eyes the shadows of people passing by and still waiting for one to stop behind me.

The waiting game allows you to think and my thoughts drifted back to the rock face deep below Roaring Water Bay. I debated whether I should reconsider the use of air powered tools to dislodge the rock-face. And then I thought of the disadvantage of trying to handle heavy gear beneath the rampant sea without a full team and quickly dismissed the idea. It would be the manual effort or...

"Well, well, well, Shackleton Speed, your ass hasn't changed a bit!"

I jolted upright. That voice? I spun round to face the woman's beckoning voice and my heart bounced so irregular that it nearly popped out of my mouth. It was her again! The very same American terrorist I'd encountered at McClusky's warehouse in London. It was the bitch herself and she was in cahoots with Deveron. She'd changed her hair colour somewhat to a strain of strawberry blonde. And by the description given at the hotel reception, I was looking at the very same short cropped strawberry blonde woman who hand delivered the letter from Deveron to my hotel. My eyes frantically scanned the bridge for her accomplices. She was quick to read my mind.

"Don't worry yourself, I'm alone."

I quickly recovered from the shock of meeting her again. "Aren't you the confident one," I scorned.

"I'm confident for a number of reasons, Buster! So don't even consider threatening me for whatever you blame me for," she warned me with acute calmness, so I assumed she wasn't bluffing.

I'm not renowned for bullying women but I did found it hard to restrain myself from exploding in a fit anger right there on the bridge. In my opinion she deserved nothing less than to be thrown over my knee and have her arse spanked in public view, and that was being kind.

I said, "Every dog has his day."

"You've lost me, Buster."

"You've easily forgotten the rough reception I received when we first met. And you left me sexually frustrated. And I almost got killed at McClusky's warehouse."

"What have you to complain about, Buster? You came out in one piece didn't you?"

"Yes, by the skin of my teeth and the rags on my back!" I snapped.

"You chose the wrong time to visit McClusky's. That was your fault not ours. So forget any schemes of retaliation you have planned."

"What and spoil the surprise I've in store for you."

"I suggest you forget any surprises? This bulge in my right hand pocket isn't just my hand keeping warm. I'm holding a small calibre hand gun; a Derringer actually, yet sufficient, I promise, to drop a full grown pig, human or animal."

She did indeed have her hand clasped around something bulky inside her jacket pocket. I couldn't tell if there was a gun present and I wasn't prepared to gamble to find out, at least not at that precise moment. If anything she interested me. There was something about her that I couldn't fathom.

I said with a touch of sarcasm, "What are the odds that you don't have an up-to-date gun licence?"

"Who's checking?"

"What happened to the frigging promise of immunity from death?"

"That's providing you keep your hands to yourself."

"I intend to, for the time being," I conceded.

There was a glint of uncertainty in her eyes.

"I promise," I reassured her.

"Follow me. I'll take you to Deveron."

"Suppose you tell me what Deveron wants or is your leader unlikely to divulge such secrets to an underling such as yourself?"

"I should imagine Deveron will explain everything to you in good time."

She turned to go.

"It's impossible for me to go with you."

She stopped and looked searchingly into my face. "You've changed your mind?"

"No, I'm concerned."

"Is it because of me?"

"Partly; I was always warned not to go off with strangers. As you have the advantage of knowing my name, how about telling me yours. I can't keep calling you bitch. Can I?"

She took the insult admirably calm. "Shayna Magginty, now can we go?"

With a wave of my hand, I said, "Lead the way, Shayna."

In spite of my initial shock at seeing her again, I definitely preferred her company than that of an old codger. There was also another point I wanted to take up with her as we crossed the bridge to the North side.

"How come I seem to have a large flashing beacon on top of my head?"

"What's that suppose to mean?"

"Well assessing the enormous size of the Irish Republic; and the estimated half a million visitors presently in the South of Ireland; how the hell did you know where I would be?"

"We've certain resources available to us. No one is untraceable."

"Are you sure about that, Shayna? I know of a fellow by the name of Lord Lucan who might just question your theory that nobody's untraceable; that's if he were to come out of hiding and tell us his secret. But that still doesn't tell me who betrayed my whereabouts?"

"Does it really matter how?"

"Yes, it frigging does!"

"Do you really expect me to divulge our operating capabilities? It may surprise you that we have a highly organized network of intelligence. And it might doubly surprise you, Buster that Irish people are not thick paddies as some people like to think."

"You're an American!"

"Irish-American," she corrected me, waspishly.

"Is that so Shayna? Didn't know much what McClusky was up too, this power of the organization shit, until it was too late."

She almost bit my head off. "Different matter!" she snapped. "McClusky was a double crossing bastard, correction, a dead double crossing bastard."

"Yes I'd heard he'd been killed in a gang war," I said. "It was headline news in every London paper. Dead people left everywhere."

"We took no casualties." There was pride in her tone.

"Didn't happen to come across two ugly bastards, who looked like vultures, during your gunfight?"

"We hardly hung about for an identity parade. Our business was concluded. We fought our way out of the warehouse and came straight back to Ireland."

"Empty handed too. That's not good business killing off your supplier."

She ignored me.

"As a matter of interest where are those inept bastards you call your brothers-in-arms? Especially the spotty faced one with the darts. I want to meet him again on equal terms"

"I'd be careful what you say. It's possible you might just do that."

"Is that a threat, Shayna? Only I've been practicing with my own set of darts; mine are called a bow and arrow."

She was impervious to my challenge.

I said, "So how did you get involved in terrorism? Or should I be asking, what persuaded you to turn into a cold blooded killer?"

She stopped at a yellow two-seater Mazda sports car. "You ask too many questions, Shackleton Speed."

"I'm interested."

"Don't be."

I nodded towards her car. "Impressive," I said. "I thought my criminal ways paid well but terrorism pays extremely better."

She wasn't amused. "Get in!"

I didn't argue. I clambered into the passenger seat and snapped on the seatbelt just before the engine roared and the car accelerated away with awesome power. She handled the car impeccably. She liked to race too. I judged that by the way she'd little respect for the road speed restrictions. She was my kind of woman; fast in all departments.

We left Dublin and headed south along the N11 coastal road. We weren't followed and if we had, I doubted that Team Ferrari would have kept up with us. I enjoyed the thrill of the ride as she crashed through the gears, which I know really pissed her off because I think it was her intention to scare the hell out of me with her erratic driving.

I said casually, "Did you find what you were looking for in my hotel room?"

She wasn't at all surprised by what I said. "What gives you the impression I was in your room? I came to deliver a letter."

"And you paid a visit to my room the other day too."

"That bump on your head has sent you crazy."

"The perfume you wear, Shayna, it's nice, but a dead giveaway. The smell choked my room."

"You've got the wrong woman, Buster!"

"What were you looking for when you rummaged through my belongings?"

"Don't be ridiculous."

"I know you did."

"Have you any proof?"

"I don't need proof, Shayna." I leaned forward so I could see the corners of her eyes. "Do you realize your eyes twinkle like two diamonds when you lie?"

"That's pathetic!" But she automatically tilted and looked in the rear view mirror. "My eyes have always sparkled. It's the amount of vitamins I take."

"Then how do you explain the smell of your perfume lingering inside my room."

"I was never in your room, period Buster!"

"You're wearing the same perfume now. Jean Paul Gautier 'Classique'."

"So you have a nose for perfume. Been around a few wearers, have you?"

I smiled impishly. "Do I detect a touch of jealousy?"

She expressed her revulsion with such a notion. "You're being ridiculous again."

"Anyway you disappoint me greatly, Shayna."

She dropped down a gear and eased the car through a sharp bend. "Why's that?"

"Well to have the audacity to sneak into a man's room and not wait in bed for him. It's shameful."

"Your mind is one tracked and disgusting."

"That's frigging heavy coming from you. I seem to recall you taking advantage of a defenceless me when I was strung up at that remote farmhouse."

"That's a woman's prerogative to do as she feels. I told you that at the time."

I jolted upright in my seat. "Hang on a minute. If the roles had been changed you would have been crying rape and I would have been clapped in irons."

She shook her head. "Wrong, Buster," and in a flash she had taken the gun from her pocket and angled it at my stomach while trying to focus on me and the road. "I wouldn't be crying rape, I'd be saying this bitch bites back twice as hard, then I would have shot your balls off."

"I believe you would be that nasty. Do watch the road, Shayna," I said calmly, and she just corrected the car's path as it nearly collided with a horn blaring oncoming truck. I never flinched once

"So where are we going, if it's not too much trouble to ask?"

"Yes, it is too much trouble."

She leaned forward and slipped a disc into the CD player which blasted out a Bruce Springsteen classic. I couldn't hear her singing along but her lips were moving.

I was...born in the U.S.A...I was...born in the U.S.A...'

I took the hint and snuggled down into the car seat to relax.

The remainder of the journey lacked any sort of conversation through no fault of mine, as she preferred to listen to the music. I took the opportunity to observe and memorized the route we were taking, as there was the possibility I would have to make an impromptu return in the near future.

We finally left the N11 at Kilmacanago, took the R755 to Roundhouse, turned into a dirt track road and came to a shuddering halt outside large ornate gates wedged between a stonewall of fortress proportion. A camera mounted on the gateway scanned our arrival. Shayna pressed the button on a remote control device and the automatic gates opened. And then with her customary wheel spin we drove down a tree lined drive till we reached a large stone built manor house of impressive proportions. Deveron had been saving his wages over the years of military service.

Shayna brought the Mazda to a skidding halt. I climbed out of the car and looked around in disappointment. I would have expected at least two armed burly guards to grab and throw me against the wall to search me for weapons. None showed. Surely I was worth some consideration for being dangerous? And Shayna, by her casualness, didn't see me as a threat either as she entered the house. I followed her through the entrance and into the hall, along a corridor and into a spacious study with a well stocked library. The walls were decorated with beautifully carved oak veneer with a scattering of oil painting hanging there merely for decoration than viewing.

Shayna pointed across the room to a frail, withered old man crunched up on a sturdy studded leather chair. She gave me a gentle nudge to make my way over to him and then without a word she disappeared leaving me alone with whom I considered to be a treble murderer.

My first instinct should have been to dash across the room and grab Deveron by the throat and start to squeeze the truth out of him. Yet looking at his frailty he probably wouldn't have survived even a short throttling. And then I couldn't be sure if he had already anticipated the idea and had placed a hidden marksman to stop me.

As for my first opinion of Dillon Deveron, it was hard to imagine him as a World War Two fighter pilot, doubling up as a stone-faced killer. His dried ragged facial features showed no hardness of a man capable of shooting his flying comrade in the back, as Billy Slade had witnessed. Though I saw no evidence of him actually smoking, he was wearing a smoker's jacket and a cravat. His head turned. He didn't rise to greet me.

"Ah! Mister Speed, I presume! We meet at last." Deveron's voice sounded just like a Dalek from a television series of 'Doctor Who'.

"Please, please, come closer. You must excuse me for not rising to my feet. Alas brittle bone disease rather limits my enthusiasm to walk unassisted unless absolutely necessary. Please, sit down. There are refreshments on the way."

I gestured to the surroundings. "This place must have put you back a pound or two?"

"Extravagance well earned, I can assure you, Mister Speed. And I've no wife to screw me for every penny in a messy divorce."

I sat, staring at Deveron in an attempt to understand the man. He took my staring as if I was confused about something

"No doubt you're wondering why my voice has a distorted sound, Mister Speed." He pulled the cravat he was wearing sideways to reveal a metallic object embedded in the regions of his throat, "Cancer has attacked my voice box. It's my own fault entirely; the legacy for my passion of Panamanian cigars. Without this voice-box device my speech would be useless."

"Ingenious invention," I said, not that I really cared.

"Do you smoke, Mister Speed?"

It was a mistake on Deveron's part to allow me the opportunity to criticize smoking as an occupational habit. I could have spent hours boring him to death on reasons of why smoking isn't big and isn't clever, but I decided to keep it short and simple.

"It smells like burnt wood and probably tastes just as revolting." I smiled and added, "I prefer drinking myself to death; far more enjoyable. And if you want my honest opinion, smokers are inconsiderate, self centred bastards, who insist on sharing their exhaled desire with other non-participating losers and then they are confounded when people object to having smoke blown in their faces. If I was to share my bad habit with others I end up pissing all over them."

Deveron was shocked by my bluntness. "Well... yes...I...er...see your point, Mister Speed."

"Good!" I said. "Now we've got that out of the way, you can start by telling me how you knew I was here in Ireland."

"Shayna told me, of course. She knew you were here somewhere."

"How did she know I was here?"

"I never asked how she knew. I asked her to find you. She's quite good at the huntress business."

"So she found me. Why?"

"So we can talk about WWII."

"You could have done that in a phone call to my hotel," I said sharply.

Deveron frowned. "You seem very hostile towards me, Mister Speed?"

"I hate mystery games. I also hate being dragged across Ireland for reasons beyond sensibility. So why don't you get to the point, and then I can judge whether I've had a wasted journey."

He raised his hand. "All will be revealed in good time, Mister Speed. The main thing is you're here. Shayna did marvellously well in tracking you down. She also forewarned me that your temperament might be a little volatile and that you also have an obstinate attitude." He snorted a small laugh. "She seems to know her men."

"Listen. I've little time for glad-chat."

"I neither have time on my side, Mister Speed...I'm a dying man. Old age is incurable. But I've had a fair run in life, I cannot grumble. So I would appreciate a little respect."

It couldn't have happen to a nicer man, I thought. I said, "That's unfortunate. Shall we get on with it then before you fade away?"

Deveron composed himself and went on. "I'm interested in the Spitfire that was unearthed in Berkshire, Mister Speed." He paused, probably expecting me to answer excitedly. "Shayna told me all about your discovery."

I superimposed an expression of surprise. "I've made a discovery?"

"You're teasing me, Mister Speed. Shayna said you mentioned the plane while you were engaged in riveting conversation with each other."

Either the bastard was taking the frigging piss or the bitch had neglected to tell him that the riveting conversation included the use of torture to extract the information.

"As I recall, we discussed what I'd read in the newspapers; old news is hardly riveting."

Deveron went on. "Mm, she assured me that you were the finder, Mister Speed."

"I can't see how or why I should have said that voluntarily."

"I read the papers too, Mister Speed. I did some checking myself through old colleagues at the ministry, but I must admit I was left a little confused with the results, especially by the name of the pilot found in the cockpit of the wreck. That name didn't match the name Shayna mentioned to me. How would she know about the name Craven when the name was never printed in the newspapers, Mister Speed?"

Checking with old colleagues! That statement interested me. Maybe Deveron had the missing documentation from the Whitehall archives?

"It beats me," I said, casually. "I don't recall mentioning any names during our discussion."

"I'm a little confused, Mister Speed."

"Aren't we all?"

Deveron probably thought he had me trapped, and to be truthful, I couldn't remember if I screamed out the name Craven while I was under duress, not unless Deveron was attempting to piece together things he wasn't sure about.

Deveron then showed me his darker side when he burst out angrily, "Let's stop the pretence, Mister Speed! Craven's name never made the newspapers for reasons I'm not sure of. Not that it would make any difference to you, as you were already aware of the name Craven. You could have only known that by the identity tags hung around the bones you found in the wreck."

I shrugged, expressing my innocence.

"I think you found something of deep interest at the crash site; something you didn't want to share with others. Afterwards you covered your tracks from the crash investigators by the intervention of a farmer and his dog who took the credit for the find. I'm well aware of your clashes with Customs & Excise and the Treasure Valuation Committee and I fully understand your reluctance to put yourself in the frame."

I'd heard that latter statement quite a few times recently. I never really looked at myself as an honest villain if there was ever such a person.

"Not just that, Mister Speed. I can't understand why you should keep silent about your abduction by terrorists which had nothing to do with the discovery of the Spitfire. You even managed to escape from the utter carnage that followed, and yet you kept the entire episode from the reaches of the tabloids. I should have thought you'd have jumped at the chance to tell your story to the papers, and the money the papers would have offered for such a story: 'man escapes the clutches of terrorism'. I think such a large financial contribution would inflate a dwindling bank balance."

"I don't have a dwindling bank balance."

"No, I shouldn't think a man with your reputation would be struggling for money. But you're missing the point, Mister Speed. I think you're searching for something more substantial; something that requires great distance from police interference. I'm interested to know what?"

"Vengeance is high on my agenda. And I don't want to be killing people in front of the Peelers."

Deveron smiled, obviously thinking I was jesting. "There's more than vengeance clicking away in your mind, Mister Speed. You're a treasure hunter. Am I jolting the correct nerve ends, Mister, Speed?"

"More like you're beginning to get on my nerves," I snapped.

"How is that, Mister Speed, we've only just met."

"Have we? Maybe we've only met face to face now, but what about your connection with events in London. Someone sent a couple of goons to extract information from the farmer whose field the plane was found in and tormented a photography friend of mine. Those friends of mine were eventually murdered because the killers thought they knew where a certain item could be located."

Deveron seemed puzzled by my accusation. "And you think I am involved in such wickedness?"

"You're standing deep in shit, Deveron. Let's start with the name McClusky. That's an easy Irish name for you to remember. Shayna knows all about him, so you must know him too?"

Deveron thought the name through. "I'm not familiar with a McClusky."

"Well they're all interested in a crashed Spitfire in Berkshire too."

Deveron went a shade whiter than he already was. "Mister Speed, you're making a terrible mistake. I would never be involved in such drastic circumstances. What Shayna does is her own private affair."

"That's frigging bullshit! Throughout your professional career you've created men designed to kill others. So how hard would it be for you to dig for some hired killers from the sewers of the criminal underworld to do your dirty work?"

Deveron was visibly shaking. He was no longer the confident man he probably thought he was a moment ago, though I couldn't tell if his shaking was responsible for his guilt or the fact that he was innocent.

"I've done nothing of the sort!" his tinny voice echoed in protest. "I'm not acquainted with any of those men mentioned, Mister Speed. I ordered no such instructions. Good god, man! I can't even get out of this damn chair without assistance."

"You don't need legs to issue orders."

"You're accusing the wrong person, Mister Speed."

"How come Shayna was there in London, at McClusky's place with her terrorist croakers? Now, strangely, she is here with you. One doesn't need the powers of deduction to connect a deceitful bunch of congregating warlords. Two and two make four and you have a team of professional killers from both sides of Europe."

"You're completely wrong, Mister Speed! There's no connection whatsoever between Shayna's misdoings and myself, I assure you. It is purely a Grandfather and Granddaughter relationship between us and no more. She is my illegitimate daughter's child, a grandchild I never knew I had until two years ago."

"How convenient it all sounds."

"It's the truth, Mister Speed! Because of my reluctance to marry Shayna's grandmother, she instead dashed off to America. It was only after I retired from the military that I found out all this. Sadly the daughter I didn't know died giving birth to Shayna. After I settled back in Ireland, Shayna became a regular visitor from America."

"And you let her use your home as a terrorist base?"

"I never once suspected she was an active terrorist until three months ago when a particular bunch of activists began arriving at my home. Friends, Shayna assured me, dressed in military uniforms and playing war-games. She forgot that my life was spent fighting unseen enemies. My eyes are failing but I know terrorist activity when I see one. I soon dragged the truth out of her. Alas I'm too old to dissuade her from her actions though I tried. And I certainly won't turn against her."

"She's a terrorist and terrorists kill people."

"I don't see her that way, Mister Speed. She's my angel. I can't betray her to the authorities; not now or ever. She is the only piece of life I have left in this world. In a way I admire her. She has the spirit of a true warrior, the same wild enthusiasm I had when

I was young; that same ego; a chip off the old block you might say."

"That's maybe all lovely to you, but Shayna and her band of merry terrorists subjected me to some unpleasant treatment and ruined expensive items of clothing I was wearing at the time."

"You can't blame me for that, Mister Speed. My only interest with you concerns Craven's Spitfire, and nothing else. I have no reason to send killers after you. I'm only interested in one piece of vital information, and I wouldn't get that if I was to kill the messenger; now would I?"

Deveron wasn't going to crack in a million years. He had too much going for him for me to lay the blame directly on him. Of course I could have been wrong that he was connected to the deaths of Tommy and Lens. Perhaps I hadn't been thinking straight; anger and revenge blanketing my direction. Deveron could be telling the truth, and then again, the easiest form of defence is to lie through your teeth. I do it myself regularly, but I still hadn't finished with the bastard just yet. I still had a nasty surprise waiting for him.

I said, "I may have misjudged you on the matter of my problems."

"Forget it, Mister Speed. Tell me about the Spitfire you found?"

A little subdued, I shrugged and said, "There wasn't much left of the plane, a smashed cockpit with a skeleton strapped to the seat, hardly distinguishable as an aircraft."

"I know all that, Mister Speed. I also knew the M.o.D. had released the wrong name of the exhumed pilot. Straight away I realized there was a mix-up. I knew Rowland. He flew a Spitfire Mark One. He's still out there, waiting to be found. But you would have already known that straightaway since you saw the name on the tags around the skeletons neck." Deveron's eyes widened slowly. "It was Craven's remains you found?"

"That was the name on the tags."

Deveron was thoughtful." After all these years lost, now he's returned."

"Under the name Rowland," I reminded him.

"And it's going to be difficult to change that without upsetting relatives."

"So you don't think it's wise to advise the MoD that they've made a huge mistake and they should put things in perspective?"

"What concerns me more, Mister Speed, is how the mistake was made when the tags around the body clearly stated the name Craven, as you have assured me."

"Somebody substituted the tags. And then that same somebody craftily switched the documentation that identified the two pilots."

"How can you be positive about that, Mister Speed?"

"I can't. But it would explain a great deal."

"Who could possibly be in a position to alter such things?"

"You would be, Deveron." I'd caught him cold. .Nobody would suspect a retired Chief Air Marshall."

Deveron expressed his horror. "Me! Is this a private joke or has someone put you up to this? Has Shayna anything to do with this? She's always playing practical jokes to cheer me up."

"I can't eradicate you from blame, Deveron? You still carry some whack at the MoD. You're probable part of the Stonemasons sect and got one of your comrades to change things discreetly."

"You're talking absolute nonsense, Mister Speed. There would be no need for me to conduct such a dastardly deed; none whatsoever! Where are you getting this pathetic information from? I demand to know?"

"Craven told me himself."

Deveron went whiter than white. "Craven's dead!"

"How would you know, Deveron? Did you see him die?"

"His plane crashed. He was listed as missing in action; it's in the military records for all to see. And you found him, Mister Speed. You brought him home."

"Yes I found Wing Commander Craven. You do remember your flying partner then?"

He looked at me suspiciously. "You've done some research and you're deeper in this than I imagined, Mister Speed?"

"I've been busy, put it that way. And the most conclusive slice of research was that you were Craven's escort the fatal day he went missing."

Deveron looked as if he was about to throw up. He swallowed hard. "Yes, that was the last time I saw him. I must admit I went cold and my spine tingled when I read about the plane found in the Berkshire countryside. Even then I knew it was Craven. Strangely I sensed his spiritual presence and that he'd returned to haunt me for leaving him behind. I shall have to seek forgiveness for not finding him at the time; that he never received the hero's burial he fully deserved."

"The dead don't forgive. That's left to the living. It's the living where you must seek your repentance. I'm afraid I don't make those arrangements."

The door to the study opened and a rather scrumptious looking maid came into the room carrying a tea tray. Perhaps growing old isn't too bad after all, I thought lecherously.

"Thank you, my dear!" Deveron said to her. "I've changed my mind. Can you pour me a neat, double whiskey, I think I'm going to need one to thin my blood, I'm beginning to experience high blood pressure again." He turned to me. "Can I offer you one or do you prefer tea?"

"Tea's fine."

I thought I caught a lecherous glint in Deveron's saggy eyes too as she poured the tea. She placed a cup and saucer in my hand and smiled, crossed the room to a drinks cabinet, returned with a glass of Irish whiskey for Deveron, and quietly left the room.

I swigged some tea. Deveron twisted the glass in his hand and raised it slightly.

"I think a toast is in order no thanks to you, Mister Speed. What I failed to do during my entire military career, you came along and found Craven's Spitfire within a day even if it was by sheer accident."

"It's a knack I have that doesn't come cheap."

"I'd always hoped Craven had perhaps survived the crash. Maybe he'd lost his memory and was holed up in some faraway hospital and had probably started a new life elsewhere after the war. It's been a hard burden to carry all these years that I never found my dearest friend."

I nearly choked on a mouthful of tea when he mentioned his *dearest friend*. I said casually, "Is it normal for a friend to shoot their friend in the back when they're escorting a fellow pilot on an important mission together?"

Deveron looked at me hard, his eyes widening. I thought he was on the verge of a coronary, especially when one side of his mouth dropped slightly. I noticed too that his hand was squeezing his whiskey glass in an impossible attempt to crush the thick glass. He snapped out of his temporary shock and swiftly gulped down the remnants of his drink in readiness for his defensive lies that he'd probably rehearsed a million times over the years of his guilt.

"I'm afraid you've lost me with that one, Mister Speed?" His robotic tinny voice actually sounded squeaky with fright. "What exactly are you getting at?"

"Which part of 'shoot friend in the back' are you struggling to understand, so I can clarify it for you?"

"Not one god damned word you've said! Do you know what you're implying?"

"That you shot Craven from the skies."

"That's preposterous!"

I placed my cup and saucer down on the table, as I calmly said, "Is it?"

"Most certainly it is, Mister Speed! Why would I want to do such a terrible thing to a wonderful man?"

"I think you're going to need another shot of whiskey?"

"Am I likely to need another? One's usually enough."

I never gave him time to refuse. In quick time I'd rose from my chair, snatched the glass from him, ignored his weak protest, crossed to the drinks cabinet and poured him a hefty whiskey, returned, plonked the glass back into his bony hand, and sat back down waiting for his bullshit excuses I'd given him the extra time to concoct.

"Isn't this all a little bit dramatic? I'm confused as to what you are insinuating I've done that is wrong, Mister Speed?"

"You shot down Craven's Spitfire from the sky causing him to crash."

Deveron's eyes flared. "How dare you even make the suggestion? Good god! I'm a man of integrity and honour. I fought to free the world from the might of Hitler. I put my life on the line countless times in many aerial battles during the war. A Battle of Britain war hero no less. And, may it be heard, my entire existence since the war has been devoted to serving the security of the United Kingdom."

"Oh I don't doubt your courage, old man. I'm just curious as to why your Spitfire fired on Craven's Spitfire."

"No! No! It's not true." He threw his whiskey down his throat, spilling a few drops down the side of his mouth which dripped off his chin.

"It happened all right, while you were engaged in 'Operation Huggermugger'."

Deveron cringed. "How…how on earth do you know anything about 'Huggermugger? That was a war time operation kept secret."

"I've done my research impeccably. Operation Huggermugger involved the hunt for a fictitious Japanese cargo submarine, the I-52. The submarine I-52 number two, that is. Submarine I-52 number one was sunk by the Americans in the Atlantic. Apparently, sub number two was never found; conclusion, it never existed. But Craven found it. His reconnaissance camera snapped the big Jap can. He wanted to tell the world and would have done so if he hadn't crashed after you shot his plane from the sky."

Deveron surprised me when he attempted to turn the tables on me. He pointed his crooked forefinger accusingly in my direction. "You-you thief!" he spluttered. "You took the camera from the wreck. Wait a minute! The photographer friend you mentioned. Good god! You've had the film developed. You've found what I spent a lifetime trying to locate." His eyeballs nearly squeezed from their sockets in anticipation; actual excitement in his voice and not one bit interested that I'd exposed him as a murderer. "The submarine is here in Ireland; somewhere in the regions of Roaring Water Bay. You're searching for it? God damn it you are!"

Frigging hell, I could have strangled the sod there and then. "Don't try to twist way from your guilt, Deveron. You're a treacherous sod and nothing else. You shot down a British aircraft and you killed a British pilot who put his trust in you to protect him from enemy attacks. And don't even attempt to deny it because I tracked down a witness to the incident."

Deveron frowned suspiciously. "There were no witnesses."

"I found one. The witness I located had an impeccable memory. He even described the action in graphic detail. It was a brutal attack on a defenceless craft and you were the hidden enemy."

What a frigging arsehole I'd have been if Deveron was to get a look at my star witness, the illiterate Billy Slade, re-enacting what he displayed to me back on the grounds of Three Trees.

In all honesty, I had expected Deveron to crack under the pressure because I knew I had him on that one, but he did the opposite and had another go at me instead. "I find it strange that you failed to disclose your imaginative theory to the proper authorities?"

"It's what happened and you know it."

"Am I to be blackmailed, Mister Speed? Money for silence, is that your game?"

Anger had me on the edge of my seat. "You frigging smug bastard, Deveron. Money won't bring back the lives of innocent people. But don't fret old man. I'm not here to bring you to justice and I've no intentions of being your judge and jury. You're dying anyway, so you tell me." I thought I was a bit callous with what I said, but isn't life a bitch. "I'm here to find out whether you sanctioned the killings of a farmer in Wiltshire and a photographer in London. That's my goal!"

Deveron was looking distinctly uncomfortable.

"You're perspiring, Deveron. I didn't think it was that warm in this room."

"To be accused of enticing murder does inevitably raise one's blood pressure."

"Or more like you're finding it difficult to come clean."

Deveron sighed heavily and put his glass down. His head dropped into his hands, his fingertips sinking into the sagging skin on his thin face. He raised his head slowly and his watery eyes stared into mine.

"It's no use me pretending nothing happened, Mister Speed. If I'm to die, I want to die in peace and with a clear conscience. I suppose the time for confession is now appropriate. But please believe me when I say I had nothing to do with the murder of your friends. I never ordered anyone to commit a crime of murder against anybody and that includes the farmer and photographer. The first time I heard your name mentioned was three days ago. I acted quickly. I just couldn't let the opportunity pass me by; the plane's discovery; the intrepid discoverer in arms reach. I had to have them"

I relented. "Okay, maybe you didn't have my friends murdered. But there's still the matter of Craven which you can't escape from so easily."

"This will be kept between us whatever I tell you?"

"I didn't bring a voice recorder if that's what you're asking.."

Deveron swallowed excess saliva. "I suppose for you to fully understand my actions I'd better start from my humble beginnings as a young teenage tearaway." He cleared his dry throat with a rattled cough. "Dublin was an impoverished place in the thirties. You'd to scratch for every penny possible; tighten your trouser belt to beat the hunger. I looked for a solution instead; a solution that would drag me from the gutters of human poverty. I found it in the brutal ranks of the IRA. I was a raw recruit with high ambitions and I was easily absorbed into the fascinating world of violence. Yes, Mister Speed, I too became a terrorist and without bragging I became an experienced campaigner with a list of atrocities behind me. It got me recognition within the ranks of the IRA. I wanted to stand high amongst the Irish people in the same way Michael Collins raised to infamous notoriety. I dreamed of being the hero. Desperate for the adulation and to have my fellow freedom fighters worship my achievement."

"It's all very poetic, Deveron. But you're forgetting that Michael Collins was executed for his troubles in 1922. Not the infamous notoriety I'd have craved."

"Nevertheless, Mister Speed, I'd already begun my ascent to power, only for it to be spoilt by the interference of the war. From there I had two choices: sit back all snug and safe just because Eire had declared neutrality or take up arms against the Germans on the assumption that Hitler would imminently threaten Irish shores anyway. Rather pointless Irish factions fighting the British to have a free Ireland, only for the Germans to suffocate us with fascism. I made my choice and with great reluctance I decided to join the fight against the Nazis. Naturally with fighting British ground troops for two years I declined the chance of joining the British army as a foot soldier. I signed the dotted line, took my shilling and joined the R.A.F. I'd plenty of flying time under my belt. My uncle taught me to fly in a First World War Bi-plane and the RAF was desperate for pilots with flying skills."

Deveron was beginning to bore me senseless. I needed to move things along. "I'm not interested how you sneaked your way into the air force. I want to know what happened on the day Craven went missing."

"You're not exactly renowned for a man of patience, are you, Mister Speed?"

"I know a professor who has the same opinion as you. His criticism I don't mind taking; yours is on the verge of making me erupt violently. So I'd appreciate if you got on with the tale!"

Deveron disapproved with my attitude with the shake of his head "Such deep ingrained hostility you have, Mister Speed. I have to confess you're making me a little uncomfortable."

I leaned back in my chair. "Does that make you feel better? Now what happened with Craven?"

He coughed twice. It annoyed me. If he'd have coughed a third time my fist would have followed his tongue back down his throat. "It was a routine reconnaissance flight to search for a Japanese submarine supposedly operating off the shores of England. It was difficult to absorb such a tale during briefing; a Japanese sub near our shores would never have occurred. All the pilots were of the same conclusion. That it was a clever piece of propaganda by the Japanese and Germans, especially when there were whispers of the submarine carrying gold. Orders were orders and you have to follow them. Craven flew his reconnaissance Spitfire and since there was still the threat of a marauding German Messerschmitt operating in the skies, I was his wing protection escort.

"During our flight my Spitfire developed engine trouble, miss-firing. It slowed me down. As for Craven he didn't hang around just for me to limp along. He was off like a rampaging bull with wings. Anyone with a decent enough engine would have had trouble flying alongside his craft, his Spitfire being lighter because a reconnaissance craft required speed and agility and all nonessential equipment was stripped out for more speed. The RAF turned the damned Spitfire into a shell; a flying coffin. It needed a courageous man to fly such a machine over occupied territory. Some pilots failed to return. Craven always did. He seemed invincible. His exceptional flying skills always guided him through the barrage of hostilities."

"You sound as if you were bitter towards him?"

"I admit I was jealous of his popularity, Mister Speed."

"So you killed him?"

"It wasn't premeditated."

"It certainly wasn't an accident."

"If you allow me to explain a little more, you may come to understand my fall from grace, Mister Speed."

I expressed his continuation with a slight wave of my hand. "Please do, Deveron. This should be interesting."

"As I was saying, I'd lost contact with Craven because of his Maverick flying. We had no air-wave communication between us, Craven's communication equipment having been removed to lighten his Spitfire.

When I finally located him, he was on his way back to the airfield, all smiles, giving me the thumbs up. I realized then that he'd located the submarine, actually seen the damn contraption and he'd captured it all on film. We'd developed hand signals to communicate between ourselves and Craven verified my assumption and signalled that the submarine had been crippled and was sinking. He just didn't say where it lay or what had caused the submarine to start sinking.

"At that moment something inside me snapped. Craven was ahead of my wing. All of a sudden I found myself in a different world; in a different time warp. All I saw in front of my gun sights was enemy aircraft carrying important information that I wanted. I suddenly hated Craven for being the hero he would be once he returned to Duxford. My thoughts switched to the counties of Ireland and the freedom my brothers in arms yearned for. I was thinking of another war and not the one we were presently engaged in. My mind had wandered back to Ireland. I thought of the gold bullion aboard the Japanese submarine and how it could be used to ensure our battle to free Ireland from British occupation once the war had finished."

"You couldn't possibly have known then that British soldiers would have been redeployed back in Ireland after the war."

"It doesn't matter what I thought at the time. It happened. In that moment of sheer madness my mind was possessed with sheer hatred. Right there in front of me was my dream of greatness and I had to stop it reaching enemy hands. I opened both guns on Craven's Spitfire. I couldn't stop myself. I remember being mesmerised by the perfect line of tracers as the bullets rattled out in cohesion. (By his expression I guessed Deveron was reliving the moment.) I hit Craven's plane with everything I had. I watched his Spitfire go into a dive; watched him struggle to control his plane, a wisp of black smoke trailing behind him. I'd intended to follow his plane down to pinpoint the crash site, and then land, so I could retrieve the cameras from Craven's plane. Alas fate played its part. My Spit's engine began playing up again. I had to deviate and quickly find somewhere suitable to land safely should the engine fail. It was pointless me crashing too. By the time my engine had recovered its capabilities, Craven had disappeared from sight. I searched for the crash site but with the night closing in fast, I had to abandon the search. The rest is history and I've wasted a lifetime searching for him since."

Deveron hung his head in shame.

I had the same amount of pity for Deveron as I would have had for a wasp that had just stung me; I'd have flattened the insect, ripped its wings off and thrown it into the nearest spider's web. I wasn't about to let him off the hook. I said, harshly. "People had crazy ideas during the war but yours was the bottom of the shit pile, Deveron."

"I know that, Mister Speed. If I could have been spared a second chance to relive the moment I might have gone in a different direction. But it happened. I can't change that now. Yet there is one important point I wish to state here and now though it probably sounds rather trivial. In my capacity as a high ranking officer in the British military, I never once passed on information to the IRA, or any other terrorist group that could have jeopardized the lives of any man, woman or child or military personal. I could have quite easily done the deed but I refrained from doing so with good reason. I soon heard about the influx of over ambitious Irish warlords who decided that terrorism was a very lucrative business: extortion, robberies, prostitution. Feuding factions fought over control of the cities; not surprising since there were no peace keeping forces controlling the streets. No, Mister Speed, I wasn't going to feed gangsters with information so they could enhance their wealth by resorting to kidnap and blackmail and the unnecessary murder of good Irish people."

"How noble of you Deveron, although a little too late for redemption, don't you think?" My tone was hard but he deserved the full delivery.

"Dreams of greatness, Mister Speed, that was my guilt. Young, proud, I wanted to be one of the great ambassadors of Ireland, a respected hero to the Irish people, to grace the same pedestal as my peers did. I wanted even greater credibility. To be remembered as the greatest fighter of Irish freedom. Gold would have achieved me that status. But world events changed those idealistic views. I changed. The older I got; the wiser I got. Wars and killings solved nothing. I only wish that I could have changed my mistake; turn back the clock."

"You kept looking for Craven's Spitfire regardless?"

"It was my intention to put the record straight and bring Craven home."

"And did that include finding the gold?"

"You've got me wrong, Mister Speed. Finding Craven became my only priority."

"If you'd felt that guilty then owning up at the time would have been more honourable than hiding behind a military rank. With more help you might have found Craven earlier."

"And face the hangman's noose for what I did in 1944?"

"Not necessarily."

"Think about it, Mister Speed. A Spitfire riddled with bullet holes from the bullets from another Spitfire; the aviation authorities would have put the pieces together. I'd have stood trial. Owning up to my treachery would be a little foolhardy don't you think, Mister Speed? I was sorry for what I did but I certainly wasn't prepared to die for it."

"You'd have probably wrangled your way out of a death penalty."

"That may be so, but I would have expected to be sentenced to thirty years stuck in a military prison. No thank you, Mister Speed, I kept my mouth shut, and after the war I kept on looking for Craven's Spitfire during my time in office. Alas the years passed and faded, as did my dream of finally finding his plane, almost forgotten until Shayna brought the memories flooding back into my senile world when she told me the story of the intrepid Shackleton Speed and the discovered Spitfire.

"But I wasn't satisfied that he'd been found, Mister Speed. I killed Craven on an assumption, now I want to know if the reason for my actions would have been justified when I shot him from the skies."

"You want to prove to yourself that you were right with what you did?"

"Is there something wrong with that, Mister Speed?"

"It sounds as if you're incredibly stupid or we're back to you wanting to find the gold?"

"The gold as well, for reasons of self satisfaction, not wealth, Mister Speed."

"Well jolly good show to you, Deveron! Only you gained nothing by shooting down Craven's Spitfire. If you're expecting to find the submarine, then forget it! Not that we can forget that you murdered Craven for nothing. There's no gold. There never was. You fell for a piece of speculative bullshit from an unknown source in another part of the world; how pathetic is that!"

Deveron smirked. "I'll lay you a pound to the penny that you're wrong about there being no gold, Mister Speed."

The crafty bastard was on the counterattack, I concluded. He obviously knew something I didn't, but then I assume that was Deveron all over and he always had a get out clause hidden somewhere up his sleeve.

"I'd probably loose the bet, Deveron."

"You would indeed, Mister Speed. I have a distinguished guest arriving later for dinner. We are old acquaintances during my final years at the ministry. He is an attaché at the Japanese embassy in London. I've persuaded him, and his lovely wife, to spend some prime time in Ireland. They arrive today. I would very much like you to meet him, Mister Speed. The conversation that will aspire should be quite riveting and should reveal some interesting facts concerning the I-52. It will be exhilarating to examine the comparisons of information you both have. You will, of course, stay for the remainder of the day, dinner in the evening, and I wouldn't dream of sending a guest hurrying across Ireland in the middle of the night. Therefore, a room is being prepared for you. I hope that is to your satisfaction?"

I hadn't planned to stay longer than I needed to. Yet the chance to exchange information with the Japanese dignitary had me hooked.

I said, "I've always been a sucker for a free dinner."

Deveron almost broke into smile. "I have one of the best cooks in Ireland, Mister Speed."

"I can't refuse then."

"I was always confident you would stay."

"Don't be too over confident. I might decide to leave early."

"And miss the highlight of the evening, a man of your endeavour? You're not the type to dismiss such an opportunity. You're a treasure hunter hiding under the banner of metal detector enthusiast. You sell what you find to the highest bidder with a total disregard to the treasure trove act. This is going to be a treasure hunt you can't ignore. You might get lucky."

"What? Aiding and abetting a criminal is lucky?"

"Come now, Mister Speed, you're as much a criminal as I, only I've retired. I know you're intrigued to hear the story of the I-52 that never was because if you hadn't been I would have expected the Garda arriving at my door instead of you, Mister Speed."

The crafty old goat, I thought. He had me sussed. Was I that predictable?

In reality, Deveron had done me no harm personally, providing he wasn't frigging lying about not being involved in endangering my life and messing up my affairs. I also thought of something else or rather I thought of someone else in particular.

"Is Shayna joining us tonight?" I asked casually.

Deveron smiled. "She wouldn't want to miss the occasion, Mister Speed. It was her idea to contact you so we could have this discussion today."

"She likes to dominate men, I can vouch for that."

"She's something special; such a beautiful woman, don't you agree?"

I'd no argument about her beauty but she was no Cinderella in my eyes. I still had the wounds to show from our last get-together and I still hadn't reverted from calling her a bitch! And after dinner I'll listen to their pack of lies.

The door of the study opened and a nurse entered.

Deveron said, "All this excitement has rather worn me out. You must excuse me, Mister Speed. This wonderful creature has just arrived with my afternoon medication. Please, feel free to wander anywhere about the house, I've nothing to hide. Examine my wonderful collection of old library masterpieces: works from all the great literary writers of our times. Feel free to roam the gardens. They are full, absorbing, tranquil, and most importantly, help yourself to the drinks. Dinner will be served at seven." He paused and looked at me seriously. "There is one more thing I need to ask you, Mister Speed?"

"What's that?"

"If I was the man responsible for the demise of your friends, would you have carried out your threat?"

I expressed my gunslingers stare, the squinted eyes, and said coolly, "Without hesitation."

Deveron nodded. "I do believe you would have, Mister Speed."

The nurse aided Deveron to his feet.

I watched them leave the study. I still hadn't acquired any sympathy towards Deveron despite his obvious health problems. I still felt that he owed me something other than dinner and a bed for the night. The moment the door closed behind them I rose and went to the bar, poured a good helping of straight dark rum and swallowed the alcohol in one swig. I twisted the empty tumbler back and forth between my fingers and thumb and thought about my next move. In five seconds flat I knew that I didn't have a next move to consider? I was here now and I could do nothing until somebody else made the wrong move first.

I left the study by the French windows and wandered out into the gardens for some fresh air, as the stagnant atmosphere of doubtfulness had stifled my lungs. The walk would give me the time to reflect on my brief encounter with Dillon Deveron the war-time murderer.

I'd no planned route for my walk I just followed my shadow cast by the mid afternoon sun. The pathway guided me down to the shoreline of a large lake and that was about as far as I could go unless I wanted to follow the shoreline to who knows where. I turned to retrace my steps and that's when I heard splashing coming from the lake.

The splashing noise came from beyond a large expansion of shoreline bushes and willow trees. I edged closer and moved around the bushes and there she was emerging from the lake, a naked bronzed sculptured goddess that left me gasping for breath. Shayna was undoubtedly a classic woman; a portrait of pulchritude. Her skin glistened as the suns rays bounced off the droplets of water dripping from her primed muscles that stretched from her shoulders to her calves. In comparison she made my body look like a wrecked temple. I had a cold sweat as I watched her. I could feel her magnetism attracting me and even though she never turned around to check, I sensed she knew I was standing there watching her.

She towel dried her body and began to dress; a striptease in reverse. She slipped into a pair of white lace panties, no bra, put on a white shirt and white pants, and soft white shoes. I found I was lusting after her despite my bitterness towards her.

Without turning round to acknowledge me, and over her shoulder she said, "What did you think of my grandfather?"

"Honest opinion?"

"I wouldn't expect anything less."

She ran a large toothed comb backwards through her damp hair.

"He's certainly eccentric," I said positively. He's possibly crackers. And he's a murderer to put it in better prospective."

"He told you then?"

"I left him no option. I already knew what he was. By the way; did he teach you terrorism or is it built into the genes?"

"Stop trying to be clever, Shackleton, or I might rip your head off."

I smiled cheekily. "Is that a promise?"

She obviously knew what I meant.

"Your mind is in a very sick condition, Shackleton."

"People I know usually call me, Shacks."

"I'll stick to Shackleton. It has that adventurous sound that impresses me. Walk with me back to the house?"

I'd nowhere else to go. "Yes...sure. I was about to head back anyway."

We sauntered back with the deliberate slowness of newly met lovers trying to make time last a little longer. And we didn't find one thing to squabble over until I decided to spoil the occasion.

"You do know Deveron is dying?"

"He's told me. I suppose that's the reason why he was prepared to tell you of his deceitful past. He obviously feels he's nothing to hide anymore."

"He could be challenging the law to come and try to get him for his crime?"

"You want to turn him over to the police?"

"He deserves nothing less."

"It wouldn't be beneficial to anyone by putting him in prison now."

"It makes me proud that I've uncovered a murderer from the past."

"He's not to blame for your loss."

"Is that your professional opinion or do you know something differently?"

"I know enough to confirm that he isn't your target. All he wants to do is rectify a mistake he made during the war. You can help him do that."

"He wants me to participate in his treasure hunt?"

"Would it be that difficult for you?"

"He might not be strong enough to survive the quest; if there is one."

"Maybe he won't but it isn't going to prevent him from trying to put things right."

I gestured toward the approaching building and said, "And when he's gone to hell what will happen to all that splendour?"

"I believe I'm the sole beneficiary of his entire estate."

"What will that gain you?"

"I'll not be poor."

"It'll be no use to you when you're dead too."

"I've no intention of dying for a long time."

"I should imagine the life span of an active terrorist diminishes with every day that passes."

"I'll retire."

"You could, but I can't quite picture terrorist chiefs leaving you in peace when there's a fight to be won. Can you? Once a terrorist always a terrorists, it simply can't be erased from your record."

"I might just surprise you, Shackleton."

"I don't think you've anything left that would surprise me, Shayna."

"We'll see."

We entered through the kitchen door and back into the hall where we met a stoutly built woman who I presumed to be Deveron's housekeeper.

Shayna said to her. "Greta, is my grandfather resting?"

Greta wasn't the prettiest of women I'd come across. She was on the plump side and had greying hair tied back, yet she spoke with such charm that if I were to shut my eyes for a moment I could have quite easily mistaken her for a younger woman rather than her fifty years of age. "Yes, my dear. And the maid has prepared Mister Speed's room as instructed. Shall I take him there?"

"Thank you, Greta, but there's no need. I'll show Mister Speed to his room."

"Thank you, my dear."

Greta smiled at me as she passed.

I followed Shayna up the stairs and along the landing like a besotted stalker. She could have been leading me into a trap but I didn't care. She stopped outside an oak panelled door, turned the handle and went inside to spring the surprise. Like a fool I followed her into the room rather hoping that when I entered she would ravage me with all that sexual starvation she had bottled up inside. She disappointed me. She didn't make any attempt to ravage me. I wondered if my expression gave away the fact that she hadn't.

"I hope you find everything comfortable, Shackleton. There are evening suits of different sizes hanging in the wardrobe. All brand new. There's a bathroom through the far door where you will find all utilities: shaving equipment, soaps, cologne, bathrobe, pyjamas."

"I never wear pyjamas," I said quickly.

"Am I supposed to be impressed? Anything else, just ask."

"This *anything*, does it literally mean anything?"

"Within reason, please Shackleton. See you at seven."

She closed the door behind her leaving me in a room of silence, so still and quiet I heard one of my shoes creak as I began to move. I had a quick shufti round the room looking for hidden miniature microphones or concealed cameras checking me out. I quickly dismissed the idea as pretty stupid. Even if the room had any type of listening device, it would be ineffective and serve no purpose as any conversation between me and my sub-conscience was solely restricted to my head. And as far as I know I don't talk in my sleep.

I'd no complaints about the standard of the room. I was going to be fed and watered, so what had I to worry about? I stripped down to my briefs and went into the bathroom to fill the bathtub. As in all my excursions into expensive hotels I always get my monies worth from the room: fill the bath to the brim with hot water mixed with relaxant salts and soak myself for a good hour. Which I did, and promptly fell asleep until the water chilled and woke me up.

Chapter Seventeen

I dressed into a crisp, fresh Tuxedo, shirt and bowtie. Satisfied with the way I looked I followed my nose to the dining room and breezed in with the charisma of a person entering a top class casino. I heard the sound of familiar voices as I went through the door.

The dining room was illuminated by an impressive crystal glass chandelier hanging over the dining table. I glanced round the room noting things: the walls were lined with maple veneer below a dado rail with decorated walls above; an assortment of water coloured painting lined the walls, openly displayed by picture lights, the extra brightness creating a spectacular phosphoresce effect. The centralized large dining table was laid with an entire set of silver cutlery and side plates for five people. Deveron was there seated at the head of the table looking rather more energetically younger than he was at our earlier meeting; it must have been his boost of medication that he'd taken earlier.

Shayna was there too, sitting on his right. To his left sat an Oriental couple. The maid began serving punch as I strolled towards the table in such a casual manner that I nearly converged into a whistled tune as I walked.

Deveron, his tinny sound prominent, displayed a joyous reception when he caught sight of my approach.

"Mister Speed. Come! Come! Please, sit beside Shayna. We're about to sample a new recipe of punch; Japanese style."

The moment I'd sat and pulled my chair in, Deveron began announcing me to his Japanese guests.

"This is the gentleman I told you about, Mister Shackleton Speed. Mister Speed, allow me to introduce a special friend of mine, Shun Tanamoto San, and his adoring wife, Ryoko."

Tanamoto raised courteously, a slight bow of his head as he spoke. "It is an honour to meet you, Mister Speed."

I returned the gesture with a simple nod of the head and avoiding any sharpness in my tone, I said, "No disrespect, Tanamoto San, but I'm afraid I've heard nothing of you."

He never even flinched by my bluntness, as if he had been warned beforehand what he could expect from me.

Deveron went on. "Ah-but you'll know a great deal by the end of the evening, Mister Speed, after Shun has relayed some fantastic information to us. Shun, fortunately for us, holds a top position at both the Japanese Embassies in London and Dublin. His position puts him well in contention to assist us in our quest to pursue the truth. He has certain privileges which allow him access to confidential information relating to secret activities during the Second World War. Isn't that so, Shun?"

"That is indeed, correct," Tanamoto confirmed with another smart bow and then sat down.

With the initial formalities of introduction completed I took the opportunity to lean across to Shayna, and whispered to her. "Wow! Shayna, you look wonderful. For a moment I almost confused you for a sophisticated and posh Lady rather than the brutal bitch I really know."

She forced a smile, as if I'd said something funny to her which I guessed was for the benefit of the others who might be watching. She shuffled in her chair and stabbed the heel of her stiletto down onto my foot. I didn't feel any pain but I got the hint and left her alone. I sipped my punch and turned my attention instead to the Japanese guests.

As characteristics go amongst most Orientals, he was short in height, had a slight chubby appearance, with heavy sacs of flesh below both his eyes. His full head of grey hair was smartly trimmed, combed back and required no generous helping of hair cream. It was hard to imagine his age was anything less than sixty, but he didn't give me the impression his life had been an arduous one. He dressed immaculately in an expensive Japanese silk tuxedo which only proved he wasn't short of money either.

His wife, Ryoko, who I guessed was at least twenty years younger than Tanamoto, was dressed in a strikingly colourful traditional Japanese costume. I thought her complexion was a little heavy in the make-up department for my liking, and from what I could make out, beneath her costume she had a shapely figure and overall she was well worth a second look at any time of the day. Her smile and her slight downward tilt of her head reminded me of a shy teenager associating with a boy for the first time; it made her look cute. Without realizing I was smiling at her a little longer than I perhaps should have done, but nobody seemed to care that I was gawping at her. Not even Tanamoto himself.

Tanamoto said to me, "Dillon tells me you have an exceptional skill in metal detecting."

"I've been lucky so far."

Tanamoto had the habit of constantly grinning when he spoke. He said, "The subject, it has always fascinated my curiosity."

"In what way does it fascinate you?" I asked and finished off the punch.

"Where do you begin such a quest? There has to be a secret to your success?"

I smacked my wet lips, thoughtfully. "The successful finders use sheer hard graft and know where to look."

It was at that moment Shayna decided to play footsy with the back of my calf. I didn't mind the attention while I studied Tanamoto's puzzled expression.

"What is-ah-this *graft*, Mister Speed?"

Deveron chuckled and stepped in. "Simple hard work! Shun. Something you and I pay other people to do."

Tanamoto, too, joined in with a brief chuckle. "Ah-yes, now I understand. Well then perhaps, Mister Speed, you could find the time to educate my ignorance on the subject and take me along on one of your treks out into the wild world."

"I'm a lousy teacher," I said, discouragingly. "Besides, no one can teach a person to be patience, which is what it takes when stuck in the middle of a muddy field on a miserable wet and windy day."

Tanamoto expressed surprise. "You would still endeavour such a task even in dreadful conditions?"

"If I thought it would be worthwhile and there was something there to be found."

"Perhaps we could venture out together soon?"

"No offence, Tanamoto San, but I don't carry passengers. I prefer to be alone. I find it more productive that way."

The maid entered the dining room pushing a large an electrically heated dinner trolley. Her timing was perfect and the smell of food distracted Tanamoto from trying to wriggle his way into my life.

After dinner we moved to the lounge for coffee and brandy. I was hoping he'd forgotten about metal detecting but once he'd settled in an armchair and sipped a wonderful French brandy, he was back on the subject. I felt like going home.

"Mr Speed," he began. "Does digging things from the ground consume a great deal of your life?"

I wondered where his line of questioning was heading. I shrugged. "I suppose a lifetime wouldn't be far wrong; since my school days most definitely."

Tanamoto was impressed. "That is indeed dedication to what you enjoy immensely as leisure."

"It's a little more than that."

"It is not a hobby then?"

"Hobbies are for weekend enthusiasts. I'm a professional detectorist and to me it's a full time dedication."

"It's more like a risk, "Shayna interrupted with a smirk.

"Life's a risk, Shayna. You should know."

"These outdoor pursuits never bore you, Mister Speed?" Tanamoto asked.

"It keeps me out of mischief."

"Until you find something that you're not entitled to keep," Shayna interrupted again. "Then you're in deep trouble."

Tanamoto grew concerned. "What kind of deep trouble, Mister Speed?"

"She's referring to the intolerable treasure trove officials sniffing into my business affairs."

Tanamoto smiled. "Ah-yes, I understand. You're not the type of man to share your discoveries with the proper authorities?"

"Something on those lines," I admitted.

"I admire a man who isn't afraid to admit his roguish ambitions, Mister Speed. You're obviously damned good at finding things. You're independent and obviously work on your own initiative. I like that. I think you're going to be our man for the job."

"The job? Tanamoto San." I enquired speculatively.

"It's a job of the utmost of importance to me and the Japanese people."

"I don't follow."

"Dillon tells me that you are searching for the Japanese submarine I-52? Is this true, Mister Speed?"

"Now why should I want to bother searching for a submarine that was sunk in the Atlantic Ocean during the war? And I'm not considered to be in the field of marine archaeology. Anyway it's already been located by an American team."

"Yes, the American team did locate its resting place, Mister Speed. And we were most grateful for the personal artefacts the American team returned to our government. But their intentions were directed to a more precious commodity, which they failed to find."

"The cargo of gold the I-52 carried, allegedly?"

"That is precisely their reason, Mister Speed. The Americans had in their possession an impressive inventory of the cargo the submarine had aboard when she sank. Facts and figures showed that the submarine I-52 was on a mission to deliver raw materials to Germany. Official war documents confirmed that was completely true. And according to the inventory the I-52 also carried gold bullion. Well, she didn't. The inventory was falsified; a white lie. I can clarify that the I-52 didn't carry gold amongst its cargo on that tragic day."

"The salvagers were convinced there was gold on board," I said. "Perhaps your government should have told them they were wasting their time."

"They wouldn't have believed us."

"No they probably wouldn't."

"It wasn't all entirely a wasteful journey for the American team. They extracted tin ingots from the wreck, and there would have been canisters of opium, which was to be used for medical purposes during the war, if only the seawater hadn't contaminated the product. Even, probably, the scattered bones of a few gallant submariners, but that's all, Mister Speed. I can verify that it carried nothing more than what I have stated. No, Mister Speed, the Atlantic bound I-52 served a more prominent purpose other than to deliver the raw materials which was listed, which I hasten to add, would have been a bonus if the I-52 had managed to escape the Allied attack."

"What was its purpose then?"

"It was to create an elaborate diversion."

I tried not to get too excited at what he'd said. "It must have been all worthwhile to lose so much?"

"It was a huge loss to Imperial Japan, but it was necessary. The diversion was to lure the Allied forces away from the main purpose of the operation. That was to allow a second type C-3 cargo submarine, bearing the same prefix number I-52, to slip through the Allied sea defences unseen. It was that submarine that held the elusive gold bullion."

"Rather an inappropriate waste of lives for a simple diversion," I said, cynically. "And then again, I shouldn't really be surprised. I suppose Japan also had idiots disguised as military geniuses who beyond their great ideas needlessly sent men to their deaths."

Tanamoto raised his eyebrows in surprise. "They were never needless deaths, Mister Speed. Ninety-four men, including officers, died on the I-52 that day and with reason. It is difficult for a person outside Japan to understand the simple existence of the Japanese people, whether male, female, or child, and their willingness to sacrifice themselves for the preservation of their country. If their life is required, it will be given with no concept of self preservation whatsoever. The crew of the Atlantic bound I-52 accepted their mission with honour. There was no need to ask for volunteers to risk their lives, Japanese people insist they are chosen for such perilous tasks."

"Please excuse my ignorance but I've always seen things a little different on that aspect." The drink was making me argumentative.

"In what way do you mean, Mister Speed?"

"That it's the natural instinct of man or a woman to self preserve unless, of course, that person is suffering from a mental disorder. No one, that includes Japanese people, is likely to throw away their lives for the sake of an Emperor or country unless unwittingly deceived or threatened by the people they trust. I think honour in death was forced upon the people of Japan by means of mind numbing internal propaganda used by the Japanese government at the time: that if the Americans landed in Japan, they'd rape your women, pillage your Cities, string Japanese men up by their testicles from the highest pole, roast their children, unless you fought to the last man. That's what I think."

Tanamoto frowned. "Your lack of knowledge of our cultures is acceptable, Mister Speed. To understand our ways can only be achieved by the ignorant person living within our communities. I also accept it is hard for you to understand a brave crew's sacrificial offerings to their Emperor; to serve Imperial Japan and achieve the highest accolade in death. Deep inside our souls we still attain the code of the Samurai."

Tanamoto's emotions were certainly running higher than mine for what I guessed to be for a more personal reason. It had me wondering what it was.

"This I-52 had some sentimental value in your life, perhaps?" I asked.

Tanamoto bowed his head slightly in respect of the dead. "Alas there is no family in Japan that hasn't been affected by some part of the war, Mister Speed. I too had a relative aboard the fated I-52; my father's brother."

"Then I apologize for my disrespect of your loss, Tanamoto San."

"I take no offence, Mister Speed. It was a long time ago and I was but a crawling infant." He dragged a leather briefcase towards him and placed it on his knees. He unlocked the case and from inside removed a thick and tatty brown paper folder which he offered to me.

"Please, Mister Speed, I want you browse over the contents."

I placed my brandy glass down on the coffee table and took the folder from him and had a shufti through the first six pages. I stopped and looked Tanamoto hard in the eyes. I said bluntly, "Excuse my displeasure, Tanamoto San, but are you trying to mock me? It's written in Japanese; a language I'm not familiar with."

Tanamoto smiled. "No, no, Mister Speed! The documents are not intended for you to actually translate, more so to prove the existence of what I am about to divulge to you. I'm authorized to allow any of the contents within that folder to be verified by any person knowledgeable in Japanese. I am merely offering them to you for your personal use."

"What would I want with them?"

"I'm hoping it will assist you to find the elusive I-52."

"You're very keen to find what most think is a mythical submarine?"

"The submarine does exist. It is stated in those documents in your hand. And it is that particular submarine that has a deeper personal importance to me, Mister Speed."

"Ah! There's perhaps a percentage of something shiny for you in all this?" I was hinting at gold bullion.

"You could put it that way, Mister Speed. My father was a submariner aboard her."

"Oh!" A gaping hole just opened up and swallowed me. "Well...that changes things. And since I haven't the time to find some educated scholar to translate this lot for me, I'll just have to take your word for what's inside these documents."

I handed the folder back to him.

"I am honoured to be in your trust, Mister Speed. Now shall we press on and seek some truths?"

"Press on, Tanamoto San, the floors yours."

Tanamoto tapped the folder as he spoke. "Everything inside these documents relates entirely to the missions conducted by the two vessels bearing the same I-52 prefix. Their codenames were 'MOMI 1' relating to Operation Atlantic and 'MOMI 2' for our main objective. The entire operation depended on hiding a submarine within a submarine. It was imperative to create the illusion that a lone submarine was heading for the intended rendezvous in the Atlantic. And it wouldn't be an easy task to conceal an additional five thousand tons of Japanese engineering without arousing suspicion of our intentions.

"This was achieved in two ways. The first was to duplicate the I-52 prefix and the other was stealth. The 'MOMI 2' was covered with experimental sheets of specially formulated rubber which made the craft practicably undetectable to sonar."

"What? Something like slipping a giant condom over the vessel?"

Tanamoto expressed surprise. "Not quite, Mister Speed. The procedure was to attach small rubber panels; a difficult task at the time, but finally solved and completed. It was highly effective too."

"If the sub was invisible to sonar then why bother with the deception of using the same prefix?"

"It was a precautionary measure in case of visual detection. And to further the invisible cloak to ensure that 'MOMI 2' successfully beat the blockades, secret correspondences were deliberately leaked over the airwaves for the Allies to decipher; instructions really, as to where they could find 'MOMI 1'out in the Bay of Biscay. The Allies took the bait."

"Authenticated by the death of seaman and tonnage of steel wasting away at the bottom of the sea," I added scornfully and sipped my brandy.

"Ruthless as our plan was, the plan worked, Mister Speed. It drew the Allies to the prescribed rendezvous."

"That intricate planning didn't exactly incorporate an elaborate escape route for the Atlantic crew."

"The submariners understood the risks. And the transferring of cargo to the U-boat was still an essential operation in the process. If we'd have broken off the transfer of cargo too early, then the Allies might have been suspicious. In war, one has to be ruthless and tough decisions have to be made. Yes, we gambled with submariner's lives and unfortunately the sacrifice was unavoidable as 'MOMI 1' failed to dive to safety and was struck with plane delivered torpedoes; a piece of bad timing. We can't change history, Mister Speed."

"No, but you tried with your deception and 'MOMI 2'."

"And even then we failed, Mister Speed. Now we know the fate of 'MOMI 1'. We are desperate to know the fate of 'MOMI 2'. I'm desperate. I want to know, Mister Speed."

"In your opinion, what do you think happened to the submarine?"

"My theories would be farfetched speculation, Mister Speed. I have to be realistic and take what I know as what's here in this dossier. We know the two vessels separated at the allocated position. 'MOMI 2' stopped her engines and drifted on the currents while the Atlantic destined 'MOMI 1' continued to the rendezvous with a U-boat. An hour later 'MOMI 2' set a course for a rendezvous with German sympathizers in the West of Ireland, at a location two miles off the Bay of Donegal. It should have been off-loaded and from there the merchandise was supposed to have been transported by land route to the North of Ireland and then smuggled into German hands. Unfortunately, all normal communications to 'MOMI 2' were severed to maintain the utmost secrecy. The only communication available was between 'MOMI 2' and German secret agents already in attendance on Irish soil.

"That was the last we heard. The communication between all parties was lost forever. 'MOMI 2' had disappeared. The secret agents had disappeared. And neither our government nor the Germans heard anything since. There was speculation of a double cross and both sides were pointing an accusing finger of guilt at each other. The submarines disappearance caused animosity between our two nations; the German high command questioning our allegiance and the Japanese government suspecting piracy. Naturally we couldn't openly condemn what had happened to 'MOMI 2' without exposing our secret intentions. Imperial Japan could do nothing more than to wait for news. It never came. 'MOMI 2' lies on our files as missing in action. Now, by some strange twist of fate, Dillon has mentioned to me in the strictest of confidence that the submarine could possibly be found. And you, Mister Speed, could be our man to find it for the Japanese government."

I noticed Deveron nodding and smiling like a Cheshire cat.

I was silent for a moment because two things had crossed my mind. Why hadn't Deveron mentioned to Tanamoto that there's photographic evidence linking the submarine to British waters? Deveron's had time to tell him. And had Professor Squires been mistaken with his shoreline prediction and instead I should have been searching where Tanamoto had indicated, around Donegal. But I've never known the Professor to wrong on any subject, and stupidly, I'd forgotten that Shamus too had pinpointed Dun an Oir from the photographs. No. I'd the right area. It was Tanamoto who was nautical miles short of its true location.

Tanamoto broke into my thoughts when he said, "For a man destined to find something of historical significance you seem distracted. I don't seem to be exciting your appetite. Mister Speed?"

"I came to Ireland for a holiday to escape the harrowing experiences inflicted on me back in London," and I flicked an accusing glaring towards Shayna hoping she'd feel guilty. I said to Tanamoto, "So where's this conversation really heading?"

Tanamoto expressed his disappoint with me. "I get the feeling you mistrust me, Mister Speed?"

"I mistrust almost everybody I meet for the first time, Tanamoto San. It's nothing personal. Now what do you exactly want from me?"

"We simply want you to find our missing submarine."

"Why? It isn't going to change anything."

"I'll rephrase the request, Mister Speed. It is the Japanese Government that wants to commission you to find the submarine. I am their representative on the matter. Our government want to know the fate of their craft and submariners. Relatives, even at this present moment, pray daily in the hope that one day they will know the outcome of what happened to their love ones. If not now, their quest will be passed on generation to generation until the mystery is solved. I too have suffered, Mister Speed. My father was on board 'MOMI 2'. I want to honour him wherever he lies. If we can locate those missing submariners then we can release their lost souls from their dark underworld."

"All very poignant Tanamoto San. What about the elusive two hundred million in gold bullion that accompanied the submarine?"

Tanamoto frowned at me, as if I'd said something accusingly or even incorrect. "Is that an estimated valuation of gold prices, Mister Speed? Or do you perhaps possess certain information you're not submitting to this conversation?"

I shrugged. "It's all rumours mostly."

"I hope those rumours don't attract the wrong attention."

"It's true then. The gold does exist. So what's it worth, approximately?"

"With today's prices, who knows what its worth? But I'll put your guess as almost accurate in today's market."

"It's a tidy sum. It would certainly influence a man's loyalty to his cause."

He looked at me speculatively. "Does that include me, Mister Speed?"

"It's not rocket science to work out that you're here tonight for other reasons than a free dinner and all this wonderful chit-chat."

"Then you don't trust my true values, Mister Speed!" Tanamoto actually sounded pleased that he had me sussed.

"It's nothing personal, as I said."

"Let me assure you, Mister Speed that besides being a guest at this excellent establishment, there is no self gratification on my part. I am here on behalf of the Japanese government to recover and return the commodity to our country, nothing else. And you, Mister Speed, I believe to be the right person to help us recover what is rightfully Japanese property."

"That might not be as easy as it sounds."

"There would be a problem in assisting us, Mister Speed?"

"Not if it's found. I'm thinking more on the negative lines; that maybe the submarine commander thought sod this for playing war heroes and scampered off to some destined land to live a life of luxury with all his merry men."

I could have sworn Tanamoto's eyes swelled from their sockets, he was that mad. He'd stopped smiling too, and he expressed his anger with me. "It's a despicable thought, Mister Speed!"

"I'm good with those; ask our host."

"Nevertheless, the situation would never have occurred." Tanamoto defended righteously.

I raised my eyebrows suspiciously. "You're sure about that?"

"I'll personally vouch that every Japanese warrior would put honour before greed."

"The criminal factions in your country might just dispute that statement."

"They're sewer rats, not honourable men, Mister Speed."

"They're profitable sewer rats, Tanamoto San."

"Every country has them, Mister Speed. Now back to my proposition. Will you assist us on our quest to find the I-52, codename 'MOMI 2'?"

"There's another problem you may want to swill around your thoughts."

Tanamoto expressed his annoyance. "What is it, Mister Speed?"

"The consequences, if the word did get around that gold bullion were up for grabs. Would you be in a favourable position to prevent an avalanche of potential gold diggers bombarding every conceivable nook and cranny looking for the wretched stuff?"

"It was never my intention to announce to the world of such an operation."

"I think the Garda Siochana should be informed." I said, watching Anamosa's reaction to my request. In reality, it was the farthest thought from my mind.

Anamosa thought it through. He finally said, "They will be informed in good time. For the moment we do nothing until we have at least located the I-52. Only then will our government liaise with the Irish assembly to authenticate the ownership of any merchandise that may still exist. The bodies of the submariners are understandably ours by rights."

I sensed there was something further bothering Tanamoto; something he was reluctant to tell me. I prompted him. "Should I expect anymore more surprises in store?"

He paused, giving me the impression that he was seriously considering if he should lie to me or not. Finally, he said, "There might be further repercussions from certain governments if they became aware of the additional cargo that was aboard."

I frowned with concern. "There was material on board to make an atomic bomb?"

Tanamoto smiled. "No, Mister Speed, it's nothing that horrendous, but then again it could be as deadly in the amount of people it could affect."

"I think I should know before I make a decision?"

"It is only right that you know, Mister Speed. There was a substantial amount of medical aid aboard the submarine that to certain criminally minded individuals could be viewed as a very rewarding package."

"How about making some sense?"

"I don't think the Garda Siochana would appreciate the knowledge that half a ton of opium, contained in airtight and water resistant containers, was part of the cargo. It could possibly, if it became common knowledge, attract an avalanche of drug smugglers."

I exhaled a huge breath. "Frigging hell, Tanamoto san, you have to be kidding me? You're saying the opium would be dry as a bone?"

"That's the outcome, Mister Speed."

"The opium would have survived after all this time?"

"In its sealed containers, providing there's no damage, it's quite conceivable."

"That kind of merchandise, well, distributed properly, it'll far exceed what the gold is worth. Are you positive there was that amount aboard?"

"The documents I believe are very accurate."

"Frigging hell, if even a third of that opium was circulated on the streets we could have a drug epidemic on our hands."

"Now you know why we have to use extreme caution until we can verify the situation."

"That's if the submarine can be found?" I reminded him.

"If it isn't located, Mister Speed, then we should have no repercussions whatsoever and we can all go home relieved that nothing untoward happened."

"That's providing nobody finds the submarine in the future, Tanamoto San."

"I'm confident that if you can't find 'MOMI 2' then nobody will."

I glanced across to Deveron. "How do you feel about all this, Deveron?"

"I don't quite follow your meaning, Mister Speed?"

"Would you like a piece of the action?"

"I'm only interested in satisfying my curiosity, as I explained to you in detail. Finding the submarine will answer a lot of questions buried within my memory. I'm fully behind Tanamoto's proposed intentions to conduct the search for the submarine in secrecy, until we can at least ascertain the truth; as Tanamoto said, if the I-52 isn't found, and then there is no need to pursue the matter any longer. And to show my allegiance to Tanamoto, and that I believe you to be the man to find the submarine, I'm going to be financing the acquisition of your services."

"Assuming I was interested," I said. "And if I was then I'd be damned expensive to hire."

"No expense spared, Mister Speed. Name your price?"

"Have I time to consider overnight?"

Deveron was quick to deny me thinking time. "No. Tanamoto has to leave this evening for an important engagement back in London. There's still a lot of work to be done behind the scenes for this operation to be implemented. You have a price in mind?"

"It'll cost you twenty thousand pound's sterling, cash of course and no tax deductions either."

I was expecting at least a gasp of surprise from one of them, but both men maintained expressionless faces, and they would have trounced me in a game of Poker.

"Per week," I added. "Until found."

There was still no disapproval from either of them. No body language suggesting I was pushing my luck. That lack of response had me worried.

Deveron reacted first and calmly said, "You drive a hard bargain, Mister Speed. This cash transaction, do I smell a touch of tax evasion?"

"You smell what you want. I call it the cost of living and you can blame the government for that. If the merchandise is recovered then it'll be worthwhile to you."

"I agree with you terms, Mister Speed. I'm sure you'll be worth every penny. I'll want Shayna to be there with you." Deveron announced.

"There's no need. I stick to my deals."

"Considering I can't be there myself, I want someone there I can trust impeccably and that is no disrespect to you, Mister Speed. Surely the employer has a right to observe how his money is being spent. Don't you agree?"

I shrugged without conviction. There was no point quarrelling at this stage of the arrangement. I could drop her later, when they least expect.

Deveron smiled. "Then our business is concluded, Mister Speed."

Shayna rose and said, "Now that you boys have sorted out your differences, I'm in need of sleep. I think we've a long day ahead of us tomorrow."

"Same here," I said, rising to my feet. "I want an early start in the morning. I'll walk you to your room, Shayna, if you've no objections?"

We left Deveron and Tanamoto in deep discussion and headed for the stairway. I would have savoured the chance to put a glass to the wall and listen in on them because I wondered how much of what had been discussed between us had been pure bullshit. In the mood I was in at the moment, if I was to believe anything Tanamoto had told me, I was going to need a lot more convincing.

When we reached the top of the stairway, I said, "Fancy a night-cap, Shayna?"

"Not really Shackleton. But if you want to fuck, your room is the nearest."

I hadn't quite expected such openness from her but neither should I have been surprised by it. I said, "I recall that our last encounter was rather a one sided affair."

"Look, if you're feeling too tired and you're not up to the occasion, then goodnight."

I wasn't tired and I wasn't going to refuse the offer of sex neither. Wild horses wouldn't drag me away from the chance of revenge. The moment we'd reached my room we were inside, the door kicked shut, our mouths crushed in embrace, in a frantic struggle for dominance, tugging to free each others clothing until we were standing there naked. Well almost naked because I insisted Shayna kept on her G-string panties.

We touched and aroused each other. Her breasts firmed. Her hard nipples digging into my chest while her fingers slipped down to fondle the length of my healthy penis. A few steps back and we were lying on the bed and I was exploring her body freely. Kissing and mouthing her neck first, I moved slowly down, kissing her breasts, licking and gently sucking her nipples, working my way down to the strip of pubic hair that guided me to the intimate part of a woman's love box. I exhaled hot breath through the material of her panties. She moaned softly, urging me to free her, so I slipped her satin panties down in one motion, the tip of my tongue penetrating the crevices of her vagina in search of the trigger button, hitting the target accurately and she responded by thrusting her clitoris hard onto my tongue. She grabbed the hair at the back of my head, pulling my face deeper into her fleshy mound, so hard that I was delightfully suffocating. At that moment I didn't care. I was lost in a world of lust.

Without even thinking about our actions we'd rolled and I found myself on my back with Shayna pressing her vagina onto my face, my tongue probing, tasting her leaking juices. She squealed with delight, moaning, talking in between the ecstasy, "Yes! Yes! Yes!" Her hips thrust faster, the texture of her juice changing. "That's how much you turn me on Shackleton Speed. Yes! Yes! Yes! Yes!"

Then slowly she ceased to a few tentative jerky movements before latching straight onto my manhood with her mouth, pleasuring me before I took control, threw her onto her back and penetrated her vagina as she gasped her approval. Sweat layered our skins, as if our bodies had been covered in silky oil. My skills as a lover were tested to the brink as she cried out for more. Positions altered, dominance changed hands, we were inseparable, two desperate lovers in deep embrace, tearing into one another. The more I rived into her, the more she opened to accept my hard thrusting shaft probing the depths of her love. The way she screamed with ecstasy had me consciously wanting to clamp her mouth shut. Yet there's certain words that make you work harder, and she knew the whole simple vocabulary.

"Fuck me! Fuck me!" She screamed, as I probed deep into her fleshy box. "Fuck me like a mad rabid dog!"

I like to please, so I did.

"Fuck me harder, you horny bastard!" she screamed, obviously almost on the verge of an orgasm.

I felt the warmth of her fluid gushing out as I moved inside her.

"Fuck me! Fuck me! Don't stop...please don't stop!"

The walls of her vagina tightened against the girth of my shaft, her nails clawing their way into the flesh of my back, tearing across, burning and I loved every moment. I pushed deeper inside her. I could tell she was struggling to maintain the pace, the pleasurable sensations too sensitive to withstand any longer. She tried to force me off her while still effectively wanting me to drive deep inside her. She pushed and screamed and pulled me back inside her. But there was no way she could stop me this time. I was no longer tied to a stanchion now. My hands were free. I wasn't going be frustrated a second time and deprived of satisfaction. I had control of the situation and I wasn't about to release my grip around her buttocks, not until I finally exploded inside of her, pumping hard, thrusting, my semen crashing against a torrent of released vaginal fluid. And when I was totally spent I collapsed onto her gasping for air like a sprinter at the end of a race.

I rolled off her and lay on my back catching my breath. I felt the beads of sweat roll down my body to be absorbed into the sheets.

She exhaled a slow long breath. "You're good, Shackleton Speed. No, you're a lot more than good. You're energetic, forceful and so exciting. You've completely exhausted me…I'm shattered!"

"I hope that's a good thing?"

She reached over and stroked my face, "Wonderful," she whispered, "Absolutely wonderful," before she yawned and faded into a bout of rhythmic heavy breathing as she slipped into sleep aided by the amount of alcohol I'd seen her drink throughout the evening.

I was knackered too, but I tend to sleep with one eye open when I'm occupying a strange bed. It's a habit that has grown on me over the years. Besides, my mind was overactive, thinking in somersaults: could I trust my new partners in crime? I say crime because I believed that sneaking around Irish waters without first informing the proper authorities of our intentions does constitute an act of illegality. It was something I'd do, but not something I would have expected Deveron and Tanamoto to hide if they were genuinely only interested in doing what's right.

And then there's Shayna and could I trust her fully; hardly. She seemed to turn up in my face unexpectedly, always in the places where I frequent, as if she was following me.

My thoughts were disturbed by the sound of a car door shutting. I slipped carefully from between the sheets, so as not to disturb Shayna, crossed to the window and slightly parted the curtains. The Japanese couple were leaving. I still hadn't made up my mind whether the Oriental guests were genuine in their pursuit to find lost relatives, or preferred the idea of gold flickering from the bottom of Roaring Water Bay. I slipped back into bed and added that problem into the blender of my thoughts. My head was still spinning when I finally fell asleep.

Morning came quick and I caught Shayna tiptoeing naked towards the bedroom door carrying her clothes. I pretended to be asleep, craftily peeping through the slits of my eyes as I watched her leave. The slight click of the door latch told me she'd gone. I closed my eyes and slept a little longer until the silence startled me awake. I hurriedly showered and shaved, and went down to the smell of breakfast with great expectancy, something like a loving, satisfied smile from Shayna. I found the dining room empty of people. I helped myself to bacon, mushrooms, tomatoes, a few rounds of toast and sat down to eat alone. Shayna never arrived for breakfast; nobody did which I thought was very inconsiderate of my host.

My isolation ceased when the maid from the previous evening entered the dining room.

"Where is everyone?" I asked casually.

She shrugged. "They've gone, sir."

"Gone where?"

"I've no idea, sir."

"I thought Deveron wasn't fit to travel?"

"I wouldn't know that, sir."

I wondered if she was under strict orders not to divulge any information to me. Then again she could be telling the truth and that she genuinely didn't know anything. Since I'd no intention of putting her under the heat of the interrogation lamp to gain the right answers, I left her to get on with her job. After breakfast I used the house telephone. I made three calls: the first call was to a local taxi firm. The second call went to a very nice woman who happened to hold a position of authority in a large law firm in central London. She was damned good at asking the right questions in the right places and poking her nose deep into other people's affairs. I gave her the relevant information she would require and I would ring her when I was ready to act. The third call went to Shamus to tell him I was on my way back to Baltimore and for him to prepare the *Muff* for a late afternoon excursion. He was more concerned over my health.

"Dashing about won't do yer system any good for diving, Shacks sir. Why don't we leave the dive until tomorrow morning when yer'll be more refreshed."

"I'm refreshed enough. You just make sure the boat's ready for this afternoon."

"I'm only thinking of yer lungs, Shacks sir. O, by the way, the harbour master tells me the *Flying Fish* is on a research programme to monitor the behaviour of underwater currents surging from the Arctic to the Southern Hemisphere."

"Believe that, Shamus?"

"I've no reason to doubt it, Shacks sir; the harbour master said their paperwork was up to date. But I gather yer're suspicious?"

"I'm always suspicious. They weren't doing much to warrant such a claim when we saw them. There was no monitoring equipment being used. More like a ghost ship if you ask me. In the meantime you watch your back."

"Yer be expecting trouble, Shacks sir?"

"I'm not sure, Shamus, all the same be careful."

"I'll do that, Shacks sir."

I replaced the telephone receiver and stood there for a moment chewing over some raw possibilities. I was still swallowing the inconclusive answers when the taxi arrived to take me to the railway station.

As the train thundered back to Cork, I could confidently say that I'd nothing to fear from Deveron, even though my testimony could send him to prison for a wartime murder. As for Shayna, she had two unpredictable sides to her; the brutal side and the loving side but I wasn't too sure which of those sides was the most dominant. Overall, she was certainly a hard picture to dislodge from my mind and I wondered in a strange way if it was possible that I was actually in love with the bitch.

Chapter Eighteen

Hamer caught up with me when I got back to my hotel. He followed me through reception. He was all riled up and I could have sworn I saw steam blowing out of his ears.

"Where the fuck did you abscond to without telling me?" He ranted, spittle flying from his mouth. "As for that thick Paddy you call a friend, he's changed his story of where you might be more times than a fucking gobstopper sweet changing colour the longer you suck on it!"

I wasn't in the mood for a verbal confrontation with slap-arsed features so I said calmly, "There's no need to insult the locals just because you've had a bad day. Let's understand each other: where I go is none of your frigging business. But if it'll stop you constantly spitting your dummy out, I've been to Dublin, sightseeing." I'd no reason to lie. I reckon Shayna was absolutely worth seeing naked again.

"You should have told me where you were going?"

"And have you tagging along? Next thing you'll be wanting me to make out a frigging timesheet."

"It would be wise to at least let me know your movements so I wouldn't be hanging about like a prize in a raffle waiting to be plucked from obscurity. Hell I was worried!"

He surprised me with that statement. "Worried about me?"

"There's something wrong wanting to look after one's asset?"

"Yes there is, Hamer. You're beginning to act as if you're my big sister."

"Bollocks to you, Speed!" And with outburst he trudged off towards the bar, weighed down by the huge sulk dragging behind him.

I said, as he strode away. "So I can take it you won't be joining us on the 'Muff' this afternoon?" Now there was a statement for open ears, which, unsurprisingly, caused a few heads to turn. As for Hamer, I considered his instant reply of a swift raise of two fingers damned right impertinent and a definite no.

"What happened to, 'stick to me like glue policy' you were so positive on applying?"

"Go and drown yourself, Speed, so I can go home with a clear conscience."

I left Hamer to decide which part of his dummy he would spit out next, went to change and met Shamus aboard the *Muff*.

*

The weather was favourable for diving; the sea considerably calmer as we sailed out into the bay, and arced towards Clear Island. Inevitably we were chaperoned by the *Flying Fish*. There was no hard evidence that the ship was actually shadowing us, yet I'd be willing to put all my money on it. And if the ship was intending to do research then I'd be sacking the crew because they were a frigging bunch of lazy bastards as there was little happening on deck. But as long as they left me alone I was content on continuing my own piece of research.

Shamus lined up the bow of the *Muff* with his pre-recorded land markers in exactly the same position as before and probably within the inch. While Shamus dropped the boat's anchor I squeezed into my neoprene diving gear, donned my equipment and was quickly into the water.

Beneath the seas and oceans of our planet the water smothers the madness of an exhilarating existence. It's an entirely different world where a person can think. Pace is smoother and more practiced; it has to be. While we are able to breathe air above the water as fast or as slow as we like, beneath the water you're at its mercy. Too fast a manoeuvre and the wrong breathing pattern is considered highly dangerous to the human body submerged in deep water. But it's not all doom and gloom and uninviting. Diving is divine, a world of excitement, and its peacefulness only interrupted by the gurgling of escaping air bubbles exhaled from my mouthpiece.

Amongst my array of diving tools I had with me a very long engineer's lever. It was heavy even in seawater and that excess weight took me down to the seabed without me having to kick my fins. It's a good thing you can't get the bends descending or else I would have been in big trouble. At least I would have plenty of reserved energy for working on the seabed. As for Shamus feeding my lifeline into the water, his hands were probably moving ten to the dozen and suffering from rope burns, trying to keep up with my rapid descent. I did warn him.

Again I located the position where the strong current flowed between the fallen rocks that I had found on the previous dive. I went to work. Rammed the tip of the long engineers lifting bar into the crack of a rock and levered hard while trying to keep my feet steady on the silted seabed. Fragments of rock splintered but nothing significant happened. I chose another crack in the same rock, again the same result. I persevered. I'd no choice because I loathe defeatism. Working on the same rock I shifted the crowbar around its circumference, levering to and fro, jerking side to side. The effort was tiring, and tired lungs use up air at a fast rate.

If the levering was to fail then my only other choice would be with a couple of sticks of dynamite, that is, if I'd any idea of using the stuff properly without blowing myself into a thousand pieces. After a little more persuasion with the lever my persistence paid off and the rock suddenly gave and rolled down causing the silt to explode into a psychedelic form of cloud as it drifted on the current.

I began attacking the next rock with more brute force, which proved just as stubborn before finally giving. Every rock after gave easily, and slowly and surely, I'd created a tunnel large enough to safely squeeze through.

I dropped the crowbar to the seabed, waited a few moments for the silt to settle before shining the torch beam into the dark void that stretched into oblivion. I half expected something to suddenly shoot out of the hole but nothing did. Still I hesitated from venturing into the unknown, wondering whether I should prop the tunnel with appropriate rigging before I entered, but that would have taken more time. I also discarded the lifeline because I thought it could snag as I went in. I tied the line to a rock so Shamus wouldn't panic if he suddenly realized I wasn't attached to the other end. Satisfied, I kicked the fins hard and slipped through the hole, pushing loose boulders aside. At first I swam cautiously slow, apprehensive of what lay ahead in the gloom. I could even admit to being a little scared.

The claustrophobic tunnel I was swimming through began to widen with every swim stroke. I would have expected to find a certain amount of sea-life, maybe a few curious fish darting into the torch beam, but strangely, it seemed devoid of anything, even vegetation. I checked my depth gauge on a regular basis. I made a quick calculation. By maintaining the direction I was heading, the readings showed that with every swim stroke I was beginning to surface. I slowed my ascent to acclimate.

When I finally broke the surface I found myself in a place of pitch blackness. I got to my feet, pointing the torch beam into the darkness to remove any concerns I had of a prehistoric beast surging towards me, though I did wonder if I should breathe the air in case there were any living parasites breeding in this hole that no scientist had ever heard of before. I took the risk and removed the aqualung mouthpiece, face mask and fins, suddenly catching a smell that at first I couldn't identify. I laid out my pathway through the water with the torch beam and waded ashore.

I'd landed on cold, dry sand that clogged between my wet toes, a secret beach with no sunshine. I dropped the fins and facemask to the ground and eased the aqualung from my shoulders along with the weight belt, and began flicking the beam in different directions in fits of organized impatience. I soon realized that someone had found this beach before me.

The torch beam landed on empty wooden crates scattered around. There was no lettering or indication of age or era stencilled on the crates so I'd no idea how long the crates had been there but they appeared quite old. I startled when the torch beam illuminated an old diving suit complete with lead weighted boots and iron helmet hanging ghost like from a rock wall. Beside the suit were what I assumed to be a hand operated air pump and coils upon coils of air pipe. There were also three tall oxyacetylene bottles with hoses and cutting tools. Everything I saw directed me into searching for a second entrance to the cavern, as the equipment had to have been transported by land and not by sea.

I moved forward.

Something snapped beneath my footing.

I stopped and took a tentative step back. I shone the torch beam down onto the broken object. I was now beginning to get used to the odd skeleton or two popping up from the ground, only this time I was guilty of standing on a skeletal frame, wearing rotting dungarees, and breaking its left tibia in two places. Slightly beyond the skeleton's outstretched bony hand there was an implement which I picked up for closer inspection under the torch beam. The shape alone told me it was a WWII submachine gun; German by its design, a substantially lethal weapon in its killing days. Not now, just rusting steel far beyond repair to be used again.

I threw the relic down and continued the search for the elusive entrance.

The torch beam landed on a waxed tarpaulin thrown over a large rectangular object and tied with rope. I pulled on the ropes; the ropes broke easily with rot. I peeled back the tarpaulin, amazed to find what I assumed to be a diesel engine and adjacent to the engine a square metal tank. I reached round and tapped the tank, estimating that it was a quarter full of what

I presumed was old diesel. I removed the tarpaulin fully and let it drop to the ground.

I was standing there admiring a 1935 Lister Cold Start six horsepower diesel engine according to the information plate attached to the machine. Surprisingly it was in pristine condition and bolted to a wooden trolley fitted with four steel wheels for transporting the contraption. Not that it would have moved easily dragging the engine across sand, I would have thought.

I looked the machine over, flicking the torch beam in every nook and cranny. I located two rubber cables attached to what I assumed was a dynamo. From the dynamo drive shaft there was a leather drive belt attached to the engines main drive wheel. On further investigation my torch beam followed the cables from the dynamo out into the darkness, each cable veering in a different direction. I ran the torch beam along one of the cables and came across a Bakelite lamp-holder, its filament lamp still wedged in the holder, although from where I stood it was difficult to assess if the filament would still burn. More interestingly, I wondered if the engine would still run and would the dynamo still generate electricity.

I tugged the leather drive belt to test its firmness. It seemed solid enough and undamaged by age. I'd once seen a demonstration of a Lister engine in operation. I tried to remember the procedure the demonstrator used to prepare the starting sequence before the demonstrator had hand cranked the engine. I looked around the machine and found the cranking handle under the engine. I retrieved it and slipped it onto the spindle of the flywheel. As I recalled, there were four stages to the sequence. First I turned the compression screw clockwise to its closed position. I found the fuel line and opened the fuel valve. Then I turned the carburettor throttle three quarters open. I took a firm grip of the cranking handle, took in a deep breath and began turning the flywheel clockwise or at least attempted to rotate the flywheel because it was partially seized. I mustered a little more effort and got the flywheel moving, gathering speed. The engine spluttered into life and I quickly removed the cranking handle and stood back. The engine spat out a gurgled sound of strangulation and belched out a cloud of black acrid smoke and promptly died a death. I closed everything up just in case the carburettor flooded with fuel, and then I tried again, mainly because my torch battery was fading fast.

I repeated the starting procedure. Cranked the flywheel with more enthusiasm, shouting encouragement for the machine to show some life, 'kick in you piece of iron shit!', and this time it responded positively. It coughed and spluttered into life, black smoke seeping from the engine's exhaust pipe; a slight groan as it picked up speed before bursting into a crescendo of clattering noise; a roaring piece of hardened machinery. Thick choking black smoke bellowed from the exhaust. The stench of burnt diesel filled my nostrils and my tongue tingled with the taste of the atmosphere. I quickly adjusted the carburettor and opened the compression screw a few turns. There was a sudden squeak from the dynamo and in seconds that too kicked into life.

Slowly the voltage built up. The cavern illuminated or in this case half illuminated because half the lamps didn't work, yet the wattage produced was far more encouraging than the weak light from a battery torch. The cavern I was inside was enormous. I turned to look around. That was when I saw it.

I think my jaw dropped to my knees at that point. It was an awesome sight. There, half submerged in the water, listing onto its portside side, was the biggest rusting bucket of a submarine that would have a salvager rubbing his hands to salvage. I saw the ensign and the flaking lettering on the conning tower that highlighted that I'd found the elusive ghost submarine, the I-52.

I just stood there numbed. Not a flicker of emotion did I display. Just struck down with an imaginary paralysis and unable to mutter a word or raise a finger in triumph. I don't recall how long I was standing there with no elation, nothing but a stare of utter disbelief but eventually I came to and exploded in delight.

Out loud, almost unheard with the sound of the Lister engine drowning my voice, I bellowed out, "Wow!"

Yet through my joy I tried to imagine how the hell the submarine got inside the cavern in the first place. How did it manage to navigate into the cave and beach itself? Perhaps it had crashed at speed, its weight momentum carrying it through and probably caused the rock fall. But I couldn't see any damage to the submarine's hull to verify my theory. But who cared! For the moment I was the proud owner of a submarine and I wondered if I should share the find with anyone.

I edged closer, noticing two rusty wire ropes which were attached to points on the bow of the submarine that I couldn't see. The wire ropes drooped down into the sand half buried. I glanced over my shoulder and soon realized the purpose of the steel wires. Beyond the clattering six horsepower Lister was a bigger Lister diesel engine, at least eighteen horsepower, and it was mounted on a large iron structure at the rear of the cavern. The big Lister was attached mechanically to an iron contraption embedded into the rock walls of the cavern. In the middle of the frame was an enormous double motor winch system operated with an array of different sized cogs. That's how the submarine had been beached, simply dragged into the cavern. The positioning of the submarine was no fluke but a highly organized operation that would have taken months to set up. This was no overnight impulsion. Extreme strategic planning had gone into this piece of historical ingenuity.

Now it all started to make sense. The wartime photographs; the vessel being deliberately sunk and hidden inside the cavern. But that didn't explain the rock-fall? Was that deliberately done to conceal the submarine? I had to assume it was, and if that was the intention, then there was definitely another entrance somewhere close by.

I resumed my search around the cavern walls for the elusive entrance and finally I came across another significant rock-fall. I shone the torch beam through the cracks in the rocks and there, lodged in-between fallen debris, I saw the protruding bones of a right hand curled round what I assumed was another rusting German submachine gun. I noticed a ring dangling on the index finger bone. I reached through the gap in the rocks up to my elbow, prised the finger bones loose from its grip on the gum, slipped the trinket from the skeletal finger and carefully retrieved the piece of jewellery for examination.

I blew the dust from the ring, wet my forefinger and rubbed away the remaining dirt. It was a man's gold signet ring, old gold and heavy too, with a cluster of minute diamonds circling the initials J.M etched on the ring's face. I'd probably found the only evidence that could identify the victim of the rock fall. Though I don't usually rob the dead of their personal treasure, bearing in mind I don't usually find bodies, what the ring could indicate was an explanation on how the submarine had arrived inside the cavern in the first place. I placed the ring in my water resistant pocket for safe keeping.

I decided that if this had been the main entrance to the cavern by land then the rock fall had ended its existence. I considered the chances of excavating the rock fall, but from where I stood any attempt to dislodge the rocks would have resulted in a cave-in. I certainly didn't want to be in the vicinity if it did and I decided I'd leave that to the experts if the situation should arise. I turned my attention to the submarine instead.

I spent a few moments speculating a number of possibilities on how I could climb aboard the submarine. The most feasible was to scramble up the side to get onto the deck or conning tower and try the escape hatches. I moved round the hull to the other side of the submarine and discovered I wouldn't need to waste that kind of energy. Where the submarine leaned over precariously, I'd found my way inside. It was a straightforward man made entrance through a section of the hull obviously cut out by the oxyacetylene. I shone the torch beam into the dark hole and cautiously entered the torpedo room. What I found inside highlighted the horrors of what had happened.

With a quick head count I estimated there were at least twenty skeletal frames and all in bullet riddled uniforms of submariners. They had dropped where they died, scattered around the torpedo room, some of the skeletons at distorted angles and probable victims of hand grenade explosions. I could only imagine the fierce gun battle that had taken place. I moved on deeper inside, carefully treading over and around more skeletons. I'd stopped counting the submariners after thirty, finding more victims around the submariners sleeping quarters and empty cargo bays. I'd the feeling that the further I ventured inside the belly of the I-52, the more bones I'd find. And I did. For a fleeting moment I wondered which one could be Tanamoto's father though impossible to identify amongst the mess.

There was no question that it had been a one-sided massacre. The Japanese submariners had never stood a chance. Blackened bulkheads and overheads showed more explosions had occurred, probably from many more hand grenades and resulting in more unfortunate dismembered skeletons caught up in the blasts and all now part of a mixed-up skeletal jigsaw puzzle. I could almost smell the gory mess of death.

The stern of the submarine, mainly the engine room and battery room was submerged in sea water and was impassable. I decided against a dive because it would have told me nothing other than confirm that the enlarged aerial photographs showing the saboteurs attaching their mines was correct and the mines had done their job savagely. I assumed there would be more victims there, if the sea hadn't already devoured the bones. I explored further rooms with the same results; death and destruction. The control deck showed signs that there had been a serious fire, some skeletons still had taut flesh stuck to their bones like melted plastic.

I looked up inside the conning tower tunnel and saw that the hatch was open. I climbed the metal rung ladder. I found a lone skeleton draped over the conning tower defence cannon. It gave me a thought. Perhaps the battling submariner had fired a couple of cannon shells that had been the probable cause of the rock fall that had trapped the person whose skeleton was embedded in the entrance tunnel. Maybe the aftershock of the cannon shells exploding inside the cavern had also brought down the seabed entrance. I suddenly had moving images of the battle inside the cavern inside my head as I put together the pieces of what I thought had occurred in 1944. It was horrific no doubt; the raging battle; the sound of bullets splattering flesh; the inevitable screams from dying men.

I broke off. I'd seen enough of the battling ghosts and returned the way I had entered, glad to escape the death hole. I also came out of the cargo hold empty-handed. Whatever had been aboard at the time of the hijacking, it had gone now. And the gold bullion too, that had gone. It meant my friends had died for nothing. It meant that my plan of luring out of hiding the mastermind behind this murderous campaign had gone too. That had been my intention all along; to dangle the pot of gold in front of the baddies and lure the bastards out into the open. Though I hadn't quite worked out how I would have exacted my revenge. I made my way out of the submarines belly dejectedly.

My feet seemed to drag heavily through the sand as I trudged away from the I-52 in deep thought, coughing with the accumulation of thick diesel smoke in the air. I was so mad with my failure to find anything worthwhile to salvage that I would have no doubt missed what I kicked in the sand if it hadn't flicked up a few inches and the glitter of light it reflected caught my eye. Natural inquisitiveness made me pick it up. It was a metal block approximately three inches long and one inch wide and half an inch thick. It had three Japanese symbols stamped in the metal. The sand had kept it clean and I knew old gold when I saw it and the ingot I held in my hand brightened my belief. I wondered how many more pieces of gold lay buried in the sand.

It was moments like these that I wished I'd brought my metal detector along with me instead of having to sift gently through the sand with my feet. But after a few unproductive minutes I realized I was wasting my time, as there were no more ingots to be found. Whatever amount of gold had been available it was no longer in this place of death and probably gone forever. More significantly, if this solitary ingot was part of the cargo then it proved conclusively that the gold had existed and Tanamoto's inventory was correct. It gave me plenty to think about. But everything led to the one question: where the frigging hell was the gold now?

I placed the ingot into the same waist belt pocket which held the ring I'd taken from skeleton, refastened the pocket securely, and then I went to collect my diving gear and switch off the Lister engine for the last time.

Within three steps my body had seized to an abrupt stop by the thunderous voice shouting over the clattering of the generator motor. It scared the hell out of me. My body felt as if someone had punched me violently in the heart region. I quickly located the source, a diver emerging from the water.

"Stand still!" The powerful foreign toned voice ordered me

I thought in my best interest I should comply with the request.

"One wrong move and you die, English pig!"

I was guessing, but by the sound of his voice I thought the approaching diver was a Russian. He was holding a polythene bag in one hand, the shape inside the bag was the distinctively shape of a machine-pistol and one that was pointing in my direction. He meant business that was for sure. I watched him remove his fins and throw them onto the sand as he came ashore. I thought about running but in what direction and to where? How far would I have gotten before he cut me down with bullets.

"Hand's high, where I can see them."

I raised them a fraction.

"You are alone?"

"No, strictly speaking."

"Put your hands higher, now!" There was anxiousness in his voice, his eyes frantically flicking in different directions while still trying to keep one eye on me. "Where are the others?"

I flicked my head in the direction of the submarine and said, "In that tin coffin over there. It's full of Japanese crewmen. But don't panic, they're not here for a beach party. They're all dead."

"You think you're funny, pig shit?"

I'd been called a few names in the past but *pig shit!* I'd no answer to that."

"Where's the gold?" The Russian spouted.

I shook my head. "There's no gold; nothing but ghosts."

The diver moved closer, pushing his facemask up onto his forehead. His expression told me he was agitated, and I was right about him being a Russian; he had the look of a Russian.

"Lying English bastard!" he shouted, the echo of his voice bouncing across the cavern walls before being overwhelmed by the noise of the Lister engine.

"Look here, "I said strongly. "English Bastard I don't mind. But I take offence to being called a liar! There's no gold, just a rusting piece of scrap submarine doubling as coffin. Why don't you go and see for yourself."

He gestured with the gun for me to move. "Towards the sub and no tricks," he ordered.

With reluctance I turned around and began trudging back to the sub while formulating a plan in my head of how I was going to relieve the Russian of his gun and shove it up the arse of his rubber suit. Even under threat I still felt confident I wasn't about to get a bullet in my back, well, at least not until he'd discovered for himself that there was nothing to find aboard the I-52 other than what I'd discovered.

When we reached the burnt hole in the side of the I-52, he peered inside, the gun still angled towards my face in case I decided to be the hero. He wasn't happy. "Where are the boxes?"

"You'll only find exactly what I told you, there's nothing here but corpses."

"Where is the gold?"

The corner of my top lip arched. "Give me a break, will you! It's a wreck, that's all. I'm just a wreck hunter. I'm not even interested in the salvage rights."

"Shut it, pig shit!"

"Is pig shit the best you can come up with?" I asked, only for the tip of the machine pistol to squash my left nostril and for me to smell the odour of a cheap plastic bag.

"You don't listen, pig shit!"

I can usually take an insult once without over-reacting. I can probably take the same insult twice with just a cringe. The third time rather out-stepped the boundaries of pleasantness, and this piece of frigging arrogance deserved a smack very quickly. I deliberated on how my plan of action would commence. In the meantime, he pushed the gun nozzle into my spine encouraging me to retreat back towards our discarded fins at the water's edge.

I decided that when the chance came I would execute a jumping back-kick. And when the chance arose I was just positioning myself for the attack when another diver broke the surface of the water and my strategy needed a rethink damn frigging quick. I could only curse the inconvenience; one man I could handle comfortably but two was risky. I held back sensibly.

The emerging diver shoved his facemask up onto his forehead. In one hand he too carried a machine pistol wrapped in a polythene bag, and in his other hand he held a rather fearsome and powerful gas propelled spear gun. I wouldn't be far wrong in assuming he wasn't after the fish. And I gathered by the smirk across his face that his sighting of the submarine impressed him greatly, but for how long?

"The contraband, it is here?" his deep voice also had the tone of a Russian.

From the corner of my eye I saw the Russian behind me shake his head. The second Russian began talking into a communication mouthpiece he had squeezed out from beneath the neck of his neoprene diving suit. It was impossible for me to hear the conversation he was having but by the look in his eyes as he talked and listened to ever he was communicating with, it sort of warned me that I might be in serious trouble and that a rethink of strategy to fight back had to mature very quick and now.

It's hard to think when you're under pressure. It's doubly hard to think when your life is in danger, and mine was seriously in that category. I'd only a split second thinking time. There was perhaps twenty feet between me and the spear gun I could see clearly being raised by the Russian in the water, its pointed projectile deliberately aimed in my direction. The twenty feet diminished to ten feet as the Russian moved towards me. I don't think he would have missed me from there.

Everyone has a right to survive the merciless intentions of a cold-blooded killer. When death threatens, the natural instinct is to either run for your life or stay and fight. Despite the odds I stood my ground in readiness.

Managing a slight glance over my shoulder I saw the sadistic grin appear on the face of the Russian who was now beside me; his slight shuffle to one side to put space between us instantly warned me that the moment was coming. I concentrated hard on the Russian in the water watching his trigger finger on the spear gun, waiting for the finger to curl and pull and when the finger did curl I reacted swiftly, surprising Mister Hapless at the side of me.

With lightening reactions I palmed away the tip of the machine pistol that dug into my ribs and dragged the startled Russian into the path of the oncoming spear. I felt the vibration of the spear penetrating Mister Hapless somewhere in the midriff. I even heard the muffled squelch as the sharp spear ripped through the neoprene of his diving suit, embedding deep into the lining of his stomach. He slumped forward as if he'd been thumped in the solar plexus. Instantly I grabbed his falling gun hand and raised the machine pistol, pushing the dying forefinger hard down on the trigger unleashing a line of bullets that zipped across the water. I hit anything that moved and the diver in the water caught the brunt of the bullets as he frantically attempted to lift his own machine pistol. I'd beaten him to the draw. The diver arched backwards spectacularly, rolled over, spasmodically jerked and laid faced down drifting in the water.

I let go of the diver I held and let the body slump to the floor. I stepped back breathing heavily, looking down at the embedded spear in the Russian's midriff, the blood pumping from the wound. I listened to the last gasps of a dying man and for a moment I didn't care less that I'd been responsible for the deaths of two men. Not that I enjoyed the moment. Far from it, as a sickly taste rose from the depths of my stomach and I almost threw up when I realized that it could have been me laying there instead of the Russian. One thing I could be certain of, I'd never make any money being a hardened killer. I'd too much of a conscience for that.

I got my brain functioning again knowing that my problems inside the cavern might not be over. I dropped to one knee, grabbed the machine pistol from the dead Russian beside me, and remained alert, watching the water with the expectancy of others. Five minutes I waited and watched. Five minutes and no one else emerged. Nothing disturbed the water with the exception of the diver's body already in the water drifting in circles. Only then did I move and quickly put on my aqualung and fins.

I never even turned off the generator as I waded back into the water but I did commandeer the spear gun from the floating diver as I passed and reloaded a spear I took from his diver's utility belt. I dived under the water quite prepared to fire the spear gun if necessary at anything that moved.

Thankfully there were no more ruthless characters waiting for me on my journey to the surface. When I finally bobbed my head up at the side of the *Muff*, Shamus had the appearance of a praying catholic churchgoer. "O' be Jesus, you're alright!"

I handed him the spear gun and climbed aboard noticing his strange look at my acquired collectable before placing it to one side. And then he was back in panic mode as he helped me aboard.

"Is everything alright, Shacks sir? Two divers from the *Flying Fish* went into the water from an inflatable. I tugged on the safety rope to warn you, I did, with no reply. Yer had me worried."

"Our paths crossed," I said.

"Well, everything's alright then, Shacks sir?"

"Yes, Shamus, everything is okay, now."

"Well it must be fine because yer here aboard safe and sound. That yer are, Shacks sir."

"Frigging hell, Shamus, whatever you want to say spit the damn thing out!"

"Well, Shacks sir. I'd be thinking they'd cause yer some bother, there being two of them."

"They did cause me some trouble. How do you think I got the spear gun?"

"Yer got into a fight, did yer, Shacks sir?"

"It was a little bit more than a fight, Shamus."

His complexion turned a peculiar shade of yellowish-white, as if he had suddenly taken ill. He raised an enquiring eyebrow and said, "There wouldn't be anything sinister going on that yer not telling me about, Shacks sir?"

"Shamus, do I look like that kind of chap that would leave you in the dark?"

Shamus glanced across the bay. "I don't see the other divers returning to the surface."

"I doubt you will for a little while. May I suggest you get the engine operational and get us out of here before the crew of the 'Flying-fish' realize their men won't be returning under their own steam?"

A wicked smirk emerged on Shamus's face. "Yer sorted them. Knocked them out for a few hours with a couple of uppercuts to the chin, did yer, Shacks sir?"

"Yes, something within that category."

Shamus looked at me suspiciously. "I'm not quite understanding, Shack sir."

"It's simple, Shamus. They're dead! Now get a move on!"

Shamus murmured the word *dead*.

"It was either them or me. I'd have thought you'd prefer it to be me."

Shamus started to panic. "Holy mother of god! They tried to kill yer, as in stone dead?"

I slashed my fingers across my throat. "Put it this way, Shamus. They'd no intention of taking me prisoner."

Shamus rolled his eye to the heavens. "O' Jesus be Jesus! Now I'm an accessory to murder."

"Stop being so dramatic Shamus. It was self defence. Nobody will blame you."

"The Garda will have to know, Shacks sir. Explain the situation."

"We'll sort that out later, Shamus. In the meantime get us out of here."

Shamus upped the anchor and dashed to the wheelhouse. I noticed he was mumbling to himself as he started the engine and got the *Muff* underway. I could tell he wasn't happy with the situation but at that moment I didn't care. I grabbed the binoculars and concentrated on the reactions aboard the *Flying Fish*. I ran the binoculars along the length of the deck which, unbelievably, had come alive with crewmen searching the waters for their men.

The *Muff* built up a good rate a knots and made good distance from where the *Flying Fish* was anchored. I did wonder how long it would be before their patience cracked and they went looking for their missing divers, and then reacted in the only way they knew; with violence; a good while I hoped, and long enough for us to abscond. Or maybe they wouldn't bother us at all considering Baltimore was bustling with activity. But I was only kidding myself. I was dealing with ruthless men. There was too much at stake. I'd be stupid to ignore that they'd hit us with everything they had. Whoever I was up against they'd already proven that they'd never hesitate to kill anyone who stood in their way. Shamus and I stood directly in their path. We'd become a hindrance to them, and I'm sure that the person pulling the strings will be so pissed off at this very moment. I didn't want to be around when they did, not yet anyway. But I was still curious over something.

I went back inside the wheelhouse and consulted the sea chart. I calculated that the cavern ran below the ruins of Dun an Oir, the fort of gold. I grinned to myself. Someone had a sense of humour, I thought.

"Shamus, is there a land route into the O'Driscoll fort on Clear Island?"

He wasn't happy with the question. "Yer've just committed a murder and yer want to go sight-seeing?"

"I need to check on something of importance."

"Forget it, Shacks sir. We'd be wasting time. Besides, the public are banned from the fort because it's falling to pieces; old buildings do that near the sea. Best we keep a direct course for Baltimore."

"I want to go and see for myself." I said commandingly

"It wouldn't be wise, Shacks sir."

"Go to the fort, Shamus, and with no deviations."

"The place is too dangerous, Shacks sir," he replied stubbornly.

"I still want to go there."

Shamus expressed his concern. "Why, Shacks sir? We're in enough trouble. We need to get far away from the *Flying Fish* as we possibly can."

"We're going to the fort regardless because by my calculations there's an uncharted cavern directly below. We've plenty of time before anybody discovers what's happened beneath Roaring Water Bay. We'll make one quick sweep of the fort and be home for tea in a flash."

Shamus was so incensed that I don't think he heard what I said about the cavern, "It's foolish, Shacks sir. It's just a mound of rock with ruins. There's nothing worth seeing."

"I'll be the judge of that, Shamus, just steer the boat in that direction."

Shamus mumbled some disapproving words but he did change course and sailed the *Muff* around Cape Clear heading for the north harbour of the island. I couldn't have complained if instead he had decided to head straight for Baltimore and hand me over to the authorities for crimes committed. But I felt he actually trusted the decisions I made. I also think it's fair to say that he also preferred the money I was paying him rather than the tedious affair of filling in witness statements. I went below, dried off and changed into walking gear.

Shamus's usual placid sailing skills had deserted him as he pushed the *Muff* towards land like a man possessed. I was bouncing around the cabin as he hammered the boat through the surging swell, the bow lifting high before slapping back down. I made a passing comment of the passage being rather rough and all Shamus did was he hit the throttle defiantly harder while bombarding me with glares and scowls and muttering under his breath, his lips barely moving as if he was practicing a ventriloquist act. As he turned his head away I managed to catch some of his moaning: "just making a living;" he said, "get meself dragged into the dirty gutters; me, Shamus O'Malley, accessory to devious mishaps beneath the waters of Roaring Water Bay," and so on he moaned.

To shut him up, I said, "By the way, Shamus, I found the submarine."

His head shot round. "Yer'll be having me on, Shacks sir?"

"Scouts honour and hope to die if I'm fibbing. But if you had listened to me instead of complaining you would have heard me mention a cavern beneath the fort."

"I'm not deaf. I heard alright."

"The submarine's inside the cavern, hidden there since 1944."

"How come it's never been discovered until now, Shacks sir?"

"The sub was hidden inside there deliberately. Remember the photographs showing the sub under attack?"

Shamus nodded thoughtfully.

"That had nothing to do with the war. It was being hijacked in broad daylight, sunk, and then dragged into the cavern by a powerful winch. Once the submarine was inside, the hijackers had all the time in the world to complete their piracy. Naturally they met resistance from the submariners; a gun battle ensued and the submariners were slaughtered and left to rot down there. But something else happened, an explosion I think, and it caused a rock fall which entombed the submarine inside the cavern."

Shamus was horrified by it all. He made the sign of the cross across his chest again and said sadly, "O' Jesus in heaven! What a terrible thing to happen, Shacks sir. Who'd want to hijack a submarine and kill the crew if it had nothing to do with the war? What reason would it serve?"

I took the gold ingot I'd salvaged from the cavern from my utility belt and held it aloft between my thumb and forefinger so he could see it clearly. "How's that for a reason?"

Shamus's eyes lit up. He let go of the wheel and stepped down into the cabin and took the ingot from me as if it was a delicate piece of Ming china. "It's pure?" He asked.

"Snap your teeth if you bite it."

He jerked the ingot up and down in his hand to test its weight. "Quite heavy too," he said pleasingly. And then his excitement was quickly brushed aside when he negatively said, "What's happened so far is hardly worth the effort of one measly gold bar." He gave me back the ingot. "Not worth dying fer." And he dashed for the wheel when the bow of boat veered to the right violently and regained control.

"How would you feel if the total weight amounted to around two hundred million pounds in English money?"

He didn't look round as he steered. Over his shoulder, he said, "I'd be doing an Irish jig around me boat, that I would, Shacks sir."

"*That* ingot you hold in your hand is only a fraction of a fraction."

Shamus stiffened as he stared ahead, then his lips moved but for a few seconds no sound emerged before he found his voice. "There's more?"

"Cases full I should imagine."

"That's a lot of gold, Shacks sir."

"Allegedly, mind you. There's no guarantees."

"Who'd want to leave all that gold behind in the cavern? A bloody lunatic, if yer ask me. Come to think of it, so did you!"

"Ah-well, that's where the mystery continues. I found only the one ingot. I assume the hijackers disappeared with the loot because it isn't aboard the sub now."

"So who do yer think took the gold?"

"The hijackers did, who else? I'm rather hoping the Dun an Oir fort can give us a few clues, if only to reveal how they entered and left the cavern Maybe we might find evidence of surplus stock they left behind. There could be some useful information. Even reveal a name perhaps."

"Yer'd be asking for a lot, Shacks sir. That coastline has taken a fair battering over the years and there's sea salt erosion to consider."

"We might get lucky."

Shamus disheartened, the gloom returned to his face. "So we're looking fer an invisible entrance and pieces of scrap material left over from the war?"

"You've got the idea, Shamus."

"So yer're still interested in finding the gold then, Shacks sir?"

"Damn right I am, Shamus. I have a more prominent reason to find the gold and it has nothing to do with money."

"Well, I'm surprised at that, Shacks sir. Another reason rather than be rich?"

"The gold is my path to redemption. Through my insatiable appetite to find things I inadvertently dragged two good people into the affray. They were murdered for knowing nothing."

I noticed Shamus gripped the wheel tightly in shock. "O me mother of god! There's death involved and yer failed to tell me you're on a revenge mission and me poor soul is stuck in the middle."

"Seeking revenge isn't exactly the first thing you tell a stranger, Shamus. I find the gold and I find the killers."

"So it's all about getting even?"

"There's nothing wrong with getting even."

"No, there's not, Shacks sir. But aren't yer taking a huge gamble?"

"Would that be on keeping my sanity or finding some killers? Whichever I care to choose, Shamus, I'm taking the biggest gamble of my life and I don't mind admitting I'm scared as hell. But it's my fight and I'm sorry I got you involved. And I've no intention of putting you in a precarious position; well not on purpose."

"I can walk away then? Steer me boat straight back to Baltimore and forget I ever met yer?"

"I wouldn't stop you if you changed course."

"Then you'd just find another mug to drag into danger?"

"I hadn't really thought about hiring anybody else."

"Well it's a good job you haven't.!" he announced. "Shamus O'Malley doesn't run from a fight. So I'll be staying if yer don't mind, Shacks, sir?"

I smiled. "I appreciate that, Shamus."

I remembered the ring I took from the corpse in the cavern. I retrieved it from my diving belt and joined Shamus in the wheelhouse. I held the ring up to the light and examined it further. On the inside of the ring, etched into the gold, I could faintly make out McCracken, which I assumed stood for the M on the ring face. I showed Shamus the piece. "Found this on the finger of a skeleton. I think it belonged to one of the hijacker's because a Japanese sailor wouldn't be wearing such jewellery. Seen anything like it before, Shamus?"

He shook his head slowly. "It be expensive I'd say, Shacks, sir."

"The initials J.M. or the name McCracken mean anything to you, Shamus?"

Shamus shook his head. "Ireland's an extremely big place, Shacks sir. McCracken is a popular name. Perhaps I should be out there making house to house calls instead of sailing me boat?"

"Subtle sarcasm isn't called for, Shamus. If you don't mind, that's my speciality. Something you're not very good at."

"Well, look at it seriously, Shacks sir. It could relate to a number of people scattered around Ireland."

"Perhaps your house calls isn't far wrong, Shamus. If we can trace the ring to a family of McCraken's then there might be a pot of gold at the end of the rainbow with a leprechaun to greet us after all."

Shamus scoffed my hopes hastily. "Who'd be that lucky, Shacks sir?"

"There's no luck involved, my distrusting Irishman. I might just know the person who can help us on the matter. He's quite an expert on bad people, especially the Irish breed before WWII started."

Deveron had come to my mind but I didn't fancy another trip across Ireland.

Something else was bothering me too. Something I'd struggle to avoid. The longer I continued this campaign for revenge, the more I'd need a pair of waders to wear because the shit piling beneath me was getting deeper and deeper and deeper and soon I would be up to my neck in the putrid game of dodging death.

As for the dead divers I'd left behind inside the cavern, if the situation should arise and I was dragged before a court, I was concerned how I would prove that I had acted in self defence, as no court in the land would believe my story. In truth I probably would never have to defend myself. Dead men can't talk.

I looked across at Shamus. I guessed he must see me as a pretty hard and ruthless character. That didn't really bother me either. Yet hiding behind my show of contempt I knew that I'd sunk low in the credibility status as I reflected on my achievements to commit enough crimes to warrant a lengthy stretch in an Irish prison. I still had one chance of reparation if I could pluck from obscurity the mastermind behind all this mess, then a stint behind bars would be worth the trouble.

We sailed into North harbour on Cape Clear just as the ferry was departing back to Baltimore.

While Shamus docked the *Muff*, I gathered a few necessities into a rucksack, climbing ropes and pulleys, hammer, hung a pair of binoculars around my neck and went up on deck. After Shamus had locked the galley door we set off up the hill and followed the road, mingling with other bird spotting, sight-seeing tourists and mixing with the local islanders.

We walked briskly along making good ground. I'd no worries about any sudden attacks from behind because Shamus was constantly glancing over both his shoulders like a man possessed, highly suspicious of everyone that we passed. He must have made himself dizzy by the time he gave up his security precautions.

We'd reached the heritage centre now. It wasn't hard to imagine the simplicity for the hijackers to conduct activities on the Island in 1944 without interference. Before tourism the island would have been practically deserted apart from the residential Islanders minding their own business. Overall it presented the hijacker's with the opportunity and freedom to organize to perfection a successful high sea robbery and with all the time they needed to ensure its success. I wondered what kind of man came up with this intriguing crime.

We left the normal pathways and crossed the foot flattened grassland path that guided us to the cliff edges which were protected by a battered wire fence and a stone wall to the right and nothing else to prevent danger. One look over the cliff edge and the sight of the rugged sea inlet below should have been sufficient to scare off anybody who wanted to attempt a crossing over to the ruins of Dun an Oir. And at high tide it was impossible to cross over on foot. That meant when the fort was built there must have been some form of bridge to cross. My guess would have been a rope and wood panelled design but it would have been suspect to swaying in high winds.

At low tide I imagined the builders would have created a stone bridge because down the side of the cliff was a narrow ledge descending to the raging sea below.

I wondered how the hijackers had negotiated the problem of crossing over to the fort, though I suppose in the forties the fort wouldn't have been in as worst state than it was now. Looking at the fort, it was hardly a spectacular piece of engineering to admire. Not a huge construction. Stone built although the battlements had almost gone. And two of the outer walls were half demolished, but strangely the fort's upper floor was still intact and now covered with a mixture of vegetation.

Shamus decided to breach the damaged wire fencing and climbed through. He risked a peek over the edge cliff. "I don't think I'd be venturing down there, Shacks sir. Not even with all the mountaineering gear in the world."

I joined him and had a shufti myself. Frightening was the verdict "I wouldn't dream of sending you down there, it's far too dangerous."

"Yer be thinking of sending me down there would yer now, Shacks sir? Now there's a surprise. But I was right about the fort. There's nothing to see but ruins and rocks and more rocks and a sheer drop into the jaws of death. This is a dangerous place."

I had to agree with him on that. I pressed the binoculars to my eyes and made a quick assessment of the ruins. It was difficult to tell if there had ever been a hidden entrance inside the fort I wondered if the rock fall had perhaps sealed the tunnel forever therefore it would be pointless for me and Shamus to waste time climbing across only to find nothing. At least I'd satisfied my curiosity and I could tick it off my list.

I swung the binoculars away from the fort and in the far in the distance I could see the *Flying Fish* still anchored. I nudged Shamus in the arm.

"There," I pointed out to sea. "Didn't I say they'd be too dumb to up anchor without first establishing the safe return of their divers. We'd plenty of time to conclude our business before returning to Baltimore."

"That maybe so, Shacks, sir. But have yer yet decided how we explain to the Garda about those dead men back there?"

"We won't have to, Shamus."

"They'll have a warrant out on us."

"Who's going to tell the Garda about us, the crew on the *Flying Fish* maybe? I don't think so, Shamus. If I'm right they won't be reporting anything untoward. The questions the authorities would ask would be far too incriminating for them to explain away."

Shamus had agleam in his eyes. "So I'll not to be standing trial as an accomplice then, Shacks sir?"

"Not a chance. They'll cut and run just as we've done."

"We should be doing ourselves right now, back to Baltimore, Shacks sir. Forget these crazy ideas of hidden passages."

"It's not as crazy as you think, Shamus. I'm willing to wager all your money there's a secret entrance in close proximity of the fort."

"Yer really convinced, Shacks, Sir?"

"Frigging hell, think about it, Shamus. No sane warrior, man or beast, even in the fifteenth century, builds a fort on a splinter of rock without having a secret means of escape in-case the unthinkable happens and the fort is attacked and taken. This fort was probably built as a bank to hold their worldly treasures from marauding Vikings plundering their lands. I think the hijackers discovered the cavern or at least knew of its existence for a long time and cleverly used it to their advantage."

"Well we're not going to find it today, Shacks sir. And yer're forgetting that the *Flying Fish* has more horsepower than the *Muff*, so we'd better get away before they catch up with us."

"I shrugged. "Perhaps we should get back, Shamus. Maybe I'm being too over ambitious in my presumption of an entrance. I have to be honest though, and what I thought was an entrance would be impassable for even a trained mouse."

"Does it really matter, Shacks, Sir? Yer said the gold wasn't there to be found."

"I detest incomplete theories of events. And not just that-," I broke off, my eyes flicking in all directions. I could have sworn something had whizzed past my cheek bone and fragmented a piece of the rock wall at the side of me. Unsure of what had just occurred I grabbed Shamus by the arm in panic, dragged him down to the ground and we both scrambled behind the stone wall like two scared rabbits.

I scanned the terrain in all directions. I was sure it had been a bullet ricochet that had been too close for comfort.

"Hell, Shacks Sir, what's wrong now, yer're turning me into a right jittery old bugger."

I gave him the bad news as softly as I could. "We're being shot at."

"What the devil are yer're talking about, Shacks Sir?"

He got his answer straight away as another bullet ricochet spat from the rock wall just in front of Shamus.

He was flat down to the ground eating daisies quicker than a magician's turn of hand.

"What the hell's going on, Shacks sir?"

Not trying to be funny, I said, "It might just be possible someone wants us dead!"

"O' Mother Theresa, protect my miserable life." He was too flat to the floor to cross his chest but he still tried.

"Keep your eyes peeled for the gunman."

"I don't wish to sound disrespectful, Shacks sir. But for an Englishman yer can attract some unscrupulous shit. Trouble follows yer quicker than sticking yer finger in a hornet's nest."

I was still focusing hard on the rocks above. "Shamus, shut up! Instead of feeling sorry for yourself, try finding where the shots came from."

He looked at me horrified. "Not on yer life, Shacks sir. Have me head blown off the moment I lift it?"

I gave him a disapproving look. "Coward," I teased.

"Coward I am, Shacks sir? And I'm willing to accept the white feather that goes with cowardice. Or would yer prefer if I was to dive from my cover and pretend I'd been shot? Yer never know it might just flush the blighter from his vantage point."

"Thanks for the offer of heroism, Shamus, but ill advised because the shooter will only put another bullet in you to make doubly sure."

"Jesus, be Jesus! I'd be joking, Shacks sir. Do I have suicidal idiot stamped across me forehead?"

I gave the pretence of looking. "You're so right, Shamus; there is something stamped there in big letters."

Shamus went cross-eyed trying to look and instinctively touched his forehead.

I shook my head in disbelief and then concentrated on finding an escape route back to the boat. I soon realized the options were limited. There was too much open ground and nothing solid enough around to use a suitable cover if we were to make a mad dash for safety. That's when I heard excitable voices approaching. I risked a look over the wall. Tourists! Lots of them! Taking pictures of the fort. Our rescuing cavalry had arrived. The gunman had obviously seen this and realized the opportunity had gone. But was the gunman still watching; waiting for the right moment?

When the tourists were closer I stood up from behind the wall and began searching the terrain through the binoculars. I saw nothing. Either the gunman was well concealed or he had made a hasty retreat, perhaps to find another firing position. And since I'd no intention of overstaying my welcome on the island, I dragged Shamus to his feet and we mingled with the group of unsuspecting tourists until they decided to move on back up the hill. We kept close, using them as a protective screen. Naughty I know, but I was confident the gunman wouldn't take the chance of a full scale security alert by shooting everyone in sight just to get to us.

Back on the pathway we had a clear sight of the surrounding area. No one approached us with any threat. No weapons shoved into our backs. After a few seconds I was confident the gunman had disappeared faster than a whippet with its tail on fire. We stayed with the group no longer than necessary, and once I verified there was no longer a danger to us, we legged-it back to the *Muff*.

I blew a huge sigh of relief when we clambered back aboard. I was probably more in a hurry than Shamus as

I quickly unleashed the mooring rope while he started the engine. I happened to glance across to a small motor launch moored close by because I didn't recall it being there when we first arrived. And when I saw *Flying Fish* in black stencil on the boats bow I knew how wrong I had been in assuming their inability to react quickly. They had obviously followed us immediately when we'd raised anchor.

I also made another serious error when we boarded. Neither of us had bothered to check the *Muff* for intruders, notably, failing to notice the galley door had been forced and then closed. I went down the galley steps unsuspectingly and was stopped in my stride by the gun shoved into my face. I back tracked into the wheelhouse. Shamus cursed as I resurfaced from the galley with my hands in the air.

The gunman, a scruffily dressed, well built man with dark hair, ordered me to stand next to Shamus so he had both of us in sight and we were both staring down the barrel of a silenced hand gun. I wondered if he'd been the same gunman on the cliffs taking pop-shots at us. If so, he must have sprinted back to the harbour to have gained such an advantage over us, but he appeared to me as if he hadn't broke into a sweat and had probably been left behind to watch the *Muff*. It meant that there were others.

Shamus broke the silence and told me off. "I thought yer said there'd be no reaction? No one would bother us. Hell, Shacks Sir, yer've got me in bloody war!"

The gunman angered, threatening wildly with the gun. "Be quiet you babbling buffoon!"

Shamus was a little upset at being compared to the animal kingdom, but I was more interested as to why the gunman's eyes kept shifting beyond us as if he was looking back up the hill where we'd just come from. It was obvious he was waiting for someone else to join us. I managed to flick my eyes in the direction the gunman was looking. Yes I was right. I could just make out the two figures hurriedly in descent and heading for the harbour. Though difficult to tell from this distance there was a similarity about the two approaching runners, but my brain was already in overdrive arranging a get-out clause and how I should deal with the gunman in front of me. By sheer luck I got my chance to make amends for my flaw in concentration when we'd boarded the *Muff*.

Two things simultaneously helped me decide my plan of action. The *Muff* rocked sharply by incoming waves at the precise moment the gunman elected to glance towards the hillside. The wobble of the boat slightly unbalanced the gunman. I reacted with the speed of electric current making contact and powered into the gunman's midriff, grabbing and twisting the gun hand away. Two shots plopped into the wheelhouse bulkhead as we grappled for supremacy. I managed to interlock my foot around his leg, nudge him hard and we crashed down the cabin steps.

I banged my head on the way down that made me groggy. The gunman hadn't been as fortunate and I think his spine had taken the brunt of both our weights as we fell. The brief fight was over and I relieved him of his gun. He was out cold. I got to my feet and kicked him to make sure. He never twitched a muscle. I kicked him hard a couple of times to recheck his response. He still didn't move or murmur. I was slightly concerned that the death count had risen until I heard him moan.

The *Muff's* engine fired up and Shamus popped his head down into the cabin. "There be two rather angry men hurtling down the hill, Shacks, sir...O be Jesus! Is he dead too?"

"Never mind them! Help me get this lump off the boat."

We hauled the man unceremoniously up onto the deck.

"What yer going to do with him Shacks sir?"

"What you should always do with stowaways. Ready? One...two...three-"

And together we promptly swung and ejected the body onto the jetty. The man moaned when he landed heavily.

I said, "Did you hear that, Shamus? Now you've observed firsthand that I'm not the cold-blooded killer you think I am. Now get us out of here, fast!"

Shamus steered the *Muff* away from the jetty. I pumped two silenced bullets into the engine of the motor launch bearing the *Flying Fish* logo, and then I tossed the weapon into the depths of the harbour. It never occurred to me if I'd done any serious damage to the launch but I was confident I had. When we'd gained good distance I glanced back to where we'd just vacated and a lump suddenly lodged in my throat when I saw them. As luck would have it, the decision to incapacitate the launch's motor proved priceless. The two men Shamus and I had seen running down to the jetty had boarded the motor launch that I'd shot full of holes. Though I couldn't be sure, taking in account the distance now between us, I could have sworn the two men resembled Damien Love and Theodore Hate, and they were in the process of unsuccessfully trying to start the frigging engine.

Chapter Nineteen

Shamus crashed the *Muff* through the waves at a top rate of knots. The ride across Roaring Water Bay is rough enough at a normal pace but the speed we were pushing caused huge waves to crash over the bow and cover the wheelhouse windows with sea spray causing us momentary blindness. I'd no complaints with the way Shamus treated his boat. I wanted the nautical miles between us and Clear Island stretched as far as feasibly possible and Shamus was achieving the feat magnificently. We approached Baltimore harbour under the cover of darkness.

My immediate worry now was the safety of Shamus. I was sure Love and Hate would have clocked the *Muff* leaving North Harbour and would now go looking for the owner. I didn't want Shamus meeting either of them in a dark alley and have his death on my conscience. With the boat tightly moored, I handed Shamus a prewritten sizable cheque for his services. His eyes widened as he stared at the figure.

"There's a problem, Shamus?"

"It's a huge mistake, Shacks sir."

"It's not sufficient to cover the costs?"

"It's too much."

"Nonsense, Shamus. You deserve it."

"But it's five thousand Euros!"

"And you find that a problem?"

"I don't feel as if my services deserved that much, Shacks sir?"

"It isn't a bribe to keep quiet about my ruthless actions, if that's what you think? It's your fee and the use of the boat, that's all. I know I've kept you in the dark about certain things that have happened but that was for your own good. The less you know the better."

Shamus smiled appreciatively. "Yer'll not have to twist me arm up me back then, Shacks sir."

"Good. Now get the cheque into your bank as soon as possible before I change my mind." I told him, sharply. "Now back to serious matters. Keep well away from the harbour; find a nice crowded bar and stay there until I contact you again."

It was never my intention to inflict fear into him, but it obviously sounded that way to him when he asked, "Why, Shacks sir? We're safe now. Aren't we?"

"I wish I could say yes, but I'd be lying."

"Holy, Mother of Jesus! Who am I to be afraid of, Shacks sir?"

I thought it best to warn him. "Remember the two men racing down the hill at North harbour?"

Shamus nodded.

"They each have a degree in unpleasantness. They hurt people. They enjoy doing it. Until I can conclude what I've set out to do, I want to keep you from any harm. Your safest option is to lose yourself among the tourists in the busiest pub. Now go. We'll meet later."

I dashed back to hotel and asked at reception if anyone had made enquiries after me.

"Only, Mister Hamer," he replied thoughtfully.

"What did he want?"

"He didn't say fully, sir. But he seemed...very agitated."

"He's always agitated. It took him a lot of hard years to develop the technique."

"No, no, Mister Speed. I mean fearful. Yes, I saw fear in his eyes. I think petrified would be a proper description."

"Did he mention what was bothering him?"

"Not to me, sir."

"Did he say anything at all?"

"Not to me, sir."

"Did he leave any messages?"

"No sir. He just asked if I knew of your whereabouts."

"What did you tell him?"

"I didn't know where you had gone."

"What did he do next?"

"He left the hotel."

"What-on his own?"

"Yes, as soon as he had booked out."

"He booked out?"

"Yes, Mister Speed."

"Did he say where he was going?"

"No, Mister Speed."

I stepped away from the reception counter thinking deeply. There was something not right here. I couldn't imagine Hamer being scared that easily. I wondered if he had perhaps clapped eyes on Love and Hate and had gone after them. But why waste time booking out of the hotel? And why hadn't he left me a note to verify his intentions. Maybe Hamer had done a runner? No, there had to be something more sinister to scare him; something more disconcerting then the likes of a couple of murdering cowards.

I said to reception, "If Mister Hamer returns, don't hesitate to ring my room. If anyone else arrives asking for me, tell the inquisitive person I'm out. Then inform me straightaway. No delays whatsoever. Okay?"

"I will, Mister Speed."

I raced up the stairs to my room not knowing what to expect in the next few hours. I wasn't sure what I was going to do either or which direction I should take to avoid any surprises, but I was about to get a surprise whether I wanted one or not.

The moment I slid the electronic key through the door mechanism I sensed or rather I smelled I had company. The fragrance from inside confirmed the human presence but it was nothing for me to worry over. Closing the door, I said, "Took your time getting here considering you left Deveron's place earlier than me."

Shayna was sitting in the single armchair with one leg out-stretched over the chair arm in a position of comfort and quaffing a glass of white wine.

"Comfy are you?"

Shayna's smile had a wicked touch. "Have you missed me, Shackleton?"

"Like a house on fire! Where's Deveron?"

"Missing him, too?"

"What part of 'where's Deveron' don't you understand? I'd like to simplify it for you."

"Ooh touchy-touchy! He's around sorting things out."

"I thought he couldn't get around? That he was dying?"

"He can still walk if it's required."

"Well tell the miserable squeaky freak that I've found his submarine."

"Tell him yourself. He's at the Quality Hotel in Clonikilty. We'd have checked into at closer hotel only everything around here is fully booked because of some regatta."

"He's closer than I thought and obviously keen too."

"He's very keen," she said, and then she sprung from her chair, shoved her empty glass into my hand, and said, "Pour me another while I use the bathroom?"

"What happened to please on both accounts?" I said.

"Please-please!" she scoffed and toddled off towards the bathroom door.

That fellow on reception had been right about poetry in motion as I watched her pear shaped bottom, squeezed perfectly inside a pair of tight leather pants, wiggle all the way to the bathroom and closed the door behind her.

I shrugged with disappointment and poured two drinks.

Her voice filtered through a slight gap of the door. "Help yourself to a glass."

"I'm ahead of you," I said, and drank my wine in one and poured another in quick succession and drank that too to ease the tension building inside me. I could have done with something stronger; dark rum, but I needed to keep a clear head to think straight.

I found myself staring into space lost in thought. Everything was beginning to come together; every piece of the jigsaw fitting perfectly. All the players had congregated either in Baltimore or the surrounding area: Deveron and Shayna, a ship full of unscrupulous villains, along with Love and Hate and me in the middle with my head spinning with uncertainty as to which direction I should take next. What I could be certain about was somebody was still missing from the party, and to induce that somebody I still needed the attraction of the gold to expose the true puppet master; the man they call the 'Housekeeper'. I felt deep down that he was close.

Shamus had been right when he said I was poking the wasps nest with a short stick and now I had it buzzing with activity and it would be up to me to silence the nuisance once and for all and without being stung. I was beginning to feel the sensation of slow strangulation by the invisible cord tightening around my neck. I glanced to the bathroom door. Once again I wondered how far I could trust Shayna. Then how far should I trust a terrorist?

When she reappeared from the bathroom all my fears of her being a threat to me diminished within seconds. She was naked for starters. No modesty whatsoever. Not an inkling of embarrassment, just that sheer poetry in motion again as she sauntered crossed the room. I could only ogle at the delicate bounce of her breasts and the twitch of her buttocks as she moved. She was certainly one frigging distraction from all my troubles and I wondered if that was a good thing or not. I poured myself another glass of wine and threw it down my throat. More noticeably, I was struggling to stop the stiffening projectile jerking in the front of my pants.

I said, "Just out of curiosity, how did you get into my room? There's no forced damage to the door. So which gel-head down at reception let you in? No doubt your charming smile did the trick."

She lay down on the bed, her legs slightly apart in a deliberate attempt to entice me. "Do I detect a hint of jealousy weakening the toughness of the treasure seeker?"

I ignored her. "I'm still asking."

"No one let me in. I'm good at bypassing electronic locks."

"Frigging hell, you don't happen to work alongside another serial burglar by the name of Hamer?"

"I don't know anybody called Hamer. Is he a professional too?"

"Even better than you, I should imagine. I've had a demonstration from him too."

"I might ask him to join our organization."

"Well you can ask him when you meet him."

"A friend of yours is he?"

"He seems to think so."

"I gather then he's not the flavour of the month?"

"To describe him in very few words, I'd say he was the most nosey bastard on this planet. Be extremely careful what you say, he happens to be government property in the form of an M.o.D. policeman and just because you don't witness him taking down notes, don't assume he's missed anything."

"What is he doing here in Baltimore?"

"Pestering me, I'm afraid."

"Have you done something wrong?"

"He blames me entirely for digging up the Berkshire Spitfire and for not telling anyone. He wants me to admit it so he can string me up by my bollocks and put me on show to the good people of London. And stop trying to change the subject of illegal entry. How did you manage to squeeze past reception without being noticed?"

"Well it's not the most difficult of tasks considering men are all of the same mentality. They see something that resembles a bit of an attractive ass and their eyes are like lumps of magnetic material forcibly attracted to the source. So much perversion goes on in the mind of a man that they send themselves dizzy as they try to watch everything in a skirt. I just waited until an attractive woman went one way and I slipped by and took the stairway."

"It does seem to be an occupational habit concerning the male staff on reception." I said.

"You going to stand there like a dumb-ass or are you going to take advantage of my vulnerability, like get your kit off and pleasure me senseless, Shackleton. Now would be nice, before we go and talk to Deveron."

At least with Shayna you know where you stand. There was no need for fumbling hands or whispers of false passion to get inside her knickers. When she wanted sex, she wasn't afraid to demand that she got it and I'm all for that positive approach. I stripped, instinctively checked my hands were clean and climbed on the bed beside her. I thought I was in for two hours of passion, but little did I know that tragedy was just around the corner.

*

I never reached the point of full sex with Shayna. I had gotten as far as oral sex on her when the sound of an explosion close by interrupted my rhythm. My head shot up from between her legs quicker than a jack-rabbit straining to hear. I twisted and threw my legs over the edge of the bed and rushed to the window and looked out. The harbour was a hue of orange and red. Something jolted my insides to move fast and I started to get dressed.

"Is there trouble?" Shayna asked as she dashed to the bathroom for her clothes.

"That explosion was too close for comfort."

"I'm coming with you!"

"Please yourself."

We left the hotel and hurried down to the quay. A large crowd had gathered to observe the spectacle of a boat well ablaze. It had always fascinated me how roaring fires attracted onlookers. That they stand there admiring the flames, and then again, maybe it was their attraction to Hell.

I found Shamus standing at the front of the crowd, his face brightly illuminated by the flames. He had the vacant stare of a man deep in shock after having lost everything he had ever possessed and I could see why. The *Muff* was on fire!

I pulled him round by his arm to gain his attention. "Frigging hell, Shamus, what happened?"

He remained mesmerized by the fire, staring into the flames, a noticeable tear or two in his eyes. He said, without looking at me. "The *Muff*, Shacks sir...she just blew up!"

"Frigging hell, Shamus, I can see that. Thank your lucky arse you weren't on it at the time. Insurance fully up to date, I hope!" I wasn't deliberately trying to be humorous just glad he was still in one piece.

"The boats replaceable, Shacks sir," he said with a lump in his throat. "It's that police chap...Hamer."

"What's he after now?"

"No, yer don't understand, Shacks sir. It's Hamer!"

I started feeling a little aggrieved with the Irishman. "What about him?"

"He was onboard when it blew-up."

It took me a few seconds to understand the consequences of what Shamus had just told me. For a moment I was stunned too. All I could do was to scan the burning deck for the shape of a burning body, not that I could see one. I turned to Shamus and said, "Are you absolutely sure he went aboard?"

"I know what I saw, Shacks sir. I found meself a nice comfortable seat by the pub window, as you told me to. I saw Hamer hurrying down to the harbour. I waited a few minutes to see if he was being followed. He wasn't so I went out to see what he was up to. In the distance I saw him moving about on deck. As I got closer..." He gestured by throwing his hands into the air a huge explosion. "The force of the blast almost knocked me off me feet, it did. Feel me, I'm still shaking."

I wondered if Shamus had seriously thought about how close he'd come to being killed because this was no freak accident. Hamer must have come down to the harbour searching for me. He paid the price for boarding the *Muff* at the wrong time and had, probably, triggered off a sensor device. He had suffered the misfortune that was clearly intended for Shamus and me. I should have at least felt some discomfort; some sort of guilt for the way Hamer had died so horrendously. Yet, in a strange kind of way, all I could think of was I'd lost my emergency pull cord to call in backup if I got into even worse trouble than I was in now.

Again I tugged Shamus by the arm. "We've got to get out of here and that includes you, Shamus."

Shamus looked confused. "What about all the mess? What about Hamer?"

I said to him harshly, "What about us, Shamus? That explosion was meant for you and me, and anyone else associated with us. We were fortunate. Hamer wasn't. We can't change that now other than to find enough evidence to flush out whoever is responsible. We can't do that if we offer ourselves as sacrificial lambs to the slaughter. And that will happen if we stay here."

Shayna backed me up. "He's right, Shamus, we're sitting ducks here."

Shamus looked at me disapprovingly. "Are yer suggesting we run away from our responsibilities?"

"We've no other choice. We're targets and the killers won't stop until we end up like Hamer."

"What about the Garda, it won't take them long to connect the boat to me."

"True. They'll probably find a badly burnt body, but they won't know who it is for a good while. They'll assume it's you, Shamus. We can use that time to finish the job."

Shamus shook his head defiantly. "Sorry, Shacks sir, I can't do that. I'll only slow you down. I'll stay and mingle with the Garda. I should be safe. After all this commotion I don't think anyone will bother me while the Garda are involved. Don't worry I'll drag the story along. Tell them I've no idea what happened, just move with their investigation."

I relented, mainly because I'd little time to lose. "Okay, Shamus, if that's what you really want to do?"

"It's better if I stay."

"It's your choice, Shamus. But I promise you, when this is finally over, and if I'm still breathing, I'll find you a new boat to compensate you for your loss."

"I can't let yer do that, Shacks sir."

"Nonsense, Shamus. I'm as much to blame for the loss of your livelihood. You collect the insurance and I'll double the cost. Have you got that? I happen to know of someone who's most willing to cover the expenditure of the entire venture and that includes the price of a new boat." I turned to Shayna at that point for confirmation. "By the way, where did you say Deveron was staying?"

I expected a verbal barrage from her, but her bemused expression rather told a different story.

I shook Shamus's hand in gratitude for his companionship and loyalty and then Shayna and I slipped quietly away from the chaos. I felt badly leaving Shamus behind to deal with the carnage, but I had to be free from involvement regarding the inevitable investigation. In the distance I could hear the sirens of a lone fire engine.

Collecting the Roadster from the hotel car park, Shayna and I left Baltimore and drove away from the inevitable prying questions, and even more significantly, away from the attention of the people aboard the *Flying Fish*, at least until I was ready to challenge the crew straight on.

It was while we were driving along the road to Clonakilty on our way to meet Deveron at the Quality Hotel, that for some unknown reason, Shayna insisted on telling me, Clonakilty was the birthplace of Michael Collins, the founder of the I.R.A., as if I really cared a frigging toss at the time!

*

Deveron greeted our arrival as if we were long lost friends. "Shayna and Mister Speed, I'm delighted to see you both."

Shayna jerked her head towards me and said, "Our 'Boy's Own' adventurer here has found your submarine."

Deveron's expressed his jubilation. "It's definitely here...in Ireland?'

"Where else would I have found it? Thailand?"

Deveron was frothing at the corners of his mouth. "You've actually seen it?"

"Naturally, since I found it."

He smiled, seemingly lost in his thoughts. And then he suddenly snapped out of his daydream. "Splendid! Splendid! Tanamoto and the Japanese government will be overwhelmingly ecstatic. You might even become folklore in Japan; an honourable guest of their Country forever."

"Forget the romantics," I said. "We need to resolve a few points of interest between us first."

Deveron's tinny voice squeaked with excitement. "I can't wait any longer, Mister Speed. Where does she lay? I have to know."

"Not until we've covered a few facts from the past."

"Do you never give up?" Deveron said disappointed. "What this time, Mister Speed?"

"What do you know about IRA terrorists assisting the Third Reich during the war?"

"I find that a rather strange enquiry, Mister Speed?"

"Did you know of any?"

"There wasn't as many as statistics supposedly recorded. Naturally there were those Irishmen who hated the British more than the Germans. But I certainly couldn't name any of them. I went to fight in the war, don't forget. After the war finished it didn't make a damn bit of difference who did what."

I held up McCracken's ring in front of his eyes, so he could have a good look at it without fobbing me off. "Seen anything like this before?"

Deveron gasped. It was a good sign that he had. "Good gracious! Where did you get that?"

"You recognize the ring then?"

"I think I do."

"Then you'll know all about an active IRA terrorist named, J. McCracken. No doubt he was causing havoc when you were involved in playing with bombs."

"There is no need to undermine my beliefs at the time, Mister Speed."

"You're talking to someone who doesn't give a frigging toss in your beliefs. Is the name McCracken familiar or not?"

"Was McCracken involved in the disappearance of the I-52?"

"Why am I experiencing problems in getting a simple answer to a simple question? What about McCracken?" I reminded him. "Did you know him?"

"I knew of him. There's not many disgruntled Irishman who were around in the late thirties who hadn't heard of Jimmy 'the merciless' McCracken, Commanding Officer of the Munster Brigade. Realistically he was nothing but a powerful warlord with big ambitions."

"World domination I suppose?"

"I hardly think so, Mister Speed. McCracken was a true patriot regardless and his main interest was a free Ireland, not to conquer the world. But he was a controversial character. He never kept to protocol. He did things his way. His contribution to the Cause was to victimize the loyal Irish people who ran shops and businesses, forcing them into paying money for protection. The protection money bought his brigade weapons to fight the British. There were many followers who fought for the Cause who believed McCracken was nothing more than a common racketeer using the backbone of the I.R.A. to fill his pockets with wealth."

I glanced at Shayna. "There you are, Shayna. Exactly what I told you when we were engaged in *riveting* conversation back at the farmhouse; terrorists are born racketeers and criminals and nothing more."

She pulled her tongue out at me which actually made her look childishly cute.

Deveron invaded our private war. "Please can we dispense with this trivial bickering amongst ourselves and concentrate on McCracken." I waved him his freedom of speech. "There was many an Irishman who saw McCracken as a born murderer and ideally suited for the IRA. His hatred for the British was brutish. He specialized in bombs; big bombs. He liked to listen to the sound of his bombs exploding. He would stay in the vicinity to witness his work. When the Second World War began he defied the agreement amongst the Irish factions for a ceasefire, so the Irish contingency could concentrate on fighting the Germans instead. Most Irishmen didn't want the Germans on their shores as much as they didn't want the British. McCracken disagreed with the decision and swore he would slaughter every Irish traitor that fought alongside the British during the war."

"He sounds like an exciting guy."

"Not a person I wanted to be around, that was for sure. What has McCracken got to do with the submarine?"

"I think he was part of a hijacking gang that made the I-52 disappear."

"But how would he know what the Japanese were planning?"

"From the Germans I should imagine."

Deveron snorted a brief laugh. "Then the rumours were true that McCracken did collaborate with the Third Reich. McCracken hated the British so much that he didn't care who stood beside him as long as he could continue his fight for freedom. But if he was guilty of intercepting the I-52, then he obviously double-crossed the Germans. Now why doesn't that surprise me! The conniving rat must have smelled some profitable arrangement."

"He wanted the gold, obviously."

"Absolutely no other reason," Deveron said solidly. "And I'm not surprised that McCracken stamped on German toes, as well as the Irish. Do you know why they called McCracken 'the merciless'?"

I shrugged, "Because he was a nasty bastard through and through?"

"That's exactly what he was, Mister Speed. In reality, McCracken practically invented the suicide bomber. He'd prime the bombs to go off the moment the bomb planter set the timer. He killed comrades to gain success. And all because he didn't want to give the bomb disposal teams any chance to diffuse the situation."

"So I guess you didn't rate him highly?"

"I was an Irishman that hated another Irishman purely because he killed innocent Irish people, and that was never part of the campaign for total freedom from British rule."

"He doesn't sound welcoming even by his own breed. Where was he originally from?"

Deveron mauled his way through the question. "He was a Corkonian…Is the bastard still alive?"

I shook my head. "Not unless someone else was wearing his ring at the time. He was the victim of a rock fall inside an uncharted cavern beneath the ruins of Dun an Oir."

"Good heavens above!"

"I thought you'd be pleased that he found his own personal coffin."

"A cavern, you say? Beneath Dun an Oir. Isn't that the old fort on Clear Island, the one referred to as the 'fort of gold'?"

"That's the one."

"How ironic he chose that particular place."

"There was nothing ironic about his choice at all. It was the perfect place and large enough to hide a submarine. The cavern isn't on any maps or charts, but McCracken knew the location and used it to his advantage when he hijacked the I-52 in 1944. Only his plan backfired. He never anticipated the possibility of the cavern tumbling down onto his frigging head."

"So the gold's still there?"

My, "no," was savagely blunt. I suspected he was treasure hunting again

"Where is it then?"

"How the frigging hell should I know!"

"Do you intend to keep looking for it?"

"Will you continue paying me?"

"If you think you can find the gold?"

"I intend to because if you weren't responsible for ordering the deaths of my friends, then the guilty bastards are going to come creeping out of their hiding places when I dangle the golden proof under their fat, greedy noses."

"Such a deep vendetta will be the killing of you, Mister Speed."

"And do I look like as if I care a frigging toss! Oh, while we're on the subject of money and wealth and that promise of unlimited expenditure. I'm going to need a substantial amount to replace a fishing vessel that was blown up."

Deveron's eyelids widened. "Good gracious, Mister Speed! You're very clumsy."

"No fault of mine. I think the intention was I should have been on the boat at the time. Now if you don't mind I'd like to wash for dinner."

"Dinner, Mister Speed?"

"Thank you for offering. Shayna and I are ravenously hungry. We'll also be staying for a while. It's unsafe to return to my hotel due to the probability of awkward police questions or a bullet in the back of my head and I don't wish to confront either of them at the moment."

Deveron slowly shook his head. "Dear me, Mister Speed, you have a remarkable knack of landing yourself in despair."

"Not intentional, I can assure you."

Chapter Twenty

Deveron protested that I should take Shayna along with me when I informed him that I'd a few things to sort out before I returned to Baltimore to face unknown resistance. I put him firmly in his place and told him I would be conducting my business alone. I never mentioned I was going to Cork City. I didn't want the cunning sod to have me followed.

I considered that my next line of action was a private matter and would be done with the least of embarrassment to the recipient of my enquiry. That's if any relatives of the Jimmy McCracken family still lived around Cork.

I parked the Roadster on a pay car park and went in search of the registrar office for birth, deaths and marriages in South Mall. I entered the building and approached the reception desk. I displayed one of my charming and cheeky smiles to the middle aged woman with a face like a Sergeant Major and built just as solid. I explained my predicament, the importance in tracing the whereabouts of the McCracken family, and were there any living relatives still in the area where I could be directed to.

I got a stern look in return and her reply was straightforward and typical of a pompous twit.

"It is against company policy to divulge confidential information to any one unless they have a perfectly good reason or have a direct family connection. Are you a family member? We would require proof of your identity."

"I have no family connections." There was no need at this stage to be dishonest as it would serve no useful advantage. I showed her the ring and pointed to the name engraved. "It's my intention to return this piece of valuable jewellery to the family of the inscribed name."

She mellowed as she gazed at the sparklers. "Rather expensive looking."

"I've no idea of its true value, just interested in returning it to its rightful owner."

"I would advise you to contact the local Garda."

"I don't think they would be much help on the matter, it's not exactly a missing person's case. I would be willing to leave the ring in your custodial safety if you could guarantee it reached the right owner. I've no other intentions other than an honourably one."

I was lying through my teeth. I had niggling questions that I wanted to ask the right McCracken's

"I'm very sorry, Mister-Ah?"

"Speed, Shackleton Speed."

"I would like to help, Mister Speed, but I can't go against company policy. And neither can we accept responsibility for returning property to the rightful owner."

I'd hit an invisible brick wall in the form of stubbornness and I'd no argument over the matter just because she didn't know how to flex a rule or two. Our short intimate meeting was cut even shorter when she blanked me to answer the telephone. I made to leave, not wanting to push hard and draw attention to myself, when another receptionist beckoned me over while iron drawers had her back turned.

I got a strong smell of cheap scent when she leaned over the counter. In a whispered voice, and maintaining a constant check that she wasn't under observation, she said, "I couldn't help overhearing your conversation. I know a lady by the name of Millie Malloy. Her mother died six months gone. Her mother's surname was McCracken. She might be able to help. Millie runs a craft shop in Corn market Street."

*

I was glad to get the information because it meant I hadn't had a wasted journey. I went straight to Corn Market Street, a tight pedestrian through-fare, all vehicles prohibited. Brightly painted shops gave Corn Market Street a sort of magical avenue. I found Millie's Crafts, a sea-blue painted shop filled with an assortment of wares. The shop attendant standing behind the counter, a red haired girl with a freckled complexion with a nice smile, was far too young to be the proprietor.

I said, pleasantly, "Could I possibly speak to Millie?"

"She's in the back baking. Who shall I say wants her?" She spoke with a strong Northern Ireland accent.

"Shackleton Speed. Tell her it concerns a piece of jewellery that I have in my possession which belongs to a member of the McCracken family. I believe Millie's nee name was McCracken."

"I'll only be a moment."

I nodded my thanks and watched her disappear into the rear of the shop. I hummed a tune to break the boredom while I waited for the girl's return, thinking how nice it was to be in an area where trust was highly thought of, since I could have quite easily ransacked the shop and till and be on my way in half the time it took her to return from the back.

My quest looked promising when she returned, because she had an inviting smile which indicated that I'd been successful with my request.

"Come through to the parlour, Mister Speed."

I went behind the counter and followed her through. The smell of freshly baked bread grew stronger as we entered an old fashioned kitchen. The podgy built woman I saw washing her hands in the pot sink had long dark hair lined with wisps of grey and tied back in a ponytail that hung down as far as her lower spine. She wore a white apron over a flowing flowery patterned cotton dress.

She looked directly at me and said, in a soft Irish voice, "Mister Speed is it?"

The suspicion in her tone matched the suspicion distorting her eyebrows. Her grey blue eyes appeared watery. At first I thought she maybe upset, only that notion was soon squandered by the strong whiff of onions that suddenly invaded my nostrils as I approached her.

"Yes. Shackleton Speed, but please, call me Shacks."

She clinically wiped her hands on a towel and gestured me to the kitchen table. "Please, sit down, Shacks. How can I help?"

I sat, took the ring from my pocket and showed the piece to her in the hope she might recognize it instantly. She didn't. Her blank expression told me the ring meant nothing to her.

She eased into a chair opposite me. "A very beautiful ring, Shacks. What has it to do with me?" She smiled. She had a nice smile, too. "I'm a little too old for the proposal lark."

"Better than that, Millie," I said. "I think this ring belongs to a Jimmy McCracken. I'm led to believe your maiden name was McCracken?"

I was expecting her to start asking a pile of awkward questions on how a complete stranger should have a dossier on her, but she didn't. If anything she was a little confused by it all.

"Before I married I was a McCracken."

"Is the name Jimmy McCracken familiar to you?"

She stared at me shell-shocked. She said slowly, deliberately, "My father's name was Jimmy."

"Maybe then I've found the right place. Does this ring look at all familiar to you?"

She shook her head. "Nothing I've ever seen before."

"And your father; would I be able to speak to him?"

"I haven't seen my father since I was a child, Shacks."

"Have you any ides on the whereabouts of your father?"

"No. According to my mother, God bless her soul, he left home one late July morning in 1944 and never returned, deserted us, my mother often reminded me. He hasn't been seen since. I was a year old when he went. I suspect he went off to fight in the war and was killed in action, that's why he never returned. Quite frankly I can't remember him being part of my life at all. There's a saying: what you don't have you don't miss! Of course my mother could have told you more about him, but unfortunately, she passed away a short time ago."

"I'm sorry for your loss."

"You can't beat the old age syndrome; the wear and tear. It happens to all of us eventually. What makes you think the ring belonged to my father?"

"I can't be sure it does, Millie. That's why I need to know more about his background. If he is the right person, then you're the rightful heir."

"How did you come by the ring, if you don't mind me asking?"

"It's an extremely long and complex story to explain properly. And I'm not sure if I have all the right pieces to fit together to make any sense of it all."

"If it is my father's ring, I think I've a right to know."

"In due course, Millie, you will be told everything that you need to know. I promise. You'll have to trust me. First I need to ask you some questions if that's all right with you, Millie?"

She smiled. "You have beautiful blue eyes, Shacks. I have a tendency to believe people with blue eyes." She paused a moment, as if she's remembered something of importance. "There's an old trunk upstairs in the attic. It was my mother's. It's where she kept all my father's personal belongings. She couldn't bear to part with his things. We could start there though I've no idea what's inside the trunk. I've never really found the time to look to be truthful."

"There's no time like the present." I prompted.

"You're right, Shacks. Follow me."

We climbed two flights of creaking stairway and passed through a small door. She blindly located and flicked on the light switch. The attic was illuminated by two pendants at either end of a spacious well maintained storeroom filled with a collection of bric-a-brac, different sized cardboard boxes, piles of neatly stacked newspapers and the inevitably scary headless corpse that doubled as a seamstress's dummy you can always find hiding away in any attic.

Millie crossed to the far corner of the room and dragged out a large hand carved wooden trunk. I marvelled at the craftsmanship, such detailed carvings delicately etched into the wood and worth a hefty price in today's antique market.

I said, "Did your mother ever mention what your father did for a living?"

She knelt beside the trunk and opened the lid as she talked. "Yes, I remember asking as a child. I suppose it was a natural thing to ask questions about your own father when you can only imagine him as a shimmering mirage. He was a stonemason and builder, my mother told me. He'd a degree in engineering too. I saw evidence of that when I came across his certificate when I was sorting out my mother's personal papers a while ago."

"That accounts for it then," I said, thinking aloud.

"You know what happened to my father, Shacks?"

I didn't want to tell her the full story just yet in case I was wrong and I'd gotten the wrong McCracken family. I said, "No, not exactly. I found this ring amongst ruins on Clear Island near Baltimore."

"It doesn't prove it belonged to my father."

"I feel confident I've found the right place with you, Millie."

"Oh look!" She squealed like an excited child. "There's a pile of journals here."

She removed the black books one by one with mild inspection, ten in all. Each dated. They spanned from 1934 to 1944. She began reading the 1934 journal.

"It's written in gaeltacht," she said.

I couldn't contradict her on that as the writings I could see had the same unappealing look for deciphering as Japanese writing. Both had me baffled. I said: "Do you know what's written there?"

She started speaking a strange dialect."

"I guess you do, Millie. Sorry I doubted you."

"My mother insisted I learned and spoke our ancestral voice."

"I don't wish to pry but what exactly did you say?"

She smiled. "I've met a very nice man today!"

I smiled and thanked her.

She began translating the first page. "It's a motto: I serve no King, nor Kaiser: I serve nothing but a free Ireland forever."

Frigging pathetic cultural prattle! I thought.

She quickly flicked through the pages, only stopping at certain chapters to read a few lines. Sometimes she cringed at certain paragraphs. I guessed she'd found that she was reading a horror story.

Journal by journal she flicked through the pages trying to understand the significance of what she was reading and again only stopping at certain paragraphs of morbid interest. It was at one point when her body stiffened and she couldn't hide her shock that she'd found something disastrously sinister.

"Are you alright?" I asked.

She said slowly, almost apologetically, "Merciful God in heaven! My father was the IRA Commander of Southern Ireland. I always believed he was a good Catholic. What did he become?"

I tried to be gentle with the truth. "A freedom fighter, from what I can gather."

Tears dribbled slowly down her cheeks "A terrorist and a murderer. These journals are confessional submissions on paper."

"It does seem to point in that direction," I said, though I couldn't be sure unless she read word for word to me.

You had to give Jimmy McCracken a certain amount of credit for a man obsessed with murder. He'd obviously been a prolific writer, though I found it confusingly strange why he should want to write the incriminating material down on paper, not unless he thought victory would always be his. And then again there many murderous minds throughout history that had the same idea in the name of fame. I suppose Jimmy McCracken was no different than the rest of the idealists for world domination.

Pushing things along, I made a suggestion. "The 1944 journal was obviously his last commitment, perhaps if we read through the last chapters properly it might tell us the last moments before your father disappeared."

"Why not, Shacks. I can't see it doing any harm" She flicked the pages to the final chapters and continued the translation with fluency. "Met German spies Harrington and Lodge for the final time." She stopped reading and looked up at me. "This gets worst."

"Don't concern yourself too much Millie. It's all in the past. What we learn today goes no further than you and me and this room. I promise. Please, read on."

She nodded and carried on with her narration. "He's written: I've convinced them to switch the rendezvous with the Jap sub to Roaring Water Bay, half a mile, South West from Cape Clear. They accepted my story that the Garda Siochana had discovered the possibility of a smuggling gang operating in Galway Bay and that the Irish Home Guard were preparing an ambush to trap the perpetrators. Both, Harrington and Lodge agreed that changes had to be made urgently. After they contacted the submarine and their task was completed, I did them in. My protector, Saint Brendan holds them safe from discovery."

Millie paused and looked up at me. "What does he mean by *Did them in!*, Shacks?"

"I suspect he killed them, Millie." I thought it best to be honest.

She recoiled with disgust. "Do you think my mother would have known about his terrible background?"

I shrugged. "Maybe she did, maybe she didn't. They were difficult times during the early forties. Your father obviously went about his beliefs in the way he thought right."

Millie sniffled back the tears. "No wonder my mother never saw him again, he's either languishing in prison or he's dead."

"I think you'll have to expect the worst, Millie." She gazed at me like a frightened child. "I took the ring from a corpse I found buried under fallen rocks beneath Clear Island. If it was your father, then I've brought you bad news, which I never intended. I'm sorry about that. But I'm confident his body will be recovered eventually even though the task will be a mammoth operation and will take a major construction job to complete."

Another lonely tear dribbled down her cheek.

From the bottom of the trunk she carefully brought out a framed black and white photograph of a group of men gathered around out-dated deep water diving apparatus. She pointed to a big powerful man in the middle.

"That's my father. My mother once showed me this very picture. It was her fond memory of the man she loved. *He was a handsome devil*, she used to say. Just look at my father's face. Is that the face of a terrorist and a murderer?"

"Looks can be incredibly deceiving. It's what goes on in the mind that counts."

Without contradiction, McCracken, in my eyes, was a brutal killer. As all religious fanatics and freedom fighters, they master the art of death and destruction. We live in a world full of madness, so what's one more dangerous freak? There are many more McCracken's out there in some dark corner of the world itching to start a war because of their beliefs and remedies. Nothing was ever going to change; not today, not tomorrow, not ever.

"At least I can put Old Willie's mind at rest," She said, which made my ears prick up.

"Who's Willie?" I asked curiously.

She pointed to the smallest member of the group of eight divers. "That's Willie. Willie Donahue. Still see him about. He's probably the only one I've ever met from this photograph, which seems strange since my mother always maintained that the eight of them were inseparable companions. How he keeps going I'll never reason why."

"What became of the others?"

"I don't rightly know. I never met any of them. My mother never mentioned them to me. It was always about Willie. My mother was always having a go at him. The harassment troubled Willie. Something had happened to him in the past but nobody knew what trouble him. Drink finally got hold of him and wrecked his life. Bit of an introvert now. Never married and doesn't seem to have any relatives. Someone gave him the name 'Wandering Willie'; stuck with him ever since."

"Where can I find this Willie?"

"What for, Shacks?"

"Have a chat with him."

She gave me a suspicious look. "I don't think he can help you with anything."

"He might be able to piece together your father's movements on the day he disappeared, especially if they were friends. He must know something."

"I doubt it, Shacks. Why do you think my mother constantly pestered the poor bloke? She spent many an hour trying to get him talk about my father. As I said, he lives in a world of his own now. You'd get more sense from a stuffed animal than get him to talk of the past."

"I'd still like to try," I persisted. "Fortune honours the brave, I say."

She was unsure what to say.

"Surely you want to know what happened to your father."

I sensed she did, but she was scared of knowing the truth.

"I'd like to try," I said.

Given time, I could have probably found him myself. I mean, how many 'Wandering Willie's' are there frequenting the pubs around Cork. But Millie pointing me in the right direction would speed things up. Mainly because I had a strange tingling in the depths of my stomach telling me that my time was running out fast and something drastic was developing that was way beyond my control. I'd been getting a few of those lately, so much, they were giving me cause for concern over my health. I always thought I was too young for a heart attack. I was pleased when she changed her mind.

"I wish you the best of luck then, "she finally agreed. "That's providing he'll want to talk to you."

"I'm confident he'll talk to me, Millie."

"His favourite haunt is 'The Ovens', in Oliver Plunkett Street. It's a nice quiet pub. He goes there more days, I'm sure."

My eyes lowered onto the journal. I noticed the last chapter at the bottom of the page which she hadn't read yet. I said, "What was his final inclusion in the journal?"

She studied the page. "A piece of redemption, I think. He's written: 'beyond the line of light is the navigator; when the sun rises and illuminates the Virgin Mary, through her eyes she will foretell my domain of madness; my future life; my dreams of stardom. The spirit of Saint Brendan will save me from destruction." She looked at me, her eyes red. "That's his final passage. No indication where he was going. His words disappearing as he had."

Part of her narrative had me wondering. "This 'Saint Brendan' seems to be a significant part of his life. Is it something special within your family?"

"In most Irish families I should imagine. He's one of the Saints of Ireland. My mother was a regular churchgoer; as for my father...I'm not sure if he'd even dared to frequent any church with his history. God would never have forgiven him."

I pressed the signet ring into the palm of her hand. "You'd better hang on to this."

She didn't fuss, just closed her hand around the piece of unexpected jewellery and clasped it tightly as if it was the most precious thing in her life.

"What do you think I should do with the journals, Shacks; burn them?"

"I'd be inclined to read them through properly before you decide, Millie. Perhaps you may find something in there that shows your father in a different light. Your

Mother loved him for something. Maybe he wasn't all bad after all."

I left her clutching the final journal to her breast and saw myself out. I couldn't be certain if the tears in her eyes were of happiness or sadness. I went to find Willie Donahue.

*

I found the pub called 'The Oven's' and ordered a Guinness at the bar, asking the barman if Wandering Willie Donahue had come in. The barman jabbed a finger towards the shrivelled old man sat alone at a table by the window, seemingly staring into his half empty beer glass he held firmly on the table. My first observations of Willie clearly indicated that he did have all the attributes of an introvert, as Millie had suggested. He deliberately kept his eyes low, avoiding staring at people in case he attracted attention to himself. His appearance was how Millie had described it, and he did indeed look like a tramp. I almost felt sorry for the sod. I paid the barmen and zig-zagged between the tables to where he sat.

He startled when I sat down opposite him, the smell of bad body odour drifting from him as he twitched nervously in his seat. What I first thought to be black lines criss-crossing his face turned out to be dirt ingrained into his deep lined complexion. His confused dark sunken eyes lifted and searched mine.

"That seat *be* taken," he said in a low, almost threatening growl.

"That's right!" I said.

"Then why don't yer move to another table and leave me in peace."

"I want to talk to you."

"I likes me own company."

"Later. We have things to discuss first."

"Are you deaf or something?"

"It might just be in your best interest if you talk to me, Willie. Because if you don't I'm going to pester you day and night until you do."

He frowned suspiciously. "Yer know me name?"

"Millie Malloy told me. She said I'd find you here drowning your sorrows."

"Millie Malloy, yer say?"

"That's right. She's Jimmy McCracken's daughter."

The mentioning of McCracken stunned Willie. I've never seen anybody as scared as he was then. His body tensed as hard as a wooden board. His Adams Apple rippled through the sagging flesh below his chin. His eyes flicked side to side in sheer panic, and then he stared hard at me searching for answers. Now I had his immediate attention. He obviously thought McCracken was a name that would never resurface again, especially coming from a stranger. But he still made a desperate attempt to squash the connection.

"I dunno that name."

"Which name don't you know, Willie; Millie Malloy or Jimmy McCracken?

He scowled in frustration.

"Surely you can at least remember your old pal, Jimmy McCracken?"

He eyed me suspiciously. "Who might yer be?"

"My name isn't important. After today you'll want to forget me."

"Yer're perhaps a relation of the Molloy's?"

"So you do know, Millie?"

"What's she after?"

"The truth and what happened to her father might be a good start."

His eyes squinted as he surveyed me harshly. "Who are yer?"

"I'm a friend of Millie. She's ever so grateful for the return of her father's signet ring; the very ring that he was wearing the day he went missing. It was a distinctive ring. Anyone whoever saw the piece would never forget it. It's the one with his initials engraved on top, with a swirl of diamonds surrounding those initials."

"Yer can't have!" Willie snapped.

"Why's that?"

"Because he was wearing it the day he-" He stopped suddenly. He'd realized his mistake that he'd said too much.

"Disappeared, you were about to say?"

"How the hell should I know? I haven't seen him for a long time."

"What do you call a long time: a week, month, year, or maybe not since nineteen forty-four?"

"Yer're not going to keep pestering me like Molly McCracken did. (I gathered that would be Millie's mother) Constantly nagging me, she was. Where's Jimmy, she'd ask. Where's Jimmy gone. Nagged me stupid, she did, asking if Jimmy had run off with another woman."

"She was concerned about him. She loved him."

"He loved her. He told me that once."

"Why didn't you just tell her the truth of what happened to him?"

"I told yer I don't know what happened to him."

"What you actually mean is you never saw what happened to him because you were too busy scampering for your life out from the secret cavern under the ruins of Dun an Oir. Isn't that how it went?"

Willie solidified into a piece of cold iron in disbelief of what I knew. Here I was, a total stranger who knew more about his life than he probably knew about himself. His complexion went a sickly white, and the blackheads spotting his face were now more prominent. I'd certainly got Willie petrified and understandable too when his past reappears suddenly into his already miserable life and confronts him about a secret he's kept to himself for all this time.

"How...come you-"

"That I know so much, you're wondering?"

Willie's lips trembled. He said edgily, "Is Jimmy alive?"

"Only in spirit," I assured him. "But he did leave behind ten confessional journals dating between 1934 and 1944, he so conveniently wrote."

Willie leaned closer to me, a concerned expression crumpling his face, his breath smelling of onions that made me withdraw slightly.

"What d'yer mean, confessional journals?" he whispered, his eyes darting around the room in search for big eared listeners.

I eased back from the smell of his bad breath and took in a mouthful of Guinness, swallowed and said, "Nothing incriminating that concerns you or the other members of McCracken's private racketeers."

He didn't protest against me calling him a racketeer.

"Doesn't rightly matter about the others...they died with Jimmy."

"When the tunnel roof fell in?"

He eyed me with a look suggesting I was thick. "They were crushed under tons of rock."

"They were your friends?"

"That they were."

"How many died?"

"Seven, including Jimmy…Hey…hold on a minute! Yer'd have known that if yer'd excavated the tunnel to reach the cavern."

"Who mentioned anything about digging?"

"Yer found Jimmy's body, didn't yer?"

"I found a skeletal hand wedged between fallen rocks with a ring attached."

"Yer'd have had to be inside the cavern if yer found Jimmy. He was last out. He always was. Always so meticulous that everything was in order for the next time. It was always going to be his secret fortress to fight his battles from."

"I went into the cavern by the sea route; the same route where you hauled a Japanese submarine inside. That was an exceptional piece of ingenuity."

Willie waved his hand gesturing his reluctance to go on. "I'm saying nothing more. Yer know where Jimmy lays. Leave me alone!"

I'd no intention of leaving him alone; not now, not until I had the true story. Keeping my temper intact, I said. "You'd better talk to me. I'm probably the only person in the whole wide world who can get you hanged. Do you understand that, Willie? Hung by the neck until you're pronounced dead."

He tweaked a cocky grin. "Hangings been abolished."

"Not in Japan it hasn't." I'd no idea if what I'd just said had any truth to it, but his look showed he was paying intention. "The Japanese will have you extradited and you'll stand trial on Japanese soil."

I'd hurt him with that. He was horrified. "I wasn't there I tell yer! You can't prove I was!"

"The Japanese, they'll use truth drugs on you."

"What do yer mean truth drugs?"

"They'll inject you with a special serum which will induce you to tell the truth to their questions."

"It wouldn't be allowed."

"Different culture those Japanese; a different culture means different laws."

"They'd be contravening my human rights."

"You have no human rights, Willie. You're a murderer! And the only one left who they can make an example of in a court."

He proved he was a stubborn bastard for his size.

"They'll not get me off Irish soil. I have me rights."

I said, "Do you think the Japanese will be bothered about your rights. The Japanese submariners down there in that horrible damp cavern were slaughtered. They were gunned down without as much as a fair fight. I think I could quite easily convince a court of your involvement to first degree murder. Maybe they'll find a trace of your DNA down there to prove your involvement. The scientists nowadays are very clever."

Willie flustered, sweat sprouting over his top lip. "Yer can't incriminate me. We worked together, that's all! We repaired quays and jetties and run down ancient buildings. Yer can't make me confess to anything else. Now leave me in peace!"

"You're lying to me, Willie. You know everything."

He shook his head vigorously in denial.

"I'm willing to make a deal."

His ears pricked up. "What-what sort of deal? "He asked cautiously.

"It'll be rewarding."

"You're willing to pay?"

"I was thinking more on the lines of non-implication to mass murder."

He scowled. He wasn't happy with his only option.

"Tell me everything I want to know about Jimmy McCracken. It's that simple. And then I'll walk out of here; this meeting forgotten; it never existed and you won't be implicated in anything. I can't be fairer than that."

I could tell by his expression that he had his doubts.

Willie shuffled in his seat thinking it over.

I could see he was going to need more convincing. "Just the whole story concerning Jimmy McCracken and I promise you'll not see or hear from me again."

He frowned. "Why should I trust you, a stranger? Shop me to Garda the moment my backs turned, yer will!"

"Millie trusted me when she gave me your name. She thought you could help me."

"Are yer in trouble?" he said slowly.

"Not just me. There are others who may depend on any scraps of information you pass on to me."

"Yer won't mention my name to anyone?"

"You have my silence."

"God will strike yer down otherwise"

"You have my word." I assured him.

"If yer do I'll kill yer! I swear it."

I stared him straight in the eyes and said solidly, "Willie, I could smash your throat with one punch, walk away and nobody will care a frigging toss; so less of your idle threats. I'm only interested in Jimmy McCracken and what happened on Cape Clear Island. Tell me what

I want to know and you can sink back into your void of loneliness. We have a deal?"

He thought about it for three seconds, nodded and leaned even closer to me so no one could overhear even a whisper, which was pointless because there was no one near enough to even hear our conversation. When Willie began his story I was annoyed with myself for not bringing a hidden voice recorder.

"It was all Jimmy's idea," he began. "We were all together one drunken night: Jimmy, me and the other lads," Willie's eyes flicked about nervously as he talked. "Jimmy asked which of us fancied becoming rich men instead of being paupers for the rest of our lives. Who wouldn't want money in their pockets? I mean...times were hard. We listened to what Jimmy had to say. He left us gasping for air.

"Jimmy was involved with the IRA. The lads knew that. He hated the Brits. Me! I wasn't one bit concerned about Northern Ireland. Neither were the other lads. What we didn't know was he'd offered his services to the Germans, shortly after the Dunkirk disaster. He was mixing it with German spies.

"Jimmy told us about a shipment of gold destined for German shores. We were flabbergasted when he said he intended to hijack the gold right from under the noses of the expectant Germans. And that we'd have to attack a Japanese submarine to get our hands on the loot. We thought it was some crackpot scheme Jimmy had made up to impress us; not that we told him that; yer didn't tell Jimmy McCracken what you thought of him because he'd bash yer face to pulp with a iron bar, that he would."

"Charming fellow playing a double role of deceitfulness," I said sarcastically.

"The man was a killer that's for sure. Stupidly we listened to everything Jimmy said. The thought of gold had us dribbling from the corner of our mouths. He relayed his intricate plan to us in detail. It seemed workable, but bloody dangerous. The dangerous part of it I didn't fancy; the strong chance that we may be involved in a mini war ourselves. We'd to kill people if necessary. I withdrew my service right away. I didn't want blood on me hands. I wasn't a fighting man. I found the courage to tell him I wanted out. Wealth I'd try to achieve later, in a more civilised manner. But no! Jimmy wouldn't accept my withdrawal. I'd made the mistake of listening instead of walking away when I had the chance. I always thought Jimmy was a friend. I was wrong. He was a bully, a dangerous bully. He said he couldn't take the risk of me walking away with the information I now had. He said he would have to kill me to maintain my silence. Well...what could I do but to participate in his scheme?

"Aye, Jimmy was a right bastard alright; a right bastard with a brilliant mind. I could only admire his skills as a master stonemason and a fantastic engineer though his talent in engineering was nothing compared to his urge for violence. As it was, we set to work on Jimmy's get-rich scheme. Three months of sweat and hard graft to construct everything inside the cavern. We had to transfer heavy equipment and materials from the mainland to Cape Clear, and then by hand-carts across to Dun an Oir. We had constructed a pulley system to transfer the gear across to the derelict fort. We'd no time to construct a bridge of sorts."

"What about the locals on the island? They never questioned your activities?"

"The few locals there at the time thought we were construction men repairing the fort. Jimmy had already warned them in advance. As for the cavern, Jimmy had discovered the place by accident, when he was doing some renovation on the ruins to prevent further disrepair. He'd discovered a tunnel that spiralled down, like a helter-skelter, a phenomenon probably caused when the worlds volcanoes divided its lands. It wasn't too steep either and wide enough to carry the heavy equipment down into the cavern.

"Jimmy reckoned the fort was used as a stronghold by the O'Driscoll's to protect their wealth from invaders and the cavern was their escape route in case the fort was overrun. Dun an Oir was a giant piggy-bank; how ironic was that."

I pushed on. "What happened once you were down inside the cavern?"

"We constructed a generator for lights and a high powered winching mechanism. We used boats to lay wire ropes on the seabed in advance. Billy-boy was our professional underwater worker. He dragged lighter lines into the cavern and we used the winch to drag the heavy wire rope through.

"Down inside the cavern Jimmy trained us to use weapons. We practiced and practiced until we were as good as any commando unit. When everything was finally in place the plan was executed with unbelievable expertise. I had to hand it to Jimmy, he was a smooth operator. I'd no doubt whatsoever that if Jimmy had managed to escape the fall-in, he would have continued his career in the IRA and would have made Commander-in-Chief."

Willie was beginning to bore me with irrelevant glorified details. I urged him along. "Never mind how good he was in murder. What happened next?"

"What Jimmy had predicted would happen. This Jap submarine sat off Clear Island as dusk began to fall. I've no idea where it came from. It was just sat there, waiting to be hit. We moved in on the sub by inflatable crafts, attached limpet mines to the propellers and fins and blew a hole in her rear end and sank her to the bottom of the sea, crippled and helpless and filling with water. Billy-boy went down and secured the wire ropes to the submarines two diving fins and then the winch did the rest, dragging the submarine into the cavern slowly, inch by inch."

"Did anyone spot what you were doing?" I asked with interest.

He thought for a minute. "Aye, there were an RAF Spitfire buzzing us at the time but it soon went; not that it would have made any difference because the sub began to sink at that point and disappeared off the face of the earth.

"Jimmy might have been a murderous, anti-Brit, fascists, but yer can't fault the ingenious piece of engineering skills in the design and building of a diesel winch capable of dragging so much tonnage. Within twenty-four hours the sub was inside the cavern and its hull beached. You had to be there to believe what we were doing, but it worked. It worked! It was a magnificent sight, she was a real beauty and we'd captured her; eight working men and seven of us with no war experience whatsoever."

"Well I can assure you, Willie, it's nothing but a rusting graveyard now. Go on!"

"We had our submachine guns in readiness in case any of the crew tried to exit the sub. We burnt a hole into the side of the sub. We knew the Jap's would be waiting for us to push our noses into their craft, but they didn't stand a chance. Jimmy tossed in a handful of German grenades for good measure; lethal things they were; blew the Jap's to pieces. And then the lads stormed inside shooting every bastard they found. I stayed outside to cover the conning tower and the deck hatches for any escapees. I listened to the raging battle inside the iron shell; heard more explosions from inside. It was a massacre. Submariners don't make good ground troops. Not one Jap was left alive. There would be no captives, on Jimmy's orders. He didn't want witnesses to the crime. But momentarily our wickedness was forgotten when we found the gold boxes amongst crates of cargo.

"Jimmy allowed us to keep one box of gold apiece; that was our fee. The remaining boxes, and there were a lot, we took by handcarts to North harbour and loaded the gold onto our boat, plus fifty smaller crates that Jimmy wanted."

"What was in those?"

Willie gave an uncommitted shrug. "Jimmy didn't say and none of us was in the right frame of mind to ask a madman. Besides, we were exhausted, just glad the job was done. Jimmy sailed away alone."

"Why take the gold alone?"

"He said the gold belonged to the coffers of the IRA to buy weapons to use against the British army once the war in Europe finished. He must have had a contact somewhere to take control of the gold. I suspected the gold was to be his elevation to the top of the IRA ladder."

"In which direction did he sail?"

"Is it important?"

"In which direction did he go, Willie?"

"North, across Roaring Water Bay; to the other side probably. That doesn't mean anything, as he could have changed course for all I know."

"What did the rest of you do afterwards?"

"Not much I can tell you. We sat around bored shitless, eating crap food and drinking bottles of beer while we waited for Jimmy to return twenty hours later."

"McCracken never told anyone where he'd taken the gold?"

"He never really got the chance did he? The secret died with him."

I got the impression that Willie was glad he was ridding the burden of the past once and for all.

Willie's mouth was flowing now. "It was after Jimmy returned when our real troubles began. Sean, he was always the obstinate one and with a bit of drink inside him, decided to confront Jimmy. In Sean's opinion one box of gold wasn't enough payment for the risk they had all taken. I thought he'd an arguable case. Jimmy didn't. He killed Sean right in front of our eyes; gunned him down, right there in the cavern. I'll always remember the sprinkling of gold bars dropping from the disintegrating box as the bullets ripped into Sean's body. And then with a smirking smile on his face, Jimmy turned to the rest of us and callously said, 'there yer are lads come and collect yer bonus.' He then pumped the remainder of the magazine into Sean's face so if he were to be found he wouldn't be recognized."

I remembered the skeleton laying in the sand when I had first landed inside the cavern. That must have been Sean's bones I'd stood on. It also confirmed to me that Willie wasn't lying to me and his memory of events that day he'd never forgotten.

I said, "Doubly charming character was our Jimmy McCracken."

"I'd befriended a madman and I don't mind telling yer I was petrified. What I couldn't believe was the other lads seemed to accept what Jimmy had done to Sean; they filled their pockets with the extra gold. I didn't. I was more worried what Jimmy would do next; wondering if he intended to kill the rest of us when our backs were turned. I had to get out of that place of death. I was first up the tunnel carrying me gold. Damned heavy it was. I thought the rest were following me. I knew Jimmy would have been last out because he'd have had to switch off the generator and cover it with the tarpaulin; always meticulous was Jimmy. I always suspected he had this insane vision of re-floating the submarine, hoist the IRA flag and use it against the Brits.

"Anyway, I was halfway up the tunnel when I heard the gargled scream echo chillingly through the tunnel. It had to have come from one of the submariners. I stopped, wondering if I should go back. I heard one of our lads shout, 'watch out! There's one on the conning tower!' Then shots were fired, and then there was a terrific explosion at the bottom of the tunnel. The entire place shook like a gigantic jelly. The tremors under me feet nearly knocked me over. When I thought about it much later I assumed one of the submariners was still alive and had managed to fire a cannon shell in retaliation. I just stood there frozen to the spot waiting for something to happen. That was when I saw the bellowing cloud of dust hurtling towards me like a sand storm."

"What did you do then?"

"I didn't hang around that's for sure. Not after the tunnel started shaking violently, as if struck by an earthquake and chunks of rock began cascading down. I was out of the there. I even threw down my box of gold because it impeded my ability to run fast. I ran. I ran for my life! When I got out I was covered in thick dust. I waited for the others, half expecting them to burst out behind me coughing and spluttering. When the dust had finally settled that's when I saw the tunnel had collapsed fully."

"What did you do next?"

"I kept on running! Back to the boat and back to the mainland. I didn't know what to do. I was so scared I deliberately disappeared for a month, waiting for news of the accident. Week after week I heard nothing. I came out of hiding expecting to suffer the consequences of my actions but all I got was Molly McCracken pestering me; asking if I'd seen Jimmy. Months went by, still nothing. Months became years, still no word and Molly McCracken's pestering finally turned me into a drunken wreck ever since."

"Why didn't you just tell somebody? Told a few lies. Jimmy and his mates had gone to the O'Driscoll's fort on Clear Island and they hadn't returned. A search party would have been formed and you would never have been suspected; simple ethics aided by a few white lies. There were no witnesses to say otherwise."

"That's easy to say when yer're not scared shitless. In the forties people were edgy, untrustworthy. Implication in a crime of robbery and murder wouldn't go down very well with the Irish Guards whether the target was the enemy or not. And with Jimmy involved with the IRA, well that definitely sealed my mouth. I wasn't going to spend the next twenty years stuck in the decay of an Irish prison. No thank you! Kept the blabbing tightly shut, and went about my business trying to be as normal as possible."

"That's everything?"

He nodded. "Now will yer leave me alone to finish the rest of me horrible life in peace?"

"It's what I promised."

"Yer won't tell Millie I ran away and didn't stop to try and rescue her father?"

"No point upsetting her more than she probably is now," I said. "One more question, Willie. Why didn't you go back for the gold boxes in the tunnel, it's obviously still buried there under the debris? Six or seven boxes would have been worth the trouble to excavate."

Willie shivered. "Not likely! Perhaps yer haven't heard of the O'Driscoll curse. Back in the thirties people died mysteriously on Clear Island in the vicinity of the ruined fort. I suspected the curse had struck again. I'd rather die in poverty than challenge the curse of O'Driscoll's. I've never been back to the island since. The cursed cargo can stop there and so can the other stuff."

It would be much later when I was to understand Willie's slip of the tongue, as we were supposedly talking about gold, yet he'd mentioned *the other stuff* which in my opinion, at the time, was a reference to another piece of cargo. At that moment I was only interested in the current information Willie had told me so far. I finished my Guinness and rose from my chair to make my exit, then checked my stride when I remembered something important that I'd forgot to ask him.

"Ever heard of St Brendon?"

"He's one of Ireland's saints. So?"

"Was Jimmy a church going man?"

"Nah! Not Jimmy. We repaired a few before the WW2 started. Why?"

"I'm curious. Can you remember which ones you repaired?"

Willie was shaking his head even though he was still thinking. "Dare say I don't...the churches were scattered...I can't be sure."

I left Willie alone to reflect on the great times he must have had with Jimmy 'the mad-man' McCracken.

*

I left Cork and drove back to see Deveron at his hotel, only he'd done a disappearing act and so too had Shayna. No message, no jack shit! I headed back to Baltimore as fast as the Roadster could move without crashing because my spine was tingling with the sense of danger, but I couldn't put my finger on whether it was my problem or someone else's. I pressed the accelerator to the floor and pushed the Roadster hard, burning fuel and rubber at an alarming rate.

I'd almost reached the turn-off for Baltimore when the in-car mobile rang. I pressed the appropriate button for two way contact. I knew the mobile number that highlighted on my screen to be Shamus's mobile, but the voice didn't match the owner's.

My, "yes," was an understandably cautious.

"Listen carefully, Speed. We've an interfering friend of yours who isn't happy to be in our company. In fact he's finding the experience rather painful."

I was baffled at first as to who the mystery man's voice belonged to, made more difficult to hear the voice because of the heavy roaring sound in the background from where the caller was calling from. To hear the voice again, I said, "I don't have friends."

"If you hurry, Speed, you may save your sailor companion from a drop to his death. Be at the fog station at Mizen Head. No police, just you, alone. I wouldn't hang about, the tides ebbing and a body smashes nastily on rocks."

The caller disconnected and my mobile went dead. The voice; the smirking tone, I was positive it belonged to Damien Love. I panicked when I realized who Love and Hate had with them. The frigging bastards had Shamus! I hadn't a moment to waste.

I raced the Roadster over to Shamus's home at Collen to make sure it wasn't a trick. I brought the Roadster to a shuddering halt outside his house and got out to check. There was no need for me to knock on the front door because it had been kicked from its hinges and lay at a forty five degree angle all splintered and battered. I shouted through to Shamus but received no reply. I went inside and looked round. The place had been trashed and Shamus was nowhere to be seen. They had him all right!

I was back in the Roadster, crunching through the gears, driving ferociously towards Mizen Head without a contingency plan to fall back on. I assumed that once I presented myself at the proposed rendezvous, the first bullet would hit me before I got close enough to plea for Shamus's life to be spared. That is, if Love and Hate had allowed him to live that long. My guts churned inside as I struggled to keep the Roadster from crashing as I negotiated tight bends and narrow country roads, heading towards my destiny with death ringing in my ears. I was also unarmed and vulnerable.

During the drive I fleetingly noticed a sign post bearing the name of a place which had recently sprung to mind, but I soon forgot the names meaning as I thought of what frightful state I would find Shamus suffering.

Chapter Twenty One

My approached to Mizen Head car-park was with understandable apprehension. There were two other saloon cars parked. Both were empty of either a driver or passenger. I looked around before getting out, closing the car door quietly and making sure the Roadster was locked while still keeping a vigilante watch. I didn't want to be caught out with a nasty surprise that Love and Hate were renowned for, and I wasn't.

Love had said to meet them at the fog station and that was a good ten minutes walking distance. I set off along the pathway towards the station. If Love and Hate weren't aware of my arrival I should imagine they would know now with the screeching seagulls circling above me announcing my presence.

Mizen Head was a place that appealed to danger. The terrain alone was an accident prone victim's nightmare and those who stepped beyond the pathways were asking for trouble. I put in a good pace, not quite a run but almost as well as one before I was forced to slow and stop. In the distance I saw Love and Hate. I couldn't really miss the two ugly bastards. They were waiting for me on the white arched concrete bridge that extended over the gorge leading to the Mizen Head fog station. The cowards were using Shamus as a protective shield and by the positioning of Shamus's hands behind his back I assumed that his wrists had been bound tightly with a strong restraint.

I wondered what my next move should be considering I hadn't forged a plan of action. I glanced down at the ground which gave me an idea. From between my feet I stooped and picked up two smooth flat stones and put one in each hand, sucked in a deep breath to steady my nerves and headed down the pathway towards them.

Love and Hate were alert as I approached. They probably had me in sight before I saw them. I'd limited options and I should have really informed the Garda of the situation and left the hostage negotiations to them. But I'd good reason to think that Love would have dropped Shamus into the gorge the moment they were challenged and with the excuse that they were trying to save a suicidal victim.

It was me they wanted more than Shamus. Now I was here to save a man's life, and on this occasion, I was on time. Besides, how could I possibly be accepted through the gates of Hell if I was to allow Shamus to perish without even attempting a reasonable rescue? I can't be an egoistic git all my life.

Within shouting distance, I yelled. "Are you alright Shamus?"

Shamus nodded, shouting back. "As fine as I can be-," before he was cut off by a hard nudge in the small of his back with a silenced gun.

"Keep walking towards us, Speed! Love yelled back. "Get your hands up so I can see what they're doing."

I raised my hands shoulder height, slipping the two pebbles between the forefinger and middle finger of each hand and gripped the stones hard, so when I showed the palms of my hands the pebbles were invisible from their view.

Love gestured me forward with his gun hand. "That's it, Speed. Keep coming!"

Stupid as it might sound, I was gambling on a hunch that I wasn't about to die by the bullet but instead Hate wanted to tear me apart piece by piece and feed me to the Basking Sharks. Hate wanted me to suffer, as he had suffered by Winston's teeth. As much as I wanted revenge on them, Hate equally wanted revenge on me. I could see the fury burning in his eyes as I went through the iron-barred gate and onto the bridge. Yes he definitely had me down for a butcher's death. But if I needed any strong encouragement to take him on, my blood sizzled when I saw the severe bruising and cuts around Shamus's cheekbones and eyes.

"Not in any pain, are you, Shamus?" I asked him, keeping a watchful eye on the fidgety movements of Love and Hate.

Shamus shook his head gingerly. "I'm Irish, Shacks sir. Me skin's like leather."

He was also a lousy liar, though I admired his bravery considering the circumstances.

Love grinned. "It's very chivalrous of you to turn up, Speed, and so pleasant to have your company."

"Crackers more like, but I'm here." I began lowering my hands, sneakily slipping the pebbles back into the palms of my hands.

Love jabbed the gun deeper into Shamus's spine. "Nothing stupid now, Speed, or I'll blow a hole threw the old man's spleen."

"Just tired arms," I said convincingly, "can't hold them aloft all day."

Hate began sneering. His fingers twitched in anticipation to get at me. For the first time I saw his recent disfigurement. The half ear was an unsightly mess, a jagged piece of purplish-red flesh that no plastic surgeon could reshape to normality. There were bite marks dotting his face and scratches criss-crossed the bridge of his nose. And then there were the deep purplish bite marks on his hand obviously from his first skirmish with Winston when they had clashed at the farm. *Do I love that dog!*

I can't say I was about to enjoy the next exciting encounter when Hate drew a long bladed knife that glinted menacingly when the sunlight caught it. There was no warning. He suddenly lunged towards me, snarling obscenities. I saw the inflamed madness in his eyes. Spit flew angularly from his mouth as he rushed towards me. I held my ground and waited for my moment. My mind was working in overdrive; only seconds to react. Instinctively I looked beyond the onrushing Hate and shouted, "Get him Winston!"

Hate fell for my lie. He slammed on the shoe leather, frantically twisting with the expectancy of seeing Winston snapping at his heels, slashing his knife downwards where he thought the imaginary dog was.

That momentary distraction even fooled Love, as he looked for the non-existent beast. Love was quick to realize my deception. His eyes shot back at me, horror across his face when I caught him between the eyes with one of the pebbles I had thrown at him. My attack copied the biblical encounter between David and Goliath as the pebble jolted Love's head backwards and he lost his balance and fell against the parapet railings, stunned, blood sprouting from the split skin and running down the bridge of his nose and dripping off the nib.

Swiftly I'd pivoted into another throwing angle and threw the second pebble at Hate, catching him straight in the left eyeball after he had turned to face me. In all the confusion I moved swiftly forward and grabbed Hate's knife arm, fighting him for supremacy. As we spun I got a fleeting glimpse of Shamus in action. In spite of his bondage he'd shoulder charged the howling Love and sent him over the side of the railing. Unbelievably, Love had managed to grab a hold of the concrete bridge support as he fell to a certain death on the rocks and he hung there helplessly, swinging and screaming for help, frantically attempting to scramble back to safety. Shamus, to his credit, did a marvellous job in preventing Love from climbing back onto the bridge by standing on Love's fingers. I got the distinct impression Shamus was beginning to enjoy himself as he shouted his own brand of Irish obscenities while stamping down his foot. Who could blame him? *Revenge is mine says the Lord!* I could have sworn Shamus was preaching.

While Shamus fought his battle I had mine to contend with, as I struggled with Hate for control of the knife. The frigging bastard was far stronger opposition than I'd anticipated and the swishing blade nicked the skin of my left cheek. The sight of leaking blood excited Hate and he fought even harder. The fight had us crashing against the parapets like two gladiators battling to the death in the centre of the arena. We were spinning, our feet shuffling for the firmness and grip of terra-firma. Our bodies rolled across the top of the railing, advantage changing constantly. Our knees thudded into each other's midriff hoping for the one fatal blow to gain the upper hand.

Shamus might have been enjoying his domination of Love, but I was feeling the strain and exhaustion, tiring by the second and I needed inspiration quickly. I got it in a way I didn't think possible, though I didn't know what possessed me to latch my teeth onto Hate's right eyebrow. But I did and I was biting hard into the baggy skin to hang on. I shook my head like a wild animal tearing the flesh from its prey. His screams sounded like a wounded wolf, but I didn't let go until my mouth came away from his face when Hate released his grip on me. He went reeling back, clutching his face. Blood pumped from between his fingers, running down his cheek and chin. I spat out the offensive lump of hairy flesh to the floor, the taste of his blood trickling down the side of my mouth as I watched the ragged piece of eyebrow twitch like a squashed caterpillar.

Hate came at me again, slashing the knife in sweeping arcs. The blood from the damaged eyebrow had filled his eye and with his other eye closed by the huge swelling where the pebble had struck, he was blind. He was slashing out at nonexistent shadows. And when he slashed the blade wildly again and it came sweeping round, I carried on the knife's momentum and forced the cold steel blade into the side of his neck. I rammed the blade home for good measure, up to the hilt with a quick, hard shove.

I pulled away from the ensuing gush of blood spewing from the neck wound, a slight splattering of Hate's blood peppering the front of my jacket. I stepped back and watched him die slowly. He made strange gurgling sounds as he attempted to reach for the knife embedded in his neck, making a desperate attempt to dislodge the blade which now prevented him from twisting his head round. Even then Hate wasn't finished. He fumbled into his pocket and began extracting a handgun. I rushed him, leaping into the air, angling my body and executed a solid sidekick into the middle of his chest which sent him peddling backwards and over the parapet rails.

For some unknown reason I made an instinctive attempt to grab his legs as he fell, but he'd gone over too quickly, only inches from my grasp. He dropped onto the rocks below, his screams smothered by the roar of the waves and the screeching sea birds as his falling body disturbed them.

I ran over to Shamus and released him from his bonds. I told him off. "I can't leave you alone for one minute-eh-Shamus?

Shamus's head lowered in shame. "I'm sorry, Shacks sir."

"Look it's not you fault, Shamus. I'm just glad you're alright."

"They took me by surprise, they did, Shacks sir."

"They're experts at that, Shamus."

"I tried to fight them off, I did. There were just too many."

I patted him on the shoulder. "I'm proud of you, Shamus. I don't have many true friends but you're high on my list."

Shamus smiled. "That I'll always be, Shacks sir."

Shamus stopped smiling suddenly and looked pass me and I saw what had concerned him. Love had somehow scrambled back onto the bridge further along and was now legging it towards the fog station. I hadn't finished with him yet. I went after him.

By the time I'd reached the whitewashed building, Love was nowhere to be seen. I kept my wits about me because he couldn't have ventured far, not unless he had the skill and nerve of a high board diver and had ignored stupidity and decided his escape was perpendicular over the cliff edge. I soon changed my theory when I heard the crack of wood breaking. Cautiously I circled the fog station, eyes and ears in tune with each other. I heard the faintest sound of shuffled feet and I knew he was close. I made a sudden jerk forward and retracted even faster as the piece of fence post tried to whack me across the head but instead crashed into the side of the building, splinters of wood flying in all direction.

I saw enough of his arms to swiftly grab him by the wrists, spin him side on and kick him in his midriff which propelled him backwards so fast that his back peddling feet couldn't keep up with the momentum of his body and he eventually landed on his arse in a heap at the side of the safety fencing.

Love scrambled to his feet and scampered over the fencing with nowhere to go, only the cliff's edge. I chased after him, closing off his escape route back through another part of the fence. His only route now was in retreat and back towards the cliffs. He realized his dilemma, stopped and turned round to face me. When I got closer to him, he made an instinctive grab for me, grasping a handful of my jacket. I had visions of him attempting to pull me over the side with him so I concentrated on gaining a good foothold before I smashed my fist into the bridge of his nose and heard bone crack. His body seemed to shudder and he lost his footing and slipped down the rock, his feet dangling over the edge, holding on for what life he didn't deserve.

"Help...help me, Speed. I'm slipping."

"Fuck off you murdering bastard!

"You can't let me die. It's immoral. It's murder!"

"No, it's revenge."

"Please…I don't want to die."

Frigging hell, I was so mad with his diabolical plea that I reached down, grabbed both his jacket sleeves and yanked him back to relative safety, well sufficient safety that still left him precariously balanced on edge by the tip of his toes while I held onto him. He didn't struggle much knowing that a mere inch separated his return down the cliff face and certain death on the rocks below.

"Right you frigging parasite, let's be having the name of your paymaster?"

"Pull me back first! Then I'll talk."

"You're in no position to negotiate terms. I'd start babbling now if I were you."

"Go to Hell!"

"That's exactly where you're going unless you talk."

He snorted a defiant laugh. "Killing me constitutes cold-blooded murder."

"So put me on trial. It'll be worth it."

"Your conscience won't allow you to kill me."

"Who's your paymaster? The Housekeeper?"

"If I tell you, what happens to me afterwards?"

I haven't decided."

"I work for McClusky."

"McClusky's dead!"

"I can't help that!"

"You kill people for money, Love. You don't work for nothing and with McClusky terminated you'd have disappeared and returned to that stench pit you call home. So you swivelling piece of shit, who's paying you?"

The stubborn bastard shook his head defiantly.

I shoved him back causing particles of rock to tinkle down the rock face. "I'm not the one dangling so close to the edge using only my toe nails to hang on."

"If I fall you'll never know!"

"Is the bastard aboard the *Flying Fish*?"

"Pull me back and I'll tell you." Love was gambling I'd agree.

I rattled him again, spittle flying as I raged, "Talk, you piece of diarrhoea! You've nothing to lose, only your life."

"That's just it, Speed. If I talk, I die anyway. It's that sort of situation. And you're just English scum who has no idea how to murder someone simply!"

"You mean there's a particular skill in killing an old defenceless farmer by drowning him in cow shit. Or perhaps killing a kind faced photographer in London, and burning him to a cinder. They were my friends you messed up."

"You can't prove a fucking thing!"

"Can't I? Your killing days are over and you're going to rot in a prison cell."

"You think so, Speed?" I didn't appreciate his cocky attitude one bit. "My appearance in an English court will be as brief as the time it takes me to explain that I'm a simple foreign tourist being bullied by a mad Englishman; that's you, Speed!"

He had a point. But his defining statement had me thinking about similarities relating to it; that I'd heard it before somewhere, but I couldn't remember where. But I'd no intention of letting him wriggle his way from the truth. "You frigging slimy leech! You murdered my friends, all right! And you'll stand trial, no problem!"

"You'll need witnesses to back your accusations. No, metal detector man, you're the murderer. I witnessed what you did to Hate. It's you that's heading for Hell!"

"Is that a fact? Well I can't have that now can I."

I looked him straight in the eyes. He wasn't going to talk in a month of Sundays. He was no use to me. I pushed him over the edge, his hands frantically clawing fresh air as he fell backwards, his deathly screams absorbed by the high pitched squawking from spooked seagulls he'd managed to scare as his body bounced against the rock face on the way down. I leaned over the edge to confirm his fate. His body was bent backwards over a large chunk of jagged rock, his back broken. He was probably still breathing but not for much longer.

I actually felt cheated that he had escaped without a trial but I certainly didn't have any regrets that he had died by my hands. The deaths of Tommy Bickermass and Lens Lazerow had been avenged. But I still had one more important engagement to attend to before I'd finished what I started. I had to flush out the person responsible for ordering the killing of innocent people. I had to find the 'Housekeeper'.

I turned round when I heard running feet approaching. It was Shamus, closely followed by another man who I assumed to be the operator of the fog station. Both were panting heavily after their sprint and both were now suffering the consequences of their efforts

The man recovered first, and said, "What was that dreadful scream?" He asked in a panic.

"Good god!" I said dramatically. "Did you see what's just happened? It was unbelievable! It seems there has been a terrible accident."

The man peered gingerly over the precipice, concern distorting his face before horror took over when he saw the disjointed body far below. "There's somebody down there!"

"I was walking along," I explained, "admiring the view when...I saw this figure standing close to the edge...well I think he jumped! I did try to save him, but he was just too determined to kill himself."

Shamus watched me with astonishment. He knew differently.

"I'd better inform the coastguard," the man said, as if the situation occurred on a regular basis.

"I'll leave that in your capable hands, my good man. Come along, Shamus, there's nothing more we can do here."

We hurried from the scene as fast as we could and back onto the walkway.

"Hang on!" the man called out. "You'll need to wait to give a statement."

We pretended we hadn't heard him and our brisk walk converged into a run.

Shamus, between gasps of breaths, said "Oh, God be praised, yer're alright, Shacks sir. I gather yer did the swine?

"What an unfortunate shame he went over the edge."

"Would that be his own choice or did he slip over your foot, Shacks sir?"

"Accidents do happen!" I said.

"Indeed they do, Shacks sir. Indeed they do."

We 'd probably made it halfway across the concrete bridge when something zinged and whipped off a chunk of the concrete railing an inch in front of me. I dropped to the floor dragging Shamus along with me and we stayed flat while I peered around.

"Where the frigging hell did those shots come from?"

"I've no idea, Shacks sir. I started falling when yer did."

There was the faintest of splutters as another barrage of gun fire chipped the concrete in a dozen places only a few feet from our position. That was when I suspected the sniper didn't have a clear view of our position, so I began to crawl along the bridge on my stomach, scuffing the toes of my walking boots as I pushed. Shamus followed closely.

As we crawled I said over my shoulder, "I think this bridge is going to need a lick of paint after this fiasco."

I heard Shamus groan with my untimely observation and he followed that with a mumbled complaint. "You're absolutely bonkers, Shacks sir. We're being shot at and you're thinking about painting the bridge!"

"I'm a perfectionist, Shamus."

We had made it to the gateway with no injuries and with no more gunshots. I listened intently before the shrill cry from circling seagulls broke the silence. In the far distance I heard the faint sound of a car engine starting, which quickly disappeared from earshot.

"I think our sniper's done a runner."

"How can you tell?"

I rose to my feet fearlessly to prove my point and I didn't get shot.

"Has that convinced you? Let's go, Shamus."

Shamus dragged himself to his feet and rubbed the grey bristles on his chin. "The gunman gave up rather too easily, don't you think, Shacks sir?"

"The thought had crossed my mind, but I've no time to ponder on fragments of puzzlement. I've a master criminal to apprehend."

It was moments like this when I realized I wasn't getting any younger. My body ached everywhere. My joints creaked and cracked. My elbows and knees had all the evidence of severe abrasions. I was definitely beginning to feel the pressure and pace of the pursuit and regretting every moment that passed.

I recovered Love's gun from the floor and tucked it away inside my jacket. My steps quickened as we headed back to the car park in a rush

Shamus, puffing heavily, said, "Those two villains back there weren't alone when they broke into me house."

"Did you recognize any of the others?"

"Two of them were crewmen; foreigners by the sound of their voices. The third chap with them-well his voice was different from the others."

We kept up a swift pace as we talked, not even a glance at each other because I was too preoccupied watching for more surprises because I didn't think we'd escaped our problems just yet.

I said, "I'd say you'd had a visit from our friends from the *Flying Fish*."

"I'd say that too, Shacks sir."

"What was different about the third person?"

Shamus blew out hard. "O he was a big man. English, sounded a bit toffee nosed by the way he talked. I didn't see his face but he was the one dishing out the orders."

"Is there anything specific you can tell me about this Englishman?"

"Yes, Shacks, sir, he'd size ten boots kicking me in the face!"

"Did you recognize the pattern on the soles of his shoes, Shamus?"

"Yer be pulling me leg, Shacks sir?"

"That I am, Shamus."

When we'd reached the Roadster one of the saloons had gone. It was then I had an apparition for disaster.

I quickly grabbed Shamus's arm as he was about to open the Roadster's passenger car door and pulled him back.

Shamus was spooked by my action. "What is it, Shacks sir?"

"You were probably right about the sniper giving in too early, Shamus. I'd take cover behind the other car if I was you. I've a very bad feeling we're walking into a trap."

Shamus didn't argue. He trusted my instincts after what we've been through together. When he was safely behind the other car I went down on my hands and knees and conducted a finger search underneath the Roadster.

I found the device I suspected had been planted there attached to the under-body of the Roadster on the passenger side. I gave the device a coat of looking at. It was oblong, roughly four inch by two inch long with two short wires linked to a pencil thin second device tucked into the bevel of the car door. I frown upon people who treat my Roadster with such tasteless disrespect.

I called over to Shamus. "Stay where you are old buddy. I think we're the proud owners of a magnetically attached car bomb."

Shamus cowered even deeper. "A bomb, yer say?"

"Well I assume it's a bomb because I didn't put it there and it would explain why the sniper didn't hang about. I think the intention was to pin us down long enough for the sneaky bastard to attach this and put the blame on Irish terrorists."

"We'd best get clear of the wretched thing before we're blown to smithereens, Shacks sir."

"What! And leave my beautiful car to be fragmented across Ireland. Never! It's only a small bomb. It's a simple device. If I keep these two magnetic contacts together and pull vigorously, like this!"

I stood up and waved the device in the air so Shamus could see I had it safely in my hands. "You can come out now, Shamus."

"Now what are yer supposing to do with that, Shacks sir?"

"Well I'm hardly going to be calling the bomb squad at this time of the day."

I walked carefully across the car-park, so as not to trip up accidentally and blow us to kingdom come. I climbed over the fence and across the grassland until I considered it was a safe place to propel the device, which I did, as far as I could throw it. I didn't hang around for the inevitable explosion as the device sailed through the air. I made a run for it as fast as I could back towards the relative safety of the Roadster. The bomb exploded behind me numbing my hearing, a shower of rock and soil debris splattering across my back; a little too close for comfort.

Shamus was furious and jumped to his feet. "What in the name of Jesus possessed yer to do that?"

"Because I want the saboteur to presume that their dastardly deed was an instant success, that's why, Shamus. Hopefully I've convinced a few people that I'm either badly injured or quite dead. Now hurry up and get into the Roadster. We've got some catching up to do."

"Were going after him?"

"We're going to follow him."

Inside the car I fumbled into my pocket for the piece of paper I'd written on earlier, and added the name of a place I'd noticed on the drive to Mizen Head. I gave Shamus the piece of paper to scrutinize while I set the Roadster in hot pursuit.

"It be a telephone number and a message, Shacks sir."

"How observant you are Shamus. When I drop you off at Baltimore, ring that number straight away. And when she answers and you hear the sweetest voice you've ever heard over a telephone, don't hang about telling her so. Tell her that Shackleton Speed said she has to start proceedings straight away without a moment to loose and relay to her the information I've written down on that paper you now hold. Is that clear?"

"What's going on, Shacks sir?"

"Stop asking questions and just do as I tell you."

"What's stopping you from ringing the number, Shacks sir?"

"I've a ship to catch before she disappears on the evening tide."

"You're going somewhere?"

"I'm boarding the *Flying Fish* tonight."

Shamus looked horrified. "Alone?"

"I haven't exactly got a commando team behind me."

"That's plain stupid if yer don't mind me saying so?"

"Have you a better idea?"

"I'll board her with yer, Shacks sir. We've come this far together."

"No," I snapped, "Too frigging dangerous. Just ring that number, do you hear? That's far more important. And tell her to arrange the rendezvous at that place on the note, urgently. Tell her it's a matter of life or death and I'm in the middle. You got that?"

Shamus read the details. "I know that place well. Why there, Shacks sir?"

"Because, Shamus, that's where I predict all this shambles finally ends, one way or the other. You just don't let me down."

Chapter Twenty Two

I dropped Shamus off at a safe place, a pub he frequented quite often, rather than risk him returning to his home. He wasn't too pleased that I'd left him behind when there was a battle to be fought. I didn't care. He was safe and that was all that mattered. While I continued my journey back to Baltimore hopefully Shamus will have begun to make important telephone calls to influential people.

Once on the outskirts of Baltimore I parked the Roadster out of sight and waited until the night was pitch black before I made my move back to the harbour. I kept a low profile as I moved along the quay, using as much cover as possible. That's when I saw the motorised inflatable dingy tied up between two large cruisers. What made it appeal to me was the *Flying Fish* logo in small white stencil on one side. I was on the verge of moving towards the dingy when I heard a slapping sound that had me looking sideways into the shadows. I crouched low and moved into deeper shadow for cover. I waited, listening hard. I heard the same sound again. This time I searched for its source. I spotted who I thought was a crewman from the *Flying Fish* sitting on a wooden crate and tapping a knife blade against his thigh out of boredom. I could only assume the dingy was the intended ride back to the ship for Love and Hate, once they'd disposed of Shamus and me.

Slowly, ever so quietly, I edged around and came in behind where he sat. The sole of my left boot caught a piece of discarded rope, which I retrieved from the ground, held it either end and moved closer to the unsuspecting crewman.

I lashed the rope around his neck and yanked him to his feet, twisted my body and threw him, judo style, over my shoulder. He hit the ground heavily. His feeble moan proved I hadn't snapped his neck with my actions. To silence him fully I instantly followed with a savage kick to his rising jawbone. I didn't like the horrible crunch I heard but then I didn't particularly like the crewman. I left him where he lay. I hardly thought it mattered whether I'd hurt him badly or not just as long as he stayed out for the count.

I clambered down into the dingy, kicked a blanket to one side, and uncovered a snipers rifle. I mumbled, *Got you fuck face!* Referring to the crewman I'd just clobbered and then realizing I might have made a huge gaff. I frantically scanned the quay expecting trouble. What I'd not considered was the crewman I'd knocked out cold wasn't waiting for Love or Hate because he'd already witnessed their execution. He was waiting for someone else. I snatched up the rifle in readiness, peering through the pitch black with the expectancy of an attack. Seconds turned into minutes and nothing happened. I eased off the rifle's trigger and slipped the crafts mooring rope from the jetty, started the outboard engine and steered the dingy towards the *Flying Fish* anchored out in the harbour. While I steered I kept the rifle handy, glancing back now and again to check if anything was happening on the quay; there was nothing I needed to worry over and I could now concentrate solely on what lay ahead.

On nearing the *Flying Fish* I veered the dingy to one side and approached in a generous arc, mainly to establish if any watchmen were present on deck. It all seemed quiet and then again what had they on board the ship to fear about? All terminations were in progress or completed. They would have thought they were in the clear, all ends neatly tied. I steered the craft towards the boarding ladder with renewed confidence, switched off the engines and cruised in toward the ship using the strong current. After tying the boat to the foot of the boarding ladder I replaced the rifle in my hand with the gun I had retrieved from Hate; it was lighter, more comfortable and quicker to swing round in the dark. I climbed the steel gangway warily, my eyes meeting every moving shadow in anticipation of an expected fight.

I reached the deck unchallenged. There was only partial illumination from bulkhead lighting and I saw no signs of life. The boat creaked as it rocked gently on the waves. The creaking would disguise my footsteps as I tiptoed along the deck but I soon halted when I got a whiff of cigarette smoke.

I froze mid-step and eased into some shadow while I listened. I could hear the smoker suck hard and deep on a cigarette, the exhaled offensive smoke clouding the night air and revealing the smokers position between two mounds of tarpaulin. Inch by inch I crept forward. Now I could distinctly hear the rattled breathing of a heavy weed user. Then the red burning stub ejected from the gap and the person moved forward into a beautifully timed right hook that I executed with power. The smoker's head twisted violently, a splash of blood spurting from split lips. He went down in a clump and when I checked him over he was out cold, wheezing heavily.

I popped my head from between the cargo to check if my actions had attracted others. It hadn't. I dragged the smokers outstretched legs back with his knees in the air so anybody passing the gap wouldn't notice him slacking on the job. If he had held a gun of any description with him I never saw it. I slipped out from the gap and kept tight against the bulkhead and made my way to the angle of light protruding from a steel doorway. I listened while I peered through the crack in the door. It was clear. I moved inside, pointing the gun forward and ready to fire if necessary. There was a companionway that led below. I crept down into the belly of the ship, glad of the cushioned soles of my boots on the steel treads. I stopped at the bottom and looked down the length of the passageway. I could hear voices coming from the opening at the far end. It seemed the obvious route for me to take which I did, carefully and alert.

When I'd reached the end I listened at the half opened door to the voices talking conversely. I immediately recognized the two voices I heard from inside the room. I angered, gripping the hand gun tight in my hand. Enough was enough and with the gun extended I pushed the door open and went inside.

There was a big man with ginger hair who had his back to me and was in the motion of sitting down comfortably in an appealing leather armed chair, holding a large brandy glass. I'd expected to find a few surprises waiting for me, but when I saw her sitting in a chair with a smug expression I was so frigging mad that I could have shot her there and then.

"Now isn't this all very sweet and cosy." I said, with rightful sarcasm. "I wondered how long it would take for all the creeps to show their true colours: red for danger and yellow for cowardice. I bet you weren't expecting me, Commander Harris Morgan or you, Shayna. Why am I not surprised that you're all here chasing Deveron's dreams. I only hope you're not celebrating too early."

Morgan's head spun round and he jumped up from his chair all in one movement, spilling brandy down the front of his jacket. "Shackleton Speed. Damn you!"

"Don't even think of twitching an eyebrow Morgan! That includes you, Shayna."

Shayna expressed sheer horror. "It's not what it seems." She blurted. "I've nothing to do with this."

I wasn't falling for her shit and made it clear to her I wasn't. "Shut the fuck up, Shayna! I hold the gun so I get the deciding vote on who to trust. I'll get to you after I've finish with frigging arse bandit here."

"My, my, Speed, such vulgarity is uncalled. I would have expected a little more decorum with a lady present and something better than 'arse bandit'."

"Somehow it suits you."

Morgan incensed me when he raised his glass and toasted me. "I have to admire you, Speed. You've been a wonderful adversary and have caused me undeniable trouble. You certainly know how to make a nuisance of yourself. Why can't you die gracefully and quietly? It's very upsetting when my plans go wrong."

"I'm in the business to annoy authority, but in your case I'm making this personal. Besides, it would have been damned right rude of me to vacate this lifetime without saying goodbye to my commissioning employer and friends who happen to be a bunch of conniving, murdering rats."

Morgan protested his innocence. "You're forgetting one important factor if you're thinking of calling the police, Speed. I haven't personally killed anyone."

"And that makes everything right?"

"It happens to be true."

I pulled a face of disgust. "You make me puke, you frigging parasite. You don't have to pull the trigger to issue orders."

"I'm not a murderer. I manipulate people, as I did with you, Mister bumbling amateur. I threw you goodies to pursue. Gave you space to search for the submarine, and then reeled you back in when the time was right. You were perfect. It's your nature to find things, and admittedly, you're damned good at finding the impossible; a magnificent bloodhound. I knew you wouldn't disappoint me in finding the Japanese submarine."

"I found a graveyard, only you weren't in it."

Morgan smiled. "You are the hilarious comedian, Speed. But I suggest you don't consider it as an alternative career or else you'll always be a poor loser."

"This gun I'm pointing at your gut puts me closer to the finish line."

Morgan seemed confident that I was talking shit. And I should have been concerned as to why Morgan's eyes kept flicking behind me and then to my chest. I said, "If you're expecting either of your overpaid assassins, Love or Hate, forget it! The blood on my clothing isn't my blood. It belongs to Hate. As you can see by my presence, he isn't coming back. And I wouldn't wait up for Love either. I took care of those two squealing bastards. You know the two. The same ones you were going to put behind bars with a little persuasion from my testimony. That was your intention when we first met. But, of course, that was the manipulating crap swirling around in your head, wasn't it. How things have changed. Here I am holding the gun. And you're in serious danger of dying where you stand."

"You're a real eager beaver, Speed, but a fool."

"I guess this means I'm not going to get paid for my services to the ministry?"

"You're attempting to be the comedian again, Speed. Yet I suppose you are entitled to that rare privilege of humour. Who am I to argue, you're the *man holding the gun.*"

"I want some straight answers from you, Morgan."

"Why don't you put the gun down, Speed? Good god man, your hands trembling so much you'll probably wouldn't be able to fire the wretched thing. Have a drink! We can talk, come to some arrangement."

I kept the gun levelled at him; a certain gut shot assured and Morgan knew it. I couldn't help gritting my teeth when I had my say. "Don't underestimate me, Morgan. You might think I'm inexperienced in the art of killing people, but I'm learning fast, no thanks to you. In fact, I'm quite open that I don't even possess a certificate to prove my capabilities of being a crack shot. Yes, the gun might wobble when I try to shoot you in the chest because I'm not used to the recoil of this handgun and the bullet might just end up in one of your legs or it might even be in your skull. Either way, I'm not fussy. I can always fire a second or third bullet to finish the job."

"You're not a cold blooded murderer, Speed. Put the gun down and be sensible."

I noticed a few beads of perspiration rolling down Morgan's forehead. Now he was beginning to worry and I was enjoying watching him squirm.

I said calmly, surprising even myself. "I've never deliberately set out to kill a man before, regardless how nasty they are. I've hurt a few whose intentions were to hurt me. I've even hospitalised a few and I never sent flowers. I could do the same to you, shit breath, but I know I would suffer from horrible nightmares and that you would come out from under the gallons of excrement that surround your murderous regime smelling of prize roses; that you'll slip away from justice with terrible ease, to live in a lavish and undeserved lifestyle." The more I talked the angrier I got. "I can't have that. I could never live with the guilt of allowing you to escape punishment for the deaths of my friends you had killed."

I started to squeeze the trigger without a care in the world.

"Don't be ridiculous, Speed! You'll be killing the wrong man! Do you want that on your conscience for the rest of your prison life?"

"What makes you think I'll see the inside of a prison?"

"For Christ sake man, I'm a government official. You'll never explain my death away!"

"I no longer care what happens to me."

I squeezed the trigger a little more. Morgan perspired from every conceivable pore in his body; his face horrified. He realized he was about to die. He flinched when I fired the gun. We all heard the metallic click of the gun firing when it shouldn't have.

For a moment I stood there dumbfounded. The click from my gun should have produced an explosion of power. But there was no kickback knocking my hand slightly. No acrid stench drifting into my nostrils of a spent bullet. I expected all three, maybe even two. I'd be unlucky to get only one; but none at all? A misfire,

I assured myself. Again and again my trigger finger repeated the firing motions only to receive the same unproductive results. Click-click-click-click-click echoed in my ears. Each click had my sweat glands working over-time. My body became tacky. I knew an empty barrel when I heard one. I looked at Morgan. He had flinched on every occasion I had pulled the trigger. But now he was smirking.

After the last chamber echoed its last metallic click, all I heard was, 'oops', and it hadn't come from Morgan's or Shayna's mouth.

There was one deformity I never had and that was having eyes in the back of my head. If I'd have been watching my rear guard I might have reacted far quicker to the piece of cold steel sticking into the back of my right ear. I was suddenly deflated.

I made a futile attempt to look round but my face was shoved back by the nozzle. I managed a glimpse of the gun's owner. I grinned in defeat and said calmly, "The miracles of modern science-eh-Hamer? I've got to admire the witch doctor that stitched you back together."

"Shut your face, Speed! When you select a gun, choose one with bullets in the chamber; a professional would have checked first."

I had to smile at that remark too because it made sense. "Why do I get this feeling that you sent out your hired killers with empty guns. Ah-yes, Love and Hate liked to kill silently: up close so as to stare in the eyes of their victim. They weren't gun merchants in any sense. Maybe the idea was we'd strangle each other to death and save you the trouble. And last man standing conveniently picked off by a sniper or the pathetic car bomb trick. But what else could I have expected from two cunning and deceitful bastards who never check their work."

"Your deductions are very accurate, Speed. You've got it in one."

I twitched in anger.

Hamer reacted quickly and pressed his gun harder in my ear. "Don't even think about using that gun as a club, or a projectile. I do possess a sharp shooters certificate that complements this gun in my hand, so drop the weapon, Speed. Do it now!"

I let the gun clatter to the floor. Morgan flew at me as if he wanted to hit me with a right hook but stopped himself; he'll have probably broken his fingers in trying to break my jaw.

Over my shoulder I said to Hamer, "The apparition of your spirit rising from the grave, Hamer, should have had me scared shitless. Strange, though, how I predicted your resurrection was imminent."

"So my horrific death on the boat didn't convince you?"

"It almost threw me," I said coolly. "It could almost construe as a nice deception, Hamer. Plant a bomb with a quick timer, slip aboard a waiting craft and sail back to the *Flying Fish*, nobody the wiser."

"It was necessary to prevent you and your seafaring partner from escaping by sea."

"It upset Shamus; he thinking you'd died on his boat. Such a nasty trick, but then your middle name is *nasty!*"

"How does it make you feel, Speed, knowing I'm alive and well?"

"I'm sick in the stomach to be totally honest. Fat bastards like you don't warrant any sympathy whatsoever."

Hamer seethed and twisted the gun barrel into the side of my head to silence me.

He'd no chance of doing that. I was too wound up to stay tight-lipped, and I was verbally at him again. "I had you down as dodgy the first moment you turned up on my doorstep; the coincidence was too great. But then I've never really trusted policemen regardless of what walk of life they descend from. I played along. It was tripping you up which proved to be the hard bit. And all that eagerness to help and the bullshit you concocted about chaperoning me for my safety; that was a real classic. Setting me up more like! When you inadvertently told me about McClusky's warehouse, stupidly, I believed you were relaying useful information, not sending me into a frigging trap to be fucked up by warring terrorists. And while I was supposedly getting shot to pieces, you took the opportunity to break into my home with the sole intention of searching my place for the aerial photographs extracted from the reconnaissance camera; remember? And all that bullshit about Winston barking, and that you were worried about me. Your problem was gaining the dog's confidence, so you took along with you a bag of dog biscuits and fed the mutt. I saw the screwed-up wrapper in your jacket pocket."

"How observant you were, Speed." From the point of facing death only moments earlier, Morgan was confidently rejuvenated. He stabbed his forefinger into my face. "You're absolutely wrong, Speed. The main intention was for McClusky to capture and scare you enough so you'd run into our caring hands for protection. Only you'd disappeared, unfortunately. It rather screwed our plans. It didn't help matters that McClusky's double crossing antics to sell our merchandise to pissed-off terrorists forced our hand dramatically and we had to send in the troops."

I sneered. "It was a diabolical disaster."

Morgan flicked his forefinger into the air. "On the contrary, Speed, it worked in our favour. All the mess McClusky created was wiped out in that gun battle at his warehouse. We couldn't have anticipated a more perfect solution. It saved us the problem of killing the bumbling baboon ourselves. The whole episode blamed on warring terrorists; you couldn't have made it up; just perfect"

"You drew lucky, that's all Morgan. What if I had been killed? Who would you have got to find the I-52?"

Morgan waved his hand in acceptance of his flaw. "Your death wouldn't be a great loss. With you out of our way we would have eventually found the photographs you had in your possession. We'd have ripped your home apart piece by piece until we got what we wanted. But never mind, everything has now fallen magnificently into perspective."

I gave Shayna a hard glare. "What about Miss blabber-mouth over there. Where does she fit into your long lost dream of heading nowhere?"

"You have me all wrong," Shayna protested her innocence.

I wasn't listening to her.

"You think you're fucking clever, don't you Speed?" Hamer seethed.

"You've got to be frigging kidding, Hamer. I'd stupidly missed a vital piece of information when we first met at the 'Greaseless Grill' in London."

"What was that, know all?"

"That you'd met Old Tom at his farm but you never even recognized his dog Winston when you saw him at my place; he's a very distinctive dog. Winston was always beside his master; always! Winston wasn't there because the poor dog had already been clobbered with a large spanner by either Love or Hate so that would put you there at the farm around the time of Tom's death. And I being an idiot allowed you to tag along when in fact it was like having shit lodged in the pattern on the sole of my shoe which was difficult to clean but the smell never seemed to go away."

Hamer smashed the barrel across my ear. "Your mouth is full of shit, Speed!"

Morgan said, "What happened to Love and Hate?"

"They're dead," I said with pride. "If you want to claim their bodies you're going to have to scrape the two bastards from the rocks below Mizen Head fog station."

"It's your doing, Speed?" Morgan asked, surprised.

"I'm here and they're not rather answers your curiosity."

Morgan shrugged uncaringly. "They fucked up! They deserved their doom. The less people I have on the payroll, the better! We should have hired you as the assassin instead, Speed."

"I thought they were the best?" I assumed Hamer was talking across to Morgan.

"They got careless and overconfident," Morgan said, impassively.

Hamer kept moaning at Morgan. "I told you at the beginning if you want a job done, then do it your fucking self!"

I suddenly understood what Hamer was getting at. I said quickly, "Kill me and the whereabouts of the gold goes with me."

"There was no gold amongst the submarine's cargo," Morgan said sharply. "Only dead men past and present; as you so stated, the place was a fucking graveyard. If there had been gold then it's disappeared for good."

I said. "I'd reconsider your assumption."

Morgan gave me a curious stare. "You're holding out on us, Speed?"

I prodded myself in the chest. "This so called bumbling amateur, you refer to, at least has an inkling of where the gold might be hidden."

I was telling them all this to prolong my life.

Hamer dug the gun barrel into my cheek. "Where have you hidden the gold?"

"Get a life, Hamer! I haven't got the wretched stuff."

"He's a fucking lying bastard!"

"I might be a bastard, but I'm no liar."

"Arrogance right to the end, hey, Speed."

I didn't like the sound of what he said, but I didn't show any fear, nor did I flinch when he began his heavy-handed Morse code on my face with the gun in cohesion with his words. "Where's-the-fucking-gold?"

"Are you deaf as well as stupid, Hamer? At the moment I don't know."

I sensed Hamer was getting frustrated and itching to pull the trigger. Morgan was thankfully calmer and finger signalled to Hamer to calm down.

Morgan actually smiled. "I'm beginning to find you quite amusing, Speed. It fascinates me the amount of knowledge you seem to have. What does disturb me is the efficiency you have shown as a killing machine. I find that rather strange for just a metal detector man. That makes me highly suspicious. Maybe you're not who we think you are, Speed?"

"I'm the genuine article alright, with a few inclusions on the art of being callous. Scum, as you are, Morgan, or better known as the 'The Housekeeper', has succeeded in turning me into a machine that I'm not really keen to be associated with. But you chose to mess up my life by murdering my friends which has done more than infuriate me. It has made me realize that my approach to life has been rather boring. I've now this sudden passion to rid dirt like you from the face of the earth with a mere flick of my forefinger."

Morgan grinned. "They're tough words coming from a man with a gun to his head. A mere click of my fingers and half your brains will be splattered against the wall. Is it your wish to die? Are you brave enough to die for nothing?"

"I take it you mean am I scared to die?"

Hamer pressed the nozzle against the side of my nose this time. "Well are you, Speed?"

"Now let me think! If I base it on the principle that a person has no recollection of being born, as they're pulled screaming from that orifice of security; therefore I doubt very much a person would remember dying. Take that into consideration, I can confidently predict I don't fear death. And I can confidently add that along with my demise nobody gets to know where the Japanese gold is or the half a ton of *opium* amongst the cargo. Now imagine the price of narcotics on the open market of this despicable world."

Morgan's eyebrows arched. "What opium?"

"The opium classified as medical supplies that was on a check list I managed to inspect."

I could tell Morgan was thinking hard before he said, "My divers didn't find anything of any value on the submarine, just the two men you eliminated and a stack of bones inside the submarine."

"That's because in 1944 a certain Irish terrorist, who went by the name of McCracken, took the frigging lot."

"What an interesting context of events, Speed. Drugs could be the icing on the cake, so to speak. There would be enough money for all of us; even you, Speed."

"You wouldn't let me live long enough to spend any." I tapped the side of my head. "But providing I've the information stored here, I'm quietly confident you won't kill me just yet. You might want to torture me but you won't kill me."

"He's fucking lying about the gold!" Hamer blurted out, his face red with anger. "He's stalling. Let's get rid of the bastard, now!"

"Be a little patient." Morgan remonstrated with Hamer. He turned to me. "You seem to be well informed, Speed. Where did you extract all this information from?"

"I was fortunate to meet a contributor to the daring hijack of the I-52 submarine, whom, I might add, would prefer to remain anonymous because of his failing health."

Hamer punched me in the side of the head. "Tell me his fucking name."

My head snapped round, teeth clamped with anger, "Do that again and I'll break your fingers and stick the digits in every orifice you have."

Morgan made a harsh gesture that Hamer remains in control of himself.

I went on. "Forget the informant. He has about as much idea where the gold is now as you two. I'm the only one alive who knows where it could be, and I can't think straight with a gun shoved in my face. So it's negotiation time."

"So negotiate then," Morgan pressed.

I didn't care for Morgan's hurriedness. "After you've given me one of your pathetic excuses as to why you had my friends killed?"

"Ah-well, Speed, that's your entire fault. When you decided to break all the ground rules and steal government property, you should have been more considerate towards who you used to lie and cover your tracks."

I felt my blood pressure rising. "They didn't deserve to die horribly."

"They were collaborators to your crime, who, unfortunately, had the same stubbornness you possess. It was you, Speed that forced us to use heavy handed tactics. It was your greed in stealing the camera from the Spitfire that put your friend's lives in danger and they paid a heavy price. So don't blame us, just take a look at yourself in the mirror, Speed."

"There was no need to murder them!"

"Yes there was!" Morgan said acidly. Professionals clean up after themselves; leave no trace of their presence at the scene. That includes no witnesses. Your friends were inconveniences. Therefore it became necessary to eradicate the problems put before us."

I never even thought about the consequences of my actions when I went for Morgan's throat like a raging Rhinoceros. But I never got further than a stride when the back of my skull imploded. I assumed at that point that Hamer had smashed his gun twice across my skull with tremendous force. I lost consciousness.

Chapter Twenty Three

I was still alive. Dead men don't feel their toes curl up inside their shoes. The cold steel beneath me and the slight swaying sensation told me I was probably still aboard the *Flying Fish* and we were still anchored. I made an uneasy movement and attempted to open my eyes. The blinding flash ripped into my iris's forcing a momentary shutdown of vision. I could still move my hands and feet, so I knew I hadn't been bound or chained. Slowly, I pushed myself up from the floor into a sitting position and opened my eyes to a squint. The sharp streak of brightness came from a light fitting on the overhead of what appeared to be a stockade of steel walls and steel bars giving the impression I was in a futuristic brig. Trawlers didn't have brigs so I had to assume I was in some sort of strong room for another purpose. Gunrunning came to mind.

I massaged my stiff neck, which hurt like hell, and suddenly aware that I wasn't alone in the room. The last two people I would have expected to see were Deveron and Shayna sitting on an old iron bed in a state of utter dejection while watching my squirming antics of a waking drunk.

My speech sluggish, I said, "Seeing your two depressing faces, I guess I'm not in heavenly paradise. Not unless you're both dead as well and this is supposed to be a jokers version of the Garden of Eden and you two are my guardian angels. Now isn't that wild to the imagination, I find you two posing as a couple of angels."

Shayna responded angrily. "Just because you've a large lump on the back of your head, it doesn't give you the damn right to be an obstinate shit!"

She may have had a point but I was in no mood to apologize. "Oh, while we're on the subject of being an obstinate shit, aren't you two on the wrong side of the door?"

"We wouldn't have find ourselves in this damn mess if we hadn't come looking for you at your hotel," she snapped. "Instead we found Morgan and Hamer brandishing steel and on the lookout for you. Good god, you make enemies really fast."

"Well that does make everything right then. I get the blame for your troubles and Deveron is blameless for something he started. This hero shit is absolutely marvellous."

"Give your sunken ego a rest Shackleton Speed. Obviously the blow to your head hasn't changed your attitude. How is your head anyway? Not that I really care a damn at the moment."

"It hurts like the rest of my body hurts. I feel as if a fat bastard called Hamer decided to kick the frigging shit out of me."

"He did," she said. "After a couple of crewmen threw you in here, Hamer spurted out a mouthful of obscenities in between kicking you about the chest. Mind you, I don't think he hurt you much, you were out cold and dumb heads don't feel much pain."

"Thanks for the compliment, Shayna. As for fat boy, I owe him one."

I noticed Shayna hadn't escaped a beating herself judging by the severe bruising around her left cheekbone. She probably deserved it no doubt. Still feeling too giddy to get to my feet I shuffled back against the steel bulkhead.

I flicked my head towards Shayna, and said, "Nasty discolouration around your eye. What's your pathetic story?"

"Do you really care what happened?"

"Step out of line?"

"What do you mean?"

I uplifted the palms of my hands to gesture our surroundings. "Which murderer or pirate or any other despicable lout did you upset? Perhaps it was Captain Morgan, who I might add, is as bent as a rejected European standard banana. Or maybe you're all just a bunch of terrorist renegades from different factions fighting amongst yourselves?"

She didn't answer me.

"What about poor old Deveron here," I said. "The instigator of this farcical nightmare we find ourselves involved in."

"You think we're part of their set-up?"

"It explains a great deal. How everybody seemed to know where to find me so easily."

"Anybody can find anybody if necessary. My grandfather insisted on meeting you. I tried to dissuade him but he can be very insistent for his age. I used certain resources available to me to find you. There was nothing sinister about it."

"And you expect me to swallow that?"

"Believe what you want, I've more important things to worry about."

Deveron stirred into life, as if someone had recharged his dead batteries. His tinny voice hadn't changed either. "You have it all worked out, don't you, Mister Speed?"

"I've worked out who not to trust and you're both in the top four."

"My actions during the war may have brought about the misery we're in. But how was I to know Harris Morgan, after all these years, would continue my quest to find Craven's Spitfire. In my latter time at the ministry he was nothing but a young pip-squeak who ran errands through the corridors of Whitehall. I misjudged the slimy toad. He obviously had a keen eye to have understood what I was doing every time a plane wreck was unearthed. Thereafter, in his position in Whitehall, he would have had a free run to finish what I began. He was on hand when you found the plane. It's Morgan that's the enemy, not Shayna nor I. When Morgan showed up in Baltimore I was as shocked as the next man. It didn't take much working out that it was Morgan who lured us to your hotel with a false message. Now he has us at his mercy here in this godforsaken prison cell."

"It's nothing more than you deserve considering you shot Craven from the sky, so thank yourself lucky prison has only just caught you up."

Shayna jumped in defensively at that point. "That makes two of you then!"

I think she must have been referring to my exploits in artefact smuggling. But I wasn't in the mood to argue with Shayna any longer because my chest was hurting bad and I'd trouble breathing. I wondered if Hamer's boot had perhaps broken a couple of my ribs.

I said to Deveron, "It seems you and McCracken had the same idealistic values; those futuristic Irish dreams of climbing the pinnacle of power to run a terrorist empire. Of course, where your dreams faded and you became the normal and responsible person, McCracken died as savagely as his dreams. But I just can't make my mind up who took the right path because it seems both of you were experts in shooting people in the back."

Deveron's face twisted with hatred. "You can be very cruel, Mister Speed. I'd hate the prospect of you running an old peoples home if I was to frequent one."

"You have me all wrong, Deveron. I like old people, especially those with pure hearts and minds. Something you don't have."

"There's no forgiveness in you, is there, Mister Speed?"

"I did try but nothing developed."

Shayna broke in. "Bickering isn't going to find us a way out of this hole!"

"Well, Shayna," I sounded cocky and I was. "Unless you can produce one of your magic door opening escapades, I can honestly say I'll listen to any sensible suggestions. Don't suppose you have any?"

"We need a diversion for when the guards come back." Shayna announced, as if she'd everything planned in her head.

"You could strip naked, Shayna, and lure the imbeciles into here. And while their hands are molesting you I can bonk them on the head with my dick because I haven't much else I can use."

The corner of her lip curled up in hatred of me. I didn't care anymore who I upset. I'd every right to be nasty. I'd been battered, clubbed, and I wanted to kill two certain individuals promptly.

There's a saying: talk about the devil and in through the door the creature walks. Only there were two devils of equal status: Morgan and Hamer; a distinguished pair of bastards between them. I'd have found a great deal of satisfaction if I could have reached through the bars to rip their throats out. Even if I'd gotten the chance, I'd have been cut down by the two armed crewmen that followed behind them.

"Well look at this," I said to nobody in particular. "We have a personal escort to breakfast. Bacon on toast will do nicely and a hot cup of tea."

Hamer put his face nearer to the bars. "Shut the fuck up, Speed!"

If I'd have moved fast enough I could have punched him through the bars and flattened his nose, but he moved away. I said, "Ah, service with a smile as usual. You can't beat such politeness from a bunch of bastards."

"I should shoot you now, you interfering fuck!"

I smirked. I had the advantage. "Think of the gold, Hamer."

Morgan, on the other hand was calmer. He said, "Speed, don't mock us. We could always revert to torture. I wonder how long you would last before you spilled what you know."

"I'll probably die."

Morgan smiled. "We could work on the lovely Shayna instead?"

"She'd die too."

"You wouldn't save her from the distress and pain?"

"I wouldn't piss on her if she was on fire."

"And I thought you were Lionhearted. How wrong I am. Of course there is another outcome for you to consider that might change your mind."

I expressed mild surprise. "I'm to be given a choice?"

"You can have a share of the proceeds for your loyalty to us."

"I thought you didn't like sharing?" I said.

"Sometimes one has to reconsider their options."

"What percentage had you in mind?" I thought I'd ask.

"Equal shares for all concerned."

By the look on Hamer's face I guessed that Morgan hadn't discussed his proposal with anyone else and had probably only thought of the solution the moment he walked through the door. I didn't like the sound of it. I said, "What about Deveron and Shayna?"

Morgan shrugged his shoulders. "What about them?"

"I want their safety guaranteed."

Morgan was blunt to the point. "I'm afraid they're not part of the deal. Now where's the gold?"

"Go and frigging stick your head up Hamer's arse! Their safety or nothing from me, it's your move."

Morgan did indeed make a move but not the way I expected. There was no warning, no verbal threat and definitely no hesitation as Morgan drew an automatic handgun with a silencer attached, aimed between the bars and shot Deveron in the middle of his chest.

Shayna screamed.

I seized.

My mouth dropped open in shock as I watched Deveron, in slow motion, slump across the bed, his body jerked twice and then coughed up phlegm mixed with blood. I saw where the bullet had hit him, or rather the red stain seeping through his clothing, spreading out like a twisting kaleidoscopic image, showed me where he was hit.

Rage engulfed me, suppressing the pains in my chest. I jumped to my feet and lunged towards the bars, spittle flying from my mouth as I screamed obscenities. "You frigging spineless murdering bastard, Morgan. He was no threat to you. He was just an old man who came to end a chapter in his life. You told me that you didn't kill people?"

Morgan angled the gun towards Shayna and calmly said, "I lie a lot; learned it from the politicians; it gets you further in life."

"Until you're caught out," I said. "And your reputation is destroyed."

"The problem with you Speed is you're getting too sentimental. I thought you were tough and resilient, not squeamish. Now I've little time to waste. The girl gets it next. Where's the gold located? I wouldn't hesitate too long because if I dispose of you all, I'll only lose a fortune I never had. I'll still get my large pension from the government. I'll still reap in money from lucrative business deals. I'll be rich and you'll be dead."

"Get rich by gun running?" I broke in, probably unwisely.

Morgan smiled confidently. "Business is business, Speed, and I'll still enjoy its rich pickings while all of you are buried in the confines of a pauper's coffin together."

Inside I was panicking, but outside I didn't show he had me worried. I had to rethink my strategy quickly.

"Hurry now, Speed! My finger is curling to the point of squeezing the trigger."

"Spare the girl!"

"You know I'll kill her, Speed."

"She can't harm you, now."

I noticed his trigger finger relaxed. He lowered his revolver. "On the contrary, Speed, she's a bigger pain in the neck than you are." His automatic rose again and he took aim. "Tell me where the gold is hidden, and you might just be in time to stick your finger in the bullet hole and prolong the death of one of the Royal Canadian Mounted Police's finest undercover operatives."

Confused, I said, "Canadian who?"

Morgan expressed surprise. "Don't tell me the intrepid metal detector man, extraordinaire, didn't know our lovely Shayna is a damn policewoman?"

I just hate that feeling when some bastard is one frigging step ahead of me. I should have refuted Morgan's claim that she was police, but suddenly things that had bothered me about her had gelled together. My head spun round to her. I paused for a moment as she desperately fought to save a dying man.

With suppressed anger, I said, "Frigging hell, Shayna. Is it true?"

She did look at me but said nothing. The tears rolling down her cheeks were genuine, and at that moment Deveron died. I must be quite hard deep down because I felt nothing towards his death. I thought it was more of an inconvenience at that moment.

As for Shayna, she had produced more twists and turns in her life that were harder to follow than a roadmap in the dark with no torch. Was she a terrorist, or not? Was Morgan simply shooting shit from his mouth about her being an undercover operative? Regardless of what was the truth I couldn't let her die too.

I turned back to Morgan. "You get the gold if Shayna lives."

"Not in the script, Speed."

"Well you'd better rewrite the script, Morgan. She either accompanies me or you might as well kill us both here and now and be done with it."

I was gambling with our lives with my fingers crossed behind me.

Shayna, understandably, was horrified, probably expecting the bullet any second when Morgan made a sudden movement. But Morgan aimed his gun at me instead.

"Don't tempt fate, Speed. Desperate men take desperate measures, and I think you're desperate. One more death isn't going to bother me in the slightest, nor am I likely to lose sleep over your death. I have my reasons why she should die. Have you ever heard the saying: 'A Mountie always gets their man?' I don't wish to be hiding beneath a stone for the rest of my life. She might have failed on this mission but I've no desire to allow her a second opportunity. She's outstayed her welcome."

My heart might have been jigging about inside my ribcage, but my expression remained defiant, calm, no emotions of fear. That was me all over, hard on the outside, and soft on the inside; to be honest I was on the verge of falling to pieces, but I kept my composure. I had to, for both our sakes. "I'm not interested in the gold, just the girl. I don't want to see her harmed. She remains by my side or nothing. You decide, Morgan."

"There's no guarantee to be any gold at all, Speed. Why should I want to spare her when she intends to see me put in prison."

It was then I remembered my get-out-of-gaol-card, the piece of Japanese gold I'd hidden in my trouser pocket. I quickly retrieved it and tossed the gold piece through the bars. Numerous eyes followed the mesmerizing gold flash as it hit the floor with a metallic tinkle. Hamer picked up the gold from the floor, gloating at the piece, a look of desire filling his fat face. Hesitantly he passed it to Morgan.

Thankfully Morgan lowered his gun. He took the gold ingot from Hamer and examined it thoroughly.

I wanted to breathe a sigh of relief but that would have only exposed my weakness under pressure, so I held my breath a little longer, exhaling slowly through my nostrils.

Morgan nodded his approval to my demands. I'd won round one. "I hope she's worthy of your gallantry, Speed. So now will you tell me where the rest of the gold is?"

"And you shoot us in the back the moment I tell you? Give me some credit, please. Besides, I can't explain exactly where it is, I can only show you."

"Okay, Speed, I'll accept that. Just remember no funny business or stupidity or the girl dies. So to what destination should we sail?"

"Head towards Crookhaven. It's on the other side of the Bay."

"The gold's in Crookhaven?"

"In and around," I said, "It's useless trying to trick me, Morgan. I won't know where the gold is hidden until I've had the chance to cast an eye over the area. I've already explained I can only show you where the gold is hidden."

Without another word they left us alone. I'd gained a stay of execution without a doubt, but for how long before Hamer came back and shot me. I knew deep down that no matter what I did or say, there was no way either of us would escape death. Just before Morgan left the stockade room, I said to him. "What about Deveron, you can't just leave the man here to rot."

Morgan glanced over his shoulder. “Of course I can. I’ll leave you two to decide which corner you put him in.”

I gave Morgan the appropriate American middle finger salute and mumbled, “Callous bastard”, as his back disappeared out of sight.

Shayna turned away from Deveron and wiped her eyes. I put the old mans legs up onto the bed before rigor mortis stiffened his aging bones, covered his body with the shabby blanket and moved away. I wondered how long we had before a body began to smell and attract flies; hopefully not until we’d reached Crookhaven.

When I looked at Shayna I saw for the first time that she had fear in her eyes which I would never have expected in a million years. I didn’t know what to say to her about Deveron. I’m pretty useless on such delicate matters. I’ve simply never been any good dealing with dead people.

She said, “I never thought it would end this way.”

I smiled. “We’re not done for just yet.”

“How come you’re so calm?”

I placed the palm of her hand over my pumping heart. “Only on the outside, as you can feel, Shayna. I can’t let these frigging shits think I’m crumbling under the pressure. But while I continue to keep them interested, we keep on living, it’s that simple.”

“You’ve obviously got something up you sleeve, Shackleton?”

“Shayna, believe me, I’m playing this minute by minute. All we can do is let fate take its course and see if we can steer it to our advantage.”

“That’s it? That’s our strategy?”

“If you hadn’t noticed, Shayna, there are bars of tungsten steel prohibiting us from doing very little else.

Besides, according to Morgan, you're supposed to be the professional. What did he say you were, Canadian Mounted Police? Somehow I just can't imagine you in a bright red uniform, riding a large horse, in pursuit of the baddies through the snow capped Rockies."

"For your information clever-clogs, we wear grey uniforms. The bright red uniforms are for ceremonial occasions and the movie world."

"Well sit on my face and smother me to death for getting it wrong!"

"Give me a break, will you!" She snapped and then sat down on the floor with her back against the bulkhead. "I'm on your side for fucks sake!"

I sneered. "You weren't exactly on my side when you kidnapped me and used my body for dart practice."

"If I'd have intervened, I'd have blown my cover." She protested.

"It still hurts in places. Which reminds me, when I catch up with your buddies, that spotty fucker is destined for my boot up his arse and his darts rammed down his throat sideways."

"You shouldn't have been at McClusky's in the first place."

"I was conned to go there."

"You're lucky I was there to protect you or you may have ended up floating in the River Thames."

"Well thanks for nothing. And that includes my captivity in terrorist hands and the abuse I was put though. And I might add, taking advantage of my weakened state by someone not too far away."

"You're still complaining?"

"Did it mean anything?"

"No, not at the time it didn't"

"I thought I'd ask."

"Look at it from my point of view. I'd spent two fucking years undercover, acting like a dyke to convince my so called brothers-in-arms I'm not theirs to touch, and then you came along and gave me an excuse to release my sexual frustrations. I couldn't resist the opportunity. I'm sorry that I used you."

"You took a chance. What if they'd sneaked back and caught you unawares?"

"I made it happen quick. No point in wasting time to get satisfaction."

"And that's it; you used me?"

"What did you want at the time, a fucking love song whispered in your ear? Can we give this entire verbal fighting a miss?"

"Frigging hell, I'm being totally selfish and disrespectful over the loss of your grandfather. I'm sorry, okay?"

Her red eyes glanced at Deveron then back to mine. "I've a confession to make."

I gave her my most intriguing look of suspicion. "It's bit late for confessions all of a sudden."

"Deveron isn't my Grandfather."

I frowned. I'd been suckered again. "You're a bag of twisted laughs, Shayna!"

"It's the truth."

"He was convinced you were. Frigging hell, you had us both fooled."

"It takes years of practice to lie through your teeth."

"I totally agree. I've been practicing the art for years but you'll always beat me hands down."

"I'm ashamed to admit we used Deveron to set up an elaborate ploy to get me inside the Irish organizations that were receiving weapons from unknown gunrunners. Using Deveron was necessary to convince the right people of my allegiance to the Irish problems, to dispense of any suspicion towards me. It wasn't easy to convince paranoid terrorists of my loyalty. Mind you, when Deveron confessed to me his involvement in the IRA in his youth, it came as quite a shock. And then you appeared and the whole operation exploded in my face. My two years of lies, deceit and hanging about with a bunch of fanatical hand shaggers, in an attempt to expose the British connection, went right out of the window. The moment you emerged into the affray with your glorified metal detector, every goddamn thing stopped. We'd have had McClusky. He'd have talked like a canary; pointed us in the right direction towards Morgan and his merry Russian gangsters."

"There's no guarantee he would have talked."

"To save his own skin he would have. It was treason he was committing. Bet you didn't know this ship is bulging with weaponry destined for numerous Irish groups?"

"Frigging hell, Shayna, you're a real dark horse with a carrot shoved up your arse instead of in front of your nose. The only sense I can make of your existence is you're on the good side of the law masquerading as a murdering misfit. And as for damaging your mission, if you don't mind, I've given you whom I suspect are your devious middlemen in Morgan and Hamer, served up on a plate. Just because you end up in the same cell as me, don't be in such a hurry to discredit me."

"Served up without the trimmings, I'm afraid. I haven't proven a god damn thing yet, and it's not looking good for us."

"You, Yanks, are always so ungrateful."

"Ungrateful Canadian, if you don't mind. At least have the right nationality."

"Whatever! So what was Harris Morgan's involvement on Canadian territory that warranted your elaborate cloak and dagger tactics?"

"Besides gun running, there's the cold blooded murder of two Canadian police officers."

"It goes deeper then? We were both on a mission of revenge."

"That we were, Shackleton."

"You never suspected Morgan's involvement before now?"

"Not in the beginning. What we had was firsthand knowledge that we were looking for somebody operating behind the protection of the Ministry of Defence in London. We had no idea of the persons rank, position, authority or department. We'd nothing. No jack shit! It could have been even the British Prime Minister for all we knew. The best way to find the seller was to follow the buyers."

"So you latched onto Big Nose?"

Shayna frowned. "Big Nose?" She suddenly clicked who I meant. "Jennings, you're referring to; the jumped-up Brigadier of the EFF-Eire's Freedom Fighters. Forget them, they're history. They were all arrested two days ago for inciting acts of terrorism."

"What a pity. I intended to pay them a visit before I left Ireland. Go on."

"We knew the Russian Mafia was smuggling weapons into Canada and then into America. From there our intelligence suspected the receivers of those weapons had a British connection and the possible involvement of Whitehall officials. Naturally we couldn't cause a stink with the British government because we didn't know who we could trust. And we didn't have sufficient evidence to pass on to British Intelligence. We only needed a name and we would have been up and running.

"The gunrunners were cunning in their use of varied routes; most were hard to follow and we failed on numerous occasions to catch them. Gathered intelligence directed us to the shores of Ireland and the weapons were destined for the developing terrorist groups who were stockpiling, hence Jennings and his gang. Along the way we suffered casualties, losing two fine and devoted policemen. Two wasted lives. There was a tremendous strain on manpower after that; facilities stretched beyond control. It was decided that we needed to send in a lone operative to infiltrate one of the Irish factions and then work upwards along the chain to reach the top men. I volunteered."

"You were taking a big risk without backup. There's been many undercover operatives murdered in the past who were better qualified than you. You lot just don't know your limitations."

"I knew the two police officers that were killed personally. Wild horses wouldn't have stopped me volunteering."

"Commendable of you," I said. "Obviously you're not married just dispensable?"

"I wasn't expecting a medal. Fortunately we stumbled across Dillon Deveron. He was in the US searching for lost relatives living there. He was the perfect choice to give me the cover I required to infiltrate a faction within Ireland. Everything was going to plan and I was confident we were closing in on the gunrunning ring leaders. And then Deveron heard about you and the Spitfire and there was no stopping him. He told me everything he had done during the war and that he wanted to put things right. He was extremely repentant."

"You should have had him arrested instead, you might have saved his life," I said condemningly. "But if I'm honest, Deveron deserved to die. He had it coming to him when he murdered a war hero on the speculation there was money to finance a war against Britain. No, I'm afraid I've little compassion for Deveron. He hasn't even paid me for my services. Do you realize I've been done twice by bad debtors!"

"You're heartless, Shackleton Speed."

"That's good coming from the woman who used the poor sod," I reminded her.

"It had to be done. The two officers of the Mounted Police deserved justice to be served. I only hope I can finish what I started."

"At least we have something in common."

"Anyway, Shackleton, you can thank me you're still alive to even get this far."

"Meaning what?"

"At McClusky's warehouse, who do you think started the carnage so you could escape?"

"My brain doesn't function under the term bedlam. I wasn't exactly watching. I was trying to survive like every other frigging idiot."

"I fired the first shot to cause the mayhem; a diversion."

"Frigging hell" You nearly got me killed. I had to shoot some maniac who was shooting at me."

"How do you think you got your weapon in the first place, by magic? I was the one who slid it across the floor to your feet. You just reacted to save yourself."

"When were you going to confide in me who you really represented?"

She shrugged. "I wasn't to be truthful. I rather hoped I'd never see you again."

"Don't you consider that a little bit selfish?"

"How could I be absolutely certain you were nothing more than just an anti-social militant against authority? Besides, you were a civilian for god's sake!"

"Thanks for the vote of confidence in my limited abilities."

"Don't be so touchy, Shackleton Speed, you're proving to be quite a gladiator."

We were silenced by the clanging sound of the anchor being raised. Morgan was going for it. I'd taken a tremendous gamble in boarding the vessel and I'd managed to survive so far. Now it was time to bring the entire nightmare to an end one way or the other and not to get killed in the process.

Chapter Twenty Four

Two armed guards fetched us from our cell and hurried us up on deck. I was a little peeved with their over zealous use of prodding their machine pistols into my back to enforce their powers of persuasion, but it wasn't the time to register a complaint or even think about retaliation. Things were happening, and happening fast.

On deck, the beginning of the day was a miserable misty grey, but I calculated that the sun was imminent within the hour. The sea air smelled good especially after being cooped up in the sweat box of a makeshift cell, and Deveron's body had begun the first stages of decomposing. I suspected Deveron's remains would soon end up thrown overboard.

From the ship we boarded a launch. Morgan and Hamer and six more crew were already aboard and all looking as pissed off as I was; not a happy face amongst them despite a possible hoard of gold waiting for them beyond the horizon.

Morgan gestured us to sit. "Make yourselves comfortable and secure yourselves. I don't want you falling overboard and drowning at such a crucial part of the exercise."

Shayna and I sat astern. She snuggled into me, which was pleasant until I understood her true intentions when she began whispering in my ear. "How long do you estimate we have before they realize there's no gold?"

I whispered back. "Who said there was no gold?"

"I thought the submarine was empty?"

"It was." I made a gesture with my finger and thumb indicating a fraction of space. "I was fortunate to find one gold ingot left inside the cavern where I discovered the submarine. While you were attending to Deveron, I showed the ingot to the greedy bastards over there. Hamer drooled over it."

"That's what you threw from the cell? One ingot proves nothing."

"It indicated to me that the gold had been moved somewhere else. It's there to be found."

"How can you be positive on a whim?"

"Call it metal detectorist intuition. We can't see it, but it's there somewhere to be exposed and closer than we think. It's my destiny to find it."

Hamer caught us talking. "Shut the fuck up, you two!"

I said, "We're flirting with each other you jealous bastard."

Hamer scowled and turned away.

We reached the stone harbour wall at Crookhaven, clamoured out of the launch and up the stone stairway. Morgan had chosen his time well; the place was practically deserted apart from the odd stray cat stopping for a nosey and the inevitable screech of seagulls in search of scraps. It was a pity the quayside pub 'O'Sullivan's' was shut, as being the condemned man I could have asked for a last glass of beer.

I led the way up the narrow road, Shayna and I remaining under the close scrutiny of the guards which stifled any chance to make a run for it. In truth I'd no intention of running. What for? I was just as excited to know if I my assumptions were correct as the next villain. I was probably more intrigued than the likes of Morgan or Hamer. In my eyes, finding the gold would be compensation for the amount of effort I'd put into exposing this bunch of murderous criminals, though the rewards I'll probably never see, but I intended to make sure neither would Morgan or Hamer.

Morgan said, "Where now, Speed?"

I pointed in the direction of the stone church in the distance. "Over there, at Saint Brendan's the Navigator church."

I was gambling that this Saint Brendon's was the place that McCracken was referring to in his journals; it was the term 'Navigator' that I'd spotted while driving towards Mizen Fog Station that had put me onto it, and Wandering Willie had said that McCracken sailed across the bay. It had made sense when I put it all together.

Morgan gave me an incredulous look. He said unconvinced: "Who in their right mind hides gold in such a small building frequently occupied by churchgoers?"

"McCracken did in 1944. Anyway, Morgan, I don't know why you're moaning, I've seen bank vaults smaller."

Hamer didn't hang around and he was off in a shot, actually sprinting up the hill towards the church. He moved remarkably well for a fat boy. He also reminded me of a thick dog chasing a stick.

Morgan said, "Remember, Speed, nothing stupid. One false move and the guards have the order to drop you where you stand. Now lead on and tread carefully; we don't want any unfortunate hold-ups."

We'd reached the small gateway leading to the church and I still hadn't any form of plan in my mind. I saw that the arched church door had been forced open, the wood split where the lock would have been located. I went inside, eyes scanning as I weighed up the situation. It wasn't the biggest church I'd ever seen nor was it the smallest. From what I could make out there was no apparent source of electric because all that hung from the ceiling was a candled light fitting and candled wall lights staggered along its length. There were rows of pews down each side with a central aisle of flags leading to the main Alter which was laid with a gold threaded cover and candle sticks on either side.

Hamer caught my attention. He was scratching around like a rampant rat in his search for the gold. It was embarrassing to watch. The poor sod actually believed my story of hidden gold. I only wished I did because my overall assessment of how the church was constructed didn't inspire me with confidence. But why should McCracken refer to this particular church in his journals; a clear indication in his writings of concealment. I could hardly imagine there would be hidden passages in the church walls; they just weren't thick enough. The floor beneath my feet revealed no hollowness. But I kept going back to the masonry and engineering skills of McCracken. What he'd created in the cavern below Dun an Oir was outstandingly real and something of such a great magnitude could have quite easily been created here in the church. Where does one start looking?

Hamer was beginning to annoy me with all his banging and clattering and stomping of his feet. I called over to him, "For a man of your brutish calibre and limited intelligence throwing things around in a tantrum won't solve a thing. And on the subject of vandalism, there are other alternatives to gaining entry instead of kicking the door in. I thought you could pick locks effortlessly?"

Hamer ignored my remarks. His expression indicated that he could smell the gold better than I could. He upturned anything that would move, fingered objects, and circled the Alter twice.

"Where the fuck is it, Speed?" Hamer's voice bellowed.

I shook my head. I thought Hamer had brains. It seems I was wrong. I said, "It isn't likely to be sitting on a pew waiting for an impatient bastard like you Hamer."

Hamer flew at me; his teeth clenched and rammed his gun under my chin.

"You're getting right up my fucking nose with your smart remarks."

I expressed surprise purposely. "Only up you nose? I want to fuck up your head!"

Morgan broke in, "I hope you haven't brought us here hoping to change our ways because I hate religion."

"I'm working on its location," I said, trying to remember the exact writings in McCracken's journals as I talked. "The clues point to this church and I can't think with Hamer rampaging around disturbing my concentration."

Morgan gestured with a wave of his hand. "Get on with it, Speed."

I recited the words of McCracken inside my head: *beyond the line of light; when the sun rises and illuminates the Virgin Mary; through her eyes she will foretell my domain of madness.*

I disregarded the words 'domain of madness', as being his hiding place. I concentrated on the line: when the sun illuminates the Virgin Mary; through her eyes…the sun was the key factor here…through the eyes of the Virgin Mary, I repeated over and over...through the eyes of the Virgin Mary…

I scanned every corner, niche, alcove of the entire church hoping to spot that one vital piece of inspiration that would lead me to what McCracken referred to in his journal. I saw a plaster cast statue of the Virgin Mary near the Altar, crossed over to where she stood. Without touching the figurine I studied the brightly painted figure for a few moments, intrigued by the two foot high beautifully crafted sculpture. She looked radiant and proud holding the baby Jesus. I began circling the statue, not really knowing what I was looking for.

'Through her eyes she will foretell', I mumbled to myself. *What the frigging hell did McCracken mean?*

And then it dawned on me that the statue I was looking over probably never existed in 1944 and could even have been placed there only a week ago. I guess I was clutching at straws but it probably bordered more of desperation, and I'd have taken anything to satisfy Morgan's itchy trigger finger. I still had to convince him I was onto something, if only to waste time.

I pretended to examine the statue from different angles. I pressed and poked different parts of the sculpture, lifting the statue to look underneath, and all the time I was thinking about McCracken's words and glancing around the church hoping for the emergence of a magical button to press.

Despairingly I glanced at Morgan. He was more than suspicious of my antics and I probably came across to him as being a pathetic crackpot on a nowhere chase. He'd have been right.

"You'd better not be stalling, Speed," Morgan said in a bored tone. "I'd hate to disfigure the beautiful Shayna's face with a bullet."

Morgan wasn't bluffing. He'd already proven his callous approach when he shot Deveron, and the way he held Shayna around her neck with the gun pressed to her cheek only confirmed he meant business.

I broke away from his stare and continued my search, but while I looked, I was also checking for an alternative escape route, quickly devising a contingency plan for when everything went sour. The main entrance seemed the only logical means of escape but Morgan had left two armed guards blocking the way, as if he was reading my mind. In all probability it would be suicidal to try and barge my way through the guards, mainly because I would be shot down before I got within ten feet of them. I considered the windows for escape but they were even too high for a high-jumper to create the momentum required to break through the glass windows successfully.

I concentrated on the task in hand even though McCracken's madness had me stressed. Again I put his words through the grinder...the Virgin Mary illuminated by the sun. Why was it so prominent in his writings? It was frigging hard to think when you're put under pressure, and it didn't help having the probing stares from Morgan and Hamer burning a hole in the back of my head.

I thought long and hard. *A virgin*-I mumbled to myself-*someone who's never experienced sexual penetration*. A virgin would be childless. Mary would be childless in image; is that what McCracken was referring to.

'Through the eyes of the Virgin Mary, She will foretell'.

And then the answer slapped me in the face. I looked towards the stained glass window to the side of me. In the centre pane, in magnificent colour, clearly depicted an image of who I visualized to be the Virgin Mary. What had brought it to my attention was the image was suddenly highlighted by a burst of sunshine illuminating the glass and spreading a colourful enchantment around the church walls. It wasn't the whole image that made me take notice but the pieces of green glass that formed her eyes, like two large emeralds, and from them, the prismatic image of colour striking down two faint lines of green light that came together when hitting a particular point on the church floor in front of the Alter.

I shifted across quickly to where the rays of green hit the floor and went down on one knee and slid my fingers over the stone flags in the area where the light concentrated. My forefinger located an indentation; it was a hole clogged with dirt. I poked the hole in an attempt to clear out the dirt and then I blew out the remaining dust. I saw what looked like the top of a rusty steel stud. It seemed natural to press which I did but nothing happened.

I turned to anybody who was listening. "I need some sort of probing tool; something thin and strong."

Puzzled faces surrounded me.

"Now would be a good time; a screwdriver or something."

There was hesitancy from everybody. Morgan and Hamer were around me now, using shayna as a shield in case I was bluffing and was about to try something drastic. They realized I wasn't and Hamer collared the guard who was carrying a tool utility belt around his waist, obviously the same set of tools that had broken into the church.

Hamer handed me a long bladed screwdriver. I placed the tip down the hole and pushed. Still nothing happened. I twisted the screwdriver thinking there might be a slot to turn the stud. Still nothing moved. I'd only one other option; the brutal way.

"Pass me a hammer," I cried out. One was put in my hand followed by a crescendo of automatic weapons having their firing pins engaged in readiness for my hammer attack. I looked at the pathetic fools, shook my head in disbelief and turned to the job in hand. I hit the top of the screwdriver with the hammer.

The first blow did nothing.

I struck again; thought I heard a noise; a scraping sound and then up popped a section of stone floor, approximately three feet square, and at a slight angle leaving a gap wide enough to get my fingers under. I slid the screwdriver between the gaps, as a precautionary measure, just in case it snapped shut again, and heaved the stone up so it stood on its end. The section of floor had been supported by an iron frame and was on a spring hinge. I stared down into a black hole.

Bodies slowly converged around me apprehensively, as if they were expecting some ghoulish fiend to suddenly spring out and scare the shit out of them. I took the initiative and popped my head down into the dark hole. I expected the smell of dampness but was surprised to smell what I thought was the smell of a bitumen.

"Someone pass me a torch?" I asked, excitedly when I shouldn't have been.

A torch was quickly put into the palm of my hand, and my eyes followed the beam of light as it hit a dusty cobwebbed wooden stairway.

Morgan said, “Do the honours Speed and get down there.”

“How considerate you are,” I said with hesitancy. “I mean anything could be lurking in the darkness waiting for an unsuspecting victim like me.”

“Stop whimpering, Speed, you’re expendable!”

“Thanks, you ungrateful bastard,” I said, and for my insolence, a guard shoved the nozzle of his machine pistol into the back of my head to encourage me down the stairway.

My first step was a tentative one, a feeler, half expecting the steps to be rotten and to collapse under my weight. I was wrong. Each step was solid, not even a suspect creak. I confidently went down into a deep cellar.

At the bottom, as I reached out to steady myself, I unwittingly disturbed a settling of thick dust which clouded the atmosphere, causing me to cough and splutter.

I received no sympathy whatsoever.

“Not dying on us, are you, Speed?” Hamer shouted down.

“Why don’t you get your frigging fat hairy arse down here to find out?”

The rest of the entourage followed. Heavy clunking as boots clamoured down, torch beams bouncing off the walls. Some scared idiot let out a screech when my torch beam illuminated the two skeletal frames sparsely covered with the remnants of large deteriorating overcoats commonly worn in the forties. Each skull had a hole in the middle of the forehead.

"Friends of yours, Speed?" Hamer asked derisively.

"German spies actually" I said. "Let me introduce Harrington and Lodge, collaborators with IRA sympathizers and murdered by Jimmy McCracken so he could mastermind the greatest hijack in all seafaring history. To be fair, you could argue that McCracken was solely responsible for preventing the Germans from continuing the war when he looted the I-52. Not that he will be receiving thanks for his contribution."

"Do I look as if I care a fucking toss for history lessons?" Hamer jabbed me in the back. "Get moving!"

"You should do," I said as I moved on. "Or else you wouldn't find yourself down this hole shuffling up to my backside."

Again Hamer jabbed me forward.

I moved the torch beam around in various directions and since nobody had bothered to clean up for sixty years it wasn't surprising we had to run the gauntlet of the inevitable dusty cobwebs and listen to the varied splutters from unsuspecting recipients as they walked into one.

Someone let out a loud whistle of surprise when they came across shelves upon shelves of assorted armaments. I estimated there was enough to supply a rampaging army and I had no doubts that this was the IRA rebuilding for the renewed conflicts with British troops that would occur after the war, as history proved. Now they were useless relics, defunct for use, scrap value and not worth me attempting to slip one of the smaller weapons into my pocket for protection.

"Welcome to McCracken's treasure trove," I said to anybody who was listening.

Hamer definitely didn't hear me. He'd scampered off around the cellar like a man possessed, pulling off tarpaulins and creating more expanding dust clouds. I stood back until he exhausted himself.

At least Morgan heard me, as he flicked the defunct weapons with the nozzle of his handgun. "It's a pile of shit that belongs in a museum, Speed. The gold seems to be missing or is it just in your imagination?"

"I found McCracken's bank. It's your treasure hunt, not mine."

Morgan ordered a guard to keep a watchful eye on me and Shayna before moving on to direct the searchers. Inside three minutes of frantic disruption someone shouted.

"There's a padlocked wooden door over here!"

There was a mad rush towards the beckoning voice, including me, though mine was an involuntary momentum as I got swept up with the euphoria. I was shoved along by the guards who were obviously scared of missing the occasion. It included me. I'd come this far and I felt I at least deserved to smell and see the success if not feel the prize.

I watched in anticipation as a hefty brute of a man began sledging the large rusty padlock that secured the door. Even though he had bulging muscles it took him a lot of effort but the padlock finally gave with a crack.

It took three men to physically prise open the seized foot thick oak door, it's creaking and groaning iron hinges refusing to give up its secrets. When the door was sufficiently wide enough, Hamer barged his way to the front and shone a torch into the blackness.

"The rooms full of wooden boxes!" Hamer blurted, and then hurried a guard to go inside to retrieve one for inspection.

Moments later the guard re-emerged carrying an oblong box with Japanese symbols stamped on the top and sides. By the way he carried and placed the wooden box to the floor, it appeared heavy.

Hamer took hold of a steel crowbar and smashed the box apart. Torch beams illuminated the contents, the colour of gold reflecting back off the collection of ingots and into our faces. I think we were all mesmerized by what we saw. The ingots matched the one I'd found in the cavern under Dun an Oir. It meant my job was done, but it wasn't over. I now feared for my life. I feared for Shayna's life too, and I wondered what Morgan had planned for us.

Without a shadow of doubt we were at the mercy of a cool customer in Morgan. Hamer was the opposite; a hothead, controlled by Morgan pulling on his restraints. The combination of the two obviously worked in the gunrunning business, notably under the cover of The Ministry. They were clever tactics by clever people. And afterwards, they simply sweep the enemy under the carpet like dust. I could see it in Morgan's eyes that he was in the cleaning mood again and we were next on his list of chores. Morgan wasn't going to let us go freely, not unless we were in a coffin and quite dead. We were witnesses to the crimes he had committed. He would never trust us to keep our mouths shut no matter how much hush money he offered.

Hamer stooped down and scooped a handful of gold and let the ingots drop back into the box. Speechless men listened to the metallic tinkling as the ingots piled. Wide eyes gloated on the wealth before them. Neither mine, nor Shayna's gloated because we were on the same wavelength and understood that this was probably the moment when our lives were at terrible risk. The look we gave each other told the same story. We obviously had the same intentions to run the moment the opportunity arrived.

"Right, men," Morgan bellowed. "Get the rest of the boxes. I want an inventory of the amount collected. Anyone found filling their pockets before the count will have their hands chopped off. The quicker you work the quicker we get back to the ship." To me, he said: "Medical supplies, Speed, doesn't seem to be available, perhaps your information was invalid?"

I expressed my surprise. "There's nothing at all there with those boxes? Maybe the supplies are stored back there on the shelving. I'll go and have a look."

Morgan shook his head disbelievingly. "Why do I get these notions running around inside my head that you're a liar?"

"I was right about the gold."

"That's true, Speed. Please correct me if I'm perhaps being a little over ambitious with my assumption, only I haven't seen anything that even resembles a medical box on those shelves."

I shrugged. "I can't always be right!"

It was the narrowing of Morgan's left eye that alerted me. It was that defining moment when I knew Shayna and I had no more than two minutes to live. The mere flick of his head to one of the guards indicated to me that Morgan had decided that this cellar was going to be our burial chamber. I never gave Morgan the chance to give the final order to his man. With lightening reactions I twisted, grabbed the guard and threw him into everybody else close enough to cause a human pile up. I grabbed Shayna by the arm and dragged her to the stairway and bolted up the steps, my shins catching two of the steps on the occasions I stumbled on the way up.

Instantly a crescendo of bullets followed our stride in perfectly formed lines either side, splintering parts of the stairs, us as we clamoured to the top.

Over the gunfire I heard Morgan scream out to his men. “Stop shooting you idiots! There are unstable high explosives all around us. Do you want to blow us to smithereens? Get after them!”

I didn’t hang about. I pulled Shayna out of the hole and we ran for the exit. A guard emerged from outside, raising his machine pistol. I was onto him before he had the chance to cause me damage and I bundled him to the floor with a good shoulder charge. We were out into the open now, running for our lives. We ran as fast as we could, down the hill towards the quay, trying to keep our feet because the terrain was uneven and rough. We weren’t moving fast enough for my liking. We were an open target now and the bullets peppering our route had only missed us by good fortunate or the shooters were terrible marksmen.

I was breathing hard both with panic and exhaustion, and more disconcerting, Shayna was slowing me down. She might be a dynamist in the sexual energy department but she couldn’t run. My strength alone dragged her along before she dramatically fell down as if tackled by a fifteen stone rugby player which only served to knock me off balance when her knees hit the ground. She’d stubbed her toe on a rock that was protruding from the ground, I learned later. I jerked her back on to her feet. Checked who was doing the chasing, and again we were running with the intention of jumping into the motor launch we’d arrived on and getting out of there fast. That idea soon diminished.

When we approached the jetty we had to dodge another volley of sub machinegun fire coming from the motor launch, forcing us to veer left and leg it along the pebbled beach.

I kept a watchful eye over my shoulder to see who was in pursuit. Hamer was surprisingly amongst the forerunners, the fat bastard huffing and puffing as he gave chase. He was keener than the rest to stop me in my tracks. And though I didn't observe it, I imagined the determination in his face, he wanted me so badly. Luckily his accuracy was thankfully hindered by his running momentum as the bullets he fired whistled past.

We were getting nowhere fast. Shayna seemed to have lost the will to run. Her legs were tiring rapidly as she struggled to keep her feet on the stony beach. Overall we were too easy of a target. We were too open and it didn't require the accuracy of a marksman to spray us with a machine pistol. I frantically searched for cover, selecting the safety of two large rocks where we cowered behind to catch our breath; where I could review our predicament in quick time, what was left of it.

I sucked in huge breaths as I thought hard, peeping between the rocks to check on our pursuers. Hamer had obviously seen our place of refuge because he was hand signalling for one the pursuing goons with him to sweep around in one direction while he went the other. The situation made my mind up for me. It was pointless to run any more because the bullet in the back would be the outcome. I had no immediate plan swirling in my head other than I certainly wasn't going to die in any cowardly fashion. If I could take Hamer or the goon down with my bare hands then at least I'd have gone down fighting.

I kept checking the progress of the two men to assess which one of them was gaining ground on us the quickest. The goon was winning or Hamer was being extremely cautious or frigging clever. I would have preferred Hamer but beggars can't be choosy. I waited, thinking through my options. If I could disarm the goon quickly enough, I might have the time to have a crack at Hamer; maybe get one clear shot before he got me. I climbed the rock in anticipation that the goon would assume I was flat to the floor in hiding.

I held my breath waiting for the right moment. Waited for the shadow of the goon's head to inch its way round the rock and then I struck. He was definitely surprised when I pounced and the first thing I grabbed was the machine pistol he held, knocking the weapon downwards, bullets firing into the ground as we grappled for supremacy. We fell to the ground, still grappling and rolling and twisting and kicking. Then the machine pistol went off again and we both stopped struggling.

I never felt a thing.

The goon's eyes slowly widened with shock, his body stiffening. I became aware of a sticky substance running into my fingers where my hand had the weapon clamped. Eyeball to eyeball I stared at the goon, the stench of his breath making me recoil slightly. He became heavier and finally flopped down on top of me. I threw him off quickly while trying desperately to wrench the machine pistol from the dead man's grip. The time it had taken me to climb to my feet and aim the gun at Hamer, was seconds too late. Hamer shot me as I twisted round.

Dead people don't feel pain and I was in agony, now crumpled to the floor clutching my left shoulder. I'd never been shot before. The feeling was weird, a sort of burning sensation where the bullet had entered, as if some sadistic torturer had shoved a red-hot poker into my flesh for fun. I grimaced, my teeth clenched with both pain and anger. Hamer was standing behind Shayna with his arm wrapped around her throat. She looked groggy and she was bleeding heavily from a cut just above her left eye. I guessed Hamer had smashed the butt of his gun into her face to subdue her.

His gun hand was angled down at me. He said conceitedly, "As I predicted, Speed; professionalism outsmarts the amateur. But before I finally kill you I would like to thank you from the bottom of a sceptic tank for finding our golden future. I'm glad I didn't kill you when I'd the chance in London. Without you I'd probably never have found the gold. Alas, Speed, death comes to you at a price and fortunately I'm to become a rich man and you'll be dead. Doesn't life stink?"

"You'll never get away with it!" I spat what seemed idle threats.

"But I am getting away with it, Speed." Hamer said with confidence. "And while I'm soaking up all that nice sunshine at some paradise location without an extradition treaty, you'll be getting lowered, along with Miss Loser here, in that pauper's grave we always promised."

"Don't count on it Hamer! I'll haunt you from wherever I am, you murdering bastard!"

Hamer smirked, his finger curling tighter around the trigger ready to shoot. I tried to be brave and keep my eyes focused on him to show my defiance in the face of death. I tensed though, my body rigid in readiness to take the bullet that was about to explode from its chamber and into my head. It was natural for me to twist my head slightly away from the oncoming death threat. When I did, in the corner of my eye, I saw my guardian angel.

Hamer was so full of himself that he hadn't seen or heard the large black shadow sweeping over him.

When he did, he was far too late to react and avoid the huge fist that smashed into the side of his face. I'd heard the smack of knucklebone hitting jawbone and its effect was to send Hamer plummeting sideways as he lost his grip on Shayna. He staggered and then dropped to the ground, knocked out, blood trickling from the side of his mouth and running down his distorted chin and in between the pebbles where his battered face lay.

I was ecstatic. Ignoring the pain I was in, my eyes flicked to the owner of the huge fist. I couldn't believe it when I saw Shamus standing there in a boxer's stance ready to throw the next punch. Satisfied he'd done his job, Shamus reached down and took the gun from Hamer's hand, but he hadn't quite finished with him.

Shamus leaned over Hamer, and said, "That yer obnoxious granite of English shit, is for blowing up me boat!"

Shamus looked at me and winked. He said, "Hullo there, Shacks sir. I didn't want to miss all the fun yer're were all having."

He hadn't finished there either as he promptly spat into Hamer's hair, (which I thought must be some sort of Irish custom) and he followed that with a kick to Hamer's midriff. "And that, you English bastard, is for giving me friends a rough and unpleasant time." He looked at Shayna with an apologetic expression. "Excuse me dreadful behaviour, Lass. It's very rare for Shamus O'Malley to conduct himself in such a disorderly manner, but I felt I'd earned the privilege."

Shayna threw herself into the Irishman and hugged him. He was slightly embarrassed by the emotional ordeal. She said, "You were magnificent, Shamus."

I could only marvel at Shamus's brilliant timing, as he had undoubtedly saved my life. He helped me to my feet, took my weight, allowed Shayna to loop her arm through his, and we trooped wearily back to the quayside and hopefully straight into the pub.

All of a sudden the place was swarming with heavily armed Garda. I heard a troop helicopter fly overhead heading in the direction of the *Flying Fish*. Motor launches skimmed across the water. Uniformed men, armed to the teeth, ran past me to drag Hamer to his feet and place him under arrest.

In a panic I stopped and said to Shamus, "Where's Morgan?"

Shamus looked puzzled. "Morgan? If he was still inside the church then he's trapped with no escape, Shacks sir. I was too busy running after Hamer to notice anything else."

"Frigging hell, Shamus, what if you hadn't made it on time or he'd seen you before you reached him?"

"O I wouldn't have worried over that, Shacks, Sir. There was a sharpshooter on standby ready to take the bastard down if necessary."

When we reached the quay the pub was still shut. Its closure disappointed me. It was the only hospital treatment I needed at that moment. I sat down on a wall because I suddenly felt dizzy. A senior Garda officer angled across to us. The officer gave a polite salute and said, "Chief Inspector, Micky O'Connor. I presume I'm addressing, Mister Shackleton Speed and Miss Shayna Magginty?"

Shayna nodded. I couldn't be arsed answering and grunted instead. I was in far too much pain.

The Garda officer went on. "You both have a lot of explaining to do when you've rested. O and there's also some representatives from the Japanese Consulate flying in insisting they speak with you, Mister Speed. I've no idea why but the Japanese have clearance to do so." He checked his wristwatch. "In approximately twenty minutes they'll be here, so I would appreciate your-" He stopped suddenly when he noticed my blood soaked jacket sleeve. "Good grief man you're injured." He raised his hand in the air to attract the attention of a group of medical staff arriving on the scene and called across to them. "Medic! This man here requires urgent attention. He's bleeding all over the place."

My mind was suddenly elsewhere. Alarmed, I said to O'Connor, "Did you apprehend someone called Morgan?"

"The big English man with red hair, you mean? We have him in custody, sir. He's not stopped ranting on about how he tracked you down, Mister Speed. That you're a thieving and murdering misfit and it should be you we put in handcuffs and not him."

I panicked. "You didn't believe him?"

"Not one mouthful, sir. He tried to shoot one of my men before we arrested him."

Chapter Twenty Five

The Bell 222 helicopter hovered before landing on the grassy knoll farther up the hill. I watched the two Orientals emerge from the passenger compartment. I recognized Tanamoto instantly. He looked pleased so he probably wasn't aware of Deveron's death. I considered it wouldn't be my place to tell him. Chief Inspector Micky O'Conner met them from the craft. They talked for five minutes. I assumed O'Connor was explaining the present situation to them.

In the meantime the medic finished off patching my wound and put my arm into a sling. He told me that I'd been tremendously lucky and the bullet had gone straight through my flesh with minimum damage, other than to perhaps have chipped my shoulder bone on the way out. It would hurt for a while but I should recover satisfactorily. It could have been worse.

Tanamoto and his companion hurried down the hill towards us, all teeth with huge smiles, with the Garda officer dragging in their wake. The two Orientals bowed when they reached us.

Tanamoto greeted me openly. "Ah, Mister Speed!" His smile dropped to a look of concern. "You've been hurt?"

"It's only a flesh wound. I'll live," I assured him.

"I wish you a fast recovery." And then he gestured to his companion. "Let me introduce to you, Haisi

Yoshimoto, military attaché at the Japanese consulate in London."

Yoshimoto bowed. "It is a great honour to meet you, Mister Speed. The entire people of Japan will be greatly indebted to the man who found 'Momi 2'."

"News travels fast but I'm glad to be of service."

Again their heads bowed and Yoshimoto said, "It is a service that will be truly honoured, Mister Speed."

I said to O'Connor, flicking my head sideways. "There's a cavern you might want to visit below Dun an Oir on Clear Island. Inside the cavern is where you'll find the submarine and the remains of the submariners. There are two entrances and both have a degree of difficulty for entry: one by sea but you'll require diving gear: the other by the fort itself only you will require excavation equipment to remove tons of rocks. Under those rocks in the tunnel are the bodies of seven Irishmen. They were the people responsible for the hijacking of the I-52 in 1944, and for the murder of the Japanese crew."

With a well rehearsed suspicious tone, O'Conner said, "How may I ask did you discover all this?"

"It was by sheer luck and guess work."

O'Conner smiled briefly. "There's plenty of that in Ireland."

O'Conner excused himself and shot off when he was called by one of his men.

Yoshimoto then reached inside his coat pocket. He produced a white envelope and bowed while he handed it to me. "Please accept the humble thanks of the Japanese nation, Mister Shackleton Speed."

I thanked Yoshimoto and tucked the offering into my side pocket without checking the contents. I should have checked the contents but I had my reasons.

Tanamoto said, "We shall detain you no longer and leave you to continue your medical treatment, Mister Speed. We shall meet later, when you have made a full recovery. We have a lot to discuss and arrange."

I nodded and smiled approvingly.

They moved away in deep discussion, returning to where O'Connor was issuing orders. They spent a few minutes talking and then I noticed Tanamoto shudder violently. I gathered O'Conner had just informed him of Deveron's death.

Shayna leaned over and said quietly. "They seemed happy with the return of their submarine and the gold too no doubt. I wonder if they'll want the opium too. Come to think of it, what happened to the opium if it wasn't aboard the submarine or at the church?"

"I haven't a clue! I've a funny feeling McCracken knew nothing of the existence of the opium. He was only interested in the gold. But I know a tramp called Willie. He knows where it is, because I suspect while the rest of them had nothing to do for ten hours, they all went searching the submarine for whatever gains they could pilfer and almost certainly stumbled across the medical supplies. Probably had knowledge of its importance and decided to stash the stuff away to be collected later without McCracken knowing. But circumstances changed Willie's way of thinking. With the others dead, he was too frightened to return to the Island to collect the stash."

"So it's still there on Clear Island?"

"I guess so."

"Shouldn't we be informing the authorities of its existence?"

"What the hell for, Shayna?"

"It's our duty."

"It's best left hidden. If that much opium was to inadvertently hit the street, I hate to think of the serious consequences and a probable increase of drug abuse."

She thought it through. "You're probable right."

"I'm seriously right," I said.

She gave me one of her curious looks that I'd grown accustomed to. "I've been wondering."

"Wondering about what?"

"The envelope you slipped discreetly into your pocket."

"What about it?"

"I noticed you never bothered to check what was inside the envelope."

"I already knew the contents. Besides, the Japanese find it discourteous if a person checks the contents in front of the giver; it's a sign of mistrust by the receiver."

"So what's in the envelope?"

I tapped my chest. "This envelope in here, you mean?"

"Will you stop messing me about."

"It's a formal invite to ex gratis, naturally."

"And what's that in layman terms?"

"It's a letter of authority from the Japanese Government approving my rights to a percentage of the salvaged gold."

Shayna frowned. "Salvage rights? Is that a legal transaction between a Country and a Commoner from another?"

"You're frigging right it is, and I expect to receive every damn penny, Shayna. I'll receive a whopping two percent of all recovered gold to be exact and kindly agreed by the Japanese government in respect of my honourable disclosure of their property."

"It's as simple as that?"

"Life can be grand sometimes, Shayna?"

"They could have disagreed and refused to pay out."

"They could have quite easily done that and then I would have pointed out a minor problem they would have experienced by refusing me my share. I would have had to apply, 'finder's keepers-losers weepers-giving back is stealing-and frigging lucky if they ever get it back-policy', if you can understand all that gibberish. But you have to respect the Japanese for their upholding of promises. I knew they'd agree. I'm happy with the arrangement and they'll be happy in Japan to have solved the mystery of the missing I-52."

"When did you arrange all this ex-gratis-thank you very much deal?"

"It came to me during one of my many sleepless nights."

Her face lit up. "How much is this two percent expected to bring?"

"I'd say roughly...two and half million."

"Is that Yen?"

"English Pounds Stirling, of course. I wouldn't have any other currency."

"You lucky Limey sod!"

"No, I'm a rich lucky Limey sod."

"Bragging rights too!"

"Not all for me. I did promise Shamus a new boat."

"I've got to hand it to you, Shackleton; you've proven to be one hell of a guy."

"And one that deserves a long rest to recover. Care to join me?"

"You have somewhere in mind?"

"Somewhere faraway and quiet where nobody knows who I am. I was thinking maybe a quiet island somewhere in the Caribbean."

"It sounds inviting."

"Then you're not too busy in the near future?"

"I might take you up on that offer."

She didn't sound convincing. I sensed something there was else was on her mind. "What's bothering you, Shayna?"

"Well, considering your reputation I'm surprised you were willing to reveal where the gold was hidden. You could have kept it for yourself; walked away and said nothing."

"The thought did occur to me, Shayna. Admittedly I was tempted. Now this is going to sound daft to you. I'd no interest in the gold whatsoever. I was angry, that's why I went after the damned stuff. Two good people died unnecessarily because of it. Finding it first gave me the impetus to expose the true villains; to dangle the golden booty in front of their murderous eyes. It worked in my favour. I'm now content. Yes I've lost two good friends, but I'm content."

"You're content because you've had your revenge?"

"I'm content because it's all over now and I can get on with my life again."

"The gold never interested you one bit?"

"Not in the slightest."

"Isn't the salvage money not in the same category?"

"Not at all, I earned that by risking my life to bring those murdering bastards to justice. Now I don't want to hear anymore about it."

For a moment my eyes left Shayna. I'd caught sight of Morgan and Hamer, both handcuffed and each man being manhandled into the rear of separate Garda vehicles. I watched the motorcade leave. Strangely, I imagined Hamer, sitting there quietly in the rear of the police car, plotting and mentally sharpening his knife in the desperate hope he could still silence me forever.

The End

CPSIA information can be obtained at www.ICGtesting.com
Printed in the USA
LVOW05s0228120713

342443LV00001B/2/P

9 781781 486191